THE RAYNE PROJECT

WEBSTERLAND
BOOKS

The Rayne Project

WEBSTERLAND
BOOKS

The Rayne Project
Copyright © 2020 by Lyna Lopez
ISBN: 9781734364507 Print
ISBN: 9781734364514 Ebook
www.lynalopez.com
www.websterlandbooks.com

Library of Congress Control Number: 2020903131

Book Cover Design by CReya-tive
Edited by MK Editing Services LLC

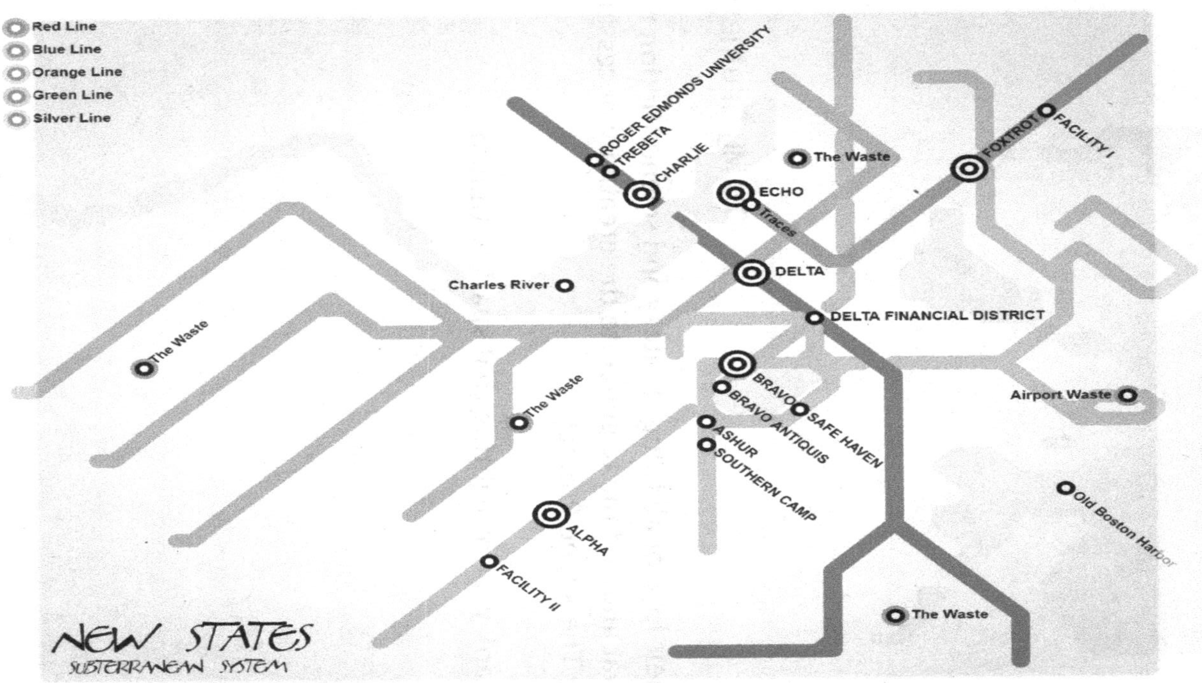
Red Line
Blue Line
Orange Line
Green Line
Silver Line
ROGER EDMONDS UNIVERSITY
TREBETA
CHARLIE
The Waste
FOXTROT
FACILITY I
ECHO
Traces
DELTA
Charles River
DELTA FINANCIAL DISTRICT
The Waste
BRAVO
BRAVO ANTIQUIS
SAFE HAVEN
Airport Waste
The Waste
ASHUR
SOUTHERN CAMP
Old Boston Harbor
ALPHA
FACILITY II
The Waste
NEW STATES
SUBTERRANEAN SYSTEM

To My Brothers.

Their love of all things fantasy and science fiction is what allowed me to generate the creativity necessary for The Rayne Project.

Thank you for lighting that spark within me.

LYNA LOPEZ

THE RAYNE PROJECT

PROJECT HERCULES SERIES · BOOK ONE

PROLOGUE

Sector Foxtrot
Facility I
Dr. Sebastian Lester

AS PHYSICALLY CAPABLE as he was striking, Hail's face was pressed against the glass of The Garden, unrealistically disfigured and distorted to anyone standing before it. Blood trickled from his mouth, following an unseen trail down the fortified glass. He pushed off the surface and ducked. Thunder missed, his knuckles leaving four parallel lines in an arch where Hail's face had just been. Hail had made it behind Thunder long enough to place him in a chokehold, cutting off his breathing. Thunder roared—the muscles and veins in his neck a vivid disparity against his tan flesh. His hair conveyed weightlessness as if the very gravity in the room had escaped, and then Hail blew back into the wall, leaving nothing behind but a trail of destruction.

To understand your parents' love, you must first raise children yourself.

The weight of the Chinese proverb flowed through my chaotic mind. I rested my chin on my interlocked fists. My beautiful children frolicked in the open space before me as I watched from behind the thick glass. Or rather, they used their superhuman abilities to train and fight one another in mock combat inside the garden intended for them to relax and enjoy. Behind the glass, The Garden was the only place in the entire facility that smelled earthy and had vibrant colors, from red roses to mauve violets and yellow dandelions. The air quality was sweet and fragrant, except for today.

The smell of the salt from their sweat and the metallic hints of their blood intermingled with the scent of bleach used for their last gory clean-up. The odor of all of the antiseptics used daily to keep the underground facility germ-free wafted through the open door. My worn, black notebook lay beside me with nothing but my trusty pen nestled between the pages marking the notes regarding Project Hercules. The military approached me years ago when they found out I had perfected a genotypic DNA coding and could splice it with animal and environmental gene chemistry and dominant allele mutations.

No one believed I would do what I said I could.

The project involved taking threads of a chromosome from animal DNA and environmental stimulants and splicing those strands with human genes. After several failed attempts—and there were many—the results stood right before me in all their glory. My babies had grown to become such healthy adolescents. I felt a lump form in my throat. The love I had for them was unconditional. I wasn't sure how it happened, but they became more than a job—they became my family.

I watched Thunder lift Hail into the air with his steady right hand and slam him on the ground. Dirt exploded all around them as if someone had stomped in a puddle of mud. Thunder took the wind right out of Hail and right out of me for that matter. From the sidelines, Cameron cheered them on, using his unique camouflaging ability to blend into his surroundings. They all carried a few abnormalities I refused to share with the rest of the facility. Hail had the added ability to freeze things with the barest touch of his fingertips. Like all of my kids, Hail manifested his skills when he turned eight years old. The little ones caused minor hitches here and there—their powers not strong enough to generate lots of damage or raise suspicion. It had been imperative I keep most of their abilities a secret from the facility's tyrannous general. He couldn't know the extent of their powers.

I shook my head. It's what surprised me most about

my children. Not only did they gain their strength from the Herculean Cocktail, but the mixtures caused random abilities. Most were specific to their animal's habitat. In Hail's brew, I added several traits of the wood frog. The amphibian could survive months in a frozen state.

Their connection to their abilities had been how I came to choose their names. Thunder laughed as he slammed his foot into Hail's chest. Hail grabbed Thunder's leg and yanked down hard. Surprised, my boy reared back and fell beside Hail. All three boys laughed in unison. Their easy camaraderie made me smile.

I wrote more notes in my book.

Although they had extraordinary abilities, the children still had to keep up with their physical training. I walked over to the gymnasium and into a locker room where I could see a few others who hung out by the state-of-the-art treadmills and large bench press. The gym had dark, padded walls and light gray, springy floors to take most of the damage when the kids got in a foul mood and objects moved of their own volition.

A strong odor of funky old socks made me gasp and cover my nose and mouth. I gawked at all of the old towels and shoes strewn about the vast interior and made a note to get someone to clean in here. My kids barely rested and consistently worked out. Leaving dirty items unchecked would be hazardous to everyone's health.

Rock and Coal spotted one another as they lifted the dumbbell with equal sides at six hundred pounds each. *They must be taking it easy today.* I watched as Rock, with his flat forehead, bawdy shoulders, and muscular arms helped Coal, the most obscene in the group, lift about twelve hundred pounds of weight. Their muscles bunched and flexed, but I knew they barely broke a sweat. The boys laughed, and it reminded me of their carefree attitudes.

The kids didn't judge one another—by looks or otherwise, except for one. My beauty Seaa hated the way she looked, and although I could not get her to believe in herself, I was glad the rest of my children never judged her. They worked together, like today with Rock and Coal, and that made me a proud papa.

Shaking off the randomness of my thoughts, I jotted down what I saw in my thick book. I felt a warm hand rest on my shoulder as delicate as a butterfly on a petal. Beside me stood one of the more breathtaking beauties amongst my children. Silk beamed down at me with those obsidian curls, very nearly blue in their coloring, bouncing around the sides of her heart-shaped face. Her skin was flawless but for a small, round beauty mark gracing the bottom corner of her right eye. Her cheeks had a permanent pink hue to them. Silk squeezed my hand, and I reveled in her silky, spider's-web-soft skin.

But as many of the staff and her brethren had come to notice, they shouldn't be fooled by her looks. She can be just as vicious as a threatened eight-legged arachnid.

I smiled back at her and watched as my teenage girl walked right over to Rock and punched him in the face with no warning. I gasped out loud and looked to my left and right as if someone would magically appear to help me. Her punch caused Rock to drop the weight on top of Coal, whose legs puffed out like air through an accordion.

Oh, dear, not again.

With eyes raised heavenward, I ran through the metal door into the room to help with the weights. I dropped my hand just before I reached the machines, realizing I was nowhere near strong enough to lift it. At my age, I could barely get myself out of bed in the mornings.

"Silk, do me a favor, darling, and please leave your brother alone."

She turned toward me with a grimace. To anyone else, she'd spark fear, but not me. The girl would not do me harm.

Crossing her arms, she growled in rebuttal, "He's not really my brother, you know, and he started it!"

I choked out a laugh at her outburst. Silk had a crush on Cameron. Cam was handsome and tall, with sharp Asian features, so I didn't blame her for being attracted. I didn't think Cameron shared quite the same attraction as Silk, but I knew Coal liked to bug her loads about it. She hated that I compared them to siblings for that matter alone.

Coal seized the opportunity of Silk being pre-occupied with me to grab the weight and throw it at her. The act made me flinch, using my hands to cover my head, laying down the white fluff I had left on my scalp. The sound of the hit resonated around the interior. I looked over to where Silk had landed. Her blood smeared under her full, lower lip. Blood anywhere in the facility was a common occurrence. The teens would wipe it off, and the wound would heal naturally.

"Kids, please," I murmured, still shaken by the experience.

Neither child listened to a word I said as they slammed one another with gym equipment. I could only hope the rest of the kids were behaving better than these. Four soldiers walked toward them with their customized Vuwands in hand. The handhelds packed triple the voltage of a regular Taser. Every child's weakness was intense amounts of high voltage electricity coursing through their bodies in large agonizing doses. Not even Thunder would be immune to them, and *he* could send exceeding quantities of electrical charge through his fingertips, like an electric eel.

The soldiers shocked my kids with their handheld devices. The sound buzzed throughout the room. My old heart took a nosedive. I hated seeing them get hurt with a Vuwand, but I could do nothing about it.

The General ruled the facility. They may have been my kids in my mind, but I was their doctor to everyone else.

The muscles underneath my skin tightened as the weight of someone watching me hit like a ton of bricks. The sensation made my skin crawl. I spotted General Brockton Braggart by the glass enclosure as he watched his soldiers drag Silk and Rock from the gym room. The rest of the room was a disaster. Afterward, he drilled me with his piercing, brown gaze, pillowed by thick, menacing brows.

It took all my willpower to hold back the vomit. General Braggart disliked me and my children. His meetings voiced how disobedient they were. I knew Braggart wanted unyielding super soldiers who never questioned his methods or orders. The kind who did as they were told—damn the consequences. But kids were rule-breakers who generally tested the boundaries. It was the general rule of thumb for their age, and attitude came with the territory. General Braggart refused to believe that.

He walked toward The Garden, with arms folded at his back. The man twirled one side of his mustache like a cartoon villain, so I sought his distracted gaze. His calculating eyes studied Rayne, my youngest child, who plucked petals off a light pink rose. Rayne was the quiet one of the bunch, who hardly ever got herself into trouble. Mostly she spent it silently sobbing, as if her body produced too many tears she could not hold back. The dear girl always did as told, and Braggart took pride in that merit. My girl sat on the stone bench beside Guy Gust and Snow—surrounded by the flowers she plucked.

My stomach churned.

The General's leering wasn't at all unusual because he had done it more than once before. There were times when I regretted doing what I did when creating her. I was a scientist. I had no power to overrule the man who signed my paychecks. Not long after, I noticed General Braggart's facial expression lose its allure. I followed his line of sight to the edge of the small wooden pergola to see Seaa's gorgeous, lavender eyes worship her brother Snow from her perch beside him. Seaa was a beautiful deity who shimmered in translucent ombré violets into turquoise, from her hair to her scales.

Unfortunately, no one else thought so—not even her.

She was more of a fish than a female, with gills at her neck, webbed toes and fingers, and the most extravagant cerulean periwinkle scales that layered her body from the shoulders down like a magical shield protecting her skin. The underside of her arms and feet had skin like an average human, but the visible parts of her skin showed mutation from the Herculean Cocktail. My fault entirely. I saw such great promise in some of the others created before her that I added too much of her animal counterparts.

The result sat before me.

I had created a technology that allowed her to receive the nutrients of water through a pack assembled at her waist. The contraption injected the correct amounts of water into her system. The cells absorbed the needed oxygen, and the rest was expelled through another tube connected at the back of her neck. The pack recycled the water through the process of condensation and evaporation. Seaa hid all of the tubing by wearing large jackets and shirts, but I figured it was more for her state of self-consciousness than the device itself.

Snow must've repeated nonsense because she smacked him across the head and stormed off. He stared at her back in shock. The girl could love her siblings one minute and slap them the next. She was a hard one to pinpoint.

A sigh escaped my lips as I jotted down more information into my book when the sirens rang off in the underground bunker. The soldiers escorted the kids in The Garden away. Goosebumps littered my flesh as I ran down the hall in time to hear the lieutenant telling General Braggart there was a riot in the dormitories.

"Sir, the experiments are trying to break down the wall separating their habitats."

Not again.

"I will no longer tolerate this insolence," I heard the General call out.

The general's second in command told him more.

"They are getting stronger, General Braggart. If we do not kill this project, we can no longer control them. We need to go with Plan B, Sir. We need already trained soldiers. The kind ready to die for their country. For our cause."

I feared the absolute worst would happen, and it would be out of my control.

"I understand, Lieutenant Charles. Contact Dr. Plumboy. Advise him of the new plans."

The name "Dr. Plumboy" came out of the general's mouth. At that moment, I knew something drastic was about to happen. I ran the opposite way and took the long way toward my office. Soldiers pushed left and right as they made their way to the chaotic scene. Once I reached the mechanical door, I punched in my code and swiped the clearance badge. The door beeped but didn't open. I tried again, stumbling over arthritic fingers in my haste. The door buzzed open. I ran in and closed the door behind me. Ready for a fight, I pulled my Dockers higher over my belly and sought around for my computer glasses.

Aching arms reached up as I searched the room for my missing lenses. My clumsy legs tripped over a few books I had stacked on the floor. I pushed two file boxes to the side, hit my desk, and grumbled at the mess of files that fell on top of it. Leaving them scattered about, I got up to think as I scanned the room, hoping they would magically appear. One wall had photos of my kids at each stage of their life from conception to the present day. Another wall had a giant corkboard with notes and essential papers I couldn't bear to lose.

Unable to make my way across the pale gray tiles to the other desk, I pushed aside more file boxes I had yet organized in my busy schedule. Underneath the books and papers, I knew a simple metal desk stood before me, my glasses somewhere within. Seeing them nowhere on the surface of the counter, I shuffled papers around and grabbed a disposable KeViewer with one hand as I continued my search with the other. I found them underneath one of the many notebooks I'd used since I started Project Hercules.

The clock on the wall ticked by the seconds, an ominous reminder of wasted time. I clicked on two programs and typed away on the computer—wiping all the information I had on the kids and my Herculean Cocktail. I made a fist and slammed it down on the desk. Papers exploded like a ripple effect.

All those wasted years! I'd be damned if Robert Plumboy came in here to take my research.

With shaking fingers, I grabbed the mouse hanging off the side of the desk. As the remaining files disappeared, I fumbled to grab the KeViewer and make a call to a couple I trusted.

I placed a finger to one side of my ear, trying to block off the loud noise. The sirens wailed throughout the interior. My heart thumped wildly behind my old ribcage. The kids must've done a number this time.

With the couple onboard, I exhaled in relief, probably my only one for the rest of the evening. I knew deep in my heart General Braggart would show them no mercy. After typing a command on the computer, I ran a hand through my thick fluff of white hair.

"Here goes nothing," I whispered to no one but myself.

Pressing the ENTER key, I grabbed all my notebooks and a bag of explosive putty I had kept in reserve for such an occasion. Nothing else mattered right now. I would give my children a fighting chance—whether it be with or without me. Hiding the goods from passing officers, I made my way through the maze of glistening white, tiled walls to the stairwell that took me to the level below. I hated it most of all. Braggart had several torture rooms and cells in that part of the facility for his many punishments. At the end of the hall on the side opposite of the General's office was a sealed-off mine shaft.

We had one chance at this.

I peeked down at my watch. The time was now.

All the doors came down around me—a security feature General Braggart placed in the facility to contain the wings under the risk of fire, which I used to my advantage. The automatic sliding doors shut down all of the other parts of the facility but created one open path toward me.

There was still a trick or two up my sleeve.

I only hoped my children would get here. A couple

of seconds later, fumes filtered through the ventilation system. The chemical mixture had been an inert gas I had created that affected humans. My kids would be immune to it.

However, I wasn't.

I placed a gas mask over my face. The sounds of footsteps headed my way prompted me into action. A putty explosive stuck to the wall covering the mine shaft. Guy Gust had been the first to come around the corner. I waved him back as the walls around me exploded and sent my old body right into the poor boy's waiting arms.

"Pops, you okay?"

Pain burst throughout my entire body. I put on a happy expression but felt nothing below my waist as I tried to wiggle my toes.

Damn.

I gestured for everyone to run out. "Get everyone out of here, my boy."

Guy tried to pick me up, but I knew nothing waited for me outside the building. The facility and the underground rooms had been my home for far too long. I couldn't remember what the sun on my skin felt like. The metal doors slowly rose. Our time was up. The sounds of gunfire rang around us. I waved Guy away while shoving my backpack into the boy's trembling hands.

"Go, my boy! Get everyone out and give this to Thunder."

The tall boy nodded and led the group out of the facility with my notebooks at his side as more gunfire surrounded us. The ammunition they used had a unique shell that penetrated their skin. The damn Dr. Plumboy invented it as a way to keep his job with General Braggart. Once buried inside, the bullet case would open and release a high dose of energy that would target their nervous system. Enough shots and my kids wouldn't make it out of here alive.

A bullet whizzed by me. The metal hit one of the kids in the leg. Tears fell from my eyes as I watched my brave Fiera drop to the floor. Her flaming red hair a sharp disparity to the white tiles. Without enough time to mourn, I heard a young girl cry and saw my little Rayne huddled in a shimmering ball of muscle and floating liquid in the hallway's corner.

Why didn't I see this sooner?

Rayne avoided conflict to keep the emotions running rampant in her mind to change her physical features. I fiddled around for the notebook. Then I remembered this was not the time to be jotting down notes. Sitting there would get her killed or captured, and I couldn't allow that. I couldn't let General Brockton Braggart get his hands on her. Using my arms, I dragged my limp lower half toward Rayne to cover her in time. Two shots fired in our direction. One hit right through the back of my shoulder. Rayne flinched but stopped crying when I shielded her. Her body shuddered in front of my eyes like waves of heat on the horizon.

"P-pops?"

Rayne was stable again. She likewise bled from her head and shoulder

No!

She had been conscious for a second to call out to me but then dropped on top of my chest. I could barely make out a pulse. I saw Thunder tossing a soldier covered from head to toe in military regalia against the wall.

"T-thunder! Come grab Rayne and run!"

It had gotten harder for me to breathe. The bullets may not have affected my nerves, but they were sure as hell doing a number on my little girl. Thunder threw another soldier across the room. The boy saw Silk on the floor. He grabbed her and urged her to run forward. She still wore the chains of solitary confinement on her wrists. Silk came flying toward me. Tears fell from those large, dark eyes.

"Pops!"

I managed a small smile for her. My worn body no longer under my control. "I h-have one more surprise f-for these bastards. Save Rayne with this." I handed Thunder a slip of paper. "Go, my daughter. G-go!"

Silk vehemently shook her head, so I gave Thunder one last plea. Thunder wouldn't let me down. He'd protect them. Nodding, my son pressed his forehead against mine as more tears fell from my eyes. Thunder tucked a screaming Silk under one arm and an unconscious Rayne under the other. He ran as if the fires of hell were upon him.

And they were.

The moment my boy was out of sight, I set off the last explosive and closed my eyes for a final goodbye.

Take that, General Brockton Braggart!

CHAPTER ONE

I STILL COULDN'T believe my luck. Inside the shell of the once-lively facility for education, in the crumbled ruins of concrete and steel, there were years of lost history. I carefully lifted each magazine from the rusted metal locker. The place was off-limits, but I couldn't care less. The twenty-first century had consistently been my favorite time in history. The abundance of freedom to go wherever you wished to go to, to eat from the variety of food stalls available on every corner. Compared to the world I lived in now, it had been a time of exploited resources and untapped knowledge.

One day, in due time, I would be able to walk inside a school and learn from other like-minded individuals. Academic centers like the forgotten one I now trespassed no longer existed in this sector. What was known as the United States no longer held states, but divisions for the remaining livable areas. The war we called Ragnarok had destroyed so much, and yet, so little had been learned from it. Instead of the people banding together to survive, each country had taken matters into their own hands and created bigger and more violent weapons to prove their dominance.

My history professor father had read stories to me every night he was home about the third millennium. I was eighteen now, but Carl Baxter used to sit me on his knee as we watched from the narrow openings of our boarded-up window on the fifteenth floor the wounded world below. Carl would explain to me how citizens used to look out their window to see the ground layered in grass so green it could have been painted. Neighbors would greet neighbors and borrow from one another without concern of ever going empty. Children would play outside on hot summer days in front of an open fire hydrant as parents looked on from the sidewalks, unconcerned. In that time, when disaster struck, the people had joined as one entity to rid the world of the inhumane and unlawful terrorist acts. My own time felt like an entirely different world—a corrupt time —where famine ruled the last remaining poor districts that espoused any vestiges of visible society.

My sector included.

I wiped away the coating of dust atop the magazines and sneezed. The air around me was so dense it was hard to breathe. The fetid scent of layers upon layers of rusted metal, dirt, and grime assaulted me. 1 distracted myself by studying my findings. The locker had to have belonged to a teenage girl. 1 came by it purely by chance, hiding under pounds of debris that appeared to have blocked most of the elements throughout the years, preserving them in their current state.

What wouldn't 1 give to have been able to go to school during this time? To have the freedom to say what you wanted and not be killed for it, to walk to school without worrying about another bomb attack on your sector. Perhaps to even be open to love. That had been one thing 1 continually enjoyed about reading my stories.

No matter how calamitous my surroundings, 1 buried my mind in the romantic gestures of young lovers through the books 1 read and magazines 1 collected. Doing so made it easier to forget about the drama and chaos of the world.

1 lifted my shirt to cover my mouth and nose from the decades-old buildup of dirt and dust. The people called forbidden places like this "The Waste." Noises from the bending metal and decaying rock structures reached my ears. Not long after, 1 heard sounds not belonging to the crumbling mess before me.

Fear practically froze me in place. Instead, 1 ducked down behind a massive steel column.

"Marie?" the voice whispered into the abandoned structure.

My hearing had consistently been sharp. My strength rivaled that of seasoned men. Gifts like my hearing and strength were a problem in our failing country. I shivered, thinking of the things they'd do to me if the government found out I had enhanced senses.

The military had apprehended several people during that disaster because of the changes in their anatomy. In our ailing land, the military ruled with an iron fist. And while the rich may have thought they controlled the military bases, they only funded them; no one out there could control General Braggart. Still, without their money, Braggart couldn't put together such elaborate schemes to take control of not just our New States but to also send super soldiers into other countries to establish fear.

Recruit or be killed was the military's unofficial motto these days.

My mom and dad told me repeatedly to be wary of who was around me and to trust no one. That is why my friend knew me as Marie and not Rayne, though I called her a "friend."

They told me to use Marie for security purposes.

The blast from the government-run lab in Foxtrot had caused me to lose my memory—all of the memories of my birth parents, gone. I knew my adoptive parents had taken me in off the streets when I was a young girl, bloodied and left for dead. I had grown into a bright and beautiful young woman with specific special abilities. My heightened senses being one. All the abnormalities I had were used in front of my adoptive parents. As long as I kept them hidden, neither my parents nor I would be in any immediate danger.

"Marie?" my friend whispered again.

I grinned as I crept along the broken glass and debris littered across what used to be the school hallway. Dead vines crept up the stone walls as if shielding the stone from further danger.

Dani searched wildly around in the dark. She lit another match. Flashlights were scarce these days. Unless you were from the prosperous electoral sectors like Charlie and Delta, you didn't own a flashlight, and if you owned one, charged batteries were impossible to find or non-existent due to acid corrosion.

The weak sectors had underground dealings they called "The Market." If we passed by some batteries or flashlights in The Market, they were wicked expensive to purchase. One of my heightened abilities allowed my vision to see clearly at night, so matches or flashlights weren't a necessity.

Dani stopped, unaware I was a few feet away from her.

"Daaaaniiiielleee," I dragged out.

Dani screamed so hard she tripped on a loose board on the ground. I made a quick grab for her and steadied her on her feet, laughing as I did so.

"That was not funny, Marie!" my friend scolded, pulling away from my firm grip.

Danielle wore a loose pair of jeans and a cute red blouse. Her sneakers were worn and dirty from years of wear and tear, which contrasted against the new shirt. Dani wore her blonde hair in a loose ponytail under a denim cap with red symbols in the front. A style so different than my dark jeans and shin-high combat boots. I preferred substance versus style. Water was scarce, and dirt layered over everything in our division of Echo, so keeping my clothes clean always proved to be a hassle—hence the darker colors. Plus, black gear prevented me from getting caught most of the time when sneaking into restricted areas. Sometimes, I would wear a gray shirt under my cracked leather jacket to change it up. My long, dark hair kept in a regular braid prevented creepy crawlers from nesting in it, and boy were there a lot of them loitering in our neighborhood.

The nuclear war killed people, not cockroaches.

The refined girl stood in front of me. Dani's father and mother worked at the same academy as my father. Her mother tutored rich kids at the university, while her father taught mathematics. Because in my household the breadwinner was my father, I didn't get cute shirts or make-up. Danielle sported pink lips and black-lined lashes.

I felt all my muscles tighten. I bit my lip. Jealousy

wasn't an emotion I felt often. The life I lived was a heck of a lot better than the one I would've had, had my parents not found me when they did.

Shaking off wayward thoughts, I apologized. "I'm sorry, Danielle. I was fooling around."

Dani pouted with an exaggerated purse of her pink lips. Her long, fair eyelashes fluttered. "You better be! Now, come on, the meal wagon will be here soon."

We walked back out of The Waste with me leading the way this time. Holding Danielle's hand, I led her over piles of broken concrete and steel. The sun was beginning to set behind the cloud-ridden sky, the cover so dense we could barely make out the bright red and purple hues the falling star provided. The meal wagon came by every night at the same time to deliver meals to each poor sector of the country. Even though Foxtrot held a massive military facility, the area surrounding it was a lot more rundown and destitute. There were deserted neighborhoods left in Foxtrot after the explosion. Many of its residents migrated to Echo, bit the bullet in dilapidated buildings, or lived underground. Not like we had exceptional living conditions beforehand. The entire west coast had been lit up by a powerful nuclear weapon that destroyed anything living in California to Kentucky. The foreign gun demolished the west and mid states and whatever other country opposed them.

We called the war Ragnarok, but it could be classified as the third world war. The weapon was unlike any we've studied. The warring nations were lucky it didn't cause as much damage as expected. Some land happened to be still habitable. When a much smaller bomb went off in the Atlantic Ocean, the explosive ended up creating a tsunami so massive it brought all of the Caribbean islands like Cuba and Haiti underwater.

I lived in a small area of what was once known as Boston, renamed New States as a way of keeping together some semblance of normality. Although the government compressed the large city due to the war-ravaged lands, instead of living together, we were split into sectors as a way of keeping the class hierarchy. It was easier to protect the one portion remaining than it was to protect the entire country. Here we were, doing anything possible to save ourselves from complete ruin, yet ruining everything in return.

Regular weapons would not help. The U.S. government had been secretly working on an experiment that would heighten the abilities of human soldiers. No matter the devastation left behind by the medical lab in Foxtrot, it didn't stop our military from creating a weapon unlike anyone else's. With few remaining livable areas, losing Foxtrot should've deterred the government away from their experimentations.

It didn't.

"So, you know that guy I've been trying to get to notice me? I think he's gonna join the military soon." Danielle broke through my numbing mental fog.

I looked over my shoulder, noting the blush on Dani's cheeks. "Oh, yeah?"

Our current military is nothing to joke about. The military's response to Ragnarok was to create capable soldiers enhanced with abilities such as super-speed and regeneration. The weapons in America's arsenal were built bigger and better and much deadlier than the other countries could have ever thought possible. The soldiers were dropped on the ground and made to fight. A successful military campaign made General Braggart the most feared man in our nation. He worked from the darkness. No one ever got to see him, and no one could ever pinpoint his location long enough to attack him.

"Yeah. He says he wants to become a super-soldier. But if he's not compatible, he was hoping to at least become a Ground Force patrolman."

I cringed but kept it from Danielle's line of sight. "Ground Force officers are wicked, Dani. You know that."

She tightened her grip on my hand as we worked our way over a corroded metal pillar. "He's not like you think. He might even cause a new trend of Ground Force officers to emerge."

General Braggart had soldiers dedicated to him and his cause. The residents steered clear of the enhanced military soldiers and the military-appointed groups of officers known as Ground Force. Their job was to keep the crime minimal in the habitable sectors. Ground officers mainly protected the rich from the poor. They were the ones who caused most of the incidents within the needy areas. The power held in their hands perpetually got to their heads.

With most of the world annihilated, everyone had been pushed to live underground or in sectors like Echo and Foxtrot. The society suffered during Ragnarok. Nobody had been safe from greedy political leaders and prideful military personnel. By adding Ground Force, they were making a hard life even more impossible to live. If rubbing the people's faces into the dirt wasn't enough, the government had split the sectors into six.

Alpha held the most potent facilities, with its top-notch scientists and politicians. The only ones to live or work there had a high rank in the government. Bravo had many abandoned, ruined areas most residents barely traversed anymore, preferring to live in the city of Ashur or the cleaner areas of Bravo Antiquis. The population of business owners lived in Ashur.

Charlie was the next important sector. In Charlie, those who worked in the education system—or were a politician with an upper-hand in our crippling government—had residences they frequented. The sole major university or education center in Charlie had been built in a spot near the town of Trēbeta. My father lived in a small hostel in Trēbeta during the week and traveled to Echo on the weekends to visit with my mother and me.

Delta was the financial district. It harbored the only two heavily guarded banks in our nation. A few legitimate traveling shops and some illegal underground markets made their home in Delta.

My residence was in Sector Echo, formerly known as Beacon Hill in the Greater Boston metropolitan area. Our governing parties split each sector, but each party was controlled by the President and his military. My father taught in Sector Charlie but lived in Sector Echo, which made his travel time a little over two and a half hours long on the shuttle. And while the people who got a university education were wealthy or their families were in one form or the other of the government, I always hoped to end up at the university too.

Making our way out of the maze of clutter and debris, Danielle and I walked down the broken cobbled road. We were surrounded by abandoned frames that were at one point supposed to have been cars, and collapsing foundations that were once known as high-rise buildings. The ever-present dust made it hard to take a breath, and the permanent stench of degradation lingered on our skins. There weren't any decent apartments or homes anymore—industrial buildings within the old city being the only structures that survived the chaos because they were built with carbon and stainless steel, among other metals. Each floor had offices and each office became a home. We had one giant mess of what had once been a thriving society left behind after the war. If the twenty-first century thought they were in a recession—they didn't know what poverty looked like.

The avarice of the country's government brought upon its barrenness and disgrace. The government forgot to fight for the people, instead opting to fight for power. Danielle jumped over a steel frame that had once held up tons of concrete and stone but was now another piece of our wrecked civilization. Another reminder we were lucky to be alive. The universe had chosen for us, but it had been better than the only other option we'd had—death. I looked around at the open courtyard in front of me.

No, the choice wasn't mine to make, but it had been mine to live.

CHAPTER TWO

A STRONG GUST of wind blew dirt around Danielle and me as we made our way toward the courtyard. Ahead, people who lived in the surrounding buildings gathered, awaiting the meal wagon's arrival. Wood from broken picnic tables loomed in one pile at the edge of a building. The citizens who lived in this neighborhood at least tried to work together to gather the bare necessities. Every once in a while, I felt a little bit of pride—a little bit of hope. Then I would see men, like the ones in front, of me fight about something as inconsequential as being bumped into, and I'd lose what little I gained. We walked around them to avoid being a part of the situation.

The three main buildings standing like towering guardians over the open park no longer appeared intimidating. Their bricks piled in different spots. Moss and algae in varying shades of black and green covered the exterior paint of the building. I could imagine the courtyard having pathways and green, fresh-cut grass at one point. The ground now had layers of trash, dirt, and sand.

When I finally made it around the struggling men, I studied the gathered citizens. Seeing them standing there for their rations struck me as ludicrous. To see how the times had changed so much from my father's stories always made it seem surreal. I looked around the courtyard, feeling the usual wave of melancholy hit me. This life had not been an easy one to live.

Clean, drinkable water was expensive, while a juice drink or soda-pop was rare for struggling civilians. The powers that be restricted bathing because of the limited water resource and the expense of being able to use it. Food came dehydrated or freeze-dried in bags known as MRE's (or meals ready to eat). You had to go to The Market underground, which had once been the sewers or subway tunnels, to barter for actual fruits, vegetables, or a rare piece of beef. Unless we knew someone or knew someone who knew someone in a position of high authority, our education ended as soon as we could count, read, and write. Most of the strong young men were drafted into the military, while single women worked the side streets as illegal paramours to make enough to support themselves or their families.

Heat was a hard commodity to come by unless it came from the sun, and even then, we rarely got to see the bright orange beacon in the sky through the thick blanket of smog. I didn't remember the last time I saw the sunshine for more than a day. Because of it, our days were cold and wet. The people turned on one another, becoming as cold as our surroundings. The world had regularly been a scary place, but now it lacked any moral fiber. The people lost their humanity along with their hope and faith. It was a dog-eat-dog world, and if it wasn't for the affection my parents had for one another, and their love for me—enough to adopt me from the streets—I wouldn't believe there was any *right* left in the world.

The smells of the courtyard assaulted my nose. From foul-smelling bodies to days-old trash, I tried to stay away from this area as much as possible. The unwashed masses stood ahead of me wore typical day-to-day apparel comprised of ripped, soiled, or stained clothes.

If someone wore new or clean clothes, it turned heads in this neighborhood. The clothes the wealthy considered fashionable differed from Echo's usual attire. The rich wore clothes that were colorful and flamboyant, with hoops to emphasize their lower bodies and colors found in the rainbow. The clothing was their way of distinguishing themselves from poverty. In one of my many books, I had read a line from William Penn that had stuck with me for years.

"Humility and knowledge in poor clothes excel pride and ignorance in costly attire."

No more-exact words could describe the sheerly

ridiculous nature of the wealthy. If they felt a need to distinguish themselves from poverty, let them run around like colorful peacocks. I wouldn't be bothered by their greed, nor disturbed by their pretension. I could not care less about what they wore so long as I was comfortable in *my* clothes. The clothes I wore kept me warm in the winter and cool in the summer.

The meal wagon arrived at its scheduled time. People shoved and surged to get to the car before others took all the meals. The wagon gave out a set amount of food every night, so some citizens still underwent hunger. Dani ran over to the cart to get her rations for the day. I held my hand out like the rest, trying to see over the chaos of heads, and hoped I would feel the familiar bag hit my hand as the jumbled mess of bodies pushed back and forth. The people around me jostled one another. The smell of their unkempt bodies and days of prolonged filth hit my nose.

My arm felt tense, and my insides had begun to swirl achingly. When the bag hit my hand, I felt myself release a pent-up breath I hadn't known I was holding and stepped out of the chaotic circle. A man shoved another down then stole his MRE as I side-stepped other residents.

The guy on the ground screamed, "Thief!" but no one ran over to help him.

To see him on the ground, gaunt limbs and sunken cheeks, broke my heart. Shoving the bag into my backpack, I knew there would be nothing I could do for him, especially when I couldn't get enough food for my mother and me. Dani made her way out of the mess, hiding her MRE inside her worn shoulder bag, pulling it over her shoulder and across her chest. I had already done that same thing, shoving my MRE right next to my old, but still new to me, magazines resting inside my tattered bag. Digging inside the bag, I found a protein bar. I watched as two people helped raise the downtrodden man from the ground. No one attempted to feed him from their own meager meals.

This had been my reality. The twisted life I lived.

The wagon drove away, leaving behind a trail of tracks in the dusty ground. The vehicle looked more like a tank than an actual cart. The metal pieces surrounding the car like a shield were riveted in place for extra protection. Steel bars covered all the windows, except for the small one that opened for the meal pouches. The tires lifted the carriage of the vehicle so high people could barely reach the opening, and they stood on tiptoes. The wagon hardly ever gave out enough meals. There were people in our neighborhood who fought with those who snuck an extra bag into their coffers or took an extra bottle of potable water.

My mother couldn't make it out to the meal wagon anymore because of the increasing severity of her multiple myeloma—a type of cancer caused by her proximity to ionized radiation. She had so much pain in most her bones and bone fractures in her back she could barely stand on her own. There were lots of times where I would tell my mother, Alice, I had already eaten so she would take her food without worry. Whenever I could sneak an extra protein bar from lunch, I would stick it in my bag to compensate for missing out on supper. I stared so hard at the bar in my hand I could essentially cut a hole through it. Not sure when I'd get my next meal, I couldn't afford to let another go hungry like that.

My mind had already been made up when I pulled the bar out.

I walked toward the man who had bent down to pick up a little boy from the ground. The boy merrily chewed on his meal. The man must've gotten enough for them both but lost his food to the thief. The little boy was skin and bones himself. He let the boy kiss him, placed him back on the dirt, and watched his boy finish his meal. I slowed down my pace as to not scare them. The older man's head shot up. He protectively placed himself in front of his son. The distance between us closed as a cloud of dust rose to greet us both. I extended my hand with the meal bar in it.

The man grabbed the bar with trembling fingers. "A-are you sure?"

I nodded and smiled. Turning around, I could hear him repeatedly thank me for the generosity, but I didn't do it because I wanted the acknowledgment. We all needed help. One way or another, we all needed to seek it out from somebody—be it an average human or an enhanced super-being.

Someone called out for Danielle. I saw my friend make her way to the stranger and hug them. From my spot a few feet away, I could hear them chat about boys. When the guy Dani crushed on approached the giddy duo, I took it as an opportunity to make my escape. Knowing she'd ignore me for the rest of the night, I waved goodbye and walked back to my home alone.

A breeze caught me unaware, so I tightened the leather jacket I had on closer to my body. The zipper broke, so I tightened the straps of my bag to prevent it from falling off my shoulders as I pulled the lapels together. From the smell of the air around me, so crisp and refreshing, I could tell there would be precipitation. I took a shortcut between dilapidated buildings until I got to the one that remained somewhat intact. Before Ragnarok, the structure used to be an office building the government had taken possession of, fixed, and rented out to low-income families.

I stared up at the building I called home. The government did enough to keep it from falling apart on the outside. However, the inside was another matter altogether. The old rugs had filth built up from decades of uncleanliness. The original color of the tiles and linoleum could no longer be made out. Rust covered the metal hinges, which gave them a copper color instead of a silver hue. I couldn't even describe the smells originating from the inside. The different scents in the building had intermingled for so long, I could only suppose they created their own fetid concoction. The residents there were cleaner than most who didn't have a government-owned complex.

It still didn't make me want to walk barefoot.

Those who didn't have a job or made money but didn't have an actual place to live were forced to squat wherever they could—most times in a section of the underground. The homeless had made it their permanent home, which provided the most shelter from the elements.

I walked into the building after punching a code into the encoder on the front door—the only security the government had put on the place. I closed the door behind me and walked up fifteen flights of stairs. My legs never could get used to the burn every time I rose up these stairs. There weren't any rails to assist you on the way up or down anymore. The rug on each floor had been worn and tattered. The walls' paint flaked and curled like a dry orange peel all around the building.

Most residents kept to themselves, preferring to post "keep out" signs on their doors. Other residents left their doors wide open as an invitation to be robbed or to cure their loneliness. I ignored having conversations with my neighbors. Being near malodorous individuals left me nauseous. This distance was a side effect of having an overly sensitive nose.

A boy sat on the flea-ridden rug on the landing before my floor with a toy car in his hand. The used vehicle once painted a vibrant red, sported three wheels instead of four. The boy barely budged out of the way as he made car noises on the dethreaded rug. The car ran over two toys—an army soldier and a one-armed Barbie. I shuddered. The scene he offered was one we often saw on the streets of Echo.

Once on my floor, the cacophony of screaming adults and crying babies somewhat soothed me. Doors slamming and children laughing were a constant distraction in my building. The smell of unwashed skin and dog feces assaulted my nose. I walked down the darkened hallway to my door.

I grabbed the small key hanging around my neck and unlocked the padlock buried within the door frame. The metal riveted to the door and the frame met when the door was closed. The lock was a way to keep extra security on the premises. My mother called out from the other side of the door.

"Marie?"

I got the lock removed as I called back, "Yeah, it's me, Mom."

My heightened hearing picked up my mother's sigh of relief from the inside of the room. I could see some movement through the padlock opening, but it was wasn't enough to have lost privacy to anyone else trying to spy. Ever since I had been old enough to go out on my own, my mother and father were always on edge with worry. At least I understood why they were still so scared. The world was a different place and not one for a young woman to be walking around alone.

When I stepped inside, I saw my mother sitting down on her rocker, knitting. I grabbed the lock and replaced it once I was inside the room. Once secured, I dropped my bag on the makeshift table behind the wall dividing the kitchen and living area. The large piece of wood from an old door served as the spot where we ate our dinners and shared stories. The wall we pushed the table against further gave the kitchen some privacy. The peeling wallpaper on the wall continued to coil down the wall like a snake. The popcorn ceiling had crumbled on one side of the living room. I made a note to scrape off more tomorrow before it fell on my mother. A torn sofa with no legs sat alone in front of the window I spent hours looking out of as if I were the eyes of a guardian gargoyle supervising the buildings myself.

I moved around the wall, looking back at my fragile mother, and made my way to her, sitting cross-legged on the floor in front of her. "I see you are using the yarn I got you for your birthday," I told my mother.

Alice Baxter grinned at me. "Winter is almost here. I was thinking of making some gloves, maybe a hat, or a scarf to keep you and your father warm."

I leaned forward until I stood upright on my knees. "Isn't it always winter in this horrid place?" Her weak hands were gently squeezed between mine. "Do they hurt?"

Removing her hand from the warm cocoon, Alice patted my hand with her own. "I love that you're so concerned for me. Do you know for how long I've loved you?"

A grin crossed my face. This interaction had been a game we played since I met the Baxters. I understood we had known one another for the last five years, but my parents constantly replied with "forever."

"You've loved me forever, Mom. Now answer the question, you old hag."

Alice grinned. "Not right now they don't, Sweetheart."

Satisfied with my mother's answer, I got up from the floor and ran back to the kitchen to get my bag. Grabbing the old thing, I rushed to my mother and reached into the bag to retrieve the dehydrated meal and mini bottle of water. "I got your food!" I wiggled the items in my hand. "Before you ask, I'm stuffed. I already ate today."

My mother lifted an eyebrow to search my face for lies. After months of lying to my mother about eating, I had become good at keeping up the poker face.

"What did you eat?"

I had a lie already marinating in my head. "I had wild rice and chicken in Thai sauce with Danielle. She was even nice enough to share the saltine crackers today."

My mother nodded, unaware of the deceit.

"Mom, stop worrying. I will not starve, you know."

Alice simpered. "I can't help but worry, Rayne."

Placing a chaste kiss on my mom's forehead, I handed off the MRE. Satisfied she would eat the food, I walked toward my bedroom with the bag in tow. There, I had ripped pages of male and female models on my unpainted walls from the magazines I had accumulated throughout the years. One side had a pile of books stacked against the wall from centuries past. I enjoyed reading them over and over again. My novels ranged from badass women to worlds full of mythological beings. Besides the books was my collection of twenty-first-century magazines still in fair condition. I had a single twin mattress on the floor I had used since I first moved in with the older couple. There were also two thick sheets thrown on top to bury myself in when the nights were too cold.

And the nights always got freezing.

I pulled out the new magazines and thumbed through them. One magazine had beautiful models on the pages and perfume ads that had long lost their fragrance. A promotional photo of a remarkable woman in patriotic gear made me stop and look further. The woman stood with her fists on her hips—so powerful and upstanding. I slid my finger down the page, pinched the edge, and ripped the sheet off the binding. Leaning over to grab some sticky tack, I pasted the glue to the back of the paper and placed it up on my wall where I could see it each time I walked out of my room.

To use it as a reminder I wasn't alone in this fight to survive.

A loud knock on the apartment door startled me out of my reverie. I walked out of the bedroom to see my mother just as frightened. A spoonful of vegetables was halfway into her mouth.

The knock came louder, accompanied by a loud voice. "Rent is due, Baxters!"

Really? Is it that time of the month again?

My mother pointed to the can under her rocking chair. The old coffee can held the cash my father had brought home for us during his last visit. He wasn't even aware rent had gone up. When Carl left us a few dollars for food or supplies, along with the balance for the monthly rent, mom and I would forgo a few things like food to complete the balance of the lease.

Alice watched from her spot on the rocking chair. I took a large wooden stick we had by the door for self-defense—in case anything happened. The military soldiers who came by to collect the rent from the tenants weren't always friendly or on their best behavior, but they were a hell of a lot better than Ground Force. One hand held the can containing our entire savings. I unlocked the door with my key and opened it a smidge.

A soldier in a pristine army combat uniform stood in front of me. He leered. I knew what he thought because it had been what most men expressed when they saw me. I shoved the can out through the crack with enough force the soldier doubled over when it made an impact with his chest. The muscles worked in his neck as he coughed and sucked in air.

"It's all there," I called out before I slammed the door in his face.

He gasped from the other side of the door and squeaked out "thanks" before he slammed the paid sticker on our door and toddled off to the next apartment. I stood with my back against the door. Relief washed through me. The abilities I had allowed me a little more room to manage simpletons like that soldier than other women, but it didn't mean I wanted to use them.

Another knock reverberated in the small room. Nervous the soldier had returned with backup, I asked for a name and gripped the weapon tighter in my hands. Hearing my father's voice, I relaxed and opened the door.

"Dad!"

I jumped into Carl Baxter's arms. The older man could barely hold on to me. He shuffled a couple feet before I picked myself up and held him straight. When I let go, Carl walked us back into the apartment. He grabbed the padlock from my hand and locked the door. Having an open door would be an invitation to get robbed, and we worked too hard for what little we had to have someone else feel they deserved our meager possessions.

"You're home early this week," Alice called from

her seat.

Her husband walked over to his ailing wife and planted a kiss on her lips. "The kids had a three-day weekend, so they sent us home on the shuttle."

The shuttle was the only form of mass transportation to and from different sectors. The machine worked like a large hovercraft over heated air—slicing through gravity without suspension cables or tracks. The shuttle cost a small fortune if used all the time. My father took advantage of it whenever the university coughed up the money for the staff.

Mom and I forever took great pleasure in these little surprise visits. It felt great when my parents were home together. They showed me the true meaning of happiness. I could only hope to one day earn someone's love and to love them in return as I'd been taught these past few years. I closed my eyes. My mind sought the silhouette of a boy reaching out to me. In my head, the boy made me feel safe, but I couldn't remember what he looked like. Whenever I tried to remember him, images of what it would be like in the tundra hit my senses.

The winter nights.

Every year since I lost my memories brought images of him and others.

After my parents shared the MRE I had brought home, Carl carried his wife to their bedroom and locked himself in the room with her for the rest of the night. I looked at the now empty room and shook my thoughts of the illusive man from my mind.

Giggling to myself, I stepped out to give them their space. I grabbed the lock, touched the key that continuously hung around my neck, and dropped a note for my parents on the small table—in case they surfaced at one point or another that night. Laughter bubbled in my throat as I shook my head. Stepping out of the apartment, I locked the door and walked down the shady hallway.

A casual walk might be beneficial for me.

Or, it might not.

CHAPTER THREE

THE LATE-NIGHT noises had died down to scuttling rats or bats screeching above my head. I passed an older male climbing the stairs as I made my way back down the staircase. He grunted a greeting as I walked past. I pulled my jacket closer together. Pushing through the front door of the building, I breathed in the cold, fresh air. It smelled like snow. The people walking around that time of night sought shelter or looked for trouble. I wanted to give my parents some privacy. My eyes sought out the window to our living space. Not knowing where else to go, I decided on a friend's bar.

I walked to Traces—a little hangout the people in the neighborhood frequented for fun. Tree limbs creaked as they swayed; the wind bit at my bare skin. The path to Traces was always easy to spot. People visited often. We all looked for a moment's reprieve from life's failings by visiting a place that appeared reasonable. I had become a regular, but because I knew the owner's son, who moonlighted as their bartender on most nights. If it weren't for him, I would find no reason to visit the only bar in Echo. Underground bars like Traces made their own alcohol to supply the neighboring citizens. I drank none of the experimental beer and could barely tolerate all of the scents gathered in that one large space. But I couldn't help the liveliness Traces produced.

The discreet building stood on the edge of town—a short walking distance from my home. Walking into the small building through a tall metal door, I spotted a heavy-set man standing by the interior doors. The locals called him Bear. He was Traces' attempt at keeping the peace. After being patted down by security, I walked toward the small bar to see my friend Thomas serving beer to an older man. Although some couldn't afford the alcohol, they still came for the fun atmosphere and opportunities to socialize.

A gentleman at a corner table nodded when he spotted me. I nodded back. He was a regular at the establishment like me. Maneuvering around a sloshed couple, I bumped into a thin man, spilling some of his drink. I apologized and grabbed napkins to place before him. Traces was a lot more packed than usual this night. I studied the interior. There were lots of new faces in the bar. Thomas grinned at a couple by the bar. He poured them a tall drink, turned and watched me approach.

The seats in Traces weren't uniform or of exceptional quality. The plaster on the walls had seen better days, holes exposing the brick in the original foundation. They assembled tables with pieces from other scraps left behind. The eclectic ambiance is why they named the place what they did. Thomas repeatedly mentioned they'd put together the pieces to recreate the traces left behind from a time of familiar faces. The burgundy of the brick gave the room its color. If not for that, the place would have been dull in its dusty beiges and browns.

A woman who wore strong perfume flittered by me. I sneezed, rubbing my nose. The room's mixed scents always assaulted my nose.

"Hey, cutie." Thomas licked his lips like the fiend he was as I sat on a wooden stool in front of the bar. "When are you going to make me the happiest man alive?"

I grinned and winked as he poured a round for a lady in a long jacket. She wore a hood over her head that covered her features. From what I could see from the rogue strand of hair escaping the hood, it contained a mixture of turquoise and teal, with strands of light purple. The color was quite an interesting blend—and scarce unless you were wealthy. Her jacket had dust marks and patches of ruined cloth. She didn't seem like the wealthy type. The rich wore gaudy colors and unusual designs. The woman, sipping beer, resembled an Echo citizen versus someone from an affluent sector.

The woman stiffened but didn't look at me. The stranger made my insides tighten and the hair on my neck rise. For some odd reason, I felt recognition from a time long buried in my mind. A weird smell of seawater in the air brought images of people I couldn't place or recognize. The room I was in disappeared as I studied the blurry faces in my mind. The area we were in was a complete mystery to me.

Why am I thinking about this now?

I gave it more consideration than necessary, so I snapped out of it.

Thomas waited for my reply.

"When you stop using tired old lines on every other female walking into this place," I joked back as I buried the uneasy feeling.

Thomas took a hand to his wounded heart.

"Ugh, you kill me, Rayne."

I flinched and looked around me to see if anyone had heard him.

The lady with the hood over her head stopped drinking her beer. Her head whipped to the side to face me, making air lodge in my throat. She had a smattering of freckles over her cheeks and nose. The woman's eyes were a light lavender. The shade one degree lighter than the purple strands in her hair and barely seen under her heavy bangs. We locked eyes before the woman pulled away first. Slim fingers slapped a few bills on the counter, and she got up from her seat.

The tall, thin woman walked toward the doors and out.

I turned my attention to my friend.

"Thomas!" I hissed through straight teeth.

Thomas shrugged his apology then made his way to another paying patron.

He poured them a drink and walked back to me. "I'm not sure why you are so scared of using your first name."

It didn't scare me to use my first name. I rather preferred it to Marie. My parents thought Marie would be safer for me to use in public since Rayne had been my given name at birth. With so many military personnel gathering exceptional people off the streets all the time, my parents thought keeping my name private would make it safer for me to travel alone. I had nobody else. The Baxters were the only family I had in this chaotic world of frenzied citizens and corrupt officials. I'd do anything for family. Thomas' nonchalant reaction annoyed me.

One night, a few months back, Thomas had walked me all the way home to my door. My mother had called out my full name, and Thomas latched on to it. I told him to call me Marie, but Rayne sometimes slipped past his lips.

I sought the door the stranger had exited. Something about the woman drew me to her. Her peculiar behavior stuck, and I couldn't shake it off.

Do we know each other? Is the woman someone I knew in my lost memories?

Knowing it would bother me until I got answers, I excused myself from the bar counter to see where the stranger had gone.

As I moved toward the door of the warm interior, a grabby drunk tried to snag my rear. I slapped his hands. The older man hissed and studied the hand I smacked—his palm bright red.

"Serves you right," I hissed right back.

The man had been about to open his mouth when I heard Thomas' voice over my shoulder. "Gifford, if you try shit like that again, I'll kick you out on your ass."

The older man retreated into his chair with his face parallel to the scratchy surface of the table. He blubbered into his drink like a child who had gotten in trouble. Thomas grinned. He got a kick out of the drunk ones. I shook my head and waved good-bye. The woman still at the forefront of my mind, I would get no sleep tonight if I didn't get answers.

Walking out of the bar, I looked to my left and right. The night was quiet. The bats I had heard before no longer swept the dark sky. Even the rats frequenting the trash cans kept hushed. Snow fell to the ground in dense clumps. I followed a set of footprints resembling those of a female. The storm roared, hiding what little I saw. The prints veered to the right of me and into the dark alley of the neighborhood. I moved to follow, getting ready to intervene in someone's secret life.

The night's breeze blew harder, and sound whistled through the buildings. A lid of a metal trash can crashed to the ground. The sharp sound echoed between the walls. Startled, I brought the worn-leather collar of my jacket up higher and tucked my head inside to avoid the cold chill and goosebumps racing down my spine. Ghostly sounds haunted me as I continued my walk in the darkness. Being able to see easier in the dark didn't help me become fearless. The night still unnerved me. I passed people sleeping along the side of the building, using whatever they could to protect themselves from the elements. Drifters huddled together for warmth. I swallowed, feeling nervous for the first time since coming up with this stupid plan.

The footsteps disappeared at the end of the alley. I placed my hands into the pocket of my jacket. The cold trickled down my veins absorbed by my bones. I couldn't shake the cold. My fingers found small piece of hard candy I had forgotten was in the pocket. Taking my hand out of the pocket of my jacket, I stared at the sweet candy sitting in my palm. The alley was full of people who could help me. I looked at the candy again. There had to be someone who would give me some information in exchange for a sweet treat. Spotting a boy digging through the trash, I slowly approached him.

Then I stopped.

The boy looked ravenous. He looked up at me through the curtain of snow like a critter caught in the act. I didn't want to startle or provoke him. Being in this part of my neighborhood was foolish enough. Several drifters watched from their spots on the ground. My fear intensified. The boy didn't move, and neither did I.

What the hell am I doing?

Not for the first time did I think this idea was ridiculous.

"Psst... You... Miss."

My entire body stiffened. Part of me wanted to look at the person calling me from behind, and the other part wanted to run away in self-preservation. I took a deep breath. My entire body erupted into more goosebumps on top of the ones I already had. I didn't move but turned my head to the side in profile.

"Yes," I mustered with false bravado.

"Are ya gonna eat that sugar there, Miss?"

I closed my hand. The candy sat inside untouched. Taking another deep breath to steady my frazzled nerves, I turned my body to the side. My legs shifted to a more comfortable stance. If someone came at me from the front or back, I could carry my weight in whatever direction I needed.

"I would eat it, but I could give it to you for a favor."

The feminine voice moved closer. "What ya want for it?"

"An answer to my question."

The owner of the voice appeared beside me. The woman had her hair cut short. She wore scars on her face like a badge of honor. There was a slight growth of hair on her chin and upper lip. "What question is that, Miss?"

I turned to face her. "All I want to know is if you've seen a woman come by here with a long trench coat and a hood over her head?"

The lady rubbed the peach fuzz on her chin. "Ah, ya, I did. She went left at the end of the alley, toward The Waste."

"Thank you." I dropped the candy into the woman's open hand.

The woman gripped the candy within her bony fingers as if the snow would melt it. Others gathered around her to see the sweet morsel. Candy was a challenge to come by for anyone living on the street. My parents had a sweet tooth, filling up a dish once a month with different colored candy pieces.

Not waiting for a response, I walked past the other squatters toward the end of the alleyway. The snow fell. Flakes gathered on the sleeves of the old leather, so I brushed them off and stuck my hands back into the pockets of my old jacket.

I walked the lonely path, looking around me for any danger lurking nearby. Unlike the other darkened corridor, this alley had no one in sight. The buildings fell apart on this side, unable to hold themselves together. It established that it was more of a disadvantage to hunker down in this area because of the falling debris.

The empty city here in The Waste felt colder, as the breeze ferociously blew through the rubble and cracks. The night sky, barely lit by the moon behind the clouds, lent a small amount of moonshine around the center of the dark alley. I watched my warm breath puff out smoke signals in front of me. The temperature had significantly dropped.

My steps halted. A racket came from ahead. I heard several grunts and what sounded like boulders hitting the brick walls of the abandoned buildings. Debris flew through the opening. My feet rooted to the ground. Whatever was happening in the area behind the buildings gave me pause. The sound of objects slamming against the building made me duck behind some crates.

The old product crates proved a slight relief. They would not protect me from whatever angry individual lay beyond the wall. In the distance, I heard a female scream. My entire body felt flushed and electrified all at the same time, and before I knew it, I was off.

I ran toward the blows resonating against the stone walls and concrete ground. Someone was receiving a beating, and I feared it was the stranger from the bar. My adrenaline surged. I hurried toward the noise. An abundance of energy coursed through my body, unlike it ever had before. Ahead of me was a discarded metal trash can used for bonfires. Not seeing a way around it, I jumped clear over it. The groans grew louder the closer I got to them. The smell of blood infused the air I inhaled.

I ran faster.

When I turned the corner, the scene in front of me made me halt my steps. I saw a man in a long, black government coat covered in insignias and military boots, pinning the female from the bar against the wall. The long strands of her bi-colored hair now wet from the falling snow. Her feet dangled in the air. Scared of what could become of her, I looked down on the ground for a weapon I could use.

I saw a large iron pipe.

Grabbing it, I ran over to the nearly unconscious woman. The man turned around right before I swung the pipe down. He held the woman with one hand and grabbed the pipe with the other. My heart dipped to my stomach. The man unnerved and fascinated me.

What the hell?

He had eyes so green they illuminated the night, and hair so glossy it seemed drenched in water. With all of the smells of the area invading me at once, I made out the scent of sandalwood and mint soap. He growled, bringing me back from my shock. This man had become feral and displeased and a hell of a lot scarier.

He yanked the pipe out of my hand. I lost my balance and fell at his feet to watch with trepidation as he lifted his mud-covered boot. My eyes closed when the man used his foot to push against my shoulder. The force was so powerful, I slid on the snow and hit my back against the opposite wall.

The wall exploded around me.

Pain registered in my body. The stones piled on my head, shoulders, and legs as they rained on top of me. With trembling arms, I tried to cover my body. My heartbeat was erratic. I could hear voices above of the rubble and over the drastic beats of my heart. Seconds after, the pain subsided.

I'm dying.

If I felt no more pain, then I had to be dying.

I tried to relax my breathing. Adrenaline ran through my veins. My senses heightened to incredible magnitudes. Reaching out through the rubble with my hearing, I heard the man talking to the woman I had tried to help. My body pulsed. Fingers shook underneath the debris.

"Do you see what you made me do?" he began. "I killed an innocent woman because you wouldn't cooperate and come, Seaa."

Seaa.

Why did that name sound suddenly so familiar?

I sniffed the air and remembered the scent of warm days on the beach. The memories Seaa seemed to awaken in me.

A strangled cough penetrated the rubble. Following a cough came the sound of a body being dragged across the ground.

"Screw you, Rome," Seaa gargled.

There was male laughter and a thud. Seaa wheezed and coughed again. I couldn't sit still any longer. I was still alive and felt fine, so I gathered all my might and pushed through the rocks above me. The clatter caught the attention of the other two people in the alley. I rose from the rubble in time to capture the confused look on the man named Rome's face and the dismay in Seaa's expression.

The frightening man removed his foot from on top of Seaa's chest. He picked her up off the ground and threw her against a different wall. Another explosion of stone and debris flew around the female. My fingernails pressed into my palm, drawing blood. I grabbed the discarded pipe from the ground, passing it back and forth between my hands.

Rome's head tipped to one side as he watched me. With no more thought to my safety, I sprinted toward the dark angel standing in front of me. He didn't expect my speed—hell, I didn't either. When I reached him, I placed one hand on his chest and pushed with all my might. There was a rush of excitement when I saw him soar through the air with arms and legs flailing for purchase. The bastard landed on his feet but skidded a few feet more from the force.

He lifted his head, but I was already there.

I swung the pipe around and made contact. The man flipped in the air and landed on the ground, unconscious. I couldn't hear him breathing but knew he would live—the faint sound of his pulse evidence. The alley was once again dark. No sounds reached my ears. There were no other people nearby, but I didn't plan on sticking around long enough to find out. Rome lay still on the ground. In a few minutes, he could be up to tear me into pieces.

I shivered.

These distractions will be the death of me.

CHAPTER FOUR

GATHERING ALL THE courage I had left, I ran over to Seaa's body, still silent under the rubble. I pushed my way through the jumbled mess and found her under a massive block of concrete. Trembling hands grabbed the stone and pulled it off her—surprised to find I had that much strength in me. From what I could gather, Seaa and Rome had similar powers to mine.

Am I something more than what I had initially thought?

I lifted Seaa over my shoulder, shaking the thought away, and ran.

There were so many things going on beyond my level of comprehension. I couldn't understand what was right in front of me. I knew deep down I wasn't like the other youths in my neighborhood, but I hadn't expected to be something entirely different. Being able to hold this woman on my shoulder as if she were a sack of flour, or survive being shoved by a grown man across an entire alley and into a wall? I had been sure my ability to see clearer at night or hear far-away sounds was a side-effect of the horrible Foxtrot fires.

But existing as more than that?

I ran past the quiet alley with its crumbling buildings, toward the end of The Waste. Once I was out of the restricted zone, I ran down the dark alley with its squatters and bums. The entire time I couldn't help but think about what had happened.

What did I get into?

Seaa felt familiar to me. More so than Thomas or Danielle, and I've known them for years. The woman bouncing around on my shoulder was someone I had locked eyes with in a bar mere minutes ago. Still, her eyes weren't the only thing comforting me. The scent coming off this woman reminded me of memories I'd long lost. The memories kept coming back to me but stayed hidden behind a locked door I couldn't pry open.

My thoughts were so entrancing I didn't even notice we had reached Traces. I was about to enter the doors to the bar when Seaa woke up and called out to me by name.

"Rayne, stop!"

Stunned, I stopped running and put Seaa down on the fluffy snow. Puffs of our warm breaths mingled with the cold midnight air were the only visible evidence we were breathing.

"Do you know me?" I asked.

Seaa straightened her coat and a large pouch hanging off her waist. She reached behind her neck, fixing what looked like a long tube. For the first time, I noticed the top of her skin had layers of colorful scales. Bright, beautiful shades of lavender and turquoise. Each intricate arch blended seamlessly into one another. I had heard of genetic experimentation conducted by the military to win the war, but I had never seen anything like her. The soldiers who won the nation's battles looked like me—normal.

Seaa stood up from the cold ground and reached out her hand. I looked at it, unable to reach out for it with my own. She saw my reaction and drew back. Closing her eyes and taking a deep breath, Seaa extended her hand back out for me to take it.

"Come on, take it. We need to get out of here."

With so many questions floating around in my head, I knew it would be a matter of time before the guy got back up and came after us. Not holding Seaa's hand didn't come from fear or repulsion. Not being able to take her hand came from confusion, pain, and sincere regret for events I couldn't summon. With quivering fingers, I placed my palm in Seaa's and held on tight.

Both of us ran through the darkened streets of Echo at speeds I'd never imagined possible. The scenery blurred right past me. I was fast, but I hadn't traveled this fast before. Right before we reached the outskirts of Sector Echo, I jerked back my hand to stop Seaa in her tracks.

"This way," I hollered.

Seaa nodded, and we ran toward the subway—a maze of tunnels and home to many of Echo's citizens. The tubes were once covered in geometric, white tiles and polished floors. There were barely any tiles left on the concrete walls, and the floors were coated in decades of gunk. The only color visible was that of dirty handprints and years of stains. Impossible to find someone down here, we ran farther down the line while still avoiding the mass amount of filthy bodies. The stench assaulted my nostrils.

Taking another turn, Seaa stopped. "Rayne, I thought you were dead."

Dead? Who's dead?

This woman came out of nowhere, bearing a resemblance to someone in my past. I didn't know who she was, but felt attuned to her somehow. Seaa knew me by name. She also thought I was dead. Things weren't adding up.

Besides, what the hell is wrong with my body right now?

My entire body felt like it was vibrating out of my skin. I was better at certain things than other kids my age, but this speed and strength was ridiculous. I feared my lost memories had a lot to do with all I couldn't understand.

I pulled my hand from Seaa's, asking, "Who are

you?"

Seaa's remarkable eyes widened, but she smiled. "Rayne, I'm your sister."

The floor appeared like the best place to handle the news. I took large gulps of air as I processed the information. Seaa leaned down in front of me. She touched my shoulder. It may have been to comfort me, but I didn't feel at all comforted. We stayed silent for a long time before Seaa took a moment to explain to me everything missing from my memory. She filled in all the gaps in my mind while I wrapped an arm around my bent knees. My other hand made it to the back of my head. Beneath the strands of dark hair that had escaped their braid lay a puckered scar beyond the thick folds.

She's right.

Sector Echo
The Waste
Operative Roman Braggart
ID: MILII6.002

MY LACKEYS RAN around the alley, looking for evidence. The soldiers found and collected several samples of Seaa's blood while I berated myself for being so damn stupid. *Unbelievable.* I got caught off-guard by a burnished-haired beauty. She had to be from Batch 001 if her strength and speed were any indications. The same batch Seaa came from. The same abomination the general warned my team had been up to no good.

Just like I rarely felt animosity from Seaa—other than she hated my guts—I felt no contempt from the new woman who showed up out of nowhere. Feeling the urge to punch things, I walked over to my van instead.

How could I have been so stupid?

I grabbed a bottle of water from the cooler in the back of the van. Popping the cap, I drank up my fill as thoughts of the girl flowed through my mind. One of the female medics from my unit came toward me with gauze in hand. She dabbed at the cut on the side of my head, her breasts pressing closely to my face. Distracted from my thoughts, I leaned away from the medic. I wasn't in the mood for pushy women, deciding I'd had enough of them the last hour. She gave me a sultry look from underneath fake lashes. If she expected to gain from this, like every other woman I'd known, she was mistaken.

Moving her hand from my face, I grabbed another bottle of water and pushed away from the van with the heat of her eyes on the back of my neck. I didn't have a problem mixing business with pleasure. Yet, I couldn't get the situation out of my mind. Ignoring the female medic, I thought back on the job.

We utterly destroyed the alley. It was a good thing it was The Waste.

Iron rods stuck out of the crumbling buildings, and the debris littered the ground we walked on. A small fissure of moonlight lit up the alleyway, showing me how my kind could demolish an entire area if we weren't careful. My men climbed over the large pieces of cement, fishing through it to find anything that would assist us with our search.

In the beginning, I hadn't meant to hurt the new woman. After all that fighting with Seaa, my adrenaline had boiled over, and I couldn't control the power coursing through my legs. I felt sick thinking I had killed an innocent woman. Notably, one that looked as insanely beautiful as her.

Strike that.

I frowned.

I'm not that shallow, am I?

Thinking about how gorgeous she appeared in the fight's aftermath could prove to be a stupid decision. Except, for her to be alive, and still kick my ass was an unpleasant surprise. My phone rang, once again disrupting my thoughts. KeViewers replaced cell phones when most of our cell towers got destroyed in Ragnarok. The KeViewers were now virtual computers that lit up the air in glittering screens. We used them to make and receive calls but through a satellite mapping system. The KeViewer additionally doubled for a camera and a camcorder. The more bells and whistles the phones had, the more money others knew we had to spend on them.

"What?" I yelled into the receiver.

The voice on the other end gave me the chills. "Is that any way to speak to your father?"

I exhaled.

Not once did it matter that I volunteered for Unit 13's Batch 002 test rounds for Project Hercules. Nor that I had the strength to kill with one jerk of my hand. Or, hell—run speeds like those of a cheetah. General Brockton Braggart disturbed me. My father had told me about the escape and destruction of the underground facility where we held Batch 001 a few years back.

The explosion rattled Foxtrot.

One of the cover labs sitting above the site received the brunt of the burst and scattered to a neighboring village. The staff behind the scenes used the explosion as an excuse and reason to collect all of the escaped creatures.

No. Creature is too much of a harsh word for the woman I saw today.

Seaa was closest to being the "creature" of the group, and I didn't even use the word to describe the mermaid-like woman. *Creature* was the word my soldiers used when talking about my father. The word we used when we didn't think he would be listening.

Unfortunately, my father knew it all.

The human-devil never let mundane things like that affect him. So long as his soldiers were faithful, Brockton Braggart didn't care one bit what we thought of him or his methods—not even the reflections of his son.

The first genetically altered super soldiers.

They were the first group ever created by the brilliant doctor, Sebastian Lester. The scientist had grown the children from Petri dishes. Five years ago, they escaped with the help of the old doctor. He died in a mining tunnel explosion, assisting them. His body had been retrieved along with the other deceased teens.

What they did with the masses, I didn't know or care.

Knowing my father, he burned them all in a pile and watched as he twirled that damn mustache of his. At most, a handful of them had been caught.

I volunteered for the new round of testing—this time for grown subjects both physically and in brainwave activity. I spent a year getting adjusted to the changes my body made. The change hadn't been easy, and several soldiers couldn't handle it. The inside of our bodies molded and shifted into something unnatural, to withstand physical strikes. It took another year to get our abilities under control. Being able to run fast didn't mean we could stop from crashing into a wall. Because we could take a hit, didn't mean we could avoid them all the time. After two years of training, the military thought we were ready to fight.

Braggart had been more than excited Batch 002 came out as he wanted—all of his soldiers dedicated to him, the Project, and our government. Even after Ragnarok happened, the nations worldwide didn't think one war had been enough to appease them. Countless battles continued, and it took our military's launch of the superhumans to make the other warring countries retreat to their drawing boards. While they sought ways to create super-soldiers of their own, my nation's military continued to excel.

We spent the last three years fighting the odd battle on foreign soil, drowning in the chaos. Afterward, the soldiers from the second batch spent it debriefing and looking for the escapees. I had tracked down Hail, who hid out in Sector Charlie. I brought him back to home base alive—although with an extensive amount of physical damage on both of us. Hail had been strong. I was stronger. I received word a fishlike human had been spotted walking near Sector Echo. So, I took the case, knowing from my briefings it had to be Seaa.

Finding her proved a lot harder than finding Hail. Seaa was a slippery catch. I looked all over Sector Echo but couldn't catch her scent. After being harassed by my father and my incompetent partner, I broadened my search techniques. Seaa had slipped up that night. I got word from Intel a woman meeting her description had walked into the building housing Traces. I watched from the rooftops for over an hour before I caught sight of her exiting the building in a hurry. I followed and thought I had her for good before she eluded me again with the help of another genetic human. The girl was no regular human female if she could throw me on my ass with one hit.

Then I remembered I was still on the phone with my father.

"My apologies, Sir."

General Braggart laughed on the other end of the line. If Braggart laughed, you needed to be miles away from him. "So, do you have good news for me then?"

I finished my drink. I threw it back inside the van before I answered, "That's a big negative, Sir."

"Why not?" General Braggart replied with an eerie calm.

I pressed two fingers to my temple, rubbing at the spot counterclockwise to relieve a colossal migraine. My father sounded ready to blow a gasket. I teetered between telling him the whole truth and giving him random bits of the night's events. I judged my surroundings, seeing again how much destruction had been left behind from my fight with the two women. Knowing my father would find out the truth, I opted for giving him the whole truth.

"Another escapee ambushed me. The woman looked a hell of a lot like one of the experiments presumed dead."

General Braggart was briefly silent before he answered, "Another experiment in Sector Echo? Two birds with one stone. Sounds spectacular. Which is she? Flora?"

One soldier waved me over. I gave him the signal to hold on. "Dark hair with big brown doe eyes," I replied. "But, no. Not Flora."

The number of women in the first batch was minimal. Most of the bunch were male, so that left a handful of choices, and the only ones matching that description were two: Silk and...

"Rayne."

My father thought of the same girl I did. "My guess exactly, General. Except, was she not shot twice in the head and presumed dead during the river crossing?"

The general cleared his throat. "Her body was never found."

I had read all the reports on the missing experiments. In Rayne's, several amounts of blood had been found on the scene of the river crossing as with Flora. The deadly rapids by the facility assisted the military in stopping the experiments before they could make their escape. Surveillance showed the girl shot at multiple times. The weapon used was a specialized Barrett .50 caliber. Those rounds were strong enough to break a bone and guaranteed to cause damage. Just because her body wasn't found didn't mean she would still be alive and well. No person—healthy or otherwise—could survive a shot like that.

I thought back to the woman I met.

Damn, but she was gorgeous.

Her hair was dark and woven into a makeshift braid. The clothes she wore looked more natural for a citizen of the sector. She ran into the fray like an innocent bystander, not once taking into account what she had gotten into by doing so. Her great dusty eyes came into my mind.

How could I forget that?

With bright, wide eyes, that look on her face told me she was surprised to be alive after I pushed her. Nobody knowing their capabilities could look as stunned as she had.

I sighed again. "Well, it seems she may have survived."

"No matter that. Don't think I've overlooked the fact you let not one, but two experiments escape."

Reminding my father I had been ambushed and caught unaware wouldn't make a difference. I became a superhuman soldier. That meant I could bring down foreign armies on my own with my two hands. Capturing another genetic experiment shouldn't be so hard to do. Except, it was difficult to contain a being who is stronger and faster than average humans. Let alone trying to catch one who has spent the last five years avoiding the military, hiding, and honing their skills. I cracked my neck. Now I had more than a migraine. I felt tense everywhere.

I looked back at the female medic. Knowing where my thoughts headed, I shook my head and ran a hand through my hair. My priority right now was to find the women and bring them back to the facility. My orders were clear. Making my way toward the soldier who had called me earlier, I noticed a trinket in his hand. The jewelry piece may prove to be of great use to me.

"I may not have a lead on Seaa anymore, but I may have found one for Rayne."

"Excellent son. Find her and bring her back." After a pause, my father added, "Alive."

I rubbed my temples again. The soldier holding a small link chain in his hand moved closer to me. Taking the necklace with a silver key attached to the end in my hand, I replied, "Roger that."

I hung up the KeViewer and studied the chain.

It seems like I found you, little Rayne.

CHAPTER FIVE

THE SNOW HAD stopped painting the sector with its white powder. The breeze still blew, and I listened as it whispered between the buildings and scattered dead trees. A Ground Force officer walked down a well-beaten path away from where I hid. I pulled myself out of the utility hole when the coast cleared. Dealing with the news of my background was more than enough for me to process at the moment. Adding a Ground Force officer wouldn't bode well for myself or him.

I got up and searched the area for anything out of place. Seaa told me to be careful heading back home. I took the advice. Two steps backward took me farther from the tunnels. From there, I turned around and beat down the streets as if the fires of hell licked at my feet.

Seaa tried to convince me the best thing to do was to leave town. But I wouldn't leave without my parents. The two people who cared for me and clothed me meant more to me than everything I had learned. I parted ways with Seaa, choosing the most deserted paths back home.

Patrol Humvees drove around in convoys throughout Sector Echo. The military spared no expense getting what they wanted, and their caravans were more than likely looking for Seaa and me. I must have been stupid to think I was an ordinary girl, albeit one with heightened senses. How could I have not put two and two together? The Foxtrot explosion wasn't an accident and the military displacing so many citizens was an excuse to cover up their mess. Now that I was a big part of that clean-up, there were a lot of answers I needed—like how I could've been lucky enough to have been found by a lovely couple—whom they took in as their own?

Instead, I had been a part of a military experiment.

I wasn't normal at all. I was a genetically altered super-human. At least it explained a lot of the uncanny abilities I had grown accustomed to over the past five years. Seaa's pure, yet beautiful form bore witness to the genetic consequences I didn't possess.

My sister.

Sister.

It was so strange to call someone that after thinking I was an only child for so long. Not like we were real siblings related by blood, we grew up together, learned together, and cried together. Although we had been separated for five years, Seaa told me no one had ever forgotten me—that others still searched for me, hoping I was alive.

I lived in an apartment with my parents as unusually carefree as one could in this stench of a nation, while Seaa felt the need to cover her body from head to toe everywhere she visited. Seaa stayed hidden to pass herself off as an ordinary human woman because she had multi-colored scales layering parts of her body with tiny webs between her fingers and toes.

I thought back to the bar. When Seaa had placed the money on the bar counter, all I could remember seeing were thin, long fingers. Not once did I notice if they were webbed or not. I held Seaa's hand and didn't notice it either. Seaa's abnormalities didn't surface because they weren't there. Seaa told me the ability to not reveal them was a power she controlled. Part of our altered DNA displayed itself in the use of unique skills. I didn't know mine, but when Seaa told me she could cast temporary illusions, I imagined something similar for myself.

Then I felt bad.

All the new information wreaked havoc in my mind, overloading my thoughts. In my mind, buried deep within its folds, was a girl full of guilt. I couldn't understand why I felt guilty. The feeling had already been there. Seaa may have filled in the holes in my knowledge of my past, but it didn't mean my memory had returned. To even imagine seeing my sister after forgetting her made me sick to my stomach.

With a beautiful round face, Seaa had gills on her neck right behind her ears and an apparatus allowing her to breathe oxygen from water and expel it through a tube connected to the back of her neck. Seaa mentioned Dr. Lester took the science of water-splitting to remove the oxygen from the water and inject it directly into her bloodstream. The device reaching around the back of her neck had fine needles making contact with her carotid arteries. The water moved constantly, allowing the process to happen over and over again. All she had to do was replenish the water in the pack to continue taking in the nutrients. The device was old but functional. Seaa couldn't survive long on land without it. The ability to process oxygen through the machine had been a gift Seaa said our actual creator concocted. She spoke of the older man who took care of us as a child would of their father. I couldn't remember anything from my life before waking up at the Baxter's door. At least now, I understood why.

A wound I couldn't explain before became much clearer.

According to Seaa, I had a bullet wound in my head. The bullet exited my skull. The memory loss I experienced made sense. In the chaos of that night, the leader, Thunder, had hoisted me over his shoulder and gotten me out of the mine alive. We got as far as making it over the river crossing when the military got the jump on us. We had no choice but to scatter. Unfortunately, we lost one another in the mess. No one knew where I ended up. Most of us found one another and remained together. I ended up on the Baxter's doorstep with no clue how.

I stopped walking and dropped to the floor, releasing all the pain and fear I had bottled up inside.

How do I explain to my parents I'm a morphed human being the government is hunting down? Or that I am a failed batch of the government's super soldiers?

Seaa warned me Rome was not a guy I wanted to confront on my own. With my element of surprise, I had gotten close enough to knock the bastard unconscious. I had a feeling he wouldn't be so easily caught off-guard again.

My new sister had planned to get the rest of the batch together. By being together, we were stronger as one large unit. Seaa hadn't been the only one searching for escapees. When I asked who else had been out there looking for me, Seaa turned mute. She didn't have a problem telling me all about the five years since the disappearance but had a hard time answering who else had been out there seeking.

Does that mean no one else searched for me? Does everyone think I was dead? Why am I even entertaining this line of thought?

Thinking about it made matters worse. I brushed the tears from my face and dusted myself off. The night would soon turn to dawn. My parents would be worried about me if they got up to see I hadn't been there.

As much as I wanted to run away with Seaa, I preferred to live my semi-human life the same way I had been living it before. Seaa must have sensed it because she handed me a small card with the name *Tutus Portus* inscribed on it. She remarked that if I needed help, to begin there. Tutus Portus meant nothing to me, but I took the card anyway and bid Seaa goodbye. As much as it pained me to see the woman go, I didn't have a choice. My heart was with the two people who had given me a second chance at life—even if that meant our rundown apartment or skipping meals now and then.

I watched the sky as night turned into day. No matter the density of the fog before me, the day invariably screamed through its barriers to envelop the earth in its rays. Deciding to stay, I ran the rest of the way back home. I avoided the watched areas. The alleyways and subterranean tunnels assisted. There was nothing out of the ordinary around my block from what I could tell, so I ran to the back of the building with its cracking gray paint and through the back door.

The building was unusually quiet.

At this time of day, children generally rose and screamed for attention. Parents made their way to their morning jobs. Doors would open and shut on all floors. However, on this morning, the building made no sound I could decipher. I stretched out my hearing. Nothing hid away in dark corridors either. Using my discovered speed to get up the stairs, I made it to my floor and halted as if a brick wall had appeared in front of me. The smell of blood hit my nostrils. My stomach felt queasy. Uneasy. Something was off.

The walls were nowhere near me, but I felt suffocated. The doors were all shut. There was no one moving about. I could no longer hear the silence. A shrill ring in my ears pulsed in a crescendo. The smells assaulted me, so my hand covered my nose. I shuffled toward the apartment door. The smell of blood grew. Shaking, I stood in front of our apartment.

Someone left the door open.

If I learned one thing in my life, it had been we never left our door open. Tears rolled down my face in fat drops. Extending one trembling hand out, I pressed my fingertips to the metal door and gently pushed it open farther. The room was in complete disarray. The table in the kitchen had been flipped over. All of its contents were scattered all over the linoleum floors. The kitchen cabinets were thrown open—the materials within all thrown on the floor. My legs gave way, so I used the wall to remain on my feet.

Pushing the door we had used as the surface of the table to the side, I stumbled into the small living space. Books were shredded apart and scattered all over the room. Curtains were ripped from their hooks and spread out in colorful piles across the worn carpet floor. A few chairs were broken. They threw miscellaneous items around. My heart squeezed behind my ribcage. My mother's rocking chair had been flipped over. Shaking my head in denial, I ran from room to room of our little apartment. My bedroom was in lousy disarray. The bathroom had seen better days. I procrastinated and knew it. My parents had been my primary concern, yet I couldn't get my legs to move toward their room.

Turning to the side, I studied my parents' bedroom door. There were dents and scratches all over the old wood I knew didn't belong there. There were moments in life where I knew the answer before it presented itself. Whether I wanted to see the answer or not, deep in my heart and mind, the answer was as clear as day. Being human meant feeling hope. Being human meant knowing that although the evidence was right before me, the reality may be different.

But I wasn't human.

I knew what lay beyond those doors wasn't something I wished to see.

The person trying to get in almost ripped the doorframe right out of the wall. I moved the wood, noticing they had barricaded the door from the inside. The smell of blood grew stronger. If I peeked inside, I feared I'd see far worse than the disaster in my home. Before even moving, I became a choked-up mess. I tried to gasp for air as I swiped at the tears falling from my eyes. My parents wanted to keep them out.

They tried to survive.

Nevertheless, nothing would stop the intruders.

Tears blinded me as I called out to my parents. My voice sounded foreign to me. Fingers trembling, I pushed my father's cracked oak dresser and jerked to a stop. I fell to my knees. Tears cascaded down my pale face. The room bore no light even though the curtains hung from one side. There was no light in the room because the room's residents shed no light of their own.

I tried to cry out for my parents but could not find my voice. My shaking fingers reached out for the two people I adored—broken sobs and incoherent mumbling the only sound in the room. My heart ached so much I thought I would die. I caressed the two people in the world I loved.

My parents lay on the floor in a pool of their blood. Tremors racked my tiny body as I crawled deeper into the blood. With all the gentleness I could muster in my current state, I lifted my mother's head onto my lap. I rocked back and forth as I whispered a prayer for my parents' souls. My tears fused with their blood. I had spent the last five years in perfect bliss. Now my world was in shatters. If only I had stayed home. This mess was my fault. My mother's hand dropped to the ground, so I picked it back up. As I moved her hand, I noticed ink that hadn't been there before. On my mother's wrist were eighteen digits.

88573947562 94405837

They wrote the numbers in ink and because I knew my mother didn't have it there before—it had to be a clue left for me. Burning the sequence into my memory, I laid my mother back on the floor. Looking at her other wrist for any other clues, I could find nothing else. Using the back of my hand to wipe away the wetness from my face, I slid on the blood to reach my father. I took a lungful of air through my mouth. Choking back sobs once more, I checked his wrists and saw an address:

14 Pier Central

The sector that had a name like that one was in the financial district of Sector Delta. What my parents needed me to do there, I couldn't quite understand. But if anyone had been more resolved and prepared for the worst, it was my parents. I used the back of my hand again to wipe my nose. None of this made sense.

Who came in here?

Who killed my parents?

What were my parents trying to tell me?

Seeing their bodies lying there on the floor made me sick to my stomach. I couldn't control my trembling limbs or quivering heart. Five years I spent with them, loved for *who* I had been, not *what* I was. They didn't care that I came from the streets a bloodied mess. My parents took me in and adopted me without worrying if they could afford another mouth to feed. I became a part of their lives as if I belonged here the entire time. I loved them. The world wouldn't be the same without them in it. And they sure as hell didn't deserve being left on the floor as they were.

I got off of my knees, standing over their bodies, wishing this had happened to me and not to them. Hoping it had been all some cruel joke they played on me and were any minute now going to jump up and yell "gotcha!" But they lay there in the same positions I had left them. My parents would not get back up and surprise me. They were gone, and some crazy lunatic had killed them in cold blood.

Feeling my blood boil, I slammed my fist into the drywall. Plaster rained all over the ground. My fist rested within the wall. I cried again.

Words could not express the pain I felt inside. So many conflicting emotions waged war inside of my body. I fought with myself to gain control. The magnitude of rage and the emptiness within tore my soul into pieces of confetti blowing away with the very haunting breeze whistling through my hollow heart. None of the stories or magazines I owned prepared me for a moment like this.

Bending down, I picked up my father from the floor and put him down as carefully as I could onto their mattress. I put a pillow beneath his head, and his favorite sheet blanketed his lifeless body. I did the same for my mother, taking extra care not to hurt her, even though I knew she no longer lived. When they were both settled, I took one last look at the room. There was nothing left for me here. All that was left for me to do was find the bastards who did this and make them pay.

I walked out of the room and closed the broken door as best I could. Walking into the adjacent bathroom, I saw in the cracked mirror my sunken eyes and pale features. There was blood on my face and hands. Leaning over the sink, I grabbed the gallon of tap water we had. Tainted water swirled in the washbasin. Tears streamed down my face, mixing with the bloody water already in the sink. I grabbed my hand towel and wiped hard on my skin, practically rubbing it raw. My hands rested on either side of the basin as I stared at my reflection.

What am I going to do now?

I got jarred from my melancholy thoughts by the sound of even footsteps. I turned my face toward the bathroom door.

Who the hell was brave enough to enter my home again?

If someone came back to finish the job, they were in for a rude awakening. I wasn't going to stand-by and do nothing. One more look in the mirror and I realized that I couldn't recognize my features anymore. Distorted waves wracked me from head to toe, like looking at a mirage in a desert. I took a deep breath.

Instead, I focused on the sounds entering the room.

The footsteps stopped.

The steps belonged to a man.

CHAPTER SIX

WIPING THE REST of the tears from my face, 1 walked to the front of the room in a turbulent mental state. My muscles flexed, ready to confront whomever dared come back to finish the job. 1 turned the corner. Rome stood on the other end of the room by the open front door. There was a remorseful set of sympathetic eyes staring back at me, which stirred emotions deep within. The man stayed in the doorway, and 1 couldn't help but notice how massive he seemed. 1 could see his muscles bunch—angry at me or getting ready for a fight. 1 made a fist, squelching down all of my bitter feelings. The devil's advocate standing before me would not confuse me with fake facades bringing forth misguided thoughts.

1 couldn't be that stupid.

Instead, 1 stood in front of Rome, bloodied and emotionally beaten. With legs braced, my adrenaline pulsed through my veins, urging me to fight my parents' killer. I took one step feeling my body shimmer with a foreign impulse, only to come to a complete stop when Rome spoke out loud.

"I didn't kill them."

Clenching my jaw to stop from screaming, I took another step toward Rome. "You bastard."

He closed his eyes, so I ran the rest of the way. Rome averted my attack by moving to the side. I slid past him. He grabbed my arm with one hand and placed his other on my back as he pushed me down. Pain shot up my arm and down my side. My arm stood erect with my wrist bent at an awkward angle. If he pushed me back down farther and my arm up higher—it would snap. My entire body tensed.

He stood eerily close behind me then leaned over. "I mean it, Rayne. I didn't kill them."

I didn't want to hear the excuses of a beast. I snapped my head up, having the satisfaction of making contact with his face. A pounding headache radiated from the back of my head before I came back to my senses. Drops of blood fell from his nose. At least the devil bled. He put a hand up and cracked his nose back into place—without a cringe or a flinch. Shocked, I ran into the kitchen, grabbing a knife on the way. I turned around and chucked it at him. His fingers caught it around the blade.

Rome was a lot stronger than I could ever hope to be. I dug my nails into the skin of my palm. For a minute there, I almost lost my confidence.

He took two steps forward. "Rayne, don't try anything stupid. Just come with me."

"How did you find my home? How the hell did you get in?" I asked as I took two steps back.

Looking behind me, I saw the window was my escape. Running past Rome wouldn't work. He had a lot more years of training and honing his abilities than I did. Mere hours of learning I was superhuman didn't make me an expert. But jumping out of the window, whether it killed me or not, was my only option.

Rome must've known what I thought because he said, "Don't think about it, Rayne. We may be superhuman, but distances like this can still kill us."

"I have no idea what you're talking about." I took two more steps back. "And stop saying my name like you know me." I hesitated, adding, "You know nothing about me!"

I turned to run when Rome stopped me in my tracks. "They shot themselves, Rayne. I didn't kill them. They saw my men and I enter your home. The male ran back to his room." He took a deep breath. "I didn't even think they'd do it, but they did."

My entire body lost its will to fight. Tears fell from my eyes in constant streams. My emotions were like ocean waves, pulling me in and out with the current of discomfort. I stared up at him, and my heart jumped behind my breastbone. His eyes exposed the truth of his words, and that made me feel naked—raw. I stood before him in all my pain. I shook my head.

The man was an excellent liar.

I couldn't trust him.

"I don't believe you. Seaa said you were a liar and someone I shouldn't trust."

He shrugged as if the words meant nothing to him. "Seaa isn't wrong about me. She's right; you shouldn't trust me."

I swiped at the salty tears on my face.

Rome put one hand up. "However, I'm not lying to you now. I got here by tracking the numbers on your house key. I have high-clearance, Rayne. I can get into any building I so please."

My house key?

I touched my neck. When I didn't feel the usual weight of the chain and key, I searched deeper. My hand clenched the shirt. I patted my entire chest. Rome dangled the chain from his hand.

"You left this behind in the alley earlier."

My anger increased. *I* led Rome to my parent's home. *I* killed my parents. I ran with all my strength. Knowing he would avoid me again, I faked left and moved right. Rome rolled to the side like I thought he would. He couldn't avoid being grabbed by the head and pushed into the wall. We both penetrated the wall with an eruption of concrete and plaster shooting out like a tidal wave. I landed on top of him. Straddling his lower waist, I didn't give him enough time to catch his breath before I punched him three times in the face.

The chain now in my hand, I lifted myself off the floor to make a run for it. Rome grabbed my leg. I came right back down to the floor with a loud thud. My side ached. I shoved the chain into my pocket and kicked up when he approached me. He grabbed my legs and grinned. I swung into another wall. Luckily for me, the wall held this time, so I dropped to the floor on my rear. Rome stalked toward me like a predator cornering its prey. My entire existence felt threatened and anxious all at the same time.

If it were anyone else, I was sure this fight would have killed them. The wall ahead of me held what little was left of my kitchen and home. Such crappy material bordered the house I lived in versus the rest of the world. I stared at Rome. If this man wanted to come into my home, my key wouldn't have made a damn difference. No amount of security would stop him. The ache in my body subsided, but the pain in my heart remained. If I hadn't lost the chain, they would have never found out where I lived. My parents would have still been alive if I had stayed at Traces without following Seaa out.

The tattoos my parents left on their wrists ran through my mind. They wanted me to see something. Succumbing to Rome wouldn't get me the answers I sought. I couldn't give up now, no matter how impossible things were. If I tried hard enough, I could distract him and get the hell away from him. I saw that the end of the hall held another window like the one in my kitchen. The result may be death, but it would be better than being captured.

I stood up, not knowing what else to do. Rome's eyes glowed like a feline in the dark. I felt captivated and repulsed all at the same time.

"It seems I caught myself a little mouse," he joked as he wiped the blood from his cut lip.

There had to be a way to distract him long enough I could make my escape through the hallway window. Boards covered the window, but I had the strength to tear through them. If I could make it through the wall unscathed, I could make it through some flimsy wood. I pushed back into the wall as Rome came closer. Fear sat heavy in my stomach. This man was no longer rational. He no longer wanted to explain what happened. His eyes glowed—a tactic that caused so many emotions within me.

I sucked in my breath the moment the tip of his boot touched mine. Along with his toes came the pressure of his thighs and the firmness of his chest. With our bodies in sync, I tried to stay rational. The sheer power cresting off him was overwhelming. I couldn't take a breath of air to clear my mind even if I wanted to. The whirlwind of emotions I hid inside couldn't prepare me for his close-hand combat. Rome didn't move. There was nothing else I could do but shock the hell out of him.

Mesmerized by his luminous eyes surrounded by thick, dark lashes, I lifted my body by the toes of my

booted feet. My lips met his. He briefly stiffened before he behaved as any other man would. He relaxed
his body and took one hand to the back of my head to
continue the kiss. I tried to remain disconnected but
had a hard time keeping any coherent thoughts with
his tongue invading my mouth and mind. I reminded
myself of my parents and raised my knee to connect
with his groin.

Superhuman or not, Rome dropped to the floor
in agonizing pain. I wiped my mouth. As the man
writhed on the floor, I kicked him once in the head for
good measure. I ran to the opposite end of the hall,
ripped the board from the window, and jumped without second-guessing myself. Feeling the weightlessness of gravity, I closed my eyes and prayed I'd make
it down alive.

Sector Echo
Operative Roman Braggart
ID: MIL 116.002

WHEN THE HELL did I become a hormonal teenager?
I adjusted my jeans as I walked over to the window
where Rayne had jumped.

Damn, but isn't she the brave little one.

I'd kissed several women in my lifetime, both before and after my genetic experience. There hadn't been a time when a woman threw herself out of the window to escape me. 1 didn't know if 1 was impressed or peeved with her tenacity. Instead, 1 wiped the taste of her off my lips and peered out the window. The little hellcat was at my two o'clock about two klicks out.

I guess she survived the fall.

1 jumped out the same way she did, landing on the ground without a problem. From this height, our type had no problem making it to the bottom. 1 tried to scare her into staying on the fifteenth floor, but she didn't give a damn for her safety. 1 sniffed the air. When 1 caught the scent of a tumultuous rainstorm 1 was coming to recognize as Rayne, 1 ran. My KeViewer rang. Searching for it in my pockets, 1 answered the call in my usual manner.

"What?"

The voice on the other end shook. "S-sir, do you need us to follow?"

1 knew my men were in the van watching the tracker move farther away from their location. Like any of the soldiers who took part in Plan B, we were equipped with trackers and kill switches. One kept tabs on where we were at all times, and the other ceased function of our bodily organs. If we wanted to get rid of the kill switches and tracker, we would have to find them. The problem was that soldiers had dug themselves up from the inside out to find them. Those who had tried

failed. Imminent death.

Still running, I panted, "Keep at a good distance, so you're not spotted."

"Roger that, Sir," the soldier replied.

Hanging up, I shoved the KeViewer right back into my pocket. I found her tracks in the snow, veering toward the right. I followed and felt horrible she had to find her parents like that. But not a thing I could do. I forced myself into their home, hoping to take them hostage. Rayne would come out for them, but it backfired on me. Those people she called her parents had an exit plan created a long time ago. If ever someone came around for them or their daughter, they'd take their own life before the military got anything out. I wondered how much they knew about Project Hercules.

That led me to believe her parents knew who and what she was. Abilities like hers couldn't be hidden from her loved ones for long. That too meant they were connected to someone on Project Hercules.

Who could it be? From what I could gather, the girl wasn't hiding like the rest of the experiments. If she wasn't in hiding, then she didn't remain in contact with the rest of the first batch. She could've hidden her talents from others in her building and neighborhood, but her parents were in on the lie.

The issue gave me a headache.

I jerked to a stop. Rayne's tracks stopped here. I sniffed the air, but couldn't catch her scent anymore, so I looked around on the ground for evidence of her whereabouts. Ahead of me was a set of car tracks. From the indentation, the traces left, and the grooves embedded in the snow, I knew she had jumped in a supply truck. Some vehicles from the twenty-first century still operated. Many farmers used them to bring supplies in and out of the city using bio-fuel. I followed the tracks down the hill and onto the road.

My legs moved faster.

The smell of her skin got stronger, so I pushed my body harder and farther down the tree-lined street. The clouds above me were dark. The air around me felt heavy. Rayne had been a symbol of her namesake. The clouds didn't bring rain or snow, but I couldn't get the scent of rainstorms amid spring from my mind. I turned the corner and saw the truck pull to a stop. Rayne jumped out the back, favoring her right leg over her left.

"Rayne! Stop!" I hollered.

She turned my direction in a panic. The moment we locked eyes, she bolted the other way. I watched for a second, knowing she wouldn't get too far. The girl was hurt. There wasn't anywhere she could hide. I ran after her while bumping into the crowd of people in the way. I saw her jump into the sewer, so I swore like a drunken sailor. The tunnels below were hard to track people in because of the onslaught of different smells. I hated traversing the subterranean levels. Reaching the same area, I cleared my mind and dived inside.

I got immediately bombarded with different scents—both disgusting and unpleasant. Homeless people, thieves and murderers, and con artists littered the tunnels. I passed person after person, struck with different smells and not one of them Rayne's.

Damn!

My KeViewer rang, so I drew it out of my pocket and up to my ear. "What?"

"Sir, would you like us to follow?" the soldier asked.

I ran a hand through my damp hair, looked at my hand, wiping it on my jeans. "What's your distance?"

A man that screamed criminal smirked at me. He studied me from head to toe and settled on my wristwatch and KeViewer. The bum turned back to his friends with a leer.

If the idiot only knew who he messed with.

"We are south of your location. About four klicks away, Sir."

"Negative, remain where you are."

The soldier agreed. I hung up the KeViewer and placed it back in my pocket as the criminal approached me. He watched me and grinned. There were missing or rotted teeth with his breath as sinful as he looked.

"That's some mighty fine watch you have there."

I wasn't in the mood. "Back off."

The guy walked around me as if measuring my strength. At six feet, broad shoulders and thick legs, the last thing this guy should have done was mess with me on a regular day. I was angry Rayne got away. Mad at myself for behaving like a teenage boy, and what better way to get rid of my stress than by punching a suitable hole in the idiot's face. Instead, I pulled out my Springfield .45 caliber pistol, customized to penetrate the skin of super soldiers. The gun was aimed right between the assailant's eyes. This baby would have destroyed a human should I have pulled the trigger. Lucky for the guy, I wasn't in the business of killing innocent people—although I was sure no one would miss this low-life.

The man raised his arms into the air. "Whoa, man! I got no problem with you."

I smirked and returned the weapon to my back holster. "Good to know."

I walked back toward where I knew the van and my men waited for me. People stared as I walked away, giving me a wide berth.

The walk back was quick. I sat down with thoughts of Rayne running circles in my mind. I told the first soldier I saw, "The Baxters must have known about Batch 001. Find out who is or was on Project Hercules connected to them."

The soldier nodded and ran off to the back of the van, where we had a plethora of electronic equipment ready for use.

I stopped another one of my lackeys. "Go comb the parents' room." The man turned to walk off when I stopped him once more. "Also, search the parents. If they shot themselves, it was because they had a plan in place for Rayne. Decode and advise."

The soldier saluted. "Roger that, Sir."

I was positive we would find out things that would lead me back to Rayne. The woman drove me mad. With her capture, I would take her into the bunker and be done with the chestnut-haired beauty who turned my stomach into knots.

CHAPTER SEVEN

Sector Delta

LOSING ROME THROUGH the labyrinth of blue tunnels helped me make my way toward the green-lined passageway that led to Sector Delta. 1 saw the signs posted against the concrete walls, labeling the streets above us. Not like all of the street names mattered. Most of them were destroyed or washed out from the remnants of a battlefield. The ones that remained intact were cleaned up or repurposed. The only thing that mattered down here was the faded colors of the subway system. Each subway was color-coded and used to travel within different areas of Boston before the shuttle was designed and implemented. Not everyone made enough money to get on the transport hovercraft, so the underground was our best bet. 1 walked down the long green-lined tunnel.

In the old days, a train would take forty minutes to guide someone from my side of town to the financial district of Delta, which used to be known as Seaport, according to old history books. I was glad walking no longer bothered me because seven miles of tunnels with the night I had was more than enough to make a regular person punch-drunk thinking about it. To the side of me were other human-made shafts the people who lived here made. The tubes weren't lit up with the sporadic lights from the government but encased in dirt and lit by fire lanterns. I passed by them without a second look.

Not for the first time had I been thankful I wore dark colors. The dried blood stuck to my jeans and shirt. If the citizens living here noticed, they didn't care or bother to say anything. I knew I was a wreck both on the inside and out. I'd stay away from me too if I looked like a homicidal maniac. My parents wanted me to go somewhere. If I did one last thing for them, it would at least be this. I saw a sign with an arrow posted to another tunnel. I weaved around a few people and continued down the dim corridor.

From the plenty of times my father and mother took me to the small village shops in Delta, I knew it had a street named Pier Central. I moved as fast as I could, as not to attract unwanted attention. I mixed my scent in with those around me to prevent Rome from sniffing me out by rubbing my clothes on the murky walls. When I made it through the underground tunnels toward Sector Delta, I climbed out of a utility hole, careful to avoid being seen by the military or Ground Force officers. The army was scary, but the Ground Force were spawns of Satan with wands that paralyzed and electrified you.

Thinking of Satan had me thinking of Rome.

So stupid.

I pulled the collar of my jacket up higher to avoid recognition. If Rome had his men send word of my escape, I needed to stay hidden. Besides, it helped block the wind from my chilled bones. I walked swiftly down the sidewalks packed with people, turning down several streets until I got to the one I sought. Once I reached Pier Central, I looked at the remodeled buildings lining the streets for number fourteen. Guessing which way to turn, I traveled west on Pier Central, looking at each building's street number.

Each building on the street had been built to withstand the elements but was still grand enough to attract the people. Marble encased the structures with decorative veins of gray and blue. Massive pillars held extended awnings surrounded in luscious green grass and remarkably vibrant flowers that withstood the cold winter frost. High society had small parks perfectly placed between the buildings as a reprieve for people on the go. In one park, a fountain graced the patrons of the district with clear, bubbling water untouched by waste.

Finding fourteen, I stopped to take in the massive

structure in front of me.

Doubling as apartments for its employees, Delta National Bank was one of the most prestigious banks in this sector.

What in the world would my parents need at such a large bank?

I couldn't quite see my father or mother visiting this place. The cash my father received for his work was shoved into a can or a trinket in our home. The government owned the two banks in this sector. They likewise had no problem taking what they needed to fund their wars. My parents would never hold a bank account. I tried to think back on the trips I made here with my parents. That I could remember, we hadn't ventured inside of the bank.

With Ground Force posted at the front entrance, I needed to get inside without being identified or mistaken for a bum. If the smell coming off me was any sign, I needed new clothes and a good rub down. On a long pasture of grass across from the marble structures stood row after row of shops that had a license to sell their merchandise to consumers. Different colored tarps provided shelter from the elements, and thin wood separated each stall from the other. Middle-class patrons shopped in the village boutiques all the time for their unique merchandise and fair prices. I turned back toward the village stands, not stopping once until I reached the spot that most interested me. The rich smell of new boxes and mothballs reached my nose. The clerk spotted me, coming to me in greetings.

"If it ishn't my little ray of shunshine." The old lady beamed a set of gums—sans teeth. "Oof, you shmell like death."

I sniffed myself. If the old lady only knew. "Hi, Agnes. Yeah, as you can see, I've been in the tunnels. Got anything new for me today?"

Agnes put down the colorful shirts she carried and grinned. "Of course, Shunshine. Beshides, you don't shmell that bad."

She motioned for me to come toward the back of the little booth. I did so with ease. I had been coming to Agnes' shop for the last three years to purchase my clothing whenever I had money to do so. The shop was a little tucked away haven with a tarp for a roof and upright pallets for walls. Agnes kept her clothing in boxes instead of on hooks, afraid they might get ruined. Her torn vendors' chair sat alone in a corner with a permanent indentation of the woman's butt. On trips with my father, I became good at bartering and haggling over prices. Whenever Agnes was involved, I paid full price for whatever she had in my size.

The citizens of the wealthier sectors like Delta wore apparel that stood out because of their bright, flashy colors or intricate designs. The wealthy preferred to set themselves apart from the rest of society. The middle class wore clothes that were comfortable and dependent on their positions. Most of the smaller shops near Agnes' sold items resembling the outfits of the rich.

Because I couldn't stand things that were too colorful, I repeatedly bought from Agnes, who carried clothes more to my tastes. Comfortable and straightforward articles of clothing were all I needed to survive. I watched the old lady rummage through a box. Hopefully, Agnes would find clothes to my liking.

Agnes shuffled her tiny frame and hunched over to the corner where she had more boxes stacked one on top of another. She struggled to pull one box down, so I rushed over to help. Taking the box from her wrinkled hands, I placed it on the floor beside the others. Agnes muddled through the articles of clothing until she came to a pair of jeans. She pulled them out and tossed them over to me. The rough material landed on my face. Agnes limped over to a different box and bent farther inside. She pulled out a dark shirt with long sleeves. I perused the two pieces Agnes had picked out for me. They were just my style. I was pleased Agnes knew me so well.

"Only pieshes I have your shize."

With everything going on in my life, I couldn't hold back the tears from my eyes. I turned into a blubbering mess. The salty water continued to flow, no matter what I did to stop it. The vendor's eyes widened. She patted the girl who had lost her parents and fought a superhuman soldier that morning even though she didn't know it. If Agnes knew how powerful I was or what I had gone through, would she still try to comfort me? I cast my eyes to the tarp serving as a roof. What a beautiful mess I'd turned out to be.

Calming myself before looking like more of a fool, I grabbed the bills I had left in my pocket and handed them over to Agnes. The old clerk grabbed a few of the bills and gave one back to me.

"For you, Shunshine. Buy yourshelf shom food."

I smiled for the first time since Traces, giving the old lady a big hug. "Ack, my old bonsh."

I flinched, forgetting I was a lot stronger than I suggested. I had even held back enough to not hurt the woman. "Sorry, Agnes."

Agnes waved me away to attend another customer who had stopped by her little booth. I watched for a minute to make sure I hadn't hurt the woman. Beyond Agnes' usual physical limitations, I noticed nothing out of the ordinary. I grabbed the clothes tighter to me. Walking out of the booth, I didn't see the man in front of me and bumped right into him. The man held me by the arms; his crisp uniform smelled like starch and detergent.

He wore a buttoned-down, burgundy jacket with black trimming. The buttons were overtly large and gold. His pants were in the same color and had a streak made of embroidered yarn down the sides in black. Steel-toe boots covered his feet, and an intimidating waist halter that carried a Vuwand rested on his hip. His grip tightened, and I flinched. I looked into a pair of unnerving, obsidian eyes. Thick eyebrows overlapped, while his long, crooked nose gave him a bird-like appearance. His hair cut tight and covered by the usual burgundy Ground Force beret.

"You trying to steal from this nice old lady?" The officer squeezed tighter. "We have punishments for pretty little girls with sticky hands. Don't we, boys?" He looked over my shoulder, and I followed the direction of his eyes.

I turned enough to see four other Ground Force officers. My insides turned to knots. I pulled against the hands gripping me so fiercely, but he resisted. "I didn't steal anything. Let me go!"

The men got closer, so I pulled away harder. He released his grip, and I bumped right into another Ground Force officer. This one rubbed himself against me. Disgusted, I jerked away. They leered. Studying me from head to toe, they may have concluded I would pose no threat to them. With all the grime and smells of the sewers penetrated into my skin and clothes, I gave off the appeal of a squatter.

But, boy, they are in for an unpleasant surprise.

I could feel the same adrenaline curl through my veins like rolling thunder.

"Hey, hey! What'sh going on?"

I breathed a sigh of relief at the sound of Agnes' crackly voice. I couldn't have been gladder to see the woman coming toward us. The less attention I called on myself, the better. With a cramp in her step, Agnes pointed her finger at the officers holding me in place. The old vendor may not have looked intimidating, but she was a recognized and respected merchant in Delta. The Ground Force officers were plenty immoral and unjust, but they knew better than to mess with the commerce merchants of Delta.

"Agnes, please tell these officers I did not steal from you."

The Ground Force officers awaited her reply. I saw in their faces they thought this would be an easy win. For them, I was a gift of a free female morsel they could punish.

"She mosh shertainly did not. She bought thosh fair and shquare."

Thank you, Agnes!

The officers unwillingly let me go. I nodded my gratitude to the old lady. The officer nearest to me was upset, judging by his drawn brows. I passed by the group but was forcefully pulled back by another.

"This is not over yet," he whispered through clenched teeth.

I yanked my arm away from him.

You're lucky it is.

Saluting Agnes, I took off once more at a run. My day continuously got worse. All of it because I couldn't mind my business. I ran farther away from the merchant shops lining the street, making sure no one followed me. I couldn't handle another incident, especially with those Ground Force officers. Rome had already depleted my mental strength fighting earlier that day. There was nothing left in me to deal with immoral pricks.

I turned into an alley between two industrial buildings. The empty area behind the buildings was void of life. Except for the steroid-induced rats and cockroaches, I couldn't sense anyone else in the vicinity. A full pit of water helped clean the mud off my boots. The weather got colder, turning the skies into overcast, dark grays and blacks. I shivered and scampered to a corner in the alley where I could change my clothes without being seen. The leather jacket fell to the ground. I studied the space around me. Not hearing or seeing anyone nearby, I changed into the new shirt and dropped the other one on the ground. The boots came off next to work off my pants. My black jeans stuck to my skin. Remnants of brown blood belonging to my parents painted my skin a ghastly shade.

Tears again fell from my eyes as I reached for some snow with trembling hands and rubbed the wet mess on my legs. Using the old shirt, I wiped at the wetness, stroking my skin sore. Little by little, the blood came off, but what I wanted to go would forever be ingrained in my skin and heart. Flesh-eating moths assaulted my insides to tear me up from the bowels.

With trembling hands, I grabbed the jeans with one and swiped at the tears on my face with the other. My heart ached—chest felt heavy. I pulled on the new, dark blue jeans. They fit me like a second skin from waist to ankles. Jackets and boots came next. I pulled out of my old pants pocket my sector identification and cash, then picked around the front pocket for the old chain.

The chain went back around my neck and underneath the shirt. I grabbed more snow and wiped down my hands and the outside of the jacket to wash out some of the smells of the subway tunnels. After feeling a little bit better, I walked out of the alley and toward The Delta National Bank. The streets were full of people marching up and down the sidewalks in their unique and colorful clothes. Women walked around with parasols and high updos, while the gentlemen held umbrellas over their heads. Their hoop skirts whisked off to one side as they nestled closer into the crook of their paramours' arms.

The smell of bread greeted my nose. My stomach growled at the reminder I hadn't eaten since the morning before. My nose burned. I couldn't afford to cry again in public at the thought of my mother and father sharing the MRE I had brought home. Their last meal.

I stopped walking and wiped my eyes. The people on the street ignored me. My mouth watered as I passed the bread vendor and his delicious treats. Remembering I had enough for one item, I pasted myself to the glass to marvel at the sweet creations.

"Off the glass. Off the glass," the vendor urged.

I moved back. Taking a deep breath, I pointed at

the item I wanted.

The owner frowned at me but grabbed the gooey cinnamon roll from the display case. The warm treat made my stomach sing again. I dug into my pockets and pulled out the bill. The owner of the small pastry shop took the money and gave me back change. A brown paper bag held the roll. I reached for the bag, but the vendor pulled it back. Surprised, I looked over the display case to the owner's face. The man frowned again and dipped his head to see inside his sample cabinet. He threw another pastry into the bag; this treat had swirls of cream and strawberry jam. He handed me the bag.

"T-thank you," I managed.

The man frowned again.

Does he even know how to smile?

"No matter how hard it gets, keep moving forward," he called out to me.

His kindness unnerved me, but I welcomed it. I wouldn't splurge on trinkets as these, but my stomach left no room for argument. With one nod at the man, I walked down the street with my paper bag of goods in one hand. I reached my hand inside and pulled out the cream and strawberry Danish. My mouth devoured the sweet, sticky pastry in four bites. I reached back into the paper bag and pulled out the gooey roll. That too slid down my throat in huge chunks. With my stomach satisfied, I walked to the nearest trash receptacle and threw the bag out.

The massive building stood before me.

I wiped off any extra mud or dust from my jacket and climbed the stairs of the intimidating structure. The Ground Force officers standing guard out front ignored me as I entered the building through the double doors. The warmth inside the building heated my chilled bones. The temperature was perfect, and it nearly made me want to take off my jacket. But I noticed what the other patrons wore and preferred not to.

The employees and clients were all well-dressed. Groomed males with deep purple or blue three-piece suits with pocket chains hanging from their lapels and shiny leather boots. The women wore bright dresses with geometric shapes defined around their hips or shoulders. Everyone socialized with one another around me. Their hair perfectly coiffed or parted. None of their clothes had a stain or a wrinkle marring their rich textures and designs. Each one of their faces was polished and preened. The entire room ignored me. I was on a mission and would not cower away because I wasn't extravagantly dressed.

A lady stood in the middle of the room. The woman greeted the customers who walked in and out. I frowned. All except me, it seemed.

"Excuse me, ma'am?"

The greeter had adorned herself with a bright yellow dress. She was encompassed by stiff material that had hoops attached at the end of the skirt to increase volume. Her hair was parted on one side and wrapped around her head like a headband with the rest of the loose hair pulled into a hair bow on the side.

The woman grimaced. I was dismissed, just like that.

Scratching my head, at wits' end, I tried again. "Ma'am, I know some numbers I need your help with, please. Eighteen digits, I believe."

The employee gave me an exaggerated sigh. "Fine, come with me."

I walked behind the haughty female, only to come to a stop in front of a kiosk counter. The computer flashed the name *Delta National Bank* around its hollow screen. "Follow the directions on the screen and print out your findings. Once you have the information you need, please make a line over there." She pointed to the other end of the room where people stood behind each other in queue.

I nodded and thanked the reluctant employee. The directions on the screen were as she said. The numbers on my mother's wrist were for a vault. Unaware of what it meant, I printed out the findings and walked over to the long line. I waited patiently, reading the contents of the page over and over again. The line got shorter. I studied the building, feeling the need to look at anything other than the piece of paper.

Inside of the large, cavernous interior with its white marble structure and sleek, shiny paint, were different paintings. Some were images of the affluent society ton with their noses high in the air and beggars at their feet. Other pictures showed the rich eating extravagant banquets as they threw scraps and the beggars eating the food from the floor. My blood boiled. The pretentious flaunted their wealth as if they were royalty. If they ever got a real taste of the miserable life, they wouldn't survive one second.

I shuddered, making it to a teller, glad to get this over with. The building secured the employees at the bank. Hidden behind an impenetrable force-field, a teller with one side of his head shaved and a wave of hair parted to the other side asked me how he could help. I pushed the paper through the open slot in the front. He took the page and typed against the holographic computer keyboard.

"Your sector identification, please."

I dug into my pocket and pulled it out. For a split second, I hesitated, afraid the military had already flagged the ID. His eyebrow rose. Taking a chance, I slid it into the opening. I held my breath and sent a quick prayer. My entire body became tense, ready to flee or fight. The seconds ticked into minutes, the longer he took with my information. I rubbed my sweaty palms on my new jeans.

The teller picked up my ID, looked at me, at the photo, and nodded. He typed more information into the computer, ran the identification card through their scanners, and nodded again. I held on to my patience, but it started to wane. Right as I was about to speak, the teller pushed the paper and ID back out to me.

He walked away. "Follow me," he called back.

Jumping into action, I followed the teller to the other side of the row. He pressed a few combinations on his door, and the tall, metal door slid open. He closed the door, shuffling his lean build toward me. He motioned for me to follow him, and I did. The clerk walked to another room, gated off with a Ground Force officer standing with crossed arms in front. The teller was not intimidated, while I shook in my beat-up boots. He scanned a pass hanging around his neck. When the door slid open, he gestured for me to go in.

"Before I let you inside, answer me this: How long have your parents loved you?"

I was confused. "Why are you asking me this?"

The teller sighed in annoyance. "It's the security question the owners on the account put in place for us to ask."

I nodded, aware I looked like a complete idiot. "Forever," I replied.

With one quick dip of his head, he escorted me into the room. "Look for bank vault B302 and enter the eighteen-digit code to open it. You are welcome to the contents inside of the bank vault locker." He snapped his fingers and walked back outside as the Ground Force officer closed the door behind me—locking me inside.

Trying to steady my erratically beating heart, I

walked over to the lockers as I sought the right one. Finding the vault, I entered the numbers I had memorized—satisfied when I heard a click of release. Pulling the drawer open, I saw three items inside: a KeViewer, a medical bracelet, and an envelope. I grabbed the things and sat at the table in the middle of the large white room. The medical bracelet read:

RAYNE ID: PH064.001 Dr. Sebastian Lester

I placed the bracelet into my back pocket. Then I slid the envelope off the table and opened it. Inside was a letter addressed to me from my parents.

To our dearest daughter Rayne,

If you are reading this, we're no longer alive. We are sorry we had to put you through this, but we had no choice. Sebastian Lester was my half-brother, whose name you've already seen on the medical bracelet. He was your creator, Rayne. The man who brought Project Hercules to life. He was the one who concocted the genome samples that made you and the rest of the super-human children. He grew you from embryos, falling in love with every one of you...

The tears in my eyes dropped like a dam flooded with water as I processed the information. I got a lot of this intelligence from Seaa, but she hadn't mentioned the older man's name. That had been the real reason I didn't fall apart. Hearing his name made it all the more real.

> ...*You were about thirteen when the military's lead, General Brockton Braggart, wanted to end your batch and create a new one he could better control. Sebastian wouldn't allow him to get away with murdering his children, so he created a plan to get you all to escape.*
>
> *Braggart is not one to mess with, dear girl. What that man wants is complete and total control. If we could've afforded to help more of Sebastian's kids, we would've. He could only get us to help one of you out. Should his selected child come to our door, we were to take you in as our own. Then you arrived at our doorstep, Rayne. We told you we found you on the streets, but the eldest boy of your group dropped you off.*

I crumbled the letter in my hands and cried even harder. My parents died to protect me. I sobbed until the tears subsided on their own. Cleaning off my face, I grabbed the KeViewer and unlocked the small screen. The KeViewer was a phone, tablet, and camera all in one. The screen lit up into the open space in front of me like a holograph. I pressed the play button floating in the holographic space in front of me. The first video had me wrapped in a towel by the tub, while my mother washed the blood off my body and hair. I could hear my parents speak to one another on the video.

"Carl, look at this. I told you her wounds were clos-ing," I heard Alice call out to Carl. Hearing their voices made my heart ache.

My father zoomed in for a closer look at the wounds on my back. "Alice, Sebastian said they had regenera-tive properties. She's healing herself."

They talked about my healing wounds. The video skipped to a different day where I beamed a full set of teeth and ate an MRE. I didn't look much different than I did now, but I could tell on the stream time had passed. Tragically, I still had a hard time remember-ing events and moments from the first year they had found me.

Alice was cleaning the living area, so Carl caught me lifting a large concrete block we used for the foun-dation of one of our chairs, with one hand, to allow Alice easier access to sweep.

"Oh, dear Lord. Rayne! Sweetheart, you'll get hurt."

The young me grinned and shrugged. The video skipped to another day where I was a tad bit older. I knelt on the floor with my butt in the air. Alice must have been the one holding the KeViewer this time be-cause my father had his butt in the air right beside me.

"What do you hear, Rayne?"

I smiled at him. "I hear scuttling noises, and I smell wet rodent. Dad, I'm sure there is a rat or mouse in the house."

This, I remembered. Thinking back, I remembered

being on the floor with my father and talking about mice.

Carl looked at the KeViewer and grinned. "My daughter has superpowers."

I heard my mother laugh and reply with, "Rayne, what does your dad smell like?"

Younger me grinned back at Alice and took a whiff of Carl. "Like three-day-old sweat and peppermint."

"Carl Baxter, where you in the candy dish again?"

Carl comically frowned at me. "Rayne, I ate peppermint yesterday. You ratted me out!"

My mom giggled off-screen. "Rayne, how long have we loved you?" she asked.

I had laughed like a girl without worries, right alongside parents I adored.

Now I was a grown woman with nothing to my name.

"Forever." The deliberate way I had said it punctuated its seriousness.

Then the video ended.

My cries turned into a watery smile. At least I knew what unconditional love was. Handling the cash from inside the envelope, I grabbed the crumpled letter and KeViewer. I walked up to the officer posted at the far gate.

"Where's the incinerator?"

He pointed to the corner at the door clearly labeled "Incinerator Room." Feeling sheepish, I walked to that end and opened the door. Inside was a large furnace roaring with fire in the middle of the room. Once near the incinerator, I opened the hatch and threw the items inside. The fire engulfed the old KeViewer and letter along with all my better memories the moment they landed inside. I closed the door on the previous chapter of my life and walked out of the room. I asked the officer to let me out and walked out of the building with one last look at the only evidence of a family I had left behind, within the burning flames of the commercial building. If the military wanted me, I'd be happy to show them how I felt about that.

CHAPTER EIGHT

LOST IN MY thoughts, I walked down the darkened streets that had been filled with citizens and merchants but were now cold and devoid of people. The breeze left gooseflesh on my skin. I pulled my jacket closer and blew warm air on my hands. Clumps of snow fell and spread over the cracked sidewalks and crumbling buildings as if bathing them in purity—trying to cleanse the cruel world of its menace. I turned into an alley and walked farther down the uneven path when I heard footsteps crunching on the snow behind me.

I stopped walking.

More steps sounded ahead of me. I sought around the darkness for potential dangers and recognized two of the Ground Force officers from earlier.

These guys have a death wish.

If I got into it with them right now, I'd hurt them,

so I turned around to walk the other way. Three new Ground Force officers who had joined in on the fun blocked off the other end of the path. I could make a run for it, but the sticks they had in their hands lit up the empty alley with sizzling sounds and shards of light. Vuwand's were used to make any regular person immobile for several hours. I wasn't sure if it worked on people like me, but I would not bet my life on it. The moment these men got me immobile, they would not arrest me and take me to headquarters. The wands lit up like a firework display. I yelped when one guy got too close, and the sparks landed on my hand. My body shivered, and I couldn't be sure if it was because of the cold or the situation.

"We told you it wasn't over yet, girly."

My head whipped to the side when a punch to the face undid my balance. Brief pain exploded inside my skull. The force of it rippled like water, getting smaller and smaller the farther away it moved.

"You must really have a death wish," I spat out.

"Oh, is that so?"

Another officer grabbed me by the shoulders, forcing me to face the others while he ground perversely at my back. I pulled away from his grip, while the corrupt bastards cackled at my expense. I turned back to the officer who held me and kicked him in the stomach. He landed against the wall spread-eagle and slid down the wall to fall on his rear. I turned around as another Ground Force officer spoke.

"What the hell?" He extended the Vuwand toward me, but I pulled to the side and knocked the device out of his hand. I turned to run, but another officer electrocuted me on the back.

Feeling spasms slither from my neck to my toes, I dropped to the ground in a jumbled mess. I twitched and shook as the seizures took over my body. One officer turned me over and stared right into my startled eyes. I was conscious but couldn't move a muscle of my own free will.

"She's a wily one, boys," he called out.

Another one added to the first's comment. "We will have fun with this one."

I finally gained control of my fingers, so I grabbed the snow for comfort until my arms responded. I tried to pull my body up from the ground. Without enough strength in my legs, I dragged myself to one end of a building.

"No!" I tried to scream out loud but could only manage a whisper.

For all my bravado earlier, I felt foolish.

The guys laughed even louder until I saw one Ground Force officer fly across the alley. The perverts stopped laughing long enough to look behind them. If it weren't for the ringing in my ears, I would have heard the extra set of footsteps joining us. There was ferocity written on Rome's face.

One that said, "Fuck off, she's mine."

There was no way or enough time to process how

1 felt about that. The sensation in my legs returned. 1 rose from the ground to see Rome fighting the five Ground Force officers on his own.

Sector Delta
Township of Delta
Operative Roman Braggart
ID: MIL 116.002

1 KNEW GROUND Force was a gang of men with no inhibitions or morals, but trying to rape a female was not something 1 was prepared to tolerate. Luckily, when my men arrived at Delta National Bank in the Township of Delta after finding the information inked into her parents' wrists, 1 had caught her scent and given chase, giving them orders to stay back. Because my team was built up of average humans, 1 left them at the bank to find out what had been stored inside while 1 searched for Rayne.

My hearing picked up her quiet "no" before 1 set off at breakneck speed. 1 jumped over fallen boulders to reach her as the officers encircled her like a piece of meat in front of a pack of wild vultures.

1 pulled another Ground Force officer off me and threw him against the wall. One of them must have

hit me with a Vuwand because I dropped to one knee. I'd been beaten by volt wands before and learned to deal with the spasms building inside my body. They weren't like the custom tasers we used in the compound, but actual fire sparks combined with a small dose of Strychnine on the tips. Ultimately, it could kill or incapacitate someone. One hit on a human, and they were unconscious. Afterward, it would be up to the Ground Force officer if he wanted to give the antidote to get the victim up, or they'd run the risk of freezing to death before they got up on their own.

Another officer kicked me in the stomach as I tried to make it back up to my feet. I pushed the assailant with my hands and got up in time to receive a punch to the face.

My nostrils flared. "That all you got?"

Before I received a response from the daring officer, I punched him.

I turned to see that Rayne had run away, and instead of feeling hatred she had escaped again, I felt a weird form of relief. She shouldn't have to deal with Ground Force. One took advantage of my weakness to zap me again with the wand. My knees quivered, but I pushed through it. Punching another officer in the face, I turned around to kick another enemy and collapsed. I got hit with two wands at once and couldn't remain on my feet. The guys surrounded me, kicking and punching me all at the same time.

Of all our weaknesses, why in the hell did it have to

be electric shocks?

I grunted as I took each kick and punch while my body tried to control the spasms running under my skin. Blood sprayed when one guy cold-cocked me with a pistol, then aimed.

"You shouldn't have messed with us," I heard through the faint ringing in my ears.

I couldn't get back on my feet. The sound of a gunshot went off. I didn't feel the sting of a regular bullet, so I stared at the officer. With a skeptical eyebrow reaching all the way to my hairline, I saw the officers all face a very pissed-off woman with long hair billowing in the wind. Her eyes were dark and feral.

If the muscles in my face weren't going wild, I would have laughed. What a twist to my night. The woman I tried to take captive came back to my rescue.

Wow, I felt emasculated.

"Put the gun away, Girly."

I tried to move but couldn't get my body to cooperate. My hands twitched, and my legs were limp like cooked noodles. Rayne pointed the gun at the closest officer.

"You first," she replied.

I laughed on the inside.

"Do you know what the penalty is for assaulting an officer?"

She pulled the trigger.

I saw when the officer closest to her dropped to the ground—grabbing his ear. "You bitch! You shot my ear off."

How lucky she missed. My custom rounds weren't meant for humans.

She pointed the gun at another officer. "Now, what's the penalty for shooting one of you guys?"

Oh, I am in love.

The saucy, little wench riled them up good. I tried moving my legs again, but they refused to budge. My arms and facial muscles gave way. I could see Rayne's fear and knew the Ground Force officers saw it too. It all happened too fast for me to issue a warning. One guy threw a bunch of snow and dirt into her face, while another ran toward her. She discharged my weapon again but missed her target. The guys jumped her, and I watched her struggle from beneath them. I took what muscles I could get working and dragged myself over to the pile-up. I grabbed someone's leg and pulled—dragging one guy away.

The man growled, "You are one persistent son of a..." as he pulled himself over me and wailed on my face.

The officer grabbed the Vuwand and took it to me over and over again on every part of me he could reach. My entire body convulsed on the ground. My heart thrummed incoherently, while the ringing in my ears returned full force. There was no way for me to move. My head fell to the side, while the KeViewer in my pocket vibrated.

I watched as Rayne got zapped by a wand, but she

seemed so fierce at that moment that it didn't even drop her on the floor. She punched one guy in the gut and kicked another in the face. She grabbed the wand an officer held and snapped it in half then threw him against the wall. The last guy standing faced off with Rayne. As much as I was concerned for her, I was a lot more concerned about what she'd do to the patrolman. He attacked her, and she shot to the side—grabbing his head from behind and pushing him toward the brick wall. He smacked right into it and fell to the floor, unconscious.

Yeah, dude. I remember that move.

One minute she had been a timid creature, and the next, she resembled a well-trained soldier.

This was why the general wanted this group captured. They possessed the same strengths of 002—without limitations. I could bet my life she didn't keep up with her training after escaping Foxtrot, so to see her fighting like someone who had made it her mission to stay performance-ready was startling in its brilliance. I needed to get my brain back in check. General Braggart said these demi-humans posed a risk to the Hercules Project. They were weapons of great destruction. I'd seen them at play. Zero-zero-one had illusions of grandeur.

The other men squirmed on the ground. I relaxed as much as I could, knowing we were out of danger, and eyed the girl from my vantage point on the ground. She was still dangerous. Rayne grabbed my Springfield

.45 from the dirt and walked over to me. She'd shoot me without second-guessing herself.

Rayne was in the perfect position to eliminate the threat to her life, and I couldn't blame her. I waited until she reached me, but she didn't aim the gun. Her rosy lips moved, but I couldn't hear a word she said because of the drum solo performed inside of my ears. She leaned down closer before, looking at the guys on the ground. I read the words on her lips.

Is this yours? Blink yes.

She asked if the gun belonged to me.

I blinked, stupefied, and saw her place my gun in her waistband.

Damn if that doesn't look sexy as hell.

Rayne dropped to one knee. Putting my arm around her shoulders, she got off the wet ground with my weight pressed against her side. The woman was a puzzle. I couldn't understand what went on in her head. We both got to our feet with Rayne carrying all of my weight. I felt her pull me up by my waistband—an uncomfortable sensation if I might add—and over her shoulder fireman style. Before I could wrap my mind around this scenario, Rayne ran down the alley at full speed. Anyone watching right then would have had a hell of a time trying to figure out how a five-foot-six, couldn't weigh more than a buck twenty female hauled around six feet and two hundred forty pounds of muscle.

She jerked me around until I felt her stop. The feeling of weightlessness consumed me. I landed on the muddy ground with a resounding thud. Rayne jumped into the same utility hole she had thrown me in. She grabbed me again and ran down the abandoned maze of rats and squatters—trying to avoid stepping on them.

After what felt like hours, Rayne kicked in a door and took us inside. She dropped me on the ground like a sack of rice and stared at me. My hearing returned, and the muscles around my face allowed for movement.

"Oh, God, what am I doing?" She paced back and forth in front of me. "I should have killed you!"

She sure should have. Her courtesy toward me would not win her any immunity because I wasn't in the business of granting wishes. I had a job to do, and she would not distract me again.

"You are the enemy," she continued. "I am being hunted down by a maniacal general who feels we are defective, and here I am saving one of his own."

I saw her grab her hair as she screamed. Rayne put one hand on my .45 caliber pistol and aimed it at me. My body convulsed as the muscles tried to relax, but I didn't feel at all calm right now. My heart made a trip to my stomach before trying to escape my damn throat. Her hands shook as she aimed at my head, but Rayne soon dropped her arm as she fought back tears. I felt a stir deep inside, but I squelched it down as soon as it flared. I couldn't afford to risk feeling sorry for the enemy.

Rayne threw the gun on the floor beside me and dropped to her knees in front of me. Looking like she had a revelation, she stared me dead in the eyes. "I'm leaving." She smirked, "Please, don't get up. I'll walk myself out." Rayne placed a chaste kiss on my lips and got up from the floor.

"If only you weren't trying to kill me," she said over her shoulder.

I *didn't* want her dead. I also couldn't help asking, "Why, what would happen?"

Rayne flinched at the sound of my rough voice, but that was the only evidence she gave of hearing me before she walked out the door. Rotating my neck, I did a body check on what worked and what didn't. Ten minutes passed by before the team burst through the metal door, guns raised.

"It took you guys long enough," I argued.

The soldiers walked toward me and helped me up. "Sir, what happened?"

I tried to move my legs, but they still weren't working. "Damn Ground Force."

The soldier nodded as if it made complete sense to him. My team dragged me out of the sewers. The moment my body came back alive, I was going back to base and taking a long hot shower. Memories of Rayne filtered through my mind like scenes of a movie, and I altered my choice. I would take a long *cold* shower.

By the time we made it back to base, my body

had ceased convulsions, but my mind wouldn't stop. I walked into the new section of the underground bunker the government had created after bombs had been set off in the old one years ago. Brilliant white walls greeted me. The walls constantly made it seem like I walked into a laboratory instead of a housing and training facility for soldiers. The moment I walked through the double doors of our wing, I was greeted by other soldiers who had taken part in Plan B. Batch 002 had been homed in one side of the facility, while the scientists and techs housed on the other. Some lifted weights while the others socialized. I saw my friend Zane jerk his chin to say "hi," and I responded the same.

I reached the door to my room and stopped right before it when I heard Trevor's voice.

"So, I heard a wizard wand brought you down."

It had been five wands and a hell of a lot more than once, but I wouldn't give in to the bait Trevor set out. I turned around to come face to face with the little piece-of-shit operative who couldn't leave well enough alone. Trevor Dallas had been one volunteer for Project Hercules and my "partner." He was an exceptional soldier—one of the best! But after Ragnarok, he, like a lot of other soldiers, didn't handle the new world too well. He took great joy in other's suffering. Unfortunately for him, I wasn't built that way. An incident years ago kept us firmly at each other's necks. He wanted the captive killed, and I wanted him saved. My father was head honcho around here, so I got my way. Trevor refused to live it down. The two of us hated each other's guts. I maneuvered one way to get Batch 001, and Trevor handled another. I was the one to bring in a genetic human from the first batch, while Trevor still searched.

I laughed mockingly. "Oh, that was supposed to be a joke? Good one, Trev."

Trevor lifted one side of his mouth, "Well, while you were busy peeing in your pants, I brought back Seaa."

His words caught my attention. "How the hell did you catch Seaa when she was on my turf?"

My partner walked over to where he played pool with another batch brother. "Seaa tried crossing over to Sector Bravo, so I caught her."

I clenched my fist. "Well, that's good. Two down." There's no way I'd ever mention Rayne to Trevor. I walked away from him and the rest of the nosy brethren only to run into my father as I opened my bedroom door.

"Damnit! Can't I take a shower first before being bombarded?"

My father, General Brockton Braggart, rose from his perch on my bed. "Son or no, Rome. You introduce yourself to me properly, you hear?"

I saluted my father, answering with a loud, "Yes, Sir."

Braggart appeared satisfied as he retook his seat on

the bed. I knew Braggart understood sarcasm. Luck must have been on my side because my dad was in a good mood. I walked to my dresser and pulled out underwear, a pair of faded jeans, and a white shirt while my father asked questions.

"What have you found out, Rome?"

I talked about the confrontation in Rayne's apartment, the parents' suicide, and the evidence left behind on their wrists. I told the general about my trip to the Delta National Bank as I stripped the dirt-layered clothes off my body. The marks left behind by the wands were slowly fading. Once naked, I wrapped a towel around my waist and slipped my feet into shower sandals.

I turned to look at my dad and noticed he was staring at the marks on my back and side. "We must have just missed her because I caught her scent in a nearby alley where she got ambushed by Ground Force. I got caught in the middle, and that's that."

I wasn't about to add how she ran off to come back and save my life.

"Then why is it they found you five blocks east of the scene of the attack?"

He wouldn't be mollified, but I had to keep my cool. I placed one hand on the door handle, grabbing my clothes with another. "No clue. You know how electricity affects us. Damn Vuwand." I grinned and walked out of the room and took pleasure in slamming the door behind me.

I walked toward the bunker community showers, receiving catcalls the whole way there. It was still pretty unbelievable Trevor had caught Seaa, and Rayne had saved my life. I stood under the showers to think and let the water drip down my body to cleanse my mind and skin.

There, I thought of a plan to get to Rayne.

CHAPTER NINE

Sector Delta
Township of Delta

WITH AN OVERLOAD of information running around inside my head, I walked the abandoned streets behind the Township of Delta, hoping to find a spot where I could rest. The cold, wet, night had exhausted me with so many things I couldn't quite believe were happening to me. That evening, I worried about what new trinket I would find and where to get my next meal. No way in hell I thought I'd meet my sister, fight and kiss a super operative, lose my parents, and learn I was a genetic experiment—not even human.

What I wouldn't give to look up and see the stars in the sky.

The clouds were dense. Snow fell. A permanent fixture in the air that moved far enough to come back around like a merry-go-round. Once in a while, the citizens were blessed with one small opening in the coverage to see one star or another. The opportunity didn't last long enough for us to figure out which constellation we watched. If wishing upon a star would make everything better, I would have done it ages ago. All I got from looking up were several snowflakes on my face. So much chaos rushed around in my mind I couldn't think straight. One thing after another didn't give me sufficient time to grieve.

Being attacked by Ground Force, and now obligated to live on the streets was not in my plans. My world turned upside down, and the only thing that made sense to me was that Seaa had answers I needed. To find Seaa, I needed to figure out what the heck Tutus Portus meant. Tired and hungry, I stopped walking when I saw a small opening between the rubble. Pushing on it to make sure it wouldn't collapse on me, I crawled inside for shelter from the night's elements.

The snow fell along with tears from my eyes. I missed my mother and father, but I was determined to be strong and handle this situation with tact and discipline. I'd get my revenge on the general who started this fiasco. Swiping at my face, I huddled tighter into myself and closed my eyes.

Night had come and gone, yielding to the sunlight filtering dim rays into my little cave. Peeking my head out a little, I squinted as I looked up. As if hearing my plea, the clouds moved away long enough to let in some sun. I could hear voices on the main street carrying on. The town had awakened, ready to start the day. There were sounds of people talking amongst one another and the joyful sounds of giggling children. I scrubbed my face to scrape off the crust from my eyes and to rub the sleep away.

The moment I moved, my entire body screamed in misery.

My stomach rumbled, but I didn't have time to go in search of food. There were a lot of things I needed to do, and stopping to find food hadn't been one of them. I needed to find someone who could translate the two words I spent the cold night thinking about. Because public libraries no longer existed, the only way to get into a library would be to become a university professor or a student. The best I could do right now would be to sneak my way in or pass myself off as a student at Roger Edmonds University, where my father had worked. This center was the closest university in Sector Charlie.

Finding an underground opening, I jumped into the sewers and walked along the tunnels. The smells started to not bother me as much as before. If I stuck around sewers or tunnels long enough, I could get used to the different nauseating smells. I searched for a sign that would lead me to Sector Charlie from where I was in Delta. The journey would be a long one. Using the sewer system like the rest of the drifters would likely be the best plan. I couldn't afford to get on a shuttle where they logged citizen profiles into their systems. Rome and the rest of the military would be monitoring the shuttle system by now.

I kept to myself as more and more bodies crowded the tunnels—whether finding a spot to camp out or using it to transit to and from sectors like me. The military and Ground Force stayed out of the tunnels because the system was too long and complicated to keep under surveillance. They preferred to roam the areas that were well populated with refined citizens or near shopping districts.

The strength of my body depleted little by little.

The walk inside of the maze had been tumultuous. No one paid any attention to me, which benefitted my situation. The worst thing that could happen to me right now is to draw attention to myself. After the fight with Rome, running the sectors, and the conflict with Ground Force, I didn't have enough left to defend myself from criminals. More people crowded the tunnels. I stuck my hands in my jean pockets and maneuvered around them. One lady bumped into my shoulder. The woman kept walking without excusing herself. The sewers and subterranean tunnels were not a place for the elite and polite.

I wasn't aware of how far I had walked before the

first sign I drew near showed up in the form of graffiti. The colorful design stated Sector Charlie would be about two more miles down the red-lined tunnel and across the Longfellow Bridge that had partially collapsed into the Charles River after the war. A few more feet down the gritty interior took me to a hall with underground merchants.

The market moved continuously to avoid detection. I had heard several stories from my parents and acquaintances about the things sold in an underground market. Feeling like I'd learn a few things by perusing, I walked toward the mess of people screaming and hollering over one another.

They bargained.

Whether they used goods or money to haggle, the markets always bustled with busybodies. Private guards posted by the booths kept thieves at bay. The merchants hired the most muscular goons they could to make sure they weren't attacked or robbed. Having them there proved beneficial.

The first booth I approached sold jewelry of all types. Costume jewelry, expensive jewelry, or anything in between lined the table in neat little rows. One man stood by the table with his arms crossed. When a small child tried to touch the merchandise, the man shoved him to the side. My legs received an alarming burst of strength, but I stayed back. Getting in the middle would be more trouble than it was worth. The child ended up jumping off the floor and growling at the man like a feral beast.

He didn't need my help. I walked to the next booth and then the next. There were many items sold, from outfits belonging to the ton to details not found in the poor districts: batteries, lighters, chocolates, and weapons. The things on the tables weren't for show, and their prices weren't low either.

I walked down the tunnel until I reached the opening to Sector Charlie's border. From here on out, I would have to sneak past a few patrolmen and down another utility hole to navigate the subway system under Sector Charlie. I climbed out of the utility hole and judged the area around me. The tunnels were so long and complicated, I didn't even realize how long and far I had walked underground because it had once again gone dark outside. I checked for trouble. Not spotting any Ground Force nearby, I kept to the sides of the buildings where others made their ways to and from the sector. If I stuck to the plan, I should be able to reach the financial district in no time. The next part of my plan was to navigate my way under Sector Charlie.

Sector Charlie
Roger Edmonds University
Operative Roman Braggart
ID: MIL 116.002

I WALKED THE hallways of the university in Sector Charlie that happened to be named after some egotistical jackass with money to burn. I hated that schools were available for the rich. Children to young adults received tutors at home until they were ready for university life. High caliber military personnel and their families studied in college, and influential entrepreneurs and their relatives. If we had money, university life was guaranteed.

The women I eyed on the school grounds wore form-fitting outfits that accentuated their every curve. None of them piqued my interest. During recon, I worked out Rayne's guardian worked for the university as a professor of history. Losing any leads I had on Rayne, I searched the large university for any sign of her. When I searched Baxter's office, I noticed several photos of him and his wife and a handful of Rayne. There were drawings on his walls decorating the bleak office with color. Other than the plethora of history books piled in bookcases, he held nothing else hinting at Rayne's condition.

My team raided the vault where the Baxters had rented out a security box, but nothing remained. Printing her picture out from the surveillance footage, I asked the Ground Force officer in charge if he saw what the woman had done with the contents. The officer told me what I dreaded.

The Incinerator.

Stopping the furnace from its fiery bursts, we found nothing but ashes. The flames had devoured our evidence. I thought back to Rayne as I walked between several young adults.

Why did she rescue me?

My first thought had been that she wanted to bribe me to let her live should we meet again, but I realized she would not stoop to that level the moment I saw her drop my gun, almost as if she had been disgusted with it. She let me live because she wasn't a murderer. My father claimed the first batch were "unscrupulous undesirables." Rayne hadn't been unscrupulous, and she was definitely desirable, and that further confused me.

What did I think would happen?

Thinking about anything that went against Braggart's orders would be a recipe for death. My father wasn't a forgiving man. It didn't matter that I was his son. I yawned, stretching my arm over the back of my head to stretch out my sore muscles.

A few of the females took second glances as I passed them. I hadn't been a student, nor a professor, but I walked the halls with authority. I had a few of my men posted in different classrooms and areas of the university, but no one chirped with good news.

The frustration I felt made me clench my fists. Trevor and I were supposed to be the ones looking for the failed Plan A beings, but I couldn't stand working beside him. The way he viewed life and humanity both disgusted and disturbed me.

My friend, Zane, was operating a job protecting a financier in Sector Charlie today, so I asked him to show up at the university if he had a minute. Zane was good at solving puzzles. His results were faster and better than the rest of the group combined. Asking him for his opinion on the projects, I hoped would enlighten me on any ideas that would break this case.

Zane walked through the front doors, past three Ground Force personnel. He wore black cargos, a crisp white t-shirt, and a large jacket hanging from his broad shoulders. Zane had his eyes covered by sunglasses; his long titian-wavy hair covered pointy ears. The Herculean Cocktail had contained a more substantial portion of cheetah DNA, bringing a more morphed change to Zane than the rest. We all looked human, except when our adrenaline brought out a characteristic of our animal brethren. Zane had pointier ears and eyes lined permanently in black. The black mark known as *tears* ran down the insides of Zane's eyes to mid nose. His vision was much better than everyone else's. The reason he covered them in public was because of the tear lines. Although we both could become our animal counterparts, it didn't mean we liked to flaunt it.

Spotting me by the library, Zane approached, all the while making me think of my own morphing. My eyes glowed in the darkness like a feline's in my human form, but nothing else would strike someone other than those involved with the project as weird—except if I got incredibly angry. The last time it happened, my animal took over. During that time, I had no control over it and no desire to play nice. The Herculean Cocktail side effect happened to me because of an alteration made to the mixture. I know the old man did it so I wouldn't turn out like Zane, but instead it caused the change to physically morph me in intense situations. I've learned to kick-ass without bringing the animal out of me.

No one wanted to see him come out.

Girls giggled as Zane passed them. One side of my lips lifted in a half-grin.

"What's so funny?" Zane asked when he reached me.

I pointed back at the gaggle of girls who snickered and eyed us both. "You have fans." I motioned toward the freshly made-up, feminine forms.

"Wish I had the time," he replied as he waved to them.

More fits of giggles. Ignoring them, Zane turned back to me.

"So, what's up?"

I sighed. "I found out there is another superhuman from the first batch on the radar. Reports claimed she was dead, but she is more than alive, Zee. Fine as hell too."

Zane smirked. "Oh? Trev know about her?"

I arched a brow.

My friend laughed. "Alright, the better question then. Do you want to catch her?"

I jumped as if hit with a volt wand.

Of course I want to catch her.

Part of the job of a soldier was to bring in these mutants and eliminate any foreign countries from getting a hold of the failed experiments. They were a menace to society. They could revolt at any moment and try to take down our wavering government. The possibilities were endless where these experiments were involved, and it had been my job to get them off the streets or permanently remove their presence from this world.

Yet, then there was Rayne.

She lived a healthy life with a couple who took her in as their own.

How could she have been a danger?

I remembered her fight with me. A shiver ran down my spine as my mind reminded me of our kiss. Then I saw her fighting those Ground Force officers. The young woman could be dangerous in the wrong situation.

The sound of Zee clearing his throat prompted my attention. Zane had been watching me with a questioning brow. Realizing I hadn't answered, I tried to play it off cool. "You know what? I can't find a reason why I shouldn't."

Zane nodded as if it all made sense to him. "No wonder you called me over. She's a puzzle, and you need to solve it."

I punched him in the arm. "I fucking hate you, dude, but you're right."

Zane laughed, knowing it was so far off from the truth. He was like the brother I never had; both of us looked after one another as if we were. There could be no way I'd ever hate him.

Ever.

CHAPTER TEN

I LOOKED DOWN at the young girl sprawled on the cold ground before me. Feeling for a pulse, I sighed in relief when I found it to be healthy. Of all of the students walking in and out of the university, she had been the only one who resembled me. The young woman had light features, brown eyes, and long, dark brown hair with the odd blonde strand. I had spent hours perusing the students coming and going through the double doors of the university, trying to find the right one. I didn't want to attack anyone, but the way to get into the university without standing out would be to blend in. The research library on campus would help me find out what *Tutus Portus* meant and how I could go about finding answers to all my questions.

I pulled the unconscious girl closer to me.

I had waited until she was alone. When I found the right moment, I cornered the girl and knocked her out. Finishing the last touches on my hair, 1 studied the clothes 1 had on. The young girl, April West, came out of the school wearing bright green stockings with black candy cane stripes from thigh to heel. A puffy poodle skirt with ruffles the same color as her stockings sat on her hips, which were much too tight on my curvier frame. 1 ran my hand down the layers of fabric. The ruffles bounced back into place the moment 1 removed my hands.

1 felt ridiculous.

A black, long-sleeved leotard completed the look. The end of the sleeves had loops that hooked on to the thumbs. 1 even took off April's huge, lime green bow and placed it on the side of my head. My knotted hair, which 1 had to finger brush, had been pulled up from the front to tumble down the back. 1 felt sick to my stomach—whether by nerves or hunger. 1 covered the girl with my old clothes to prevent her from catching her death and gave my cracked leather jacket one last once-over.

1'd miss it.

Hoping 1 could pass as April West, 1 grabbed the girl's books from the ground and her student ID. Digging into the small clutch that belonged to the West girl, 1 found a bottle of perfume and spritzed a good amount of it all over myself, trying to drown out my scent with April's.

Ground Force patrolled the front gates of the school, but 1 swallowed all my fears away. 1 couldn't afford to trip this up. Sneezing, I rubbed my nose. The girl's strong perfume made my nose itchy. The mixture smelled like alcohol and chemically altered flowers. The cute little backpack had a couple notepads and pens, untouched now on the mushy snow. I picked them up to complete the student façade. Feeling uncomfortable, I moved the clothes on my body around.

How do wealthy women walk around in these unflattering ensembles?

Stepping out of the bushes, I climbed the path leading back to the university where my father had worked.

I wonder if they already know he is dead or if they even care.

My nose burned with unshed tears, but I bit them back. I had done enough crying. Being upset right now would not help the mission. I needed to look less conspicuous. I was confused studying my new outfit. We avoided attention the more ridiculously we dressed. The students walking toward the university and those walking out didn't pay me any attention. So far, the plan worked. If I could make it past the armed Ground Force officers guarding the front of the school, I should be in the free and clear. Avoiding the eyes of the officers, I walked to the gate leading the way to the front doors and put April's ID into the computer system right beside it.

One patrolman watched me. He eyed the outfit

with a leer plastered on his thin lips. "Forget something?"

I froze.

What the hell could I have forgotten that the guard noticed? The door beeped my entry, so what did I miss?

The bag was over one shoulder. My skirt and stockings were in the correct order.

The other students scanned their cards as I did, so what could I have forgotten? Afraid I would have to fight, I feigned shyness toward the officer who spoke to me. His beret shielded his eyes, but there was no mistaking his appreciation.

"Pardon?" I asked in a voice, not my own.

He pointed with his thumb back toward the school. "I saw you walk out."

Damn!

My entire body went from coiled to loose and limber muscles. The man had noticed April walk out. I didn't appear as a red flag. He had been paying attention to April West. Or rather, her ridiculous outfit. I batted my eyes at the officer. Every single one of these bastards I had come across had only one thing cross their mind when a pretty girl came around. Biting my lower lip to be as coy as I could, I eased into a conversation with the patrolman.

"You noticed me?" I giggled like I figured April West would.

Inside I wanted to punch him in the face.

He scuffed the toe of his shoe on the ground like a teenager. "Yes, ma'am."

Well, I'd never in my life think I'd see a bashful Ground Force officer. Maybe the guy liked April, and this wasn't the first time he noticed her. I studied the floor to avoid eye contact. If that was the case, I could get myself into a lot of trouble if he comes not to recognize me. I couldn't afford to ruin this now. Not when I was so close to finding out what *Tutus Portus* meant and get closer to stopping—

Stopping?

Stopping who? The general who started this whole damn thing? To avenge who? My parents? My other siblings? Our creator?

So many thoughts ran through my mind at that moment I forgot where I stood. I ran my thumb under my eye. I didn't want to ruin the makeup, but I also needed to prevent myself from crying right now.

Not wanting to encourage him further, but not trying to anger him either, I pouted. "I have a boyfriend."

He frowned.

I put a finger up. "But if we ever split, I know whose shoulder to cry on." Sending him a wink, I walked through the gates. The last image I saw was of his grinning face.

When I walked through the double doors, I expected to walk within a hallway to get to different rooms. Instead, I walked right into a glistening green courtyard with towering trees giving off the scent of the forest. The heady combination of oak, pine, and sage wafted around me to cocoon me in its rich fragrance. The tri-colored, stone-paved ground was smoothed out from years of being walked on. Underneath all the branches were a frenzy of wildflowers and trimmed bushes. A large, glass dome covered the entire courtyard. Bowed white buildings surrounded the dome opening to an area outside of the yard. The premises must be where they housed the classrooms and offices.

Looking at the curved buildings, 1 walked through the courtyard. A simulated projection of a campus map glistened and glittered a few feet away in the exact center of the university forest. 1 made my way toward it, noticing the library sat right beside me with its prominent sign over the front doors. 1 took one last look at the map. Knowing where to go, 1 kept my head down and bypassed a few students chatting on a bench.

How great would it be to live so carefree?

The students laughed or walked to what could be their next class in focused steps. With the courtyard behind me, 1 reached the library's building. 1 moved to the side to prevent getting run over by a distracted young man. The tall, lean man shoved the spectacles he wore back up his nose and rushed into the library as if on a mission.

A student walked out the hydraulic sliding door, a whooshing sound following in his wake. 1 rushed forward and slid in after him. The warmth of the room sank into my cold bones. I stood in awe of the traditional floor-to-ceiling bookcases that reached the ceiling of the building. The books rose from the ground upward in a never-ending staircase. The middle of the room had virtual computerized systems dedicated to research. Two students worked there, while the rest sat at tables or plushy cushions to read or study. I walked the extensive library, looking for the area containing all of the foreign language texts. Several students and staff sat around, reading, or writing at the floating tables. The chairs stood on four metal legs with thick leather-covered cushions, but the tables hovered, suspended by air, crafted from the same metal as the stools.

A Gidget, which had a large round platform hovering over the ground, rose to the second and third floor of the building. Like an elevator of the past, a Gidget took you from one level to another. I saw an empty Gidget and climbed on. The portal hovered, encasing me in the mounting bars so I wouldn't fall out. The sound of escaping air had the Gidget moving upward.

I held my breath to the second floor and released it the moment we came to a stop. The bars came down, so I climbed out to see everything labeled. Strolling down the bookcases lined up against the wall, I passed thrillers, historical fiction, and suspense. A sign on the wall showed that foreign books were on the third floor. Avoiding students who gawked, most likely at

the fit of my borrowed clothes, I made my way to another Gidget at the end of the cavernous interior of
rising books.

A few girls stood at the edge of the floor, giggling
as they stared over the balcony. They pointed to the
bottom floor. Taking a quick note of their pink cheeks,
I wondered what it would be like to laugh and fall in
love. I wondered what it would be like to be with your
girlfriends at a little café and giggle at handsome
boys walking past. Instead, I stole clothes and snuck
into private libraries under a false name. I shook my
troubled thoughts and walked to the Gidget. A female
walked out with three books in her hands. I moved
out of the way and got on the Gidget before it moved
again.

Once on the top floor, I walked to the area for foreign books. I needed to figure out what *Tutus Portus* meant or even what language it was. I noticed
the same young male who had very nearly run into
me earlier, sitting cross-legged on the floor. The boy
had hair strands about two inches long, scattered in
a mess of interwoven locks of hair all over his head.
There was no sign he had done anything to it when
he got up that morning and got out of bed. Thinking
he couldn't be too dangerous, I approached him. He
looked up at me, fixing the frames of his glasses as he
slid them back up the bridge of his nose.

"Excuse me, could you help me?"

He looked around the room and then behind him.

I smiled, noticing there were only more books behind him against the wall. There wasn't any room for people.

"Me?" his voice squeaked with the high-pitched sound of amazement.

I knelt, careful to not show anything underneath the tutu. "Yes, you. There's no one else here."

His wide eyes grew wider. "Uh, yeah. What do you need help with?"

"Could you tell me what this means?" I pulled out the card that contained the two words I couldn't decipher.

He glanced at the card, handing it back to me. "It's Latin."

A frown marred my face. I barely knew how to read English well; any other language threw me for a loop. The boy once again shoved the glasses up the bridge of his nose. What had taken me days to figure out took his two seconds of perusing the card.

"Would you happen to know what it means?"

He shrugged, his narrow shoulders going up and down beneath the baggy cloth of the shirt. "If my Latin is on point, it should mean *safe haven*," he replied.

Safe haven? What the heck were those words supposed to mean? I would assume it meant safety, but where would that take me?

The knowledge of the words left me with more questions than before.

If my father were here, he'd know what to do.

"Is it a place?" I questioned out loud.

The boy looked up from his book again as he uttered, "A haven is a place where a person can take refuge or feel secured. Now, is there a place like it now? Doubt it. This whole country has turned to hogwash. I don't think we are safe anywhere nowadays."

God, don't I know that already. Safe Haven sounds familiar. A town maybe?

"However," he continued unaware of my internal dilemma, "there used to be a town nearby on the coast called Safe Haven before Ragnarok eliminated the states."

A genuine smile graced my lips.

Yes, I remember a town by that name from one of my old textbooks.

The boy blushed.

Clearing his throat, he continued. "The town was small. But during the war, soldiers created a secret underground base there when they were in connection with the Navy. The place no longer exists, having been wiped out by our militant forces."

"Yes! I think the base might be the key."

He shrugged again. "Anyways, that's all I know. Professor Baxter started the lesson before the holiday, but we haven't gotten into it yet."

My heart ceased to function. There was a second... two... even three... that ticked by without it thumping wildly in my chest. My father. The boy had been from his class.

Does he know my father is dead? Did he appreciate my father's lessons?

Tears fell from my eyes. That I couldn't control my emotions pissed me off, and more tears fell. I had cried so much already. I was surprised the world hadn't already drowned in my tears. A dam had burst inside of me, and it refused to stop since that night with Seaa and Rome. I tried to wipe at the constant stream of salty water.

The boy jumped from his seat on the floor, shoving skinny fingers into his pockets. He pulled out an embroidered handkerchief and pushed it into my hands.

"Shit. Did I say something wrong? I usually talk more than I should. I said something, didn't I? I'm sorry. Shit again."

I wiped the tears from my eyes, giving him a gentle, watery tilt of my lips. "You didn't say anything wrong. My dad was Carl Baxter. He died the other day." The boy's eyes grew rounder than before.

"Mister Baxter is dead?"

I nodded.

The library's interior soon exhausted his attention.

"Please say nothing. I think no one at school knows yet."

I placed a comforting hand on his shoulder. Something about this guy made me feel relaxed and in control. The distracted boy from earlier seemed to have so much going on in his mind, and I finished troubling him with some of my own. But I felt comfortable around him. I squeezed his shoulder.

The boy was weighted down by the new news. "I won't say anything," he promised.

Whispering my thanks, I got up from the floor. According to the young boy, Safe Haven could have meant the town. I needed to search the geography books for that kind of information, but the only place with geographical maps would be at the GeoScience Center in town. Before trying to head out, I asked him if they had any other information regarding Safe Haven in their library.

He shook his head. "No, we have small clips here and there in our history textbooks but nothing extensive. A lot of those items got destroyed throughout the years. The GeoScience Center might carry that kind of geographical mapping you need."

Exactly what I thought.

Leaning toward the boy while using my hands to cover the back of the skirt, I kissed him on the cheek.

He blushed again.

"Thank you," I whispered.

I walked away but stopped when he called out to me.

"Miss, I'm Gavin Foxhand. If you," he took a deep breath, "ever need help again. I... you know?"

I nodded.

"Oh!" he called out again, writing inside one of his notebooks. "Here's my number, in case you need it." He ripped the small brown sheet out and passed it to me. Gavin Foxhand had to be one of the many rich kids in this school if he owned a KeViewer to make and receive phone calls.

My parents KeViewer had been the oldest model on the market and a gift from the university. Not a "good job" here's a phone, but more of a "we were about to trash this, do you want it" kind of gift.

"I'm..." I had been about to give him Marie, like I usually did, but decided it didn't matter anymore. "Rayne," I said to him as I took the small paper.

With a finger to my lips, I gestured for him to keep our conversation a secret. Turning around, I walked away from Gavin and toward the Gidget. I got more than I thought I would, visiting this library. I may not have found Safe Haven, but I thought I might have found a new ally.

I turned around one last time and saw him watching me walk away. He simpered and put his head back down. Either he had been quick to smile, or I looked even more ridiculous in this getup than I thought. Feeling self-conscious, I sucked in my tummy and pulled the puffy skirt down a little more to hide my butt.

What I wouldn't give for a pair of jeans and a long sleeve shirt. When I left this campus, I would take great pleasure in burning the big green bow in my hair. I didn't know April West, but I mentally thanked her for unwillingly giving up her identity. The road would be tough ahead of me, and I knew it. The ability to move forward through all the bitterness and biting cold came from a swollen heart full of love, desire, and revenge. The love of family. The desire to move ahead instead of giving up. And the ability to get revenge on those who'd wronged us.

Those who had wronged me.

CHAPTER ELEVEN

I MADE MY way back to the first floor of the library, feeling better than I had before. It was about time I was one step closer to solving the Safe Haven riddle. The front rails of the Gidget opened with a burst of air. My entire body stilled. Two men stood in the middle of the warm building. The blood from my face rushed toward my toes. Nausea rose in its stead. The man with orange-brown strands in his hair had his hands inside of his coat pockets, while the other man with dark, thick hair and vivid, emerald eyes rubbed his hands together to warm them. His long black coat dragged on the ground as he leaned down to tie the laces of his boots.

How did he find me? Was Rome here because he caught sight of me, or was he here on a hunch?

The other man looked around the vast library while Rome focused on his boots. I couldn't afford to stand here and gather dust. If Rome got up from the floor, he would recognize me, no doubt about it. The April West façade wouldn't work long on him. The man was a beast. My skin ran hot and cold, which made me shiver. Gathering my wits about me, I studied the floor and made my way forward to go around them.

Walking ahead, one foot in front of the other, I hoped I wouldn't trip and fall flat on my face. The tension in my shoulders made my movements awkward, but I moved forward regardless. He rose from the floor, staring right at me. I needed to leave without looking him in the eyes. I didn't want to get caught—not now. I was so close to figuring out where Safe Haven was to meet up with the rest of my siblings.

There was a gaggle of teenage females gathered on one side of the men. I could see from my peripheral vision they giggled and tried to grab the men's attention. The doors breezed open, and a cold wind blew into the interior. A group of students walked into the library together with their bags hanging off their backs and textbooks in their hands. They walked to the other side and parked there, which left me with nowhere to go but between the busy men. One watched the upper levels while Rome watched the people in the research center and beyond.

The time was now.

Using the same voice I applied for the Ground Force officer, I squeezed between the two massive men. "Excuse me, please."

Both men moved to the side to let me pass. Rome sniffed the air as I passed him. Screwed, I turned my head to glance at him. The guy beside him likewise sniffed the air, but he only paid attention to Rome's reaction, while Rome stared dead at me. There was a quick second interlude between us as his eyebrows narrowed in recognition. I bit my lip, turning around to run. My entire body lit up with unlimited energy. I felt the strength of that energy coalesce in my legs.

April's items fell to the ground in my haste. Rome cussed, but I didn't bother to wonder if he gave chase. I knew he would. Another set of rapid footsteps reached my ears, and I knew his friend gave chase too. Scared, my adrenaline increased as I fought my way through bodies. There was no way I would make it through the front gate alive. I turned toward the side of the buildings to avoid the courtyard. The open space would be my best bet right now. Past the courtyard dorm and beyond the arched structures stood a high concrete fence that barricaded the school. There were hovering picnic tables ahead of me, so I ran toward them—feet burning from the tight fit of April's shoes.

I jumped on top of the table, my speed giving me some momentum. From there, I leapt again to the top of the roof of one of the academic buildings by using the table as a springboard. I didn't look back, afraid he'd gain distance. There was no noise other than the gasping sounds of students below and our thumping feet on the corrugated roof of the classrooms. Seeing the end of the building ahead, 1 felt a small wash of relief. So close. 1 had been about to jump over it when an arm wrapped around my mid-section. Pulled into a firm body 1 didn't recognize, 1 struggled to get loose. 1 grabbed the bow in my hair with my free hand, slamming the pointed end into his arm.

The guy screamed.

He let go as Rome arrived to grab me. 1 dipped to the ground to avoid his hands. Rome reached and missed. My elbow pushed into his mid-section to flip him over me. The other man got up from the ground. 1 spun behind him. He turned and got a kick in the face. The partner slammed into Rome. Both men straightened themselves. 1 saw no way past them.

"Give it up, Rayne."

The partner stared at Rome in disbelief.

1 didn't know what he saw, but what 1 saw was two fully grown men standing in my way and a dome shield covering my exit.

"Tell me, Rome. Would you?"

Clenching my teeth, 1 braced myself for what would come. Rome's partner ran toward me. At the speed he was going, 1 used it to grab his arm and propel him around and into Rome. Both men flew back and into the bottom of the dome. Their bodies slammed into the glass, cracking it, and onto the ground below. 1 ran again and jumped toward the top of the wall. The material burst as my body pushed through it. Weightlessness consumed me. The ground came toward me.

The dirt exploded all around me from impact.

I gave a loud cry as pain swallowed my senses. A bone stuck out of my skin. Hearing the voices of Rome and his friend, I ignored the wound and dragged my body toward a man sitting on a hovering scooter. I cried louder as the pain shot up and down my body. My vision went in and out. The man watched me, eyes wide with fear.

"Please, they're trying to kill me. Help me!"

Bless him, it took him but a second to process the situation. When he saw Rome and his friend come out of the gates at breakneck speed, he pulled me to the side of his vehicle. He got on the machine and floored it. The guys grew farther away from me. Looking tinier, the farther away we drove, compared to the hulking bulks they were.

The man yelled over the sound of his hovercraft. "I'll take you to the law enforcement center, Miss."

"No!" I turned my body enough to move his steering wheel to the side.

He tried to maneuver the scooter straight again, but I had pulled myself over enough to push him off. The guy fell to the ground, tucking his body to protect himself from the fall. I yelled, sorry as I pulled my leg over one side, straddling the machine. I increased the speed of the vehicle, maneuvering around the people in town and then turned into an alley when a bubble of delirious laughter burst from within me. There had to be a spot to park, heal, and process the situation. I'd gone nuts if the mess I avoided could make me laugh.

I turned around in time to avoid a large dumpster. Turning too quickly sent the scooter into an abandoned building. My body flew over the motorcycle, slamming my petite frame against the wall. An explosion of bricks was the only evidence my body had hit the obstruction. More torturous agony swallowed me as I lay on the debris-ridden concrete floor, staring at the rusted ceiling.

Harsh breaths assisted me in steadying the nerves running rampant under my skin. The seconds turned into minutes. No one else was around. I pulled my upper half up and slid on the dirty ground toward the retaining wall. Blood ran down my arm, but I didn't know where it came from. I hurt everywhere. The area shimmered in and out of focus as I tried to concentrate on my surroundings.

Rome and his friend were as fast, maybe even quicker than I was, and it scared me.

How am I going to continue to outrun this guy?

The debris in front of me doubled before my eyes. I blinked. No matter where I hid, he was one step behind me. But if I gave up now, I wouldn't get my revenge on the man who made me this way.

How was I going to do this?

My head felt fuzzy—thick with nonsense and irate senses.

So occupied had I been with my thoughts, I did not hear the heavyset man approach. I shook my head. He ogled and licked his lips—a drifter or thief who found me to be easy prey. I'd prove no challenge for his size with my injuries. I backed up closer to the wall. There wasn't enough bite in me to fend him off.

If it isn't one thing, it's another.

"You seem to be far from home, doll face."

There was no weapon around I could use. My wounds were excuse enough for him to attack me, but being female and wearing the clothes I wore was more than enough temptation for him. I stared at my would-be attacker, tired of all the crap I kept going through. My strength depleted itself in long, tumultuous waves away from my body. He was about to reach me when I saw a flash of movement, and then the drifter dangled from the air. Rome had him by one hand, hanging precariously over an opening on the ground.

He growled at the man. The sound emanated from deep within his belly—animalistic and primal. "Run very far and quick. If I see you again, I'll tear you limb from limb."

The man cried, agreeing with anything Rome said. Moving away from the hole, he dropped the guy on the ground. Rome hadn't even turned toward me before the guy had run for his life. Pressure built behind my eyes. I felt my ears flush red, so I gathered all the energy I could to brace myself for what would come.

I sank deeper into the wall. "Back away, Rome," I yelled at the dark form approaching me, whose eyes glowed neon in the growing shade.

The man didn't care less about what I said and knelt down in front of me. "What did I tell you about jumping from tall distances?"

I couldn't help it as another bubble of laughter escaped. "God, you're such a charmer."

Rome grinned. He studied me, looking at the blood on my arm and my foot bent at an awkward angle. "Let's set this bone back before you heal."

I pulled my leg away from his nearing hand. "Hands off, pervert."

Another grin lit up his face. "I'm only trying to help, Rayne."

I looked at Rome, seeing something in his face that made me feel comfortable at the moment. He got closer to me again, reaching out for the injury on my ankle. He prodded around the bone, making me flinch from the rapid succession of pain shooting up my leg. Rome grabbed either side of the break, staring at me.

"This will briefly hurt. I recommend you look away."

I wanted to see what he would do, but I didn't like the pain I felt. Any more of it and I'd pass out. There was brief silence as the sensation of his fingers remained on my injured leg. A loud snap and my screams drowned out everything else.

"Shh, shh, shh, Rayne. All done. Turn here so I can see where that blood on your arm is coming from."

My head swam after momentarily blacking out. I finally came to my senses to see the wound bandaged with a piece of cloth.

"Damnit, w-who taught you how to show girls a fun time?"

One side of his mouth lifted. Tears fell from my eyes as he leaned forward.

"I know how to show a girl a good time. But if you keep running away from me, I might question my prowess."

I snorted. Rome's gentle fingers prodded around my shoulder. He grabbed a chunk of the ruffles of my skirt and ripped them off. A bizarre feeling filled my chest—not at all as unpleasant as I thought. Rome leaned over me again, his head beside mine. His male scent imprinting in my nose.

Oh, no, not at all unpleasant.

Dressing the wound on my back with his makeshift bandages, Rome pulled back to look at me. We stared at each other as time slowed down around us. The tension brewed. The air became thick. I felt him lean toward me. Rome licked his lips as he stared at mine.

Was he going to...?

Threads of electricity latticed throughout my body as it covered me like a second skin. The high energy I felt filled me with sensations I had never felt before. When I settled on the thought of his lips on mine, his KeViewer rang.

"What!" he bellowed in the abandoned structure, pulling away from me.

The voice on the other end said things I couldn't quite understand. I took a moment to rotate my broken ankle, feeling nothing but a small twinge of pain. I slid my leg underneath me, trying not to jar his attention away from his caller. Once I had my legs underneath myself, I jumped off the floor and turned to run. A hand clamped down on my wrist. Rome had the KeViewer at his ear but stared at me as if I had committed a grave sin.

Hanging up with his caller, he tsked in my direction. "Shame on you, Rayne. Where do you think you're going?"

I pulled at my arm with no success. "Let me go, Rome. I didn't go through all this crap to get caught right now," I yelled. "All so what? So you could look good to that pompous prick of a general?"

Sector Charlie
Edge of the Academic District
Operative Roman Braggart
ID: MIL 116.002

WHAT THE HELL is she going on about? Is she talking about my father?

I tightened my grip on her wrist the more she attempted to pull away from me. When I faced Hail, I didn't hold back my punches and brought the man into custody where he belonged. When I fought with Seaa, I didn't care for one minute about what she had to say. Now I had another superhuman from Batch 001; except, I couldn't seem to bring her into custody.

What the hell was it about this girl that made her so different? She was beautiful, granted no one can say otherwise, but she was additionally as beautiful as the other women who have come and gone from my life. She was feisty, but I've slept with women soldiers from Batch 002 and damned if they weren't feistier than Rayne.

While I had waited outside, freezing my butt off, talking to Zane, the same thoughts I had now troubled me then. Zane had told me that maybe she threw me off guard. I could also be tired of following the rules and saw this as the perfect opportunity to rebel. Either choice I made, Zane supported me. But I needed to make sure it was worth risking my life for. The kill switch embedded somewhere deep inside my body prevented me from ever living a life away from Unit 13. Just having those thoughts would get me killed for treason.

"What do you know," I asked. Already frustrated beyond reason, I knew letting Rayne go would affect me, and bringing her into custody would too.

Rayne tried to pull her arm away again, but I refused to let go. The crew was on their way to my location. I looked at my watch as I waited for her to reply.

She has less than five minutes before I either hand

her off to my team or... I couldn't even finish that thought.

She stopped pulling to yell, "Your goddamn general killed the only man who loved us, regardless of what we were! Now he hunts us down, uncaring of who or what he tramples along the way. My parents included."

Rayne looked down at the floor, taking in a lungful of air. "My memory is still a little hazy, but anyone's would be after getting shot in the head."

I'm sorry, someone did what?

A feeling akin to anger for her well-being seethed from deep down within me like a geyser. Oblivious to my feelings on the subject, she continued.

"We were about thirteen when the general decided we were a liability and began procedures to eliminate us and start over."

What?

From my briefing on Batch 001, the project experiments tried to kill the underground staff. They had gone rogue. But in all of my reports, none of them were children. The brief said they were full-grown adults who no longer aged, but mutated. I saw Hail, who looked like an average man, but closer to the build of a man who worked out—like a bodybuilder. Scaly skin and webbed fingers and toes made Seaa very much mutated. Thinking back, I'd wondered why they used digitally aged photos of the Plan A superhumans and why I hadn't put that bit of information to better use before. Braggart had said everything concrete disappeared in the explosion, but now his story seemed more and more absurd.

What the hell am I doing?

Ridiculous to even fathom that my father was a sadistic child murderer.

He couldn't be that uncaring.

I sought back to memories growing up with my father, and none of them were pleasant. He had never been the type of man who played catch or took me out to events we could share. The world gave in to chaos way before Ragnarok ever happened. General Braggart had forever been very much involved with his job, hardly ever his family. I never even knew my mother. Couldn't even think of a woman bedding that man. The thought alone repulsed me. But Braggart was honest, and that had been the main reason I joined the service and why the rest of the team followed my old man.

We thought him a hero.

Having heard enough of her lies, I dragged her toward the opening in the building to the alley where my men would pick us up. She yanked and pulled, uncaring she would pop her wrist out of place. I still couldn't believe her strength. Our tough skin prevented regular bullets from penetrating it, but to see her stick the metal tip of her barrette into my friend's arm had been miraculous. Zane cursed like a drunken devil walking into a church. From what I could gather, it seemed like the first batch might be a tad bit stronger than we were. Regarding speed, mine was far more superior.

More reason for me to get rid of her already. Rayne was a menace to our healing society and needed to go away. I had no ties to this woman.

"Rome, please! Please!!"

Her words pierced me somewhere near the vicinity of my heart.

When did hearing my name make me second guess myself?

Rayne needed to stop begging me. I would not cave in to her lies and manipulations. I didn't even know what got into me if I doubted my job and duty for even a second.

"Sebastian Lester was my mother's half-brother. He told her what happened. Please, Rome!"

I stopped walking, kicking an upturned stone across the alley. The rock aimed true toward one of the windowpanes of the warehouse. The resulting explosion of glass shards had me turn my back to it, sheltering the woman in my arms. I watched her gorgeous, large eyes shift from the broken glass and back up to me. Rayne blinked, and I felt like a giant pile of mush.

My eyes drew down the gentle slope of her nose to her lips. Without even the evidence of stain to enhance the color, I could see her voluptuous upper lip in the shape of a hunting bow. My mind took me back to the two times she had planted those lips on mine.

The first time she did it, I fell all over her. Then there was a gentle peck on my lips after she saved my life, and I couldn't help but want more. Shaking away those awful thoughts, I took in a lungful of air.

I looked at my watch again. Two minutes. "Speak quickly."

Rayne realized it had been fruitless to continue pulling as she took in a large gulp of air. "Sebastian Lester created us from embryos. That man raised us, and then he's told to end us because the general wanted a group of soldiers he could control. He died for us!"

Rayne's eyes grew wider as her other hand traced the back of her head. "I remember. He placed his body in front of me to protect me from a bullet."

Her adorable face looked up at me—eyes warm and trusting. "I remember, Rome. I remember."

Not knowing what persuaded me, I let go of her hand and watched several emotions cross her face. "Go, leave."

Rayne stood there in her little lime green getup, frozen still as my words penetrated her daze. I didn't know why I let her go, but I felt like she had told me the truth.

What if my father really is a murderer?

I hated this job. At first, I thought I had done something positive with my choice to take part in Plan B—not like my father gave me much choice.

But to be used to hide a mistake?

No wonder there had been a limited handful he trusted with their retrieval. I couldn't fathom it. I joined the military to protect what was left of my country, not to cover up my dad's bad choices.

"Come with me."

I lifted my head, startled.

Why would she ask me that? How can she be so trusting when I single-handedly brought the military to her doorstep? I've ruined her chance at normalcy.

The familiar sounds of the team vehicle filtered through the craziness of my thoughts. "Rayne, run now. My team will be here in thirty seconds."

She said nothing, just nodded and ran. I looked at the mess I had made. I let my responsibility run from me. Pissed, I punched the remaining wall of the building. My fist broke through; the debris burst toward my face and body. I felt the bits cut at my skin, but I knew they would heal before the crew even walked toward me. Our ability to regenerate made us an enormous asset to our government. In my line of work, being able to recover after being wounded had been a bonus. Still, sometimes, I wanted the cuts and wounds to feel alive—to know I could feel pain and that I was human. My men ran toward me with their weapons ready. Looking around for Rayne, I shook my head.

"She escaped."

CHAPTER TWELVE

Sector Foxtrot
Unit 13 Headquarters
General Brockton Braggart

MY FISTS HURT, but 1 refused to show my ungrateful son mercy. The General was law. 1 expected to be obeyed by everyone. No one was above me here. No one. 1 pulled back my right, sending the fist flying toward my son's face again. Roman had been taught a lesson first by the aluminum bar 1 carried on my waist. Afterward, 1 let my guard beat him with his mutated fists. 1 watched my son with distance. 1 felt no regret. Roman Braggart would learn that messing with me had been a mistake. 1 kneed him in the nose, watching my son's head whip back from the force. Roman Braggart may be genetically altered, but he bruised and bled like all of them if softened enough. Their abilities were only as strong as they were.

And Roman had been weak.

I had two soldiers hold him down on his knees, but Roman had been too worn to fight back. Taking each swing, I taught my son a lesson in power and control. I had the power here. I controlled everything. Everyone obeyed me. Bending down to face my son at eye level, I grinned when I saw the blood pour from his nose and mouth. Swelling formed around his eye, and even though I knew Roman would heal—it was pleasurable to see him in pain.

The team sent in with my son had said he had Rayne in custody, but when they arrived, she had escaped. I tired of them escaping. I wanted to see my little Rayne in person. To see how she had grown up. Unequivocally one of the more charming females of the freaks. Then Roman dared to come at me with questions regarding the failed batch. He had gotten closer to the truth I spent years trying to hide. The first batch had been a failure I refused to accept. If that ridiculous doctor would've avoided getting so involved with the assets, those kids wouldn't have been such a liability.

I yelled profanities in my head, punching my son one more time to relieve the absurdity of the situation. Failure would not be an option. My superiors depended on me to keep the rest of our country safe. No matter how I secured our freedom, I would not let my government down. Roman Braggart would be taught my law was absolute. No one would ever dare question my motives again. Grabbing a pistol, 1 shot my son.

No one.

IT WAS COLD. The wind bit at my arms and legs through these awful borrowed clothes. The breeze howled as it blew between the large trees surrounding the front gates of the university. After leaving Rome, 1 ran back to the school, hoping 1 would see Gavin walk through the gates. 1 hid far from view, my vision helping me seek my charge from a distance. No one spotted me. No one looked for me. 1 shivered again and coughed. The cold wrapped me in its dark embrace, snow falling from the cloudy evening sky.

Several students walked in and out of the school, but none resembled the skinny boy from the library. He could've left the grounds while 1 evaded capture. A couple of minutes later, he walked out of the gates. He had three books in his hands, and a bag slung over his shoulder. His glasses slipped off his nose, so he pushed them back with his free hand. Knowing 1 needed to get to him quickly before he boarded the shuttle or got into his ride, I waited until he walked right beside my hiding spot and snatched him with a quick hand.

Covering his mouth, I shushed him from screaming. He struggled once before he stilled at the sound of my voice. "Please, Gavin. It's Rayne."

Gavin tried to turn his head, but the position I held him in prevented him from moving.

"I'm going to let go now."

He nodded, mumbling behind my fingers.

I let go of him as promised, watching as his eyes registered me.

"What are you doing here, Rayne? The school is on high alert. You were seen running from some guys and jumping the wall. Jumping. The. Wall!" he reiterated.

Shaking from the cold, I dropped to the frozen ground to hide from the breeze and to wrap my arms around my half-naked body. The fight had caused my wardrobe to malfunction. There were severe rips in my stockings and tears in my clothes. If anyone spotted me, I'd be immediately reported. Hunger pains racked my stomach. The cold hardened my skin. No woman should have skin so rough.

"I n-need your help, Gavin. I have n-no one else."

Gavin knelt down in front of me. I heard rustling, and then his school items dropped to the frozen ground beside me. Like a true gentleman, he shrugged his shoulders out of his jacket and placed it over me. I was thankful because I couldn't handle the bitter air any longer.

"I-I'm not sure how I can help, but I'll try."

I wrapped his jacket closer to me and inhaled the scent of old books and roses. "I need to find out about Safe Haven, and as you can see, I'm not dressed for the GeoScience Center." I smiled, but it didn't quite reach my eyes. "Besides, my picture is probably posted everywhere by now."

He nodded. "Yeah, they have a photo of you at the gate. April West is the daughter of Councilman Rupert West, and he was not happy his daughter got assaulted on school grounds." He studied me through the thick frames of his spectacles. "First, we need to change your clothes. Come on." He stood from the ground, pulling me by the hand.

I had had a long few days, so I swayed precariously on my feet. The feel of Gavin's hand on my forearm kept me from passing out. I watched as he fed my hands through the sleeves of his jacket, buttoning it for me, I couldn't help but wonder why this boy was so kind to me. Grabbing his discarded books, Gavin put his backpack back on and pushed it higher on his shoulder and extended his hand to hold mine. I didn't know if he was about to help me or walk me straight into a Ground Force patrolman's arms. But I was hungry, cold, and tired. I didn't have the strength in me to fight right now.

Avoiding the more populated areas, Gavin walked us along the narrow sidewalks of Sector Charlie. He approached a large building seemingly made out of glass, with two large titanium doors in the center ground-level. Two bodyguards stood in front of the doors beside a bellman. Pulling on his hand, I feared he geared to feed me to the wolves. Gavin turned to me, pushing his glasses back up his nose. I stared up at him. He smiled shyly. Swallowing my foreboding, I choked on it as I moved along with Gavin. Whistling a jaunty tune, Gavin walked past the two guards as if they didn't even exist.

The bellman must have recognized him because he called out to him as he entered the double doors. "Mister Foxhand, how are you this evening?"

I could only see the back of his head, but I sensed his sizeable bright grin. The guards studied us.

Oh, God. I'll get caught.

My heart hammered in my chest as if getting pounded on by a live, thumping rabbit's foot.

"I'm doing great, Arthur."

Arthur expected more, asking, "And who is this... uh, young lady?"

"A female companion." My head shot up at the mention of the new title. Arthur watched me with distaste but nodded as if he had already come to terms with my profession.

"Please, make sure we are not disturbed."

The man bowed in half with his right hand over his heart. "Right-o, Young Sir."

I didn't appreciate being called a hooker, so I

squeezed his hand a little more than I should've to let him know of my dislike of the term *female companion*. I would have laughed if I didn't feel so insulted right now. Gavin flinched and registered my drawn eyebrow.

But only shrugged.

We were going to have to talk about all the shrugging he did.

Walking me toward a large hovering Gidget, we set foot on the platform. As the bars lifted from within the platform, a projected image of numbers floated in front of him. He touched a numerical sequence, and the screen disappeared. The Gidget moved upward at rapid speeds. Feeling like I would fall over the edge, I held on to Gavin's arm. He seemed thrilled at my weakness. If I had the strength to punch, I might have.

We arrived at the top floor of the glass building and disembarked the Gidget. I held his hand, as two more men in suits were plastered to the door at the end of the hallway appeared. The door we happen to be approaching. The men in suits barely batted a lash, seeing Gavin walk in with a girl.

Does he bring women to his home often? Am I going to be in trouble for trusting this guy?

He unlocked his door, gesturing for me to proceed inside before him. I'd never seen a home like this before. The small palace looked as I imagined a wealthy patron's home would look. The floors were tiled in pale gold—solid pieces covering every surface I could see.

Massive chandeliers hung from the ceiling, glittering with their bright icicle-shaped bulbs, lighting up the room resembling a colorful Indian harem. There were dark ruby reds and fiery oranges with splashes of royal purple in the mixture of throw pillows and drapes. The pale windows dressed in lengths of gold and red fabric. Thick cushions on the floor and on top of what seemed to be a sofa called attention to the room—giving it an inviting feel.

I passed an open doorway, spotting a large black marble kitchen with actual appliances to cook on and store food. I'd hardly ever seen any of it before. My sector was poor. MRE's were our saving grace—and the occasional visit to The Market for other essentials. A bowl full of fruit sat on top of the counter separating the kitchen from an area to eat. My stomach growling, it reminded me I hadn't eaten in a while. A dining table hovered beyond it with a creamy gold fabric hanging from its surface. Wildflowers and the smell of spices accented the room's ambiance. The interior blew my mind.

Is this what real living feels like?

I drew in on myself. The little apartment I shared with my parents *was* living. A lone tear escaped my eye as a memory of us in the tiny apartment came to life. I missed them so much.

Waving to me—"This way, Rayne"—Gavin led me away from the foyer.

I nodded and followed him to another room in the

spacious interior. Gavin's room was much simpler than the dramatic spectacle of his living and foyer, inviting me to its warmth and prompting me to climb in the bed and sleep. I heard Gavin speak, but the pillows called my name. A melody I had to insist on listening to. I dropped on the boy's bed. My eyes felt heavy—weighted down by anvils. My breathing grew more relaxed—a whisper in my ears. Eventually, I forgot it all and fell asleep.

I ran faster.

I could see the girl running as fast as I was through the darkness as I held on to another's hands. The girl was beautiful. She had a dark beauty about her. A mysterious goddess, but with a sinister aura surrounding her. Her hair bounced in large curls—the black ten times darker than my color—almost blue in their hue. My hand was so tiny, so inviting in the large palm enveloping it. The girl's eyes beside me were dark, practically black as they blended with her dilated pupils framed by long, whispering lashes. I struggled to keep up with the person pulling me, but I felt even more tired the more we ran. A warm thick substance ran down the side of my face and neck, but we ran so fast I couldn't look at what it was. My legs gave way.

I was picked up by the boy with blond hair. We moved so fast he jostled me around his shoulder. Fast objects whizzed by us at massive speeds. My entire body burned and ached. My head throbbed. The girl called my name, pulling closer alongside me. Other kids ran around us, but I couldn't figure out who they were.

Everything looked murkier, but the girl wouldn't give up. There was yelling, grunting, and the sounds of explosions all around me. Of everything, I felt the sensation of paper gripped tightly in my hands. I pulled my hand up as the person holding me jumped over a log. I didn't know why I had this in my hand—its importance had to be significant.

"Keep going, Silk!"

"I'm too tired, Thunder. So tired."

Silk.

Thunder.

Were those their names? I must have known them.

We ran faster and harder than before. Someone in front of us turned back to help, but a shot penetrated his right thigh, and I felt the person who held me dip down to drag him back up to his feet. He teetered back and forth, trying to gain his balance on the edge of the riverbank, but failing. Someone pulled Silk forward. The momentum tripped her. She had been whipped around to the other guy. Silk held on to his hand before he fell back, but I wasn't as lucky. The person holding me slipped on the muddy ledge. We both fell, I screamed, and blacked-out as the running rapids swallowed me up.

Jolting out of bed, drenched in sweat, I looked around at all the foreign furniture.

Where am I? Whose room is this?

The feeling of being watched propelled my body out of bed—practically back-flipping toward safer ground. I straightened, trying to make sense of the unfamiliar surroundings. My chest felt heavy; my muscles were tight. I focused on the boy in front of me as he slid his shiny spectacles up the bridge of his nose. The gesture sparked the return of my wandering mind. I remembered meeting Gavin yesterday at the university. This was his home. I had fallen asleep on his bed. Running a hand through my damp hair, I grimaced as Gavin stared at me in intrigue.

I leaned forward toward the edge of the bed, burying my head in the thick blanket. "I am so sorry, Gavin," I mumbled.

The sound of repressed laughter got me to look up. "Wow, Rayne. You are the most interesting person I've ever met."

"I didn't mean to fall asleep on you as I did. I was so..." I fought around with my brain for the right word to describe the fatigue.

Gavin spoke for me. "Pooped?"

I snorted. *Yeah, pooped is a good enough word.*

He waved my worries away. "While you slept all night and day"— He walked over to his desk.

Did I sleep all night and day?

I looked out the window to see the sun beginning to set.

—"I went to the GeoScience Center in town and got the information you needed."

His news got my attention.

"It seems Safe Haven is in Sector Bravo. And because you were so interested in the Navy base I told you about yesterday, I looked into more information about it for you. You need to find the old underground bunkers the Navy used during the beginning of the Millennium. Years ago, during the war, it was claimed to be filled in, but you might find what you are looking for there." He handed me a copy of a map.

I could hug him. He found out all that information while I lay unconscious on his bed. Walking around the bed, I sat down on the edge while I pulled off the irritating stockings. He turned as I pulled the last leg off, blushing to the tips of his ears.

"Um, well, hopefully, you find what you need."

"You said that already," I couldn't help teasing.

He reddened further. "Oh! I also picked up clothes for you. Hopefully, you'll find items in this box that fit because I kinda guessed at your size."

Gavin handed me a box full of assorted tops and bottoms. There were two types of footwear—a pair of boots and sneakers. I laughed, genuinely feeling like I made a real friend in all of the chaos. His kindness made me think of the friends I had left behind. Dani and Thomas struggled daily to have a semi-normal life. My drama wouldn't do them any good. Digging through the box, I pulled out a pair of tan, stretchy pants and a black and beige, long-sleeved blouse that fell a little past my rear. None resembled the clothes

I usually wore, but they were clean and in one piece. Grabbing the shoes, judging both, I chose the shin-length boots over the sneakers. These boots were one part of my realistic style I would never change. There were undergarments in the box, so I grabbed a pair and dangled them in front of Gavin.

He chortled deep within his throat but stayed mute. I struggled not to laugh at how uncomfortable he seemed.

"Oh, I almost forgot." He rummaged through his closet and pulled out my old leather jacket. "I saw this fall from the bag April West gave the authorities before it was passed on to those scary dudes chasing you. I thought you might have wanted this back. Seemed special. But what do I know? I cleaned it though..."

I hugged him to stop him from talking. I couldn't believe someone as lovely as Gavin had made his way into my life. After letting him go, I grabbed the items and searched the room for the bathroom.

Gavin jumped off the chair he sat on. "Ah, the bathroom is down the hall to your right. There's a towel, and essentials and such for a shower. Take your time."

Feeling blessed, I leaned over and kissed Gavin on the cheek, making my way toward the bathroom to shower and change. While in the bathroom, I enjoyed the warm water sluicing down my bare body. My ankle had healed—as if it hadn't broken in the first place, and the deep laceration in my upper shoulder showed a slight faint line. Nothing else was out of place, but I did a double check in case.

After absorbing as much hot water as my skin could take and lathering myself twice with the rose-smelling oils, I stepped out of the shower feeling refreshed. I took great fulfillment in shoving the borrowed clothes in the trash receptacle, which burst into flames the moment the items fell inside.

Small incinerators, how neat.

Brushing my teeth—twice—I combed the knots out of my hair. Toweling off the ends of the strands, I heard a happy tune whistled from the kitchen area. Taking one last look in the mirror, I placed my chain back around my neck, satisfied.

Gavin made dinner because of the late hour. I walked over to him, wondering why he lived in this prominent place all by himself. Unless I missed someone else during my sleep-induced coma, he was all by himself. I sat on one of the air-suspended stools in front of the divider separating the kitchen and dining area.

He smiled at me. "Feeling better?"

I grinned back. "Yes, lots. Thank you."

Gavin grinned as he reddened.

I shook my head, saying, "No, Gavin. Really, thank you for everything."

The boy shrugged his narrow shoulders up and down. Today he wore a buttoned-down shirt with vertical stripes and loose-fitting dress pants. He looked very homely and sweet. His glasses gave him trouble as if he couldn't quite get the hang of them. Each time he pushed them up made him endearing to watch. I felt a bond with the handsome man.

"Regardless if it was to ask me a question, you talked to me. A lot of people ignore me or go out of their way to pretend I don't exist. I'm my dad's skeleton in the closet. His mistress' child. He's wealthy and powerful, and so his image of me goes as far as keeping me clothed, fed, and sheltered. I'm lucky to be educated. I have like three other siblings, but they ignore me too. You were the only one who had spoken to me in a long time who genuinely needed my help. Others who talk to me want in with the family."

I felt for this poor soul. To be deprived of someone's love and still turn out to be as sweet and caring as he was—it baffled me to see such a man turn out so great. "Well, I like you, Gavin. I needed a friend, and you befriended me, no questions asked."

He offered me a timid tilt of his lips and pushed a lock of hair from his face.

Which made me ask, "Now, why didn't your guards out front bat an eyelash at seeing you with a girl when you rarely have people around you?"

Gavin blushed brightly. "My, uh, father, thinks it's time for me to spread my, uh, you know..."

One eyebrow rose in question. I enjoyed making this boy speechless. I watched as he squirmed. "Dad hires hookers for you?"

His face shot up and stared at me. "Uh, yeah, sort

of. My siblings are all girls. He wants the last name to continue. But I don't..." He waved his hands in front of himself.

I shook my head. The information was too much to process with the smell of herbs wafting up my nose. Taking the offered plate of food, I ate as if my life depended on it. Not remembering the last time I had eaten so well, I dipped the delicious bread into the flavorful broth and placed pieces into my mouth.

"This is so good," I said between bites.

The last topic forgotten, Gavin's face showed relief we had moved on to other subjects.

He seemed lost in thought at my previous statement about the university. "You said you were Professor Baxter's daughter. He was my favorite teacher. If you're anything like him, then you're someone I'd like to get to know," Gavin admitted.

God, I hope even a bit of that couple rubbed off on me.

"I'm not...normal, Gavin."

"Neither am I."

I put down my spoon. "I'm sure I'd surpass even your wildest imaginations."

He nodded. "Anyways, what happened to you earlier? You were tossing around and moaning while you were sleeping. Did you have a bad dream?"

The dream. Silk. Thunder. Running away from something or someone. Bullets were whizzing by us. A man shot. Silk and the guy who carried me running to his rescue. How I had fallen in the water and drowned. The dream seemed so real, so vivid. I pondered the vision further, realizing maybe it hadn't been a dream, but a memory—a memory long forgotten because of my head injury.

Unconsciously, I rubbed the puckered scar on the back of my head. "I think it was a memory."

"A memory?"

I rose from the chair to walk around to the kitchen. Washing my bowl, I explained what I could to Gavin. "I got shot in the head a long time ago."

Gavin dropped his bowl on the floor. The pieces crashed against the tile, scattering across the room.

"You were shot in the head and survived?"

I knelt to help him pick up the pieces. "I've had a lot of things happen to me, Gavin, that no other rational human being could've survived. Would you like to know?"

Gavin stopped moving, watching me with visible curiosity. At least, I hoped he was curious and not at all as intimidated or as scared as I felt.

Not enough to run from me.

I hoped.

CHAPTER THIRTEEN

Sector Charlie
Edge of Academic District
Gavin Foxhand
New States Citizen ID: CH.JJ49.GL-Rank A

GASPING, 1 TURNED to face her.

Having picked up what 1 could from the tiles with shaking fingers, 1 placed the pieces on the counter and wondered what she was going on about. I've never met a girl like her. From the moment her warm nature graced me, 1 was awestruck. Rayne was sweet and beautiful. 1 could even see it through the awful outfit she wore when 1 first met her.

"It was about five years ago," she began.

1 watched with utter curiosity.

"1 was adopted by the Baxters after the original organization 1...lived with decided my siblings and 1 were more of a liability than an asset. The organization's leader tried murdering all of us, but our father refused and died in the process of saving us."

I looked into her eyes, seeing the truth that lay there. Moving toward the counter, I sat on one of the hovering bar stools. "Mr. Baxter tried to save you?"

Rayne's head shot up from her distant reverie. "No!" She looked to the side. "I mean...Yes, but not like you may think." She leaned over on the counter.

"My real dad tried to save us and died in the process. Well, some of us that is. The Baxters took me in and died to protect me. But before that, someone shot me twice. One bullet hit me in the head. Two people saved me afterward. At least that was the memory I had last night."

She was blabbering, and it made it difficult for me to understand anything. I shook my head, confusion written in my drawn brows and pinched nose. "You can't be more than seventeen—"

"I'll be nineteen soon."

"—years old. Oh, so you were a teenager when someone tried to kill you and your siblings? Oh, shoot. I mean, damn. Rayne, why would they try to kill you? Oh! And who were those guys chasing after you yesterday?"

"They belong to the organization. The cleanup crew, I guess."

I moved back and forth in the small kitchen. "Rayne, those guys were intense. I hardly ever see a government super-soldier up close. And you." I pointed at her as I paced. "You jumped the wall and survived. Are you one of those...you know the government super people?"

She shrugged. "Kind of. I have certain...abilities which help and hinder me."

I folded my arms across my chest, expecting more from her. The soldiers with abilities seemed like a myth to our world remnants, but they did end the big world wars—they ended Ragnarok. However, no one got a good look at them, and they didn't walk around advertising who they were.

"Abilities? What did they do? Run experiments on you or something? It wouldn't surprise me."

She arched a brow. "Oh? Well, it surprised the hell out of me."

I walked to the fridge and pulled out a bottle of water. "Professor Baxter said the military had tried everything from weapons to experiments to conquer the Ragnarok War. I mean, the people know super soldiers were created to beat the foreign territories. I wouldn't be surprised if you know...they like... did something to you."

She burst out laughing, catching me off-guard.

"If I tell you, will you keep it a secret? Forever?"

If she only knew how miserably alone I am.

I gestured to the large empty space that reflected my empty life. "Rayne, I didn't even speak to anyone before you came into my life, and I don't share secrets even if I did. You can trust me."

Edge of Academic District
Gavin Foxhand's Apartment

I NEEDED TO trust someone rather than trying to hope Rome was different than Seaa had said. Motioning Gavin to follow, I led him into the living room toward the vibrant sofa. I positioned my body beside the couch as Gavin watched me with wonder. Bending my knees, I placed my hands underneath the sofa and lifted. He didn't look impressed. So I lifted it vertically, dropping the pillows on the tiled floor. I bent farther and raised the entire couch with one hand with little exertion. The gasp coming from Gavin was proof enough it surprised him.

I put the couch back down in its original position, leaning over to grab the cushions from the floor.

Gavin approached me, squeezing my upper arms. "Wow, I'm impressed. What else?" He looked like such a nerd to me right now.

Smiling, I turned to Gavin, lifting him off the floor like a child. An unladylike squeak came from his lips before he slapped a hand over his mouth. I ran to his room using my increased speed, laying Gavin on his bed before he could even grasp the situation.

"What the...How the heck we ended up here so..." He looked at me. "Wow."

"Safe Haven has to be the spot where the rest of my siblings are in hiding, Gavin. I need to find them. My sister Seaa said if we fight together, we might rid ourselves of the organization trying to end us. Besides, my parents' deaths should not be in vain."

He slid off the bed. "Then, I'm going with you."

I shook my head. "No, Gavin. I would rather you not get involved more than you already are. I need to get to Sector Bravo. You being with me will get you killed."

Gavin tried to argue.

"No. I can't take you with me. You saw how I barely escaped with my life yesterday. If you are with me, I'd worry about your safety along with mine."

"I figured," he added, dejected.

I ran toward him and wrapped him in my arms. If the world ended today, I'd be happy I at least made one true friend even though I may have lost two of them back home. Hoping to uncover the truth, I put on my sturdy leather jacket, smiling a farewell to a good friend. I needed to leave. Nightfall approached and painted the sky in its dark ambient beauty. The time was now.

THE PAIN IN my leg was uncomfortable, but I sucked it up and walked the perimeter around the shuttle station. I received word from one of the men patrolling the station in Sector Charlie he saw a woman who looked like Rayne aboard the shuttle, but the names didn't match.

Because of my probation, General Braggart advised the team I used they needed to report to both me and Trevor. I cringed as another bolt of pain shot up and down my body. My sadistic father thought his particular plan to make me submit would work—well, it had the opposite effect. I now knew General Brockton Braggart would do anything to gain control of a situation—even kill a bunch of teenagers and his son. I didn't even get enough time to heal the wounds my father and his goons inflicted before he sent me out to retrieve Rayne or others from Batch 001.

Like a twisted, diabolical joke, my father thought leaving the bullet in my body would be better than removing it. The metal a reminder they watched me, and I would be removed from the case should I make the wrong choice, failing my father again. Keeping my current aggression in check, I spotted Trevor walking toward me. The man walked around like a pompous rooster in uniform.

Holding a hand on his weapon, he approached me with a calculative glint in his eyes. "The Freak"—I made a fist to prevent myself from pummeling the little prick as he spoke.

—"was spotted getting off the shuttle near Bravo, so I'll scope out that division while you continue checking here in case they were mistaken."

Damn me if I let Trevor take the lead on this mission, especially when it pertains to Rayne.

I'd missed several opportunities to capture a super-human from Batch 001, but it hadn't gotten me the punishment my father had handed out for letting Rayne slip through my fingers. This beating had to do with her. There was something about *her*. Whether the old man harbored illusions about her or it annoyed him that she very nearly slipped undetected, thus ruining his perfect military record—I wouldn't know. But Trevor knew General Braggart had me on probation, so he would try to twist things around to further his accomplishments, leaving me in a hell of my own making. Not today. I hadn't been top in my field for nothing.

Studying Trevor's reaction, I replied, "Roger."

If it weren't for the one light twitch of the nerve under his eye registering his irritation, I would have thought I made the wrong choice.

Looking as if he would say more, Trevor stayed mute for once and walked away, talking to one of our personnel members before heading out. I wasn't an idiot and knew Unit 13 watched my actions. They had one hand on the equipment and the other on my kill switch. I needed to outmaneuver them.

I tried to think as Rayne would in this situation. She should know they posted her picture at the university. Or that my entire team and Ground Force operatives knew what she looked like by now. The guys were human but merciless. Thinking of how Rayne would travel, I sought the nearest utility hole leading to the underground tunnels in Sector Bravo.

Sector Bravo
Bravo Antiquis Subterranean System

SOMEONE HAD BEEN following me since I disembarked the shuttle in Sector Bravo's rural town known as Bravo Antiquis, bringing me an overwhelming anxious sense of foreboding. I looked everywhere around me, using my superhuman abilities to wheedle out the military and Ground Force personnel. Other than some Ground Force officers in the area, whom I avoided, nothing else struck out at me as odd. Now I walked the tunnels underneath Sector Bravo to see how near to the coast they would take me before I had to surface.

The smells made me queasy.

From what I could gather about my unique abilities, in the last few days, my sense of smell increased incredibly. The unwashed bodies, rotting earth, and putrefaction assaulted me. I passed more and more settlers who paid me no mind but overlooked my shoulder to the character stalking me.

If I hadn't been sure then, I was sure now.

The sensation increased, causing the hairs on my body to stick up like pine needles. Thinking my best bet of survival would be to run, I spotted a crate full of scraps. I walked past it, turning around in time to snatch it and throw it behind me. In the quick instant, it took to turn and throw, I made out several bodies ducking for cover, while one stood out above the rest. The stranger's eyes were the palest blue I had ever witnessed—the irises almost appeared white. A hood covered his head, but I could tell from the strands escaping its confines that his hair was of the purest white. Skin relatively clear in definition, a scary contrast to the dark colors he wore to cover his body. Lips were rosy, the sole color on his entire frame. He had to be the man following me, and I didn't bother to stick around and confirm it.

I bolted.

He followed, but I didn't check once, afraid it would give him even the slightest advantage. I darted down another tunnel, my breathing coming out choppy. Anxiety built further, tightening my chest as I ran for my life. I took off down another tunnel, but this one led to a dead end. I hit the wall, searching everywhere for an escape I hadn't seen earlier. My heart beat harder. I punched the wall in anxious energy. There was nothing but a massive wall and people running away from me.

The man spoke, the chill of his voice bringing shivers down my spine. "Stop running, Rayne." I turned around, ready for a fight, but he wore a crooked grin as he said, "You never could beat me during training."

There was a moment of recognition, but it disappeared to wherever my lost memory lay in hiding. The stranger pulled his hood off, showing me his hair was indeed all white. I had the sudden image in my head of this man at a young age, blending with the snow during camouflage training.

Why does he look so familiar?

"Seaa was right when she contacted us before her capture."

Did they capture Seaa? Did Rome catch her or kill her?

As painful as it was to think about, I hoped he had nothing to do with it.

"You lost your memory, didn't you?"

I couldn't be sure if I wanted to trust this guy right now with information, but he knew me, and he knew about Seaa. He further knew I had lost my memory, but so did Rome, and I didn't know if I trusted him right now either.

"My name is Snow."

Snow. The name so familiar to me, yet so far out of reach. My head tipped to one side as I pondered the meaning of the name. Silk was an element made from spiders, earthy. Seaa could be a feminine description of the sea and its creatures. I knew Thunder would be loud and intimidating with its splendor. They spelled my name differently, but it too described an element. Now the surname Snow. He had to be from the first batch.

"You're an escapee like me?"

He beamed—straight, white teeth. "That's right, Rayne. We grew up together up until five years ago. We all thought you were dead."

Well, I'm not.

His Cheshire grin disappeared as he cocked his head to one side. There was a moment where he resembled an owl as he listened to sounds around him. Eyes narrowing, he ran toward me, wrapping me up in his arms. But when we turned, a man I didn't expect faced us. My heart dived into the depths of my stomach, only to rise right back up. Rome's face was emotionless as he met Snow and me with his usual faded tan features, paler than I'd ever seen before. I could tell, Rome was in pain. I needed to realize he had come right then because I was his enemy.

"You don't give up, do you?" I asked.

Rome stared at me but didn't respond. Sweat dripped down his temple and gathered in the creases on his face. Something was up with him. I saw him take one step closer. My skittish heart jumped. What if he was regretting his decision to let me go earlier? His being here meant our fragile truce had ended, and he would bring me in.

Well, that sure as hell isn't happening.

I came to terms with the impending fight when I realized Snow's grip around me refused to loosen.

Rome had one hand on his gun while the other curled into a fist at his side. I tried to unwind the arms banded around my chest. The more I struggled to move, the tighter Snow's arms became, with his hand splayed across my abdomen. I tried to tell Snow to let go, but Rome's voice reached our ears first.

"Let her go."

Surprised I was caught off-guard, I stared back at Rome. Snow growled low in his throat, placing me behind his body as if protecting me from the super-soldier. "Over my dead body, Roman."

I watched Snow. *Does he know Rome?*

"Aw, c'mon, Snow. You know I'd love to play with you, but I have bigger things on my plate."

"Like capturing two live specimens from the first batch?" Snow pressed closer to my body with one arm bending back to hold the side of my midsection.

Rome's expressionless face turned feral as he stared daggers at Snow. "Get your hands off of her, Snow. I'm asking nicely."

What the hell is going on?

I had landed one hand over Snow's when Rome pulled out his weapon and shot Snow in the leg. His weight plunged toward the floor. I screamed as Snow fell on top of me. He roared with pain, but he didn't stop studying Rome from his precarious position on top of me. I looked up at Rome from over the back of Snow's shoulder. For the first time since everything happened, I feared this would be the end before I got my revenge.

Seeing him approach us, I noticed how he favored one leg over the other one. His weapon drawn, I closed my eyes, ready to get this over with.

"I told you to get your hands off her, Snow."

Snow's weight above me lightened. If possible, Snow laughed. I opened my eyes to first look at Snow and then at Rome.

"How cute, Rome. Are you crushing on our Rayne?"

Startled, I saw the grin on Snow's tinted lips and pale face. "What the hell are you talking about, Snow? We're enemies."

Snow pulled himself up with my help. I studied Rome as I straightened Snow, trying to glimpse a sign Snow jested. I instead saw him holster his weapon, crossing his arms over his chest. His muscle definition outlined through his shirt.

Rome stared into my eyes. "I'm thinking of changing that."

I stilled while Snow laughed like a hyena. The interior of the walls helped his laughter bounce off them.

The echo resounded around us as if taunting us.

"Shit me if I ever thought to see the day."

"I'm not on your side, Snow. You can go to hell for all I care." He took one step closer to me, limping. "But I'm on hers."

Lots of emotions threatened to rise to the surface, but I clamped them down. I couldn't afford to believe Rome right now. He had a chance to leave with me before, but he chose Braggart.

What would have changed his mind from then until now?

"Quit the lies, Rome. I don't have time for them."

His KeViewer rang. I knew what the KeViewer call meant.

He picked up, "What?"

Leaning on me for support, Snow looked at me and then back at Rome as he spoke to the caller. "Yeah, I was giving chase, but I must have lost it. I think it was male. No, it wasn't Rayne. I shot him, so I'm following the blood trail now. Give me ten and then come to my current location to gather evidence." Silent again. "Roger that."

Hanging up the KeViewer, Rome approached us. Grabbing me by the upper arm, he pulled me closer to himself.

"Snow, how do we get out of here? I bought us ten minutes before they come down here to investigate."

Snow grinned. "You're serious, aren't you?"

Rome didn't smile back.

"I told you, Snow. I'm doing it for her." He stopped to stare at me. "I owe you, Rayne."

Rome took me farther away from Snow, dragging me down the cold, damp tunnel.

Instead, I pulled him to a stop. "Stop playing with my head, Rome. Stop playing the superhero."

Rome opened his mouth to speak. "Now we have less time to get out of here." Grabbing my hand, he pulled me down the low-lit tunnel as Snow followed behind us.

Rome and I are enemies, right?

His fingers had intertwined with my own as we trekked forward. Snow led us through several tunnels, looping us around as he left smudges of his blood for Rome's team to follow. As we emerged, Snow had already stopped the bleeding. Darkness enveloped the night sky, with stars barely visible through the thick clouds. Rome hadn't let go of my hand at all since we left the old subway tunnels. Not like I wanted him to. He was such a mystery to me. I couldn't help wondering if he was serious in helping or playing a game.

We walked in different paths so the people giving chase could not decipher our location. I saw that Snow sped around in circles behind us, jumping onto a large jagged piece of metal from what may have been part of a frame for a large structure at one point in time. I tried to move my hand away from Rome several times, but he refused to let me go.

I was tired of the silence. Feeling an overwhelming

need to know the soldier's thoughts, I pulled on my hand one last time. "Rome, stop. I'm not going anywhere with you until I know what plan you have."

"As much as I'd like to know this plan of his, let's first get on the supply truck," Snow interjected.

Wondering what supply truck he talked about, we turned a corner and saw just that, its solar engine idling. The man seemed to know the schedules around this area because the truck was about to leave. Running, we grabbed on to the back of the truck bed as it sped down the road. I held on as Rome held on behind me, pinning me to the hovering vehicle. Barely anyone lingered outside as the truck made its way around twists and turns, passing empty buildings along its route until it approached an area near The Waste. The entire ride made me less aware of my surroundings and more aware of the man pressing his body against my back.

Snow grinned the entire time. I could tell there was a firm plan in his mind. I feared where this headed but didn't even have time to voice my concern before the truck stopped. A woman jumped down from a window frame of an abandoned building about twelve flights up, coming toward the truck we were on. Snow pulled me closer to his lean frame, distracting Rome from the approaching woman. I watched as the female slunk undetected, dropping Rome to the ground. I heard sounds of doors being slammed shut and turned my head to see two men disembark the vehicle.

I held my breath as one guy pulled down the hood covering his face. He looked like a gorgeous model with his blond hair and light gray eyes—glowing with repressed energy. The model was tall and muscular, but not as big as the man coming up beside him. The man's forearms looked more substantial than any average man should have—closer to a genetic mutation. His forehead was a flat surface as if molded to stay that way after years of being hit with a blunt object. His eyes were angry. As he clenched his fists—fear built inside of me, like the adrenaline of anxiety I couldn't control.

My throat felt raw from all the screaming for them to stop, as Rome lay on the ground, being pummeled by the three unannounced visitors. I could hear Rome grunt from each hit he received, but I could no longer see him, as tears blurred my vision. Afraid he'd get killed, I dug deep into my reservoir of strength. Feeling a sense of euphoria, I grabbed Snow's hand and ripped his fingers back. The group moved away. Rome had curled into a ball on the ground, bleeding from the cuts on his face.

Seeing him in pain infuriated me further. If Rome had to bleed, it would be because I did it. I turned my body and kicked Snow on his injured leg. He dropped to the ground and hissed in pain. Looking back at the others, I noticed they had taken one step closer to me. They stopped when they saw me pull out the sharp blade Snow had in a holster on his waist. I dropped behind Snow and put it to his neck. The woman whose face was covered by a large hood had Rome's gun pointed at his head, while the other two men drew closer to me.

Knowing I would have to fight and maybe fail, I tightened the knife to Snow's neck.

"S-stop," Snow croaked.

The two men stopped walking.

"Let him go, and I'll release Snow." I tried to sound obstinate, but my voice cracked.

The woman cocked the gun, sending my body thrumming with apprehension. This was a battle of wits, and I feared I didn't quite muster up.

Rome stayed put, and Snow spoke. "Silk, let him go."

The name weighed heavily on my memory as the vision of a young, beautiful woman with dark curls ran behind me through the woods—eyes pitch dark with porcelain-smooth skin. Silk had been a part of my memory, so I turned to look at the woman who had Rome's life in her hands. The cloak covered her features, so I couldn't see her face. If this was my sister, I'm sure we could come to an understanding.

"Silk? Are you the same Silk who ran with me through the woods five years ago?" I asked in a low voice.

The woman made no move, but her body tensed. Her free hand reached up to pull the hood off her head. The moment she did, the vision of the girl who saved my life turned into reality. She had hair twisted into a dark French braid hiding inside her cloak. Her skin looked like butter from where she stood, so smooth and moist. I recognized the woman who had followed us to safety. The only face I could remember in my vague memories.

"Rayne?" Even her voice was similar.

Silk turned her head when Snow spoke up from his awkward spot on the dusty ground. "That's why I said stop."

Silk didn't discontinue her aim of the weapon, but walked forward, her arm bending back, the gun locked on Rome. The two men dropped back as if choreographed, hovering over Rome. Silk dropped her arm, standing in front of me now. I trembled with the knife still at Snow's neck.

"Little Rayne? God, look at how big you've grown."

I wanted to let go of Snow and hold the only woman I remembered close but feared to lose the only leverage I had keeping Rome alive. "I remember little, but I had a memory of you the other night."

Silk nodded in understanding. "Seaa told us you lost your memory from the bullet wound in your head."

"Ah, hello? Knife to my throat here."

The beautiful woman looked down at Snow and back at me. "Right. Guy, Rock, let him go."

The guy named Rock spoke up. "Are you nuts, Silk? This guy is being tracked. Dudes could be on us at any minute."

Silk's eyebrows drew in anger; her voice got high. She must not have enjoyed being called crazy. "I said," her voice dropping to a normal tone, "to let him go. We'll bring him to Thunder. He'll fry whatever chip the guy has on him."

Taking a leap of faith, I dropped the hand holding the knife.

Snow coughed as he lifted himself from the ground. He grinned a sexy, sly smile at me, turning to look at Silk. "Rome seems a changed man because of little Rayne here," he said as he pointed at me with his thumb. "He even told his people he was giving chase but gave us enough time to escape."

Silk looked down at his thigh. "So, why is there a bullet hole in your leg?"

"I didn't let go of her when he asked me," Snow replied with a grin.

I turned to look at Rome, who sat up to spit out the blood in his mouth.

"Yeah," he coughed, "and I'll reshoot you if you put your hands on her again." He shrugged, the picture of being so at ease. "Even then, I might still shoot you."

Silk shook her head as Guy laughed along with Snow while they walked back to the truck. Rock didn't crack a smile. He stood there with a Gargoyle-like grimace on his face. I knew I was as red as I could get as the intent of his words penetrated my baffled mind. No man had ever shown his jealousy for me as Rome did. Passing by my siblings, I got to Rome as he stood on shaky legs. He practically ended up right back on the ground, so I wrapped my arms around his body and buried my nose inside the mid-length coat draped around his lithe form. I took in his musk of sandalwood and mint, hoping this was where I belonged. He held onto the truck with one hand to keep his balance, but the other held on to me.

Before anyone could say anything, his KeViewer shrilled again. Rome pulled it out of his pocket, staring at the bright screen. Shaking his head, he held it out to Rock. Rock may have been briefly confused, but his large hand grabbed the KeViewer, as if waiting for instructions from Silk. She nodded at him, so he answered.

"Too bad he wasn't fast enough. If you want your boy back, let Seaa and Hail out."

Rock was silent for a minute before he spoke again. "I don't make deals with you dickheads. Call me back at this number if you want to see your punk-ass super soldier again." Hanging up, he handed the KeViewer to Silk.

Rome nodded. "They won't trade me for Seaa or Hail. I guarantee it. But they'll be convinced you have no idea about my kill switch and tracker. Once they track me to your hideout, they'll kill us all."

I was afraid they might do that when Silk spoke. "How far back you think they'd be?"

Rome let go of me, making me feel bereft. He stood beside me and clasped my hand. "I had them gathering evidence, so I'd say another fifteen minutes before they catch up to my whereabouts. However, Trevor Dallas is on the move too. The faster we get out of here, the better."

Guy nodded. "That should be enough time to get Thunder to work his magic."

Rome looked perplexed. "Wait, what magic?"

No one answered.

Instead, Rome's head whipped back when Rock punched him in his face and knocked him out cold.

CHAPTER FOURTEEN

Sector Bravo
The Waste
Operative Roman Braggart
ID: MIL 116.002

WHEN GUY SAID Thunder could work his magic on me, they weren't too far off from the truth. After sending Guy Gust over to get Thunder—whose speed was unparalleled to that which any of us from Batch 002 could ever dream of reaching—he returned with Thunder. The lightning leader was not happy to see me. For years, I had caused this group of biological soldiers grief, capturing one, and getting a second one caught by my partner. The experiments had no reason to trust me, but because Rayne was on my side, they allowed me to live for now.

Except, the pain I felt all over my body, causing me

hardships to breathe, said differently about my time around these genetic beings. Death knocked at my door, seeking entrance to what little life I had left. I couldn't breathe, couldn't stand as I crawled over to a stump on the ground to use as leverage to lift myself off the ground. Rayne stood to one side, her beautiful hazel eyes open wide. Her hands covered her mouth as Thunder sent current after current of electricity into my body. Zaps of lightning were at this man's disposal. His powerful hands sent currents into my body in small doses so it wouldn't kill me. The hits felt like a Vuwand would feel if it zapped me over and over again—*which they have.*

I coughed, gasping as I tried to suck in some much-needed air. "Give me more than that if you want to fry the tracker. Vuwand's pack a stronger punch and don't mess with our trackers."

Thunder grinned as he looked over at Silk and Snow. They both nodded in unison and walked over to where Rayne stood. I knew what it meant, so I held on tight for a wild ride I may or may not come back from. Thunder held his hand out, sending strikes of lightning to my body at full capacity. Seizures wracked me, while the sounds of rolling thunder rang in my ears. I could feel warm moisture run down my ears and nose as spasms vibrated my every muscle and bone. Arching up high as another shock ran through me made me scream in response. My heart felt like it would burst from my chest. I had already slipped from the stump, writhing on the ground.

Taking a small reprieve from this latest attack, I turned my head to stare at the woman who had turned my entire world upside down. Rayne screamed, but I couldn't hear her. There was a high-pitched sound in my ears. The spasms attacked my body, praying they would kill me to end the misery. Opening the door for *Death*, I blacked out.

FEELING WORN DEEP down to my bones, I sunk into the cushioned single sofa chair in the small room. The wall was layered with different pieces of metal like a jigsaw puzzle gone wrong. The area was barren, but for the small sofa, a cot, and a desk with a plethora of paperwork scattered on top. The floor was dark and made of stone. The small interior smelled of old gym clothes and mold. I sighed again for the billionth time as I watched Rome's motionless body on the cold cot in front of me and shivered as I remembered the beating Rome took to get the tracker fried.

Thunder was merely playing games with him as he zapped him over and over again the first times. To get the tracker Rome had in his body fried, Thunder had to kill him. With all of the electricity coursing through his body, Rome's heart had stopped beating. The area containing his tracker and kill-switch burned a mark on his body so we could locate them. Guy had leaned over Rome's dead body as I screamed for Silk to let me go. Instead of leaving him gone as I first thought, Guy bent over and started chest compressions. I was relieved for a split second. Guy grabbed a blade at his ankle and stabbed the two marked areas on Rome's skin with his sharp edge.

I still couldn't get the screams I'd heard from my mind as Rome cried over and over again in agony. Guy removed the tracker and kill switch, and Rome passed out again. After what felt like hours, the team gathered together and drove off to a different location, skipping from one point to another. We got on a boat headed toward an uninhabited island, and then took a smaller rowboat to the other side of the coast where they opened the ground and walked underneath the earth.

Underground, a doctor with a bald head and thick, round-rimmed glasses met us at the entrance and ran to Rome's side. There were hours of surgery to connect the main artery in his leg where the kill switch was attached and an additional hour to remove a roaming bullet from his leg. Afterward, the doctor stitched up the wound in his neck left behind by the tracker. Two days had gone by, and I refused to leave his side.

The other sound in the room aside from my breathing was Rome's, and I turned when footsteps greeted the silence. Thinking it was Silk again trying to get me to go shower and sleep, I called out, "Stop wasting your time, Silk."

"It's not Silk," a rough voice called back.

Jumping out of the chair, I turned to stare at Thunder. The massive, six-foot-five male stood with his arms crossed in front of him. He had long, light brown hair with a long streak of blond running down one side. He wore dark jeans with a white shirt that showed every muscle definition on his chest. He had roped muscles with veins showing through his skin. Thunder's eyes were like a stormy night that shot sparks when intense and angry.

I feared this man and his power.

With my heart doing everything but escaping my chest, I spoke. "H-hello, Thunder."

Thunder led the rest of the group as the eldest. The underground bunker we were in harbored Silk, Guy Gust, Rock, Snow, Thunder, and a senior doctor named Ferdinand. A young woman with a patch over her eye and a bum leg did the cooking and was, from what I could tell, Rock's lover. I think they called her Beatrice. Seaa and Hail were, too, a part of the location before Trevor captured Seea, and Rome won over Hail. Two others came around sporadically, Cam and Blister, but they were so deep undercover the facility counted them as dead, as they had me.

I looked back at Rome, who had barely moved all night.

"He'll survive, Rayne."

I turned back to look at Thunder and nodded. I hoped so.

"I came to get you. We need you to remember what you have forgotten. You need to understand the gravity of this situation. That Rome is alive right now is because Silk and Snow saw the way the man feels for you. I, for one, would have killed him without a second's hesitation."

I understood that about him. Thunder didn't look to have one kind bone in his body when it didn't involve his family. Silk briefly mentioned that everything was meticulously thought out for benefits and calculated for risks.

"I don't understand how you expect me to remember anything. It was recently I got snippets out of dreams that were locked away memories."

He leaned against the metal wall. "Ferdinand thinks I should use my power on your brain."

"O-on my brain?" I nearly tripped on the sofa, not knowing I had taken a step back in fear.

He nodded.

"I saw what you're a-ability did to Rome. I won't let you anywhere near my brain, Thunder."

For the first time since we'd met, he looked amused. "It wouldn't even be as bad as all that. You might barely even feel it. All it would do is cause the nerves in your brain to work in the area that had blocked off your memories."

Is that all it will take to bring my memories back? To remember everything that happened before I met my adoptive parents?

Before I could reply, Rome stirred on the cot. I left Thunder where he stood and turned to watch Rome move from side to side. He groaned softly. With fluttering eyelashes, his beautiful jade eyes took in everything around him as they searched the small interior, landing on me. A small quirk graced his lips as he worked his hand to reach out to mine.

"Hello, Gorgeous."

This time I sighed in relief. "Rome, how are you feeling?"

Before he answered, Thunder had come around my shoulder to look down at where he lay. "Yeah, Roman. How are you feeling?"

Rome took his eyes off me, placing them on Thunder. "I'm sure you took great enjoyment in my suffering, Thunder."

Thunder grinned, but it wasn't at all friendly. "I'd take more pleasure in knowing you, and the rest of your group is dead, but it seems I was overruled. For now."

"Lucky me," Rome replied, coughing.

Thunder walked out of the room, taking one last look at me. "Remember what I said, Rayne, it might help."

I nodded but said nothing, turning to look at Rome.

"What did he want?" Rome asked.

I shrugged, and the act brought Gavin to my mind. Leaving him behind was the correct answer. "To help me with my lost memories, but don't worry about all that. How are you feeling?"

Rome didn't look like he was at all thrilled at my clipped response, but he didn't push further. Instead, he rose from his position. He stretched his muscles, not once flinching from the pain of his wounds. He felt for the gauze pads that were placed on his healing injuries and ripped them off. The skin underneath held a faint scar.

"I feel fine now. I assume they got them out?"

I nodded. "Yeah, they weren't easy to remove. Guy got bits out, but Dr. Ferdinand did the rest. We also found a bullet wound in your leg, so he took it out too." Rome nodded and moved the leg in question around.

"Yeah, the bullet was my father's own sick and twisted punishment for letting you escape the last time."

"He shot you?"

"Yup, after he beat the shit out of me."

I couldn't quite understand why someone's father would hurt them like that. My adoptive parents never laid a hand on me. I couldn't imagine ever getting punished as he had been, and I wasn't even their flesh and blood.

"I'm sorry," was the only response I could give.

Rome shrugged as he leaned around to plant his feet on the cold, stone floor. I jumped from my spot to turn around as Rome threw the sheet off his naked body. With a pair of boxer briefs to cover his nudity, I couldn't contain the blush adorning my cheeks. Men like him had only ever graced the pages of magazines, and seeing a man like him in person made me breathless.

He had a very intricate tattoo covering the majority of his left arm to the wrist. The lines of the symbol flowed over his shoulder and blended seamlessly into the other marking over his left pectoral. The black panther on his breast had his mouth wide open as if frozen in a mid-roar. The ends of the panther blended into another marking covering the entire left side of his chest and stomach and hid behind the elastic of his waistbands.

I wonder why he wears such a magnificent creature on his skin like tapestry.

He rummaged through the clothes at the end of the cot and slipped them on. I didn't even know when he had finished dressing. I was turned around by the shoulder and dragged into a long, deep kiss. His lips moved over mine with years of practiced skill and precision. He fisted one handful of my hair as I clutched his shirt. I could feel a wildfire burn inside me. We both pulled each other closer. Someone cleared their throat, so I pulled away from the toe-curling kiss—the magic broken.

The man would be the death of me.
He'll be the reason I fail.

Batch 001 Headquarters
Roman Braggart
ID: MIL 116.002

EVERY TIME I wanted to taste this woman, someone or something impeded it going further. I still didn't know how the hell this woman even got to me as she did, but I was dead tired of fighting it.

Hell, I've already died for her.

After what I learned from Rayne—and the actions my father took on me—there was no doubt in my mind they had wrongfully accused this batch, and if they were dispensable, so was the next installment. I trusted Rayne, but looking around me as we walked down the darkened halls of the underground bunker, I sure as hell didn't trust the rest. In a large room sat the rest of the Plan A genetics, eating food, and it occurred to me that for the past five years, I was trained with the thought to eliminate the experiments. Now that I had them all together in one room—I couldn't get the urge to care.

Led into the dining area by Rock, I looked around

at all the faces. With not so much as an introduction, Rock turned away from us and headed toward the petite woman sitting at the corner of a table with an overused apron wrapped around her thick waist. She didn't look familiar, so I assumed she was a girlfriend. Rock was the Herculean Cocktail gone wrong with his sizeable, flat forehead and Popeye arms.

The guy in question turned to look at me, flipping me off. I grinned. Rock had an attitude problem. Beside the woman with a patch on her eye ogling Rock sat Guy Gust, who was ordinary compared to the rest. He was the average American golden boy of the twenty-first century with blond hair and a slim, muscular build. The only difference was the golden boy had gray eyes, not blue, and he eyed Rayne like a piece of meat, and he the starving wolf.

I studied Rayne, who stood next to me at the entrance of the dining room. She, too, had nothing to say as she looked around her. I still couldn't get over the fact I was in their headquarters, standing beside a woman who threw me for a loop. Just the other day, I had given chase and told my friend she was the enemy, and now I was fascinated with the small woman. The Thor-looking Thunder sat at one end of the table, discussing political matters with a bald man Rayne had described as the doctor on-premises, responsible for the surgical procedures conducted on me a few days before.

Farther down the table sat the beautiful and elusive Silk—her jet black, blue hair lying down her back in a French braid. Silk was beyond beautiful, but from what I had read, she had a mean temper on her, rivaling the grizzliest of men. From the looks, Snow, who was as pale as the substance, with long white hair, was on the receiving end of her fury.

A startled snort escaped me when Silk grabbed her fork and stabbed Snow's roaming hand. Beside me, Rayne gasped, assuring me she saw the same thing. Our sounds alerted the group of our presence; all heads shot up from their plates and conversations. Silk gave me a fierce stare down then turned to look at Rayne, and the anger vanished. So the black widow had a soft spot for Rayne. I confirmed this when I wrapped my arm around Rayne's shoulders and Silk hissed, slapping her hands on the surface of the table.

"Relax, Silk," roared Thunder.

Rayne shrugged her shoulders, dropping my arm back to my side. She looked up at me, and my heart skipped a beat. This woman had intrigue, beauty, and a fascinating world unseen by the norm surrounding her. She stood out to me amongst the rest. Rayne placed a comforting hand on my arm and walked toward the table where the rest of her family sat. I followed, but the stares around me told me where they'd like me to be right about now.

SILK PULLED ME into a firm hug, caressing the hair down my back in a comforting gesture. There was something about Silk—her scent, her touch, her warmth—that brought me peace, regardless of how much I knew or didn't know about my family. I returned Silk's hug with one of my own, hoping I could remember everything I had forgotten about the few around me.

"Little Rayne, I'm so glad you found us."

I let go of Silk. "Me too, Silk. I don't remember anyone else, but I had a memory of you. That counts, right?"

Before Silk could respond, Thunder broke in on the conversation. "You might be able to gain them all, Rayne."

Yes, I could, if I allowed Thunder to zap my memories into place. I saw what the man could do with his ability. I feared him.

"If you could get your memories back, Rayne, you might remember me a whole lot better," said Guy.

I stared at Guy, his beauty light as Rome's was dark, but I felt nothing for him. "I'd like to remember everyone, Guy, not just you," I countered.

Ferdinand, the doctor, got up from his seat next to Thunder and walked around the table. "Rayne, is it?"

I nodded.

"I believe Thunder could restore your memories." He stared up at the ceiling as if finding the words on the carved-out rock. "The memories you harbor can arguably be stored in your amygdala." He stared back at me, pointing at different spots on my head. "Sparking the cerebral cortex could help the amygdala react. From what I gather, you had a bullet wound to the head which didn't kill you but must have healed around the bullet, or it may have exited your skull. I'm not so sure yet without analyzing the area myself. You lost your memories like operative Rome lost function in his leg. We can spark up your memories and get those nerves firing."

I almost choked on the bread roll on its way to my mouth, but Rome saved me from saying anything.

"Brain surgery? You must be fucking kidding me, old man. You're not going anywhere near her brain with a scalpel and Thundergod over there."

I agreed, though I didn't show it. But I wanted my memories because roaming around in the dark without being able to make sense of the chaos around me was exhausting. Silk grabbed my arms and looked me in the eyes.

"Rayne, trust Dr. Ferdinand. He knows what he's doing. If not, trust me. I would let no harm come to you. Not again."

The memory of Silk and me being pulled by some unknown man as we ran from disaster flittered in my mind. There was a guy with blistering red skin, made brighter from the taxing run, being shot, and Silk trying to stop him from falling into the raging river. Instead, the river took *me* as a victim.

Feeling a need to protect Silk from that kind of pain, I blurted out, "I'll do it!"

Rome roared from his seat, about to jump over the table, but Thunder zapped him with a volt that made Rome writhe around on the floor. I could hear him trying to talk me out of it, but I needed to do this. Not for Silk, but for myself. Gaining the last bits of my courage, I walked over to Thunder, glancing down at an immobile Rome. My heart ached for the man, but I couldn't remain clueless. I wanted revenge for the death of my parents, for my creator, for the rest of my family. No, not just revenge. I needed this craziness to end. I needed to remember those lost memories.

Thunder clapped my shoulder, I flinched but nodded as he led me to a backroom in the cavernous dining area. The doctor followed close behind, murmuring so quietly I could barely hear him through my keen senses. Unaware of where I'd go, I walked into a sterile, white room, small, with a sink and medical supplies. Beyond the room was a wall made of glass, which held an even more sterile room with bright white walls and brilliant white tiles. A table made of stainless steel hovered in the middle of the room, medical equipment all around it. The room was like a hospital would look like in the twenty-first century, except for the holographic screens our generation used and the sporadic hovering stations throughout the room.

The room was pristine.

"Please, strip down, and jump into the Hydro Chamber."

I looked at Silk and Thunder, who stood as if the doctor had said nothing indecent. "I am not taking off my clothes in front of all of you."

Both the doctor and Thunder frowned, but Silk grinned. "C'mon boys. Let's give her a minute." She handed over a paper gown. "Put this on to cover the goods as soon as you are done. The chamber is set for a thirty-second steam wash to cleanse the grime and buildup on your skin. Just press this button," she pointed at a blue knob, "and it'll steam up quick." She told the boys, "We'll be back in five."

No amount of courtesy would help me feel at all better. The butterflies ate away at my stomach as bile rolled up my throat. I needed to get this over with, so I took off my boots and peeled the clothes from my body. I stared at my reflection in the small mirror near the Hydro Chamber. There were bags under my eyes and stringy clumps of my hair plastered around my face. I looked like a wreck. I pulled the chain over my head. Naked, I walked into the small Hydro Chamber and slid the door closed. Pressing the knob, a blast of warm, wet steam spouted from every direction of the interior. The moisture clung to my skin, sliding down in droplets as it took all of the filth from my body. I could feel it scrubbing each dead layer of skin off, leaving behind a light pink tint to my body.

When the chamber finished, 1 slid open the door to find a towel sitting on a hovering stool. The moment the door slid open, a vent of warm air pushed through, drying off all the leftover water from my body. 1 worked the towel into my hair. Amazed at the technology, 1 grabbed the paper gown and wrapped it around me, tying the ends together. 1 was about to tighten the last bow when noises outside the door caused me to look up. 1 heard screaming and shattering glass. People shouted all at once so 1 couldn't make out any words. But one voice called out to me.

Rome screamed out my name, and all fell silent. 1 felt the urge to run to him, but 1 stayed rooted as tears fell down my cheeks. Ferdinand and Thunder walked through the door as 1 wiped my face.

"Let's get this over with."

CHAPTER FIFTEEN

THERE WAS PAIN.

Lots and lots of pain encased every muscle in my body.

I couldn't open my eyes, and I couldn't scream even though I wanted to. None of the muscles moved in my body, even though I felt like kicking the person inflicting the pain.

My head ached as if someone had slammed it repeatedly into a wall. There were sparks of light like a kaleidoscope of color behind my eyelids when shapes took form. Voices jumbled together as I tried to decipher who they belonged to.

The movements around me came into focus little by little until I could see a younger version of Thunder standing in front of me, laughing as he played with his brother. He had Hail in a headlock, while Hail had Sandman in his own headlock. I remembered Hail with his short-cropped hair and a crooked smile. He looked up at me and winked. I could feel the heat in my cheeks and the steady beat of my heart. Our dear friend Sam, whom we nicknamed Sandman, laughed as he disintegrated into pieces of sand through Hail's strong arms. I giggled loudly. Hail flipped Thunder over his shoulder, slipping on the sand left on the concrete floor. Another voice spoke from beside me, so I turned my head to see Flora place a beautiful flower behind my ear. The smell of roses and lilies perfumed the air around the young girl. Flora had orange, auburn-colored hair in massive waves around her small heart-shaped face with eyes the color of moss. She was lanky but just as strong as the rest of us.

A soldier passed us with a long look to make sure we didn't misbehave. Flora giggled alongside me as Sandman got back into his human form and punched Thunder in the back of the head. Dr. Lester hated it when we used our abilities around the soldiers. He told us to make sure no one else saw. Even though security in this place was tight, Pops always had our back.

I saw the doors swish open that led into the faux courtyard created for us to run scenarios and Guy Gust coming into the large room with his blond good looks. Flora had a massive crush on him. The womanizer preferred to ignore the signs right in front of him, instead opting to flirt with essentially every other female in Project Hercules. He came directly toward me in his baggy shorts and swagger, but he didn't make my heart flip around my chest as Hail did.

Guy placed his arm around me and whispered stupid nonsense in my ear. He did it to piss off Hail. And boy did it work. Hail got off the floor and sauntered toward me. Guy removed his arm from my shoulders before Hail even said anything. I assumed he preferred to live.

"Hands off my girl, Guy."

I wasn't really his girlfriend. Not like in those magazines, our pops allowed us to read every once in a while to have some connection to the world outside of our bunker. More like someone who shared the same interests he did that weren't military-related. This fight wasn't my choice at all, but we knew what our orders were and what consequences we faced if we didn't obey.

"We cool, Hail. I was just keeping her warm until you showed up."

I felt my cheeks burn once more and was about to shy away from the flattering comments when the doors swooshed open again, and General Braggart walked in with one hand on his weapon and the other twirling his mustache. My stomach dived as bile rose. The General was not a friendly man and much feared throughout the facility. Pops said we were better off doing everything the General wanted, or he'd end Batch 001 permanently.

The man in question walked the Elements Courtyard, taking in each one of us teenagers with a wary eye. Except, when they landed on me, the gleam in his eyes was more maniacal and predatory. The greed I saw creeped me out, and he'd been doing it more often now than before. The day before, he had walked into the girl's locker room, claiming he had been making sure no boy's hid inside.

"You experiments have had enough fun for today. Get back to work! Guy Gust and Rayne? Go join Snow in the Tread room for a speed check." Both Guy and I nodded and practically ran out of the room as the General told Hail and Thunder to go into the Tactics room for a one-on-one fight.

The memory ran seamlessly into another one as screams and outbursts filtered into my ears. I cowered in one corner of the room. The girls chanted and got the boys excited like they usually did when they got rowdy. The wall behind me kept vibrating as someone on the other side continuously banged on it. The concrete and metal burst apart, and the girls ran through the opening into the boy's dorm. Fiera came toward me, grabbing me by the arm and yanking me up.

"Let's end this now and get out of here, Rayne!"

There was the hope of freedom in those words, prompting me to move and join the rest of the fight. Nonetheless, regardless of our strength, the General was consistently one step ahead of us.

Braggart's officers attacked the rest of my siblings and me. They had custom tasers and pistols that *penetrated our thick skin and caused a lot of damage. Most of the kids dropped on the floor, writhing in pain, or remained still. Lights flickered, and walls closed together, separating a lot of the children from the military. Another room exploded outward. I could see some of the teens fall out of the massive hole in the wall. Guy saw Pops before any of us did and called everyone to follow him.*

All I saw were faces full of fear and excitement. I was scared as I ran down the corridor away from the soldiers and their weapons. Chaos rang around us the faster I ran down the hall into an old mining tunnel the doctor had talked to us about. Kids fell injured and dead around me, further scaring me. I hid behind a boulder, afraid to move ahead, but a blur carried past me, a sting in my head, and my pops took a bullet meant for me. I saw two of my siblings jump over us to stop the soldiers as I held Pops in my arms—tears mixed with blood cascading down my ashen face.

I sat upright as I inhaled the stale, medicinal air around me. My eyes were unfocused, but I no longer felt pain. Looking around me, I noticed this was the same sterile room where they had performed the surgery on me.

Dr. Ferdinand stood in front of me with a broad grin on his face. "It worked?"

Silk and Snow were on the other side of the large glass pane. They were curious.

I stared back at Dr. Ferdinand and said, "Yes."

Sector Bravo
Headquarters Holding Cells
Roman Braggart
ID: MIL 116.002

I HOWLED AGAIN as I tried to break through the bars of the jail they had placed me in. I didn't know what the hell these things were made of, but they wouldn't budge, so I ran a hand through my hair in frustration. No one said anything to me. It had been over a day since Rayne walked into that surgical room. I was well aware of why they had me in captivity. I didn't blame them. But I was worried about Rayne. I wanted to make sure she was alright, and that the lunatic doctor didn't hurt her.

Dr. Plumboy, back at the military headquarters, was sinister and cruel. I knew how nasty these scientists were with their experiments. I slammed the bars again.

This is bullshit!

I was about to vent once more when the door at the end of the broad corridor swung open.

My senses breathed her in before I saw her. "Rayne?"

Rayne ran toward my cage, gripping the bars. God, she was beautiful. I didn't know how badly I wanted to see her until she stood right in front of me.

"Rome, I'm so sorry!"

"Are you okay?"

She studied the dirty floor, scuffing the toe of her boots on the cement. "Yeah, I'm fine."

What did that mean?

"Rayne, did you get your memories back?"

Rayne nodded. "Yeah, I got them back."

I gripped her hand with mine as we held the bars. "I'm glad, Rayne. I'm happy you are okay."

I *really* was.

Rayne deserved her memories, whether they were good or bad. She earned the right to know the truth about her birth, instead of all of the secrecy the military had raised me around. Rayne sighed as she ran her thumb across the skin of my hand. Her flesh on mine sent shivers down my spine.

Damn, I want her.

"Silk, get him out of here."

Silk dropped from the ceiling, landing on the balls of both feet. I judged how high she had been and the mere fact the poisonous spider was hanging upside down. "Please tell me you spit a web out your mouth. Or..." I winked and left it to her imagination.

Silk hissed. "No, but I *am* feeling carnivorous right now."

I laughed as Rayne frowned. "Please, you two."

Silk opened the door leading into the cage with a sneer.

"Damn, these are strong bars. *I* couldn't even break through them."

The black widow didn't even flinch. "Yeah, several have tried and failed."

I bet they did.

Now, if I could get Rayne alone and talk because we had much to discuss.

An hour later, Rayne sat on a bed in her little room. I sat in the small chair across from her. Both of us looked confused, conflicted, and battered as we recalled our latest conversation. I couldn't believe everything she had told me about Batch 001 and the abuse they had undergone in Braggart's care. Rayne was upfront about her feelings about the General from the beginning, but my feelings for her were undeniable, and I knew the moment she found out I was Satan's son, Rayne would push me away. I couldn't allow it to happen.

If I was honest, I thought her getting her memories back would make her a different Rayne. That wasn't the case. Rayne was still the same sweet but tough female who drove me insane with her touch and smell. I couldn't help it. Rising from my seat, I sauntered over to her like a cat to milk. As I approached, her large eyes grew. Telltale signs of her swallowing, rapid eye blinking, and tense fingers showed me I excited her as much as she aroused me.

Rayne leaned back as my massive frame enveloped her vision. The woman would be the death of me, and she knew it. Leaning down, I swooped in and claimed her lips for my own. She purred, and I responded with a growl buried deep in my chest. My long-repressed panther blood hummed with excitement. Rayne's taste filled me with euphoria, and her skin drove me insane. She rubbed her chest against mine, molding our bodies in complete synchronization. I tried to take the kiss deeper, but she pulled away from me, pushing me away.

"I c-cant, Rome."

I felt more confused now than before, knowing our feelings for one another were mutual. Then it clicked. "Does this have anything to do with your memories?"

There were things she wasn't telling me, but the fear of losing her was more significant than her withheld information. Rayne averted her eyes, looking everywhere but at me, and I knew this was worse than I could have ever expected. Running a hand through my hair, I straightened and walked back to my chair.

"What's his name?"

Rayne froze but eased her body as she blew a breath out of her mouth. "Hail."

I stiffened as I clenched the end of the seat between my fingers.

Shit, it had to be Hail.

The first genetic human I captured from the group because I was lucky enough to catch the guy off-guard. Hail wasn't an easy target, and I knew I would have died if it weren't for my own genetic abnormalities.

Hail was the first fight that stirred my panther DNA. If it weren't for the team following me sedating the panther, who knows how much worse I could've made it. Protecting his brethren, Hail took a hit from my bullet and a beating from my fists. To top it off, I handed Hail to General Braggart, and after another blow from the General, Hail had been dragged off somewhere—to a cage or his death—I didn't know, and until now, I didn't care. Rayne would hate me.

"I captured Hail, Rayne. I'm sorry."

She nodded but didn't say a word. Seconds passed between us, but it felt like minutes before Rayne spoke. "I know. Seaa told me a lot about you before we met in my apartment, Rome."

"He may not be alive."

"I know."

"I may have led him to his death, Rayne."

"I know."

Her clipped responses unnerved me more than a fight would have. "What will happen to us now?"

"I don't know."

My heart beat like a rogue drum, but ignoring how badly I wanted to shake her and make her mine, I got up from the seat and walked back up to her. "My feelings for you haven't changed. When you are ready to open yourself back up, let me know."

I refused to look back as I walked out of her room through its only door.

The cavernous hall was long and dark as I walked

down the beaten path. I had excellent eyesight in dark spaces, but I sensed another watched me and prepared myself for a fight should the need arise. I was in enemy territory, and although the experiments were no longer my enemy, I was still an enemy to them.

I tried to pinpoint the scent to a specific person, but like before—I couldn't. This genetic human could mask their identity. The familiar sensation reminded me of my incarceration earlier and the fact Rayne came in and identified Silk without me even realizing she was there.

"You can come out, Silk."

The black widow dropped from the roof of the interior and smirked. "It seems the second batch is a tad bit more reliable than I thought."

"We have a unique ability to connect scents to memories—even if there aren't any specific scents to begin with."

"You are mistaken, Rome. I do have a scent, like everyone else, but my job is to make you feel relaxed and place you off-guard."

I smirked. For a second, a split-second, she gave the impression of a normal girl. Silk was quite the fascinating creature as she walked beside me. She seemed as if she wanted to chat, but her dislike of me must have kept her quiet. There was no other reason to believe she needed to speak to me otherwise.

My background eliminated any chance of camaraderie. My choices would not open them up to me.

It would be several days before any of them would trust me, even if a little. I was sick and tired of my father's orders. I could only wait to see if they saw it. When I had been forced to volunteer for this project, I thought I would at least be able to make a difference in this chaotic, dystopian world, not add to the frightening circumstances we already faced daily.

"Hail didn't give up on her."

This was a conversation I hadn't expected to come from Silk, but I was far too curious to tell her to mind her own damned business.

"He loved her," was all I could say.

In the darkness, I could hear the echo of our footsteps and see the slight nod she gave. "He blamed himself for not saving her from the raging river after the escape. Hail was there when Blister got shot in the leg. When I grabbed Blister, Hail watched in horror as Thunder slipped on the mud, and they both fell into the river. Thunder came out of it. She got swallowed up so quickly we thought she was dead. Following the escape, Hail wanted to look for her body, but the heat of the escape was way too fresh. Thunder was the one to go out and search. He didn't find her, so after spending a long time in hiding, Hail went off on a search for females who looked like Rayne—just in case. He refused to give up."

"Then, I came around."

Silk cracked her knuckles as we continued our walk down the dark space. "You took Hail away from her.

Away from us."

"Yes."

"Do you feel any remorse?"

Do I? I want Rayne to be happy, regardless if that means with me or without me.

"Yes, I think I might. She means a lot to me. But to be fair, at the time, I thought I was doing the right thing."

A smile ghosted on her face—there one second and gone the next. "Good. Maybe you can do something for us."

I nodded.

"Follow me."

Safe Haven Headquarters
Planning Room

I SAT CROSS-LEGGED on the large couch inside the room where my family held their meetings. I could see an old conference desk. There were no longer chairs surrounding the giant, wooden masterpiece, but it wasn't like any of us needed to sit down. Well, except for me. I think I sat out of habit. Those gathered around the table had so much pent-up energy it made it impossible to sit still. We've been in this room for the past two hours, discussing the latest phone call received on Rome's KeViewer. Guy amped up the device to prevent our location from reading off the KeViewer in case they tried to track it.

The military thought Rome died. His tracker was offline, and so was his kill-switch. Thunder made up lies about making an example out of him and left it at that. Rome had been freed from their clutches, so I felt guilty he stuck around, even helping us free Seaa and Hail from their prisons—if they were still there. Rome made my heart hitch as I watched him arguing with the others about the best battle plan.

I felt horrible I couldn't give Rome the attention I knew he craved of me. He didn't force himself on me again after the conversation in my room, and I didn't know if it upset me or made me happy. The memories of Hail affected my heart, and I didn't want to be confused when I gave in to Rome. For me to settle this, once and for all, I needed to see Hail again.

"Well, what do you think, Rayne?"

Lost in my thoughts, I didn't even realize someone talked to me. I looked up, blinking in confusion. "Uh, I wasn't listening."

Thunder gave me a quick glare, but this time it didn't scare me as it had before. The man who had carried me out of the old facility was Thunder, after I had gone unconscious from the bullet in my head. I remembered our fights, our apologies, and how much we cared about one another. I was glad to have part of my family back, even though none of us were related. It would've been ten times better if I had the Baxters too.

"Earth to Rayne," he continued.

I noticed Rome watched me too. He gave me a half-grin, and it made my heart flutter. I saw Rock comforted by Beatrice, her gentle caresses expressing how much she loved him. Guy and Silk stood beside Thunder, waiting for me to speak.

"I'm sorry. I was lost in my thoughts."

Thunder crossed his arms before speaking again. "What part didn't you hear, Rayne?"

I blinked. "Uh, all of it?"

Rome snorted, while Rock's girlfriend giggled. Silk sighed, and Guy grimaced. Thunder stomped over to where I had sat down. He gave me no warning when he swooped in and lifted me unto his shoulder. I saw the concern on Rome's face as Silk held him back.

Thunder jostled me around, walking down the dimly lit, rocky interior. I did not understand where he was taking me. I pinched and yanked on his shirt, but he refused to let me go. We passed Guy's room on my left and turned down another corridor. This one was encased in steel, an area not destroyed by the bombs set off inside the bunker.

"Damn, Thunder. Let me down!"

He did as I asked, but only once we were inside of a different room. I recognized nothing in here as I stared at the surroundings. "Where..."

He stopped me. "Maybe looking around would help you remain focused. When you are done in here, walk through the adjacent door to the other room. I guarantee when you come back to us, you will be more prepared to listen."

I didn't get to say anything else. Thunder backed out of the room and closed the door. I studied my surroundings. The blue sheets on top of the bed were crumpled from what suggested a fitful night. The dim room glimmered in a soft blue glow from a small rotating water tank with little neon fishes swimming around inside.

Seaa.

This room belonged to her. I saw pictures coming in and out of focus on a large screen on the wall. Someone set the television on standby to shuffle different photos of her and the rest of the group in varying positions, doing a variety of different things. I came upon one with Seaa and Hail, grinning side by side with the beach as their background. When I saw him, my heart dropped into the depths of my stomach. I hadn't seen him in years, but he had barely changed. Although he was a lot more grown now, Hail still looked handsome and sturdy.

I ran my fingers across the small dresser with little bits of make-up and hair accessories. The perch that held Seaa's clothes stood right before the adjacent door. The rack held a variety of clothes, but all of them would cover most of Seaa's body. I felt for my sister. To have to feel she needed to hide how she looked. Opening the door beside Seaa's rolling closet, I walked into another dim room. Some lights ran around a mirror hung from the concrete wall as the only light in the space.

Unlike Seaa, Hail's room was a lot barer and less colorful. His bed made. The urge to sit on its crisp, linen sheets, plagued me. Instead, I ran my hand on the surface of the bed and made my way to a long dresser he had at the end of the room. They had perched a smaller version of a television screen on top, and next to it, two photos. In one, there was a miniature version of him and me before we escaped. He had his arm around my shoulder and looked down at me while I stared straight ahead at the camera. The picture was old. They placed photos on holographs these days.

I remembered my Pop's old camera. I also remembered posing for that picture.

The other photo on his dresser was of all the experiments together. So many of us, now reduced to handfuls. Hail had refused to give up on me, going as far as to go on the run to find females that looked like me. I needed to go back to Thunder and be as dedicated as Hail. I wanted to save him just as he tried to do for me. Thunder was right. Being inside these two rooms reminded me of what we fought for.

Pushing all of my feelings aside, I pressed a kiss to the tip of my fingers and ran them down a photo of Hail and Seaa together.

I would get them back.
That was a promise.

CHAPTER SIXTEEN

Sector Foxtrot
Unit 13 Headquarters
General Brockton Braggart

I TWIRLED ONE side of my mustache, feeling the satisfaction I received when the tip curled precisely as I liked it. Below me, staining the floor with his blood, was the soldier who came to tell me he believed Batch 001's leader, Thunder, killed my son. I invested a lot of time and money on the boy and would be damned if someone told me Roman was dead. Before I shot the soldier for giving me such inadequate news, the boy had rushed out Thunder had made an example of him.

No one makes an example out of Roman, but me.

To hear he might be dead didn't make me sad. The thought of it made me angry. So angry, that if Roman weren't dead by their hands, he would be gone by mine. I heard the sweet sounds of torture. Walking over to the next hallway where we stored our prisoners, I gestured to an incoming soldier. I left an injured one behind me. The guy didn't even bat an eyelash when he saw the shot militant—just as we trained him.

The sounds of a woman's screams plagued the hall with her melodious song of agony. I walked in as a group of soldiers electrocuted Seaa over and over again, her body squirming on the floor she dropped on. This latest capture disgusted me. The only thing pretty was her face. I placed one hand on my pistol, watching from a distance. I simply took great enjoyment in their suffering, especially with the fish girl. Hail wasn't an easy one to crack. Torturing didn't work on him, so I had to resort to other means to get him to comply.

Placing him back on their experimentation floor, I had the wily Dr. Plumboy conduct his experiments with the captive. Last I checked, they gave Hail a stimulant that progressed the mutated cells throughout his body. It excited me to see how it came out. The soldiers filed out of Seaa's cell, smiling at one another. They spotted me, immediately wiped the grins off their faces, and deposited into a straight line. I walked by with my hands behind my back, perusing my well-trained soldiers. These men weren't volunteers for experimentation, but they underwent vigorous training to get the position they held.

"I see the fish has been acting up again?"

The officer with the most rank stepped forward; his eyes stared straight ahead. "Yes, Sir."

I approached the clean-shaved man. "Now, what did she do today?"

The officer swallowed. "She was screaming out for the other captive, refusing to follow directions."

My eyes took in the motionless girl. "Well then, good. I'm sure you've taught her a proper lesson."

"Yes, Sir," they both replied in unison.

I was about to turn around, when two soldiers and one operative came around the corner. They dragged Hail by his armpits, his hair disheveled, and the fresh wounds on his body puckered and alive. I recognized those gashes anywhere. One of his favorite operatives, Roman's friend, walked behind the two guys with seriousness on his face he couldn't deny. Braggart dismissed the rest of the soldiers, walking over toward the cell holding Hail. Zane noticed me standing there, waiting to hear the news of the experimentation.

Zane saluted and remained there until I released him from his acknowledgment. When I did, we both turned to watch the men drop Hail on the floor and walk back out of the room, locking it behind them. We watched Hail through the impervious glass window.

"Any news, Zane?"

Zane turned to look at me. "Yes, Sir. Dr. Plumboy said his cells mutated another thirty-eight percent.

Then they rejected the mutated genome. Instead, he planted the control chip and is planning to alter the juice in the next doses."

His words caught my attention. "Rejected, you say?"

The large man nodded. Zane was a lot thinner than Roman, but the operative was taller and a lot faster than my son. Zane always slicked back his hair. Tear drops came down the side of his nose; his eyes reflected the hallway's lights. The usual sunglasses he wore to hide the markings on his face hung from his shirt collar. Behind his lips, I knew Zane had four sharp canines he kept hidden from the rest of society. Zane was a favorite and was usually hired to do more private work for wealthy families living on the surface.

Which reminded me, "Weren't you on the job? What are you doing here?"

A few days ago, they brought Zane in with a hand injury. A metal trinket was embedded in his hand, seizing its functions until they could remove all the fragments. The novelty was so cheap in material, the pieces of it remained inside his hand, not allowing his mutation to regenerate and heal the wound. I looked down at the faint scar left behind by my sweet, young Rayne.

It irked me she was still nowhere to be found. According to Roman's last transmission, he gave chase, but for Snow, not Rayne.

"Yes, well, the governor didn't need me tonight. Where he was going, he didn't require help. I had gotten back a few minutes ago and was called down to Dr. Plumboy's office to retrieve Hail."

I looked at Hail, who let out a weak moan from the floor. I didn't notice the changes from the mutation. Hopefully, that would change with Hail's next doses. I planned to send Hail out into the field to capture his brethren with the new programming we'd implanted.

"Which reminds me. Your friend has been killed from what I've gathered."

Zane did a double take, pausing to see if I lied.

"Rome is dead?"

I said nothing, turning to look at Hail. With a little more improvement in the cocktail, he'd be ready to send out into the field. The chips we implanted inside the killer would keep him doing exactly what I wanted him too. The team of scientists had implanted a new brain-washing procedure chip during the last round of genetic mutation. When he wakes, he shouldn't remember anything from his past. The one thing this super-soldier would know was how to fight for me.

Noticing Zane waited for an answer, I replied, "It seems so" as I turned around and walked away.

GUY APPROACHED THE group after being gone for the past hour. I sat next to Silk, awaiting our next orders. Thunder had already gone to a higher spot to watch over us from a vantage point. Rome sat in front. Once more since waiting, he ran his hand through his hair. A nervous twitch I'd come to adore. Rock and Snow stayed behind at the bunker, awaiting instructions. Guy would head into town and find out where their nomadic camps stayed for the night.

"Trevor's camp is hunkering down in Ashur tonight. He refuses to move from here, probably thinking he'd come across more of us that way."

Rome rose from his spot. "Let me at Trevor. I'm looking forward to beating the shit out of that asshole."

Guy frowned. "We aren't hunting little fish, Rome. Our ultimate goal is the facility."

Rome's body language implied dejection. He appeared antsy and ready to fight.

"Your job is to get back in, Rome, even if it means sucking on Trevor's big toe."

He gave Guy a look that would've brought down someone weaker. "That is not happening."

I giggled. Rome looked at me at first with a frown plastered on his face. Those lips transformed into a grin with a wink for added effect. I could feel my heart flutter behind my chest. Instead of succumbing to his smile, I wiped my sweaty palms on my borrowed jeans.

"I will get into the camp, but they won't tell me anything until I'm debriefed."

Guy nodded. I hated we were sending Rome back into the wolves' den, but I couldn't very well stop him. This is what I agreed to during our tactical meeting. This is what Rome wanted to do. Who was I to stop him?

"Silk will be watching you, unseen. Rayne will be with me—ready to provide back-up if need be. Remember, only get the necessary information."

Rome yawned, more than likely tired of being repeated the same information over and over again. He stretched his muscles, then cracked his knuckles and neck. When he lifted his hands over his head, I enjoyed seeing the tan skin right above his jeans and the design on his flesh hiding behind them. My fingers itched to touch him in that exact spot. Rome noticed the exact trail of my thoughts because he gave me a double raised brow, followed by a broad, tell-all grin.

He walked over to me, placing the briefest of kisses on my forehead. As much as I wanted more, I would not complicate matters any more than they already were. Rome turned to face Guy, and before he got a word out, he got punched in the face a few times. I knew it would come, but it still didn't make it any more comfortable to watch. Silk smirked, watching as Guy pummeled Rome. He had been thrown to the ground, the shells and rocks on the beach burying themselves in his skin and abrading the surface where they pierced it.

Rome got a few hits in, making sure his knuckles bore the evidence of a real fight. Guy punched him twice in rapid succession on his nose. It broke, and blood gushed down his face. I squirmed on my perch. Silk held my hand, seemingly more afraid I'd jump in and tackle Guy down. Another kick to the gut made me flinch.

Silk raised one hand. "That is enough, Guy."

Both men breathed heavy. Both were bleeding as if close to death, but neither one was anywhere near it. Those wounds would heal in a matter of minutes.

Rome nodded his head, gave me a half-lidded smile as blood covered the entire surface of his face. Before I could reach for him, he ran off at top speed.

Sector Bravo
Town of Ashur
Roman Braggart
ID: MIL 116.002

WITH EVERY MUSCLE in my body burning in pain, I ran

as fast as I could. I knew one of Trevor's men would be posted in the center of town, so I aimed to get there. I made a swipe at my face, coming back with blood all over my cut hand. I stopped in between two buildings to catch my breath. I didn't want to cause panic by scaring the clueless citizens walking around town. My back slid down the wall. Blood fell from my broken nose. I reached up and fixed it back in place.

I could breathe a little better. The area sizzled with new energy around me. I knew when I got spotted, and Braggart's men closed in quickly. The next step was to stay put. They got nearer; I could feel them approach. I flexed my fingers and stretched out the kink in my legs. Touching the side of my abdomen, I judged I had at least two cracked ribs. They'd heal quickly, but if I didn't get those bones set first, I'd have to get them re-broken to treat correctly. I looked up. Trevor's expensive cologne smacked me senseless.

"Well, well, well. Look who we have back from the dead."

I moved my head to one side. The pain in my neck was aggravating the hell out of me. "I think I died quite a few times at their hands."

Which isn't so far from the truth.

The rest of the team gathered.

"You expect me to believe you escaped?"

My shoulders shifted up and down in a fashion I knew he'd comprehend. I didn't enjoy getting questioned by this jackass. "Not as easy as it looked, I'll tell you."

Trevor crossed his arms and leaned back against the wall. "Clearly."

I tried to stand up, but the pain in my chest made it hard. Trevor gave a quick lift of his chin to two soldiers. The goons walked over, lifting me off the floor.

"Broken rib?"

He dripped sarcasm after every word. "Two or three, actually."

Trevor pushed himself off the wall, slowly walking toward me. "Well, then I guess we're going to have to get those fixed." He moved his hand around the area that hurt.

I flinched but bit down on the pain.

Trevor shook his head. "It seems they aren't healing properly. Here, let me help with that."

Before I could process the information, Trevor punched the area so hard, he re-cracked the ribs, sending copious amounts of pain to every part of my body. The blood loss and immense pain had bile burning in my throat, and then darkness took me down.

When I awoke again, I sat on a chair we used to interrogate criminals. Luckily, my hands remained untied, so that meant they didn't *not* believe me. We were outside. I could see the soldiers laughing and eating what smelled like chili around a fire. None of them paid me any attention, but someone watched me. I could not only feel ominous eyes on me, but I could sense Silk's presence nearby.

I turned to the side, seeing Trevor watch me with a half-smile on his lips.

"Welcome back to the living."

I ran a hand through my hair. "How long have I been out?"

"Long enough to be dragged back here and cleaned up by the medic."

I nodded. "You call General Braggart yet?"

Trevor's grin widened. "Yes, as a matter of fact, he wasn't too surprised."

The words made my entire body stiffen. If my father did not emphasize my capture, then he already knew we premeditated it. I knew that asshole, and I further knew this conversation would not go well. The plan failed.

I tried to play it off. "Yeah? Well, go figure. Not like I expected the man to give a shit."

My ex-partner whistled, and the entire team surrounded us.

Damn.

I knew this would be trouble. No one made a move to approach me, but I would not take any chances. My eyes immediately studied everyone's movements and judged their distance. I was confident I was still safe. Being the best didn't make me a complete fool.

"No need to feel so shaken, Rome." Trevor walked closer. "None of us will hurt you. However, we need you to prove your loyalty to the cause."

That meant someone else would do the job for him.

A path opened right in front of me. Soldiers stepped aside, making room for the last man 1 thought I'd have to fight again. The guy was tall. 1 knew firsthand he was strong. 1 also knew Rayne would kill me if 1 killed the dude.

Double damn.

SILK MOVED AWAY from her spot, taking quick steps toward me. Something was wrong. 1 could see it in the black widow's eyes. Guy moved in the opposite direction. Dread had me biting my lower lip. Silk got close enough to grab me, dragging me farther away from the camp we had earlier followed. Rome's former partner had talked to him, and 1 watched as he punched Rome in the stomach, knocking him out. 1 wanted to run down there and kick all of their asses but remained calm. 1 didn't want to be the one to ruin the plan. Now, 1 stood to the side, waiting to hear what Silk had to say.

"They are testing Roman's loyalty."

1 felt awful. "What does that mean? He has to give

us up?"

Silk shook her head. "No, Rayne, they are making him fight Hail."

My entire body shook, and my legs trembled, dropping my whole weight to the floor.

Silk turned her head to the side, listening to the comings and goings around us. I couldn't let him do this on his own. Rome gave up his freedom for us and now would be tested by killing the man for whom he knew I harbored feelings. Deep feelings. Ones I still couldn't quite get a handle on.

"The fight has started."

I wiped at a lone tear. "Rome won't kill him. For me, he won't kill Hail."

Silk placed a comforting hand on her shoulder. "I know Rayne, but this changes the plan."

"Why doesn't Hail run?"

Silk turned to listen once more. "They have altered Hail. I smell it on him."

I couldn't handle it anymore. I got up from the floor and moved closer to the camp. Hiding behind a pillar, I watched as Rome and Hail exchanged punches. I saw Hail, and my mind exploded with memories of our time together.

I watched from the rooftop as Rome placed his hands around Hail's neck, pinning him against a concrete wall. I couldn't sit by and do nothing. Sensing what I was about to do, but unable to reach me in time, Silk swore as I dropped from the building and landed right behind a group of soldiers. I kicked one in the back and backhanded another when he turned to attack me. Two others brought out their weapons. I was about to stop them when Silk dropped on top of them.

Chaos broke out around the camp. Several people ran around, grabbing their weapons. A few men jumped on top of Rome, trying to bring him down for a kill. I didn't want that on Hail's hands either. I punched someone else, grateful I didn't feel the hit. We needed to do something to stop this, and this wasn't it. Looking behind me, I saw Silk bringing down soldier after soldier, oblivious to my warring thoughts. Guy sped around several others to avoid their attacks, having been brought into the fight too. I looked back at the mess ahead of me, watching a group of soldiers pin Rome down into the bits of gravel and dirt. Hail moved to crack his neck, his hair longer than I ever remembered seeing it. Farther below the tips of his hair, a tiny tattoo of a raindrop in the middle of his upper back almost shimmered from the sweat dripping down his neck. The dramatic drop reached the part where strong shoulders met and splashed out as if landing on a puddle.

Hail grabbed a random soldier holding Rome down and threw him off to the side. For a moment, I thought he was back to normal, but then I saw him get down on one knee and punch Rome in the face. Rome gripped the arm Hail used to hold him down, trying to dislodge it. The distortion I saw in Hail, in this battle of strength, made me sick to my stomach. My hand clutched the fabric of my shirt, trying to calm the quiver deep inside. I could barely swallow down my anxiety when a soldier came running to the side of me with a weapon in hand. I turned in time to dodge a bullet. Shock crossed the man's features. With my left hand, I grabbed the barrel of the gun. With my right, I hit his wrist. I straightened the weapon and aimed. The man stopped moving, hands flying up in the air.

Not in the business of killing for the hell of it, I spun the gun around in my hand. The barrel again in my hand, I swung and clocked him across his temple. With the guy incapacitated, I threw the gun far away from prying hands. Weapons were not my thing. I turned to look at the two men who held a piece of my heart and panicked when I saw they were no longer in the same spot.

My eyes landed on an unconscious Rome being dragged by Hail toward a protruding iron bar. The rusted metal jutted from a crumbling piece of con-crete as an invitation to evil thoughts. I screamed for them. Running like a bat out of hell, I pushed aside the other soldiers in my path.

Ignorant of everything else around me, I only had eyes for the man I cared for, about to get impaled by the man I had loved since childhood. Using both hands to lift and throw a random soldier away from me, I watched as he hit the side of a collapsing building. The debris rained down around me. I turned to see Hail lift Rome off the bloody ground. Rome's limp body fell back, his fingers and the tips of his boots dragging on the dirt below him. I ran faster.

My heart ached.

My lungs burned.

The tears falling from my eyes shot back toward my ears.

Hail swung his arms down—a listless Rome in his grasp. I lowered my body and lifted a tad when I felt my right shoulder connect with Hail's mid-section. He grunted. Rome fell to the ground beside the corroded rod. With my right arm banded around his waist, Hail got locked against my body. He pushed at my shoulders. When I wouldn't budge, he drove his elbow into the muscle in my neck. Pain shot down my entire body, which could not hold up. My shoulders bunched, and weak legs crumbled beneath me. I fell at his feet.

Hail lifted his left boot and sent it right to my head. Stars floated around my pounding head. Trying to drag myself away from him, I felt my body lift off the grime beneath us. I turned my head to see Hail's features askew with anger as he raised me in the air. My heart hammered in my chest. Then an impact on my back had me greedily coughing up oxygen. Seconds later, there was weightlessness as I landed on the ground a few feet away, head hanging between my bent legs.

Hail stalked me, his movement slow and calculative. I saw him—watched as his eyes glimmered like a wolf's underneath the moonlight. He took one step closer. I sucked in a breath. Another step and I exhaled. My body shook as he glared.

There was no recognition in his face.

Hail dropped to his knees. He knew and sensed I'd be no threat to him. With one raw, bleeding hand to my neck, I closed my eyes and waited for what was to come. I didn't want to see him hurt me. This wasn't what was supposed to happen. I tried to swallow. My breathing shallow. I remembered the way his cool fingers had felt on my skin or the smell of him—all my senses absorbing the smoky, worn leather aura that was him, and the new camphoraceous scent of myrtle I had never noticed before. Memories ran through my mind of our time together, and a new wave of power surged from within me. He squeezed my neck tighter. I clawed at his arms, to no avail. My small frame hummed with foreign energy I hadn't felt in a long time.

The tingles reached each tip of my fingers and toes.

I knew of everything at once.

With tears in my eyes, I looked back at Hail.

Then dissolved into water.

CHAPTER SEVENTEEN

I FELT MY entire body liquefy, slipping through his fingers and sliding underneath to resurface right behind him. Hail's arms moved away from his body as he sought the spot I was in. I tried to gain my bearings when he abruptly turned around and tackled me down to the floor. A rush of air escaped me. I drew my arms up and covered my face. Hail used his left hand to pull down my arms, while the right flew straight at my nose. With my adrenaline running rampant, I heard rather than felt the break on my face.

I cried out, blocking him with my free hand.

"Hail! Stop! Please!"

He didn't.

I pulled my hand free, turning to block my face. "Hail, it's me!"

He didn't stop.

I reached up to place timid fingers on his flushed cheek. The muscles in his jaw clenched. He shivered. Blood ran down my face, but through it, I caught Hail staring into my eyes. I felt his body stiffen above me. He shook his head as if fighting with his brain for control.

By then, I had both hands pinned above my head. His free hand balled into a tight fist. Hail straddled me. His weight pinned me from the waist down. I could do nothing but turn my head, watching my sister fight off herds of soldiers. Guy knocked another soldier down. A few feet away lay Rome, still unconscious. His former partner trudged toward the comatose Rome. He pulled a knife from a holster in his boot. I cried deep sobs as I tried to move my hands again.

"Hail," I cried harder. "Please come back to me. You found me! You found me!"

I couldn't save either of them now.

So, I struggled again. "Oh, God, no! Hail, please save him. Please!"

I felt Hail lift his weight off me. He grabbed his hair with both hands and watched me. There was a moment of clarity before I saw the shadows fall back over his eyes. I took his distance as an opportunity to get to my hands and knees. Limbs shaking, I looked up at Hail to see he studied me.

Ignoring him, I sought Rome's partner, watching as he made it to Rome, raising his arm to bring the blade down into Rome's chest. I moved to propel myself forward when the entire area around me frosted over like a glimmering kaleidoscope of silvers and whites. Every one of the soldiers and warriors in the position they were last in, except for me.

A voice penetrated my thoughts. "Rayne?"

Hail sought me with the same teal colored eyes he once used to. Tears intermingled with the blood on my face. The area, unlike anyone, had ever seen before. Everyone in the camp had completely frozen in place. Last I remembered, his powers weren't ever this strong.

He leaned down, gently pulling me up from the tundra before us. We faced one another for seconds before his hand rose to touch my face. His fingers trembled. Noticing the blood cascading down my face, Hail ripped a piece of his shirt and wiped off what he could.

I was tired. Today had taken a turn for the worse.

Hail placed both hands on my shoulder and studied me as if not quite believing I was here and alive. "Rayne?" He eased a rogue strand of hair behind my ear. "I can't believe it's you."

The real question was how everything got frozen. "Uh, Hail?" I gestured to the rest of the human popsicles.

Hail turned to see. "Ah, well, look at that."

My head shot up to look him in the eyes. "Why does it sound like you didn't know you did that?"

Hail grinned, and it sent butterflies on a never-ending path inside my body. "I'm stoked your alive, Rayne."

He moved to hug me, but I shuffled away. "Hail, we'll hash this out later. Right now, I need you to tell me how long this will last for?"

Hail's face screwed up as if he had tasted something terrible. "I don't know. Never done it before."

Pinching my nose to stop some of the bleedings, I flinched at the pain I felt instead. "We have to get out of here. The little things you've frozen before lasted for minutes."

Instead of doing as I asked, Hail pulled me close to his body and placed a chaste kiss on my lips. This time, I was the one who felt frozen. I saw him walk away from me, whistling a jaunty tune as if nothing had happened. Shaking my head, I jogged up behind him. Water dripped from the buildings. I feared we wouldn't get out of there in time. I ran past Hail, dropping to the floor next to Rome's prone body. Hail walked up beside me, still uncaring of the melting ice.

I hit the ice, breaking off piece by piece until I got to Rome's neck. I checked his pulse.

"What the hell are you doing?"

I turned to stare at Hail. "We need to get him out of here."

Hail crossed his arms, legs braced apart. "The hell we are, Rayne. You know who this bastard is?" I chipped away the ice. Large chunks fell off.

I took a deep breath of courage. "Hail, Rome came back here to save your life and Seaa's. He's not with them anymore."

He placed two fingers around his nasal bone and frowned as I pulled Rome to my body to lift him.

"Fuck, man!"

He gently pushed me to the side and lifted Rome over his shoulder, fireman-style. He said nothing else to me, leaving a trail of frost as he walked away. The ice melted off the people around us, making me anxious. Hail didn't care. The ice stretched and cracked off Trevor's body. Little bits dropped to the floor. I wanted to run and get the heck out of there, but Hail wasn't in the same rush. Squinting at Trevor's frozen body, Hail shifted Rome to his other shoulder and pulled back his right arm. When he let go, the punch sent Trevor to the other side of the alley. There was an explosion of ice, and then Trevor's body, face blue from the cold, dropped on top of all the debris, unmoving.

I ran ahead of him. "Silk is here too!"

Hail walked up to me. "Where?"

I perused the different frozen sculptures and spotted Silk. Grabbing a rock from the ground, I hacked away at the ice surrounding her. I got most of the pieces off without an issue. Hail sighed behind me, irritated with my lack of speed.

"Here, let me," he said as he handed me Rome.

I awkwardly grabbed Rome's still body, and in the next second, I gasped at Hail's audacity. He shoved Silk against the metal trash canisters, laughing as the ice cracked from her body, and Silk's legs flew over her head. He laughed again, pulling Rome off me and placing him back on his shoulder.

"You ignorant son of a..." My eyebrows rose as Silk came back over the trash cans with a flurry of words I hadn't heard before.

Silk glared once more at Hail, grabbing my hand.

"Y'all gonna stay down there, or we gonna get out of here? Thunder has given the signal, so we need to move quickly."

Guy had already climbed on top of one of the buildings completely untouched by the frost. With one nod, we knew what we had to do. All of us ran off down the empty alleyways and over structures. With my hand in Silks, I couldn't be happier. We got one ally back, out of the two missing. Little by little, we would succeed. I felt things would be fine.

I was sure of it.

FOR THE TENTH time since being back, Hail and Rome stood chest to chest in a power struggle for male dominance. The tension was thick in the air. Thunder had already given up on separating the two guys. He sat at one end of the large table with his feet propped up on the cracking wood. I was surprised the thing hadn't splintered into tiny pieces by now. Silk was frustrated, and Snow added fuel to the burning blaze. I watched the two prancing peacocks, sighing for the umpteenth time.

"You're a damn traitor to your military," Hail yelled. "What's to say you don't betray us too?"

Rome pressed even closer. I was afraid they'd become one if they kept this show up. "You're right," he yelled back. A finger came to point in my general direction. "I am here because of her. I give two flying fucks what happens to all of you. She's my only concern."

I could feel the warmth of a rising blush on my face.

Hail wasn't at all too happy to know he had a rival for my affections. The moment we had gotten back to base, the group had welcomed Hail back with open arms and cheers, while Rome and I had made our way to Dr. Ferdinand. Laying Rome on a large cot, he'd placed a thick, white block over him. I watched as it hovered over his body. A shimmer escaped the box and lit his body below. The stream of light ran from the top of his head to the tip of his toes. As the object, he later called an Ultrigraph, highlighted the length of Rome's long, thick legs and firm torso marked with tribal tattoos, Dr. Ferdinand had come over to me.

I had let my nose heal for way too long in that position. For the following hour, the poor doctor had to re-break my nose and set it again. The pain I had gone through was more than enough for one night. Since Rome's awakening, and Hail's knowledge of his betrayal to Project Hercules, the bunker had been in a non-stop debate. I sighed again. The cook made me a sandwich, so I sat cross-legged on the little sofa and finished the delicious combo as the two bickered like an old couple.

"You don't belong here, Rome. You aren't one of us."

Rome let out a sarcastic laugh. "Again, my being here has nothing to do with you."

Hail's hand fisted at his side as the other pinched the bridge of his nose. I could tell this would not get us anywhere. I looked over at Thunder, pleading with my eyes to get these two to stop their bickering, but he shrugged. I polished off the last of my food and moved around on the sofa. When I did, my knee rubbed against an upended spring. The metal scraped the skin of my knee and ran down the edge. I yelped and jumped off the couch.

Both men were at my side.

Each bombarded me with questions. Each looked

at my wound.

I slapped both away.

"Look, I am so fed up with this macho power struggle thing you guys have going on." I grabbed the napkin I had used to clean myself after the sandwich and dabbed the bleeding cut until it healed. "I lost my memory, Hail. I'm sorry about that. Rome chose to be here. I didn't coerce him, nor did he plan some elaborate scheme to get in here."

Hail turned his head to face me.

I blubbered. "I didn't ask him, Hail. I also didn't ask to get shot in the head. If you two would stop fighting for one minute and focus on the real creep behind all this, we'd be better off."

Hail threw his hands up in the air. "That's what I'm trying to say! The goddam creep is—"

I noticed Rome stiffen, but it was Thunder's reaction that had everyone in the room go quiet.

"That is enough, Hail!"

Hail turned to face his longtime friend. "Are you serious?"

Thunder slammed his hands on the surface of the table. The wood groaned and creaked but didn't break. "I said, that's enough."

The weight in the tone of his voice left no room for argument. Hail turned to look at me. His firm, careful fingers, slid along my jawline as if memorizing my face. I could feel Rome's intensity scarcely managed to keep itself in check.

"Rayne, I'm sorry." Hail placed a rogue strand behind my ear as he always did and always would. "I missed you."

I wanted to tell him I missed him too. Even when I had lost my memory, I still held to my feelings for him—feelings for a man I didn't know and couldn't remember. There was so much I wanted to say, and so much I wanted to ask him, but this wasn't the time. Instead, I reached up to touch his face; my fingers flitted across the delicious stubble until they met nothing but air. I couldn't understand the secrets present in my heart.

Two very different men.

Two emotions I couldn't place.

Too many days holed up with so much testosterone around me.

THE NEXT COUPLE of days passed by in a blur. Silk stood in a cavernous room with its rocky interior and leaking walls. The large space made my sensitive nose twitch. There was a strong smell of built-up moisture and sulfur—surprisingly earthy, as this was not a volcanic area I knew of. Lights and cables streamed across the walls and low ceilings, which had layers of stalactites dripping from the years of mineral deposits. The smooth ground held several pieces of exercise equipment and punching bags. I walked toward my sister taking out her frustration on a free-standing punching bag.

The team had a lot of technology in their possession, but I knew Silk preferred the original equipment to the new. The worn bag had been sewn and taped up from years of abuse. It so happened I had to train in The Arena today where said technology frustrated the heck out of everyone with its crazy-ass opponents and sneaky computerized tactics. Silk's damp curls bounced around her head. Sweat dripped down her temple. She took one look at me and arched a shaped eyebrow.

Silk jabbed a right fist into the bag. "Where are you going dressed like that?"

I looked down at the borrowed clothes I wore. Although I wore a camisole underneath, I had on a loose t-shirt and some sweatpants I found in the extra wardrobe box. My hair was in a low ponytail.

"Uh, The Arena?"

Silk laughed as she shook her head. "Not like that, you're not."

In a matter of seconds, she had me ready to train in The Arena. The training was a nightmare. A colorful array of holographic enemies appeared in various faux environments chosen by the device. The hits felt like the real thing, and no matter how many I ticked off the counter more appeared in their place. I realized during our training Rome was an excellent shot, and I was lucky to hit a target by accident.

I wasn't exactly sure when it happened, but Rome became a beneficial ally to our group and someone very important to me. If only Hail and Rome got along better. Both guys were different in their own way, but they were still very similar—brave, handsome, sweet, and committed to whatever they put their minds to.

I should know.

Right now, they both had their eyes set on me.

Regretfully, it wasn't as thrilling as one would think.

CHAPTER EIGHTEEN

Sector Bravo
Safe Haven Headquarters

I LEANED AGAINST the wall of another tunnel as I searched for the exit. The sirens wailed inside of the bunker. Bright, pulsing lights flickered on and off, bathing the hallways in reds and yellows. For the third time, I turned down an abandoned corridor, my muscles aching from training in The Arena—lost in a maze of hallways and empty rooms.

Where the heck am I and why is the alarm going off?

The meteoric play of the lights wreaked havoc on my vision. I needed to use my other senses. My abilities crept from within me like vines, trying to pick up anything new. Nothing. My hearing didn't pick up anything but dripping water.

Lots of dripping water.

Remembering how my body had disintegrated into water made me shiver. It was a sensation I couldn't risk happening again. The thought scared the hell out of me. Pops had repeatedly told us letting others see what we could do would bring dire consequences. I forever hid them at the facility. I hated the way it made me feel. Touching my body, I made sure I was stable and human. The moisture came down faster. The sound of rushing water came toward me. With a fluttering heart, I closed my eyes and braced for impact. The liquid hit me, reaching my ankles. I stumbled, trying not to fall in it.

"Rayne?"

I heard my name and looked up, relishing in the scent of leather and camphor and knew it was Hail. My stiff joints relaxed as he came up to me.

His arms wrapped me around his chest. "Oh, baby, you're alright."

The embrace was swift and unexpected. He was wet and blistering cold. I could barely wrap my arms around Hail before I let go. Hugging him felt like wrapping myself around an ice block.

"How the hell did you get all the way out here?" he asked.

I didn't know where I was and voiced it. Hail grabbed me by the hand, leading me down the halls.

I realized he was still dripping with water. "So, why are you all wet, and where the hell did all this water come from?"

Hail grabbed my hand, running his fingers through mine. "Dr. Ferdinand was trying to adjust and study the mess Project Hercules did on me while they locked me up in their cells. They injected me with a stimulus agent that sped up the mutated cells. He triggered one, and I turned into one giant piece of ice."

"Hail, you're telling me you turned into hail?"

He looked even more embarrassed now. "Uh, yeah, pretty much."

I laughed so hard I almost slipped on the dripping water.

"Why did the alarms go off?"

"No clue. I was in the lab when it went off. You were my first concern."

"You ran around the compound looking for me in your ice form?"

He laughed. "When you make it sound like that, it sounds like I ran around in here like a snowman."

I shrugged. "Yeah, pretty much. And Hail, in case you didn't know, I don't need a hero."

The smile that lingered wasn't confirmation he understood, but I could only hope he came to realize it. The male superhero thing was long gone. We females were plenty capable of kicking ass all on our own.

Hail squeezed my hand, leading me out of the dimly lit hallway. "I'm not sure if the group realized what the threat was, so we need to be careful. We might head into anything right now."

We walked. I tensed, trying to come to terms with a potential fight. Kicking ass and taking names—*yup, that's me*. Voices reached my ears as we rounded the corner. Right in front of me, with a timid, glasses-less Gavin kneeling on the floor, stood Snow and Guy holding him down. Thunder stood behind them with arms crossed, his legs spaced apart. It shocked me to see Gavin didn't look as scared as he should have been in this situation. He held himself back, giving Guy and Snow his version of a death stare. The sight of seeing him stare daggers at the two made me laugh.

"Oh, wow, Gavin. How'd you find me?"

Thunder spoke first, asking, "You know this boy?"

The boy in question turned his head, looking back at Thunder as if ready to rip him apart with his own two hands. I couldn't help but laugh. This façade was a side of him I had not seen. I knew Gavin was brave, judging by the way he protected and helped me. Only, I didn't realize the same shy, easily flustered guy had so much bravado inside of him.

"A real man wouldn't need two goons to subdue the boy," said Gavin.

Hail laughed, slapping a hand on his knee. Thunder simpered.

With one nod to his "goons," Gavin was let free. He wiped off the grime from his jean-clad legs and stood up straight. He stared straight at me. I grinned. An overwhelming urge to hug him overpowered me. I ran toward him, wrapping him up in my arms. He hugged

me right back. Gavin's hands splayed out, encompassing my upper back.

"I'm so glad you're okay," he whispered in my ear.

I nodded, happy tears running down my face.

Gavin pulled me away from himself. "So, these are
your siblings?"

I nodded again, wiping the tears from my face. I
looked around myself. Hail, Thunder, Guy, and Snow
stood around us. The curiosity on their faces said they
wanted to know how he knew about us. Right then, I
didn't care. I was so glad to see the friend I made after
losing my parents.

"Come on, Gavin. Let's get to the Planning Room,
and I'll introduce you to the rest."

Sector Bravo
Safe Haven Headquarters
Gavin Foxhand
New States Citizen ID: CH.3349.GF-Rank A

I RAN A hand through my hair as several intimidating men walked into what Rayne called the Planning
Room. These guys were plenty abnormal. I stood off
to one side, with Rayne standing right beside me, in a
show of unity. It felt great to have found her. For days

I wondered what had happened to her. There was no way for us to get in contact. She had my number but didn't call me. I knew where she headed, and because I feared something awful had happened to Rayne, I went on my own mission to find her. I fidgeted with a loose strand on my shirt because I was nervous. Rayne held my hand, and I could feel all of those nerves settle down.

Then a raven-haired beauty walked into the room with curls bouncing with each step she took. Rayne was beautiful. But this woman made my heart skip a beat, unlike any woman had ever done before. There was an insane need to both possess and protect her. I shook my head as if it would clear my physical response to the woman. I watched, in utter curiosity, as she walked toward Thunder.

Wicked thoughts played games with my head. My hands almost reached for her on their own. She stopped talking and turned to face the others in the group. Her eyes landed on me. I knew she could sense my thoughts, and she was none too happy with them. Not a second later, the feeling that washed over me was gone. Taking a deep breath, I turned to Rayne. Gauging my reaction, Rayne nodded and let go of my hand. I watched my new friend walk toward the table, placing both hands on the chipped, flat surface. The room we were in was encased in dull, gray metal with rivets and bolts holding the panels to what I assumed was the stone interior. There was an old couch at one end, and a few scattered chairs throughout. They looked abandoned and decaying.

"I wanted to invite you all here to meet my friend, Gavin Foxhand."

I sought everyone's reaction. I was incredible at watching people around me. In seconds, I could tell when they didn't like me, or when they were lying. Years of being cast aside, I built quite a handy talent for knowing when someone wanted to get to know me, versus wanting to be connected to a Foxhand heir. My father was powerful and wealthy. However, they didn't know I had more than enough money of my own. Many people thought I was a pushover. This ideal protected me from the vultures in my school. I was good with technology and research. That personality of mine was my own best-kept secret.

"How in the world did this guy get here?"

My thoughts flittered to the back of my mind as I looked up at the woman who spoke. Her voice was husky and hauntingly beautiful. "I was the one researching this place for Rayne," I replied.

The Thor look-a-like, Thunder, who seemed to be the leader or eldest of the group, and respected by most, spoke first. "Yes, and how many people did he tell?"

I shook my head. Rayne watched, seeking the answer for herself. "No one followed me, and I told no one of this place."

"I don't believe him."

Rayne looked over at the woman with a frown on her face. "Silk, I trust him."

Silk.

Since the moment I read up on her, I had been intrigued by everything about the woman. The research the military had on Silk was minimal. She was hardly ever approachable during training, and although she had the same sensory output as the rest, any talents of hers remained a mystery. Hail could create ice or freeze things with the slightest touch. Thunder could create a phenomenal amount of static energy like a lightning storm. Guy had increased speed and agility, and so on. But not Silk. Silk, like Rayne, was a mystery to the government.

I shoved my hands into my pockets and watched as the group argued back and forth. The only one quiet was a man sitting on the armrest of the couch. He had dark hair and a few days' worth of stubble on his face. He was tall and built as the rest of the men in the group—sans me. He would watch Rayne but didn't make it too apparent. I knew this man was in love with her. There was no doubt about it. I saw it in the way he watched her, and in the way he carried himself around her. When others spoke, he slumped uncaringly. But when Rayne lit up, he straightened and focused all of his attention on her. I looked over at Rayne, wondering if she knew.

Thunder slammed his hand on the table. The old thing shook but remained upright. "Enough!"

The group settled.

"Let him talk. I am curious to find out what he knows."

I saw everyone's eyes travel back to me. I didn't care what the others thought. My concern was for Rayne and now weirdly, the woman standing on the opposite side of me. Letting out a deep breath, I began with, "I am your ally. Ever since meeting Rayne, I have been curious about this organization she spoke of. My life revolves around research." I held a hand up when one man with long silver hair tried to speak. It was obvious what he was about to say, and I was ready to ease their troubled thoughts.

"No, my research raised no suspicious eyebrows or interest. I know how to research the web through a backdoor. Several backdoors that can't be traced. I don't care how powerful a company you are or how many talented tech scientists you have on your payroll." I took a deep breath, now with their attention all on me again.

"These people do not have me." I looked at Rayne. "When Rayne met me, I was researching in the library. I was learning a new language to decrypt a secured file I was trying to hack into."

Rayne looked at me, shock written on her pretty features. I held her hand again and looked straight at her. "I'm a hacker, Rayne. My job is to break into things no one else can. I am an introvert, preferring my own company versus anyone else around me." I squeezed her hand. "Then you came and genuinely asked me for help. You weren't trying to gain my father's attention through me."

I heard a snort from the corner where the guy sat on the armrest. Everyone turned to look at him. "No wonder you sounded so damn familiar. Gregory Foxhand III is your father?"

I nodded. *What does this man know about my father?*

The man got up, stretching a hand over his head. "His father is one of the main supporters of Project Hercules."

Everyone spoke at the same time. Thunder put one hand up. He didn't need to say a word this time. The entire group fell silent.

"Let him speak."

I nodded again. There was no turning back now. "After Rayne left, I did my own research. First, you needn't worry. The organization knows nothing of your whereabouts."

With those words, the group collectively sighed as if afraid they would finally be found.

"Second, I researched how you were all created. I read every file. I know what they know about you." I looked over at the man now standing in front of the sofa and knew exactly who he was. "Roman Braggart."

The entire room felt frozen in place. The space chilled, and I involuntarily shivered. Rayne was so stiff beside me I thought she would splinter off into pieces if someone flicked her with their fingers. I wasn't sure what I had said wrong, but I knew this moment became a pivotal change in all. And from what I could sense, the difference was be between Roman Braggart, the son of General Brockton Braggart, and my friend, Rayne Baxter.

Rayne spoke up first. "B-Braggart?"

Rome took two steps toward her. He stopped when her hand flew up. "You are the son of that asshole?"

Rome's shoulders fell. I watched as he deflated at her rejection. "I am," he replied.

She looked at everyone else in the room. "You all knew this, didn't you?" She looked at Hail. "You tried mentioning it before, and they stopped you."

Hail spoke, running around to comfort her. I watched as she allowed him to reach her and hold her. I fell awkwardly to the side because she refused to let go of my hand through the action.

"Baby, I'm sorry. I wasn't allowed to say anything."

She looked at him with distant eyes. I knew this man felt as strongly for her as Roman Braggart did. I couldn't blame them. Rayne was as peculiar as she was stunning. I looked over at Rome, who had hands fisted to his sides. This man would unravel, and when he did, everyone near him would be victim to it.

Rayne turned to Rome again. "Why didn't you tell me?"

Rome rubbed his beard. "I didn't want you to question my being here."

Rayne shook her head when he tried to approach again.

He sighed, and I could see the immense pain he hid under controlled features. "I wasn't lying when I said I am here because of you. That hasn't changed, and it won't change."

She squeezed my hand before letting go. Rayne walked around everyone, leaving—her booted feet echoing as she exited. Hail ran over to Rome with speed I wasn't used to seeing. He lifted Rome in the air by his shirt. Rome grabbed the hand entangled in the cotton but did nothing. I didn't know how good Hail was in a fight other than his scores during training when he was younger, but the highly decorated Rome was quite a threatening foe.

Silk spoke, and I couldn't help but be mesmerized by the sound of her voice. The music was ethereal and lyrical. She pulled me in without even knowing it. "Leave it alone, Hail."

Hail dropped Rome and moved to leave the room when Thunder spoke. "Leave her alone, too, Hail. Give her time to seek us out. Do not push her."

Hail wanted to argue from the way his brows drew in and his nose flared, but I knew by now no one went against Thunder's orders. Not even Hail.

Thunder turned to me. "Please, Mr. Foxhand... I apologize for the interruption."

I looked around the room again. No one seemed comfortable with the situation, and I felt a spark of the blame. I should've kept quiet about Roman's last name. The guy wasn't sent undercover. The story is true. Labeled as a traitor in the system and presumed dead, they set Roman Braggart for a shoot-to-kill versus capture. The military wasn't even sure if he was still alive or not, so that should count. I felt responsible for upsetting Rayne and would tell her as soon as I was out of here.

"Uh, they consider Roman Braggart a traitor in their files. They have a large reward on your head. The group doesn't even know if you are alive or dead after some huge battle in Ashur."

He came back to his senses, asking, "Who's leading the charge?"

"Trevor Dallas."

He shook his head with a tight press of his lips. "That prick."

I turned to the rest of the group. "I'm here to help. Like I said before, I have lots of information that will help you. Rayne is my friend and the only true one I have, so let me stay."

Thunder shook his head. "We can't allow it. Your father is too powerful as it seems, and if he looked for you, we would be in more jeopardy than we are now."

Before I could argue, he put a hand up to stop me. "However, we will take you up on the offer to help."

The man turned to the woman beside him. Silk had a hand on her cocked hip. "Silk, you will take him back to his home in three days. You will watch over him for the next couple of days afterward to make sure he wasn't followed or spied on."

Silk was ready to argue. "That is not going to—"

"Don't even try to fight me on this, Silk."

She frowned, staring daggers at me.

Thunder turned to speak to me. "We appreciate you extending your talent our way. In three days, we will take you home. We will use those three days to gain any information we can. It is also enough time not to raise any red flags. Where does your father think you are?"

"I told my guard I was going on a research trip for a project at school. I do them often; no one questioned me."

Thunder nodded. "How long do these trips take?"

I shoved my hands inside my jeans' pockets again. "Um, about four or five days give or take."

Thunder smirked. "Perfect."

The group took it as a sign to walk out of the Planning Room, leaving behind nothing but stares and the sound of their feet on the pebbled ground below them. Rome stood to the side, watching me as they led me out of the room. I felt awful. I wanted to go back and talk to the man and tell him I'd explain things to Rayne, but I wasn't sure I had enough courage to do so. My unexpected appearance had quite an effect on those around me.

I transcended from being oblivious, to quite the novelty act.

We rounded the doorway leading out when I heard objects being thrown across the room and splintering off into thousands of pieces.

I gulped, afraid the chair could've been me.

CHAPTER NINETEEN

Sector Bravo
Safe Haven Headquarters
Roman Braggart
ID: MIL 116.002

I THREW ANOTHER chair, feeling better after the second one splintered. This shit was all my fault. I should've told Rayne a long time ago, but I rarely thought about it. I don't remember ever having a great relationship with the man I called Father, so I didn't even feel like his son. Weird as it sounded to even me, I felt more at home here than I did with the others of Batch 002. My friend, Zane, must be damn disappointed to know they were after me now because I had decided to leave the organization.

Although Zane *would* be the best person to talk to about this entire thing.

There was hope Zane would choose our friendship versus turning me in to my father. Suddenly tired, I dropped into the worn cushions of the couch. I had a hand over my eyes, a migraine forming. This wouldn't go well. I knew everyone watched me, and to head out of here to seek an actual operative for Project Hercules, would be akin to treason within this group. They wouldn't believe anything I'd say after that. With Rayne against me, I couldn't risk giving the others any reason to feel betrayed.

Rayne.

I glanced over at the opening, hoping she would come back and talk to me. My wait was in vain. She wouldn't come back. I gave her no real reason to trust me. She still felt guilty for caring for me after what happened to her parents. Not like I had anything to do with it. I sighed once more in the vast, empty interior. I needed to prove to her I would not betray her.

When a thought fluttered to the forefront of my mind, I sat up on the couch, the migraine long forgotten. I needed to find this friend of hers. Gavin was the start of this whole thing and would sure as hell help me end it. Cracking the bones in my neck, I got off the couch and out the door.

I walked down the quiet halls of the old bunker. Other than being encased in metal frames here and there, the old place still had evidence of what it once had been, before humans interrupted its centuries of dormant sleep. The hallways and rooms in this bunker were intricate because of the old caverns once domi-nating the area. Some corridors weren't even covered in metal. They were left untouched.

In return, these mazes of stone gave what was once the United States military an opportunity to seek shel-ter and provide storage for weapons and food and any-thing worthy of survival. Thunder and the rest were lucky to come to a place like this. The caverns were far away from populated sectors and accessible through a boat past The Waste. Before the beach was a thick forest, and after the forest were dozens of crumbling buildings and warehouses bordering the general area of the bunker. The city was unfit to live in and bar-ricaded from the rest of the human population. The new military and Ground Force didn't patrol these ar-eas. The amounts of rock and water also barely left a trace of the unique scent any one person carried.

I saw Guy walking Gavin down the dormitory wing, so I whistled to get their attention. The sound was so loud it bounced around the empty walls of stone. Guy narrowed his eyes, and Gavin twitched at the pierc-ing sound. I wasn't sure if Gavin wincing was because of the whistle or the fact he saw me coming straight for him. The young man may be a hacker and good at digging up information, but he was still timid and facing a pissed-off genetic human was not something he wanted to handle.

"I need to speak to Gavin, Guy."

Guy's eyebrow shot up as if he was trying to determine if I would kill Gavin the moment I had him to myself. That made me want to laugh. The thought occurred to me, although briefly.

Gavin looked over at Guy, gauging his response. "Uh?"

I looked at Gavin again. "I won't kill you."

The boy swallowed. Guy turned to face us both. "Look Rome, I don't doubt you're pissed off with Gavin mentioning your last name and all, but he's under Thunder's protection, and..."

Guy trailed off as I put a hand up to stop him. "As I said, I'm not gonna kill him."

"Yet," both Guy and Gavin reiterated.

I grinned.

Guy shook his head, a glimmer of a smile on his lips. "Alright. When you are done, take him to the room next to Rayne's."

My body turned as hard as a stone around us. "The hell he'd be staying in the room adjoining hers."

Gavin glared at Guy, but the idiot found the situation funny. "Oh, please. According to Gavin, she's already slept on his bed, so..."

The move was instant. I had pinned Gavin against the wall, cutting off his airways. Guy's hands were on my wrists, trying to remove Gavin from my tight grip. Gavin gasped for air, trying to claw at my shoulders and t-shirt. Guy wasn't strong enough to pull my hands from Gavin's neck. Guy punched me on the same side I had broken my ribs. The pain shot down my body, but I refused to loosen my grip. Black spots covered my vision. All I could see was Rayne in this man's bed, and it infuriated me.

"Dammit, Rome! Let him go! He didn't sleep with Rayne. She slept on his bed while he slept in the living room."

My ears rang, but I could hear Guy's plea to let him go. Removing my hands from Gavin's neck, the boy dropped to the floor like a rag doll. I twirled on Guy. Guy put his hands up in the air in surrender with a Cheshire grin on his face.

"Whoa, whoa, Rome. It was just a joke."

Gavin sputtered and coughed on the ground. "What the hell, you two!"

I stared at Gavin, feeling a slight twinge of guilt. "I'm sorry." I held my hand out for Gavin to use to get up.

Rayne's friend looked at it for a long time before he took it. He turned to face me as he wiped off the dust from his clothes. "Look, Rome, Rayne is my friend. Yes, she's beautiful, but I don't feel anything more than that. I care about her and want to protect her, but I'm not looking to start a relationship with her."

His words made me feel ten times guiltier. "I apologize, Gavin."

Gavin glared at Guy, who laughed as he turned around and waved goodbye. I motioned for Gavin to follow me. My heart raced at the thought of the possibility of seeing Rayne. I half expected her door closed and half hoped it was open so I could see her.

When we approached her side of the wing, her door was shut and had a sizeable metaphorical "keep out" sign keeping the likes of me from coming anywhere near it.

My hope deflated.

Gavin must have noticed, because he said, "I'll talk to her, Rome. This is the least I could do."

I nodded but said nothing.

Closing the door behind us, I flicked on the switch for a light in the center of the room. The light bulb buzzed and hummed with the energy flowing through it. The room smelled untouched, but for the fresh lavender scent on the sheets Rock's mate had washed.

"Listen, Gavin, I need answers."

Gavin turned to look at me. For the first time, I noticed the backpack Gavin carried around. The boy dropped it on top of the bed and rummaged through it.

"Yeah, what you need to know?"

I dragged a chair hiding in the corner and sat on it. "What did the report say?"

Gavin turned to say, "On you?"

I nodded.

The boy took out a notepad and gadgets. I knew one was a holographic tablet, the same as we used, that would open and manipulate the space around it to come up as a visual representation of the small piece of technology. Gavin pressed a button at the corner of the device. When it lit up, the entire area in front of Gavin as he sat on the edge of the bed, lit up like a station full of computers and monitors. There were six screens in total. Three on the top and three on the bottom. They curved to encompass the space around him. He had two ergonomic keyboards curling on either side. Gavin typed on the images representing keys, maneuvering his fingers on the screens to move documents around.

I got up from my seat and came around to where Gavin sat to get a closer look. "I never saw the KeViewer look like this before. The one I used when working for Braggart had one screen and set of keys."

Gavin nodded but didn't look at me. "Mine is the same as yours. I tweaked it a bit." After a few more keystrokes, he turned to look at me. "Okay, look here." He pointed to a file he had opened.

It read:

Braggart, Roman Julian

ID: MIL116.002

Project Hercules volunteer 116.002 was injected with 10CC of the Herculean Cocktail with predominant genetic conjointment of a South American Jaguar and the African Leopard to create a new Panthera series. Unlike volunteers 0 to 115, Braggart was not given 15mg of impetus agents at risk of physical abnor-

malities seen in the other volunteers,
per General Brockton Braggart orders.

I read down the list. The screen contained more information on the effects and how quickly they saw abilities present within me. Bright red words on the corner of the screen caught my attention.

Operative Braggart on the run; Possibly dead. Tracker and Kill-switch deactivated and unresponsive. Update: Last seen on the outskirts of Sector Bravo, Town of Ashur, while infiltrating the southern camp. Operative Dallas failed to apprehend and dispatch. General orders to eliminate the threat on sight if the suspect is still alive. The reward for his extermination extended to private sectors.

My stomach twisted in knots. I knew my father was a prick; I wasn't sure of how much until now. Gavin swallowed as he turned to face me. He said nothing to me, and for that, I was grateful. The information hurt to read, but I wasn't seeking sympathy. All this meant to me was I needed to be more careful while out in public. I was one of the best at this job. In no way, shape, or form would I be caught dead by these bastards. If I didn't before, I knew now I had made the right decision in joining forces with Rayne and her siblings.

I turned to Gavin. Gavin paced the floor. I knew the boy's fears extended to Rayne, for that I had no doubt. Knowing this was the only way to help the group, I took a deep breath and hid away all of the concerns sitting at the base of my skull. Not only should I do this for Rayne, but I needed to do it for myself.

Sector Bravo
Safe Haven Headquarters

SHIVERING, I WASHED off the sweat from my skin. There wasn't any hot water, and the cold water affected every nerve ending in my body. I quickly swabbed the surface of my skin with liquid soap, rinsing it off in small bursts. My teeth chattered. Finally done, I turned off the spray and shook the water off my body. The plush, clean towel fell off the hook. The mind of a burdened soul had so much going on in it, that nothing, in particular, could scratch the surface. With my mind blank, I grabbed the towel and shook it out to wrap it around my sore body.

The open showers and locker rooms were empty. The only other woman in the bunker I talked to was

Silk, and she protested the fact she had to watch over Gavin when he returned to his home. A secret smile graced my face as I thought of the reaction Gavin had when he saw Silk. His eyes followed her around the room as they discussed pertinent information he had in Thunder's place. Silk's room was right next to Thunder's, so she had headed directly there after walking out of the Planning Room. The slinky spider knew no one would dare step into her domain, so she had hidden in there like a petulant child. I didn't count on the party continuing their discussion by Thunder's room either. There was importance in being in the meeting, so I risked a peek, satisfied Rome was nowhere to be around.

Roman Braggart.

All this time, he was the son of the crazy, sinister general controlling Project Hercules. I didn't know what to do about this little tidbit of information. Instead, I swallowed the lump stuck in my throat. My stomach cramped again. I sat on the bench between the lockers. After gathering my wits about me, I pulled a clean shirt over my head and slipped on a pair of underwear. The muscles in my stomach hurt again. I pitched forward, wrapping my arms around my midsection. This entire situation was causing me indigestion. Sharp pain wracked my midsection again, letting a tiny moan escape my clenched teeth.

In a bat of an eye, the door of the female locker room slammed open. I shot up from the bench, expecting to be attacked by soldiers and operatives, and instead came face to face with a concerned Rome. I quickly realized I was partially nude, so I fumbled around for some pants.

"What the hell are you doing here, Rome?"

Rome looked around for potential dangers, and when he found none, he ogled me from bare feet on up. He flushed to the tips of his ears.

Seeing him so vulnerable pissed me off. "Why the hell are you the one blushing? I'm the one naked here."

Smiling, Rome turned around but didn't leave the room. I quickly put my feet in and pulled up the pants. As I buttoned them, I looked back up at him. "Why are you in here?"

"Can I turn around now?"

I wanted to say no, but I was curious. "Yeah," I uttered through partly closed lips.

Rome turned around and took a few steps closer to me. He looked as delicious as he usually did and smelled just as tasty. I hated myself for feeling that way. With arms banded across my chest, I placed space between us.

He didn't venture farther. "Rayne, I'm sorry I didn't tell you about my father. I mean, it's hard even to count him as family." He ran a hand through his hair. "I'm sorry, Rayne. I truly am."

I wanted to cry. Since finding out about my lost memories, Seaa, and then my parents' deaths, I'd done nothing but complain. Sometimes I wondered if that was the reason I had been named Rayne. "I'm trying to understand why you didn't, Rome. Just... Did you lie to get here?"

Without a moment's hesitation, he called out, "No, of course not!"

Taking swift steps to approach me, Rome wrapped me up in his arms. All I needed was five seconds to get my fill, and I'd push him away. *4.* I took in his woodsy scent and fresh linens. *3.* I weaved my fingers into the thick of his hair at the nape of his neck. *2.* I rubbed my nose at the skin below his ear. *1.* I sighed in contentment. *0.* I finally returned to my senses, dropped my hands, and pushed away from him.

Rome placed trembling fingers to my cheeks. He leaned in slowly as if asking for permission. I wanted to scream no. The words were on the tip of my tongue. He lied to me. I couldn't trust him.

Then he whispered, "I think I love you, Rayne," and molded his lips on mine.

CHAPTER TWENTY

ROME DIDN'T GIVE me a chance to protest. My thoughts and objections lost on the very breath he took from me. When he angled his head slightly to consume more of my mouth, I couldn't help the bubbles of excitement tickling deep in my belly. The little euphoric orbs seemed to have fluttered out of me and enveloped us within one giant bubble, creating a space where we belonged. Our breaths intermingled. The sweet air around us lingered. Then I remembered how mad I was at Rome, and the bubble popped.

After pushing him away, I reeled back and punched him. Rome got caught off guard, taking the full hit without preparing himself for it. I waited for him to speak. When he didn't, I ran off like a scared creature. There needed to be boundaries. It was necessary to make choices quickly. Tears fell from my eyes, and it pissed me off even more. As I wiped one cheek off, I ran into Hail. I looked up at the man I had once forgotten. His hands were on my shoulders with a thick frame of concern lingering in his eyes.

I watched in slow motion as Hail narrowed his eyes at whatever was behind me. His grip tightened. My eyes registered what he was about to do right before he swooped in and kissed me. There were those rare moments growing up when he touched me. He once kissed me on the cheek, and I wondered what his lips would feel like on mine.

Would they be warm, or would they be cold?

But this wasn't the time or the place to steal kisses from me.

I pulled away from him, slapping him in the face. "Shame on you, Hail. I thought you were better than that."

I stepped around him and walked away. A few steps ahead of me, Silk rounded the corner and leaned against the crumbling wall. With a shake of my head, Silk nodded, understanding everything I wished to say without saying it. My friend, Gavin, turned right behind her. His mouth opened to talk, but I saw Silk cover his mouth with her hand.

She whispered, "Leave her alone for now. She needs some time."

Exactly what I needed. More than once now, I was thankful for my beautiful sister's incredible intuition. There were random bits of chaos and conversation I caught before I walked out. Rome argued with Hail.

Silk argued with Gavin about leaving her alone. Silk broke up the fight between both Rome and Hail. I wanted to get out of here and take time for myself.

The night air shimmered over my exposed skin, causing me to shiver. There were no clouds in sight. The sky above me was clear. Stars sparkled and glistened in their large, open space. The biggest astronomical satellite out there was full, encompassing its scope as it rotated around the Earth. The night was correctly set for me to settle my thoughts and get things straightened in my mind and heart before I walked back in there. It had become a rare sight to see the night sky. Stuffing my hands in the pockets of my jeans, I walked to the edge of the shore and took the small dinghy toward the other end of the island.

Once there, I tied up the small boat and covered it up with the old, draping tarp we used for it. I walked off the beach, noting the various seashells crunching underneath my feet. Movement out of the corner of my eye caught my attention. I turned to see a small crab traipse over the seashells and pebbles as it made its way toward the water. The breeze blew around me, whistling through the trees and long blades of grass. I maneuvered my way through the small forest before me while still fighting the urge to rub my lips together. Both Rome and Hail clung to my lips, and no matter how many times I rubbed the sensation away, the weight of them stuck.

What the hell am I going to do?

I cared about both of them, so I couldn't deny the feelings held deep within. But this wasn't the time to get into all of this melodrama. We had more significant problems out here than worrying about romance and relationships. My parents sacrificed their lives to hide information from Project Hercules. Memories spent with them made my nose burn with unshed tears. God, I missed them so much. Every time I felt determined to do something about it, I became bombarded with all of the current crap in my life.

There was rarely a real moment of reprieve.

Not even now.

The streets were empty at the edge of Beta Antiquis toward the border of Ashur. There were barely any citizens walking around the sector that night. The ones I saw were huddled within themselves, protecting their bodies from the cold wind. I noticed some of the buildings had light shining through their windows, and I wondered if any of them carried as much weight as I did. A Ground Force officer turned the corner as he merrily chatted with his partner. Knowing I would stand out if I lingered, I took to a corner. Disappearing within the dark, abandoned alley, I walked over tipped-over trash barrels and broken glass. I worked my way around broken piles of concrete and exposed iron rods.

The sound of movement behind me stopped my feet from moving. Turning to look over my shoulder, I saw two drifters digging through the trash barrels in search of food. Judging them not to be a threat to me, I walked again. Going down one alley, I caught sight of a hanging metal ladder that would take me up to one of the buildings' roofs. Jumping up to reach the metal rung, I swung my weight and brought down the rest of the ladder. With quick agile steps I ascended the ladder. I made it to the ailing metal balconies and continued my flight up. I would briefly look through the windows, watching as different families moved around.

One man, around the fifth floor, read to his boy, while the mother cleaned a spill on the floor. I placed myself in that scenario. Nostalgia made me warm even though the night chilled my bones. I could see in my mind's eye my father reading me a book on the floor of our small living room. My mother would have been cleaning up another spill she made from laughing so hard at one of Carl's jokes.

I smiled as I watched the strangers.

Those moments often happened in my home. My dad would come up with the funniest quips, and Alice couldn't contain her laughter. She spilled many things, many times throughout our years together.

Shaking off the memory, I walked up the steps. I looked down and noticed the drifters were below me, rummaging through old boxes and trash bags, so I ignored them and kept moving. Once at the top of the ladder, I paled. Lines of soldiers watched from every visible surface. My heart dropped, chest heavy. With shaking fingers, I tried to turn back down the stairs and noticed the drifters standing on the metal balcony, watching me too.

They weren't bums.

These were soldiers in disguise.

Not one to wait for the fallout to happen, I ran toward the edge of the building, coming to a dead stop. More soldiers surrounded and aimed their weapons from the buildings bordering this one. I turned to see one man pull away from the rest. I dropped in shock because I recognized the man from the university when I had stabbed him in the arm.

He was Rome's friend.

"Hello, Rayne. We meet again."

Unlike Trevor's soldiers, this man had his people ready to handle anything. They were precise in their movements and detailed in everything they did. I looked for a weakness or an opening but couldn't find anything. My mind whirled. There was no way I would get through this alone, and I couldn't sense any of my siblings around.

I stood up straighter. "You know my name, but I don't believe I know yours."

He threw his head back and laughed. The man was a lot smaller in build than Rome but made up for it in his height. His dark skin contrasted with his white shirt. I noticed the dark lashes around his eyes because he didn't have sunglasses on this time. The same ones he had been wearing the first time I saw him, hung off his shirt, and tears like those of a wild cat ran down the lines of his nose.

Pulling his open jacket over his weapon, I saw him adjust it and drop to his knees. The methods were tactics to both intimidate and ease my nerves. Neither worked on me at the moment. I was disappointed with myself. Of everything I knew, I should've seen this coming.

"Ah, my apologies. I'm Zane. You're more than welcome to call me Zee."

He waved one hand around, and his soldiers moved back one step like a choreographed dance number. Looking around, I noticed the groups he had posted on the other buildings still kept their aim.

I closed my eyes and took a deep breath. "I assume this is where you take me captive or kill me, right?"

Zane seemed quite put out by the idea but didn't reject it. "If need so, yes, I will have to kill you. However, I have orders to bring you in alive."

I shuddered thinking about who gave those orders. "You are merely a tool for the tyrant."

Zane didn't even ask me who I meant. He studied the same night sky I had enjoyed mere moments before and spoke as if speaking to them. "You had my friend killed. None of you deserve to live."

Rome's friend narrowed his eyes at me—more laborious than before. He was well and truly upset with me right now.

Should I mention he's alive, or should I keep it a

secret?

I struggled with my indecision but didn't think this was the right time to say something to him and the open, calculated ears around him.

Rome trusted this man.

I couldn't mess anything else up, so I responded with, "You know nothing," and ran toward the nearest soldier.

The man didn't expect me to be so bold. Caught unaware, I rammed into him and threw him to the ground. I punched him once in the face and rolled away before another soldier came down for me. My nerves wailed. My heart hammered wildly. I got off the concrete floor, and my head made impact with another person.

Three down, I counted.

Except, three more landed on top of me, toppling me over. I growled. I fought. My body arched as I tried to shove them off. More and more descended upon me. I couldn't lift my face off the hard surface. The small bits of dirt and debris bit at my cheek. I grunted when another body landed on top of mine. I was strong, probably just as strong as a lot of the other genetic experiments. But I was most definitely not strong enough to unload several strong soldiers from on top of me.

I stopped struggling long enough to see a pair of boots come into view. From my position, I could look up as high as Zane's knees. The more I moved, the farther they pushed me down. Zane bent down in front of me. His hands hung from his curled knee.

"I give you credit for trying."

I tried to move again. My breathing labored. The soldiers tied my limbs together before pulling me up. I wanted to punch Zane in the face, but I couldn't hate him for hating me. He thought I killed his friend. The last time I saw this man, he didn't carry so much turmoil in him as he did now.

Trying to pull myself away from one soldier, I looked into Zane's feline eyes. Biting my lower lip, I dropped to the floor. The movement caused two soldiers to trip over themselves. With more momentum now, I pushed off the ground and toward Zane.

He opened his arms and grabbed me as I made contact with his chest. The strength of his body had my soft curves molded around him. My face landed right by his ear as we both fell back onto the roof. I could smell his sweat and cologne now. Feeling hands all over my body, soldiers tried to raise me from on top of him. I whispered too low for anyone else to hear, "He's alive and lives with us."

When Zane's body froze, I knew he had heard me. The rest of his soldiers pulled me up and tightened their grip on my upper arms. I stared at Zane as he rose from the ground. He wiped off the dirt from his pants and watched me. I didn't know if he searched for the truth on my face or if he saw it before he turned around and walked away from me.

I turned to yell at the one holding on to my right arm. Before I could see the person, an elbow came toward my temple and made contact. I could feel nothing but blinding pain. My body dropped to the ground at awkward angles.

THE DOCTOR'S EXPLANATION was nonsense. The Herculean Cocktail wasn't perfect. I knew without Lester's notes, nothing would go right. I detested the kooky doctor and disliked this one just as much. Dr. Plumboy looked precisely as his surname reflected. The man was short and plump with arms waving like a primate's when he walked. The only thing worthwhile in the odd man was his lack of morals.

It pissed me off that these idiots lost all those important notes belonging to Dr. Lester before he offed himself. I could barely recreate the cocktail from Sebastian's leftovers. We were at least able to fix some of the old doctor's genomes, but now his soldiers lacked what the other experiments didn't—elemental abilities.

That's not to say we didn't create something a little...wilder.

Ready to rip the old man's throat out, I raised one hand to shut him the hell up. "I want my operatives to gain these abilities, Dr. Plumboy. I will not listen to your excuses again."

The doctor paled. He knew I was serious and would not hesitate to replace him. Trevor's group saw my little Rayne melt into a puddle. One minute she was there, and then everything had frozen over. Plumboy received a hell of a nasty surprise when I found out Hail fought his way out of the mind program. So, the doctor currently skated on thin ice with me.

I'd seen those kids use tiny bits of their abilities before. Dr. Sebastian Lester noted the changes in their abilities were small and not enough to cause as much damage as Hail had. I knew the alterations we made in Hail increased the strength of the power. I wanted to know which strand in the cocktail caused the skills.

I wanted that power.

I wanted the ability to win the war for good.

I'd be unstoppable. Unbeatable.

My receiver beeped. Static filled the air around us until voices came over the line. I pulled the walkie-talkie off my belt and held it up. The doctor ran off, taking advantage of the opportunity they called me. Words came over the line, and I was startled still.

"Repeat."

What I heard couldn't have been correct. If, in fact,

it was, then I would have a great night's sleep tonight for the first time in a long time.

"Sir, operative Mueller brought back one of the fugitives. A Rayne Baxter was apprehended earlier this evening."

I didn't even wait for the man to say anything else. "Where? Where was she taken?"

The line crackled as I anxiously awaited the response. "She was taken to Cell 3B, Sir."

I said nothing else to anyone, moving swiftly down the halls and deeper one floor to the cells keeping our criminals after implantation in Alpha. The determination was present on my face. No one dared stop me. One of my secretaries stayed with papers in her hand, but she saw I wouldn't break my stride for anyone. The woman pushed herself against the wall to avoid me.

I moved down another hallway, looking into the security room for the cells. One cell had Seaa. She leaned against a wall, gasping for air as the men controlled the moisture in her room. I turned to look at another cell. His men laid my beautiful and elusive Rayne out on a cot in a small cell. I could see her chest rise up and down. For years, the memory of her haunted my every dream. She belonged to me and no one else. Sebastian thought he could take her away from me like he did, but she had found her way home.

No one will take you away from me again, Rayne.

She had a mark on the side of her head by her ear.

Seeing it made my blood boil to know someone had dared put their hands on her. My hands tightened into giant fists. Although she needed to learn her place, the discipline would come from me or from someone of my choosing. Pulling out the receiver, I called for Zane to come down to the cell's security room. Deep breaths helped me squelch the anger burning inside. I despised it when my orders weren't followed precisely to the letter.

A matter of minutes passed, and I heard Zane enter the room.

"Sir."

I pointed to the screen. "I said unharmed, didn't I?"

Zane knew what I was talking about because he didn't deviate from looking me in the eyes. "The soldier responsible has already been disciplined."

I nodded, content enough Zane handled the matter. Nevertheless, he was the lead on the case and punishment needed to be dealt to him as well. "Soldiers, please escort operative Mueller to one of the gas chambers for his punishment."

Zane stiffened but showed no other sign of fighting my commands. The operative was much stronger than the soldier escorting him out of the room, but he dutifully took his punishment and walked over to the chamber we used to send toxins into the genetically enhanced soldiers. The poison filtered through their lungs and caused them massive amounts of pain. The strong ones made it out of there alive. The weaker soldiers couldn't handle the pain and practically gutted themselves to be rid of it.

They never survived.

A lock of her hair fell over her face. My fingers itched to move it from her soft skin. My little Rayne was back in my possession. No one would ever take her from me again. My desire for her encompassed my entire being. I placed my hand on the other guard in the room.

Startled, the man looked up. "Any matters regarding this experiment go through me. No one may open this door unless I have cleared it. Understand?"

The man nodded. "Yes, Sir."

I removed my hand and cleaned it on the fabric of my slacks. "Unless told otherwise, keep the temperature in her room normal."

Another affirmation. I walked out of the room toward Rayne's cell.

My measured steps took me to her cell in no time at all. I looked through the shatterproof glass. The glass material was stronger than steel, impermeable to the strength of my mutants. I stood near it, knowing no one would break it and get to me. My eyes roamed over her with malicious intent. I whispered to the glass separating one from the other, "Pitter-patter, pitter-patter, listen for me, Rayne. Pitter-patter, pitter-patter at your windowpane."

Her chest rose and fell. She had one arm around her waist—the other underneath her. Rayne was filthy.

Her clothes did not reflect the beauty I knew this girl possessed from the tip of her head to the soles of her feet.

She moved again.

This time, Rayne's beautiful eyes fluttered open, and she stared right at me. When those mesmerizing eyes stared into mine, I could not control the yearning coursing through my veins. Not once had a woman made me feel this intensely.

She immediately recognized me, breaking the spell I was under. Her eyes narrowed, and she jumped from her spot on the cot and toward me. Rayne slammed into the glass. Her fists wailed on the thick material. I grinned as I watched her scream in frustration.

"Welcome back, my little Rayne."

She was home, where she belonged.

CHAPTER TWENTY-ONE

A THROBBING HEADACHE wailed. I stood in front of General Brockton Braggart; warning signals screamed louder than the pounding in my head. The look in his eyes told me more than I needed to know. I studied the confined space and shivered. Being around such tall and large men all the time, General Braggart didn't seem equal to their imposing height. Yet, I knew this man wielded a lot more power than the others did. The General stood erect with hands folded behind his back.

I can't see Rome anywhere on this man.

For that, I was thankful.

As if reading my mind, Braggart dropped one hand to his side, slowly raising it to twirl that god-forsaken mustache. His thick brows rose, and a glimmer of a wicked grin rose from behind his hand. "Now, how is my son?"

My entire body petrified.

Does he know he is alive, or is he testing me?

In case it was the latter, I narrowed eyes at the crazy bastard and wailed at the glass walls. "You had him killed, you psycho!"

The General dropped his hand, placing it right back where it was behind him. "Ah, so he's dead, you say? Again?"

I dropped my head, wiping the tears from my face. For once, I was glad I cried so much. The effect benefited me. "You're an animal," I whispered.

General Braggart laughed. The sound was harsh and grinding. Every nerve in my body withered under the sound like a human exposed to nails on a chalkboard. "My little Rayne, between you and I, I'm led to believe you possess more animal than me."

I ran a hand through my messy hair and pulled it from my face. With eyes that could kill, I approached the glass protecting the General from all of his wrongdoings. My entire body shimmered with a free spirit. I've had enough of holding back my abilities when I felt my body erupt in a wave of energy.

"The only animal here is you."

General Brockton watched me as I uttered the words burning inside of me. I didn't want this to happen again, but I couldn't fear it my entire life. Unable to control it, I pulled my arm back, feeling the flow navigate through my veins. Like a coiled spring, my fist flew toward the glass enclosure. My entire body liquefied, slamming on the glass like a rogue tidal wave. The water cascaded in all directions like practiced dancers, rolling back into a solid form. Legs were the first to appear. The water opposed gravity as it rose from my toes and up to the tip of my head. I stared at the man in front of me, who, for the first time since coming to see me, showed he was cautious of what his experiments could do.

The entire episode made me jittery like an addict deprived of his drug.

Shaking himself off, Braggart walked to the other side of the glass. My eyes followed him, but I didn't move from my spot on the floor as my body put itself back together. There had to be an explanation for these changes, but I couldn't figure out what it was. One minute I was a solid, human girl—albeit enhanced—and the next, I turned into rushing water.

The general straightened his jacket.

"You do understand I require information."

With my body put back together, I walked to stand right in front of Braggart. "You aren't getting anything from me."

General Brockton Braggart was not easily swayed. "Oh, I will, my little Rayne. I'm sure living the sheltered life you've led until now hasn't hardened you to the harsh realities of our world like the others have had to endure." He pressed a button and the wall beside me shimmered. "I still can't break her." He looked back up at me. "But I'm positive I can break you."

My knees buckled. Seaa lay sprawled out on the floor of her cage. Her skin was a sickly pallor; her scales had lost their luster. There were patches where she had lost most of her scales. The only color visible on her body was that of the bruising on her skin.

I could tell from looking Seaa had become dehydrated and in so much pain. I ran to the shimmering wall, trying to break through it. The field was as strong as the steel had been before it changed. I pounded on the iridescent image, but all my efforts failed.

"Seaa, can you hear me?" I called through the transparent obstruction.

There was no movement on Seaa's end, but for the labored rise and fall of her chest. The entire image disappeared, and I came face to face with nothing but a steel wall. I looked back at the General. My anger was evident in every part of my body from my locked legs to my cold eyes.

"Now, do you understand where I am coming from?" I tried to sound harsh, but the anxiety was eating me alive. "Y-you don't scare me."

He smiled, and I could see the General had a gap between his two front teeth. "Well, we'll see. You must learn somehow, my dear. Torture it is." He drew his arms back as he had done before and whistled an old nursery rhyme I had heard before.

He walked away, singing, "Pitter-patter, pitter-patter, listen for me, Rayne. Pitter-patter, pitter-patter, on your windowpane," before he was out of sight.

Minutes felt like hours and hours felt like days. No one approached my cell. They left me alone in the small interior with nothing but my crazed mind as a companion. For the umpteenth time since waking up in this dreaded room, I had run to the glass, trying to break through it. I noticed a gray sliver of metal embedded in my underarm during one of my fits and ripped at my skin to remove it. When I couldn't, my entire body exploded in rage. I grabbed the bench, ripping it from its bolts on the ground, and slammed steel against steel. But mere scratches were the only evidence of my anger. The chair hit the glass next. The room clanked and pinged, but nothing proved merciful.

I screamed at the top of my lungs. My throat abraded and burned, and my chest heaved with the strength of my wail. Nothing worked in my favor. I pulled at my hair and had fingers that were raw and bleeding, with knuckles cracked and bruised. The pain didn't even register. Not for the first time had I wondered if the rest of the group knew of my capture.

Did someone follow me out?

No, I replied to myself.

I would've sensed them.

They gave me the space I needed, and what good did it do me?

It seemed pointless to have been so ignorant of the strength of my heart. My old feelings for Hail superseded those new ones I had for Rome. True, I hadn't remembered him for a long time, but my heart hadn't forgotten him. The love I felt for Rome was of a whimsical little girl oblivious to the world around her. Those feelings were in the moment's heat. I scratched my head and sighed again, dropping my weight onto the cot.

But then, why does it hurt so much to tell my heart Hail is who I am supposed to love?

A laugh interrupted my musings when it filtered through the interior of the wrecked room. Trevor stood in front of the glass. I stared at my surroundings, noting for the first time how stiff I felt. God knows how long I'd been sitting here, thinking about the most mundane things.

It goes to show my inadequacy. "What are *you* doing here?"

Trevor Dallas stood tall with his worn cowboy hat planted on the top of his head. I could tell his hair was dark from the little tufts seen around the hat, but upon closer inspection, I could see the strands were a brownish-green. He was unshaven and wearing way too much cologne. The last time I saw him, he wore similar jeans and a jacket. He tapped on the glass like a petulant child in front of a wild animal he wanted to provoke.

His mouth opened into a giant grin. "I'm here to see

if you changed your mind about the whole 'I'm not telling you a thing' thing?"

The bench was within kicking distance, so I shoved my foot forward, and the steel bench pushed ahead with so much momentum the room vibrated with the strength of it. Trevor flinched but didn't move from his spot.

"I'm not telling you a damn thing."

"Are you sure?"

I leaned back against the wall. "Oh, I'm sure."

He beamed. "So, if that's the case, I guess you and I could chat a little bit here." He leaned against the glass. "You know, like we were old girlfriends catching up."

I grimaced. The guy was as insane as Braggart, and I told him so.

Trevor put a hand to his heart as if wounded by my words. "Oh, c'mon. My partner is dead, and I have no one to chat with anymore."

My eyes narrowed.

Trevor pulled his hat off. He ran a hand through his hair or what was left of it. I could see two receding hairlines where I was sure the hat rubbed. He placed the damn thing back on. "Now, the least I could do is let you go first. How 'bout it, doll?"

I crossed my arms instead.

He lifted one side of his lips as silence filled the room. Neither one of us spoke for a long minute. He gave first. "Okay, okay, I guess I can start." He pulled away from the glass. "So, I've been having a hard time sleeping. I mean, I should be happy, right, that I caused so much damage in that traitor Rome, oh, and the fact I caught that slimy fish."

My shoulders tightened.

"Right, the fish." He shuddered, and I wanted to punch him. "That is one disgusting freak. I mean, I've been drunk out of my mind and screwed lots of women I've regretted the next morning, but hot damn..." He whooped. The sound echoed off the metal interior. "I'd get straight sober if I had to touch that thing more than necessary."

I shook with repressed anger.

"Yeah, so back to not sleeping. I captured her, and I have tortured her every day since she's been here, but man oh man does she got resilient, thick skin." He put his finger to his chin in deep thought. "Oh, wait, I guess she doesn't have skin now, does she?"

Right then, I pushed through everything and ran to the glass. For a minute, I forgot the glass was even between us. I slammed into it so hard I bounced back on the floor. The pain of my broken nose sent sparks down the rest of my body. The back of my head slammed on the concrete. Blood poured down my face.

Damn.

I was dang tired of my nose breaking. Getting it re-broken by Dr. Ferdinand had been way worse. Gaining a little bit of courage, I looked up at Trevor, who grinned from ear to ear. I snapped the bone back in place, able to breathe once more through it.

"Well, that must've hurt a tad."

I got off the ground and dusted myself off. "Why don't you come in here and I can show you."

Trevor shook his head before I finished speaking. "Nah, I think I like it right here." He shifted his feet and looked over to the side. I knew Seaa was in the room next to mine. "Well, lookie here. The fish is up."

I ran to the door and punched it, calling out for Seaa over and over again. My body was tired beyond belief. Worry for myself and Seaa filled me with dread. There was so much I wanted to know. We needed to get out of this place.

Trevor laughed as he watched Seaa and turned to look at me. "Poor thing can't speak anymore." He slapped his knee, shouting even louder now.

She can't speak?

Wild eyes searched for a way out of the room. "What did you do to her?"

Trevor shrugged. "What wasn't done?" He laughed again. "Now you really look like a fish in a tank."

I screamed to my sister. I cried, trying to compose myself enough to get more information out of Trevor, who was readily willing to give up the bad bits. Giant sobs burst from within me. I hated them poking at Seaa as if she was an animal at a freak show.

"I guess all those torturous screams do a number on your windpipe."

The rage inside of me exploded, and like a tornado let loose in a metal trailer park, I wreaked havoc on everything inside. I twisted off a steel leg from the curved bench and stabbed the glass repeatedly. My rage blinded me. I saw nothing but the maniacal cowboy in front of me. For the first time, I saw his eyebrows dip, and concern painted his features a pale yellow.

He nodded to one camera, and a thick mist enveloped the room. There were two vents at the top of the ceiling letting the fog roll in and fill the place with its noxious fumes. I wavered on my feet. My eyelids repeatedly blinked. I tried to cover my nose and mouth. Trevor moved back and forth, but that could have been my eyes playing tricks on me. My hand dropped the metal tool. I heard it ring in the small interior. The room waved, and I felt a lot more tired than I had before.

My muscles weakened.

My knees buckled.

My entire body fell sideways toward the ground.

Before my eyes sealed shut, fatigue rendering me immobile, I noticed I had cracked the glass and felt a lot better than I had before.

There was still a chance.

Sector Bravo
Safe Haven Headquarters
Roman Braggart
ID: MIL 116.002

I SCRATCHED MY head and rubbed a hand on my chest for the third time since being in this room with the rest of the genetic experiments. My heart ached, and I wasn't sure why. The only thing making me so uncomfortable was Rayne's disappearance. The woman had serpentined her way into my heart through sheer serendipitous methods—damned if I wouldn't do it all over again just to feel her breath on my skin.

"Roman, are you listening?"

I had no idea what they were talking about, so I looked up at Thunder. "No, I wasn't listening."

Thunder took a deep breath as if controlling himself from electrocuting the hell out of me. I'd been on the receiving end of those shocks and didn't look forward to a repeat performance. "You wanted this meeting, Rome."

I nodded because I did want this meeting. Silk wanted her sister to have some privacy, but it wasn't smart to leave Rayne alone for so long. She may be tough as hell, but she was not wise to deception like we were. "Rayne hasn't checked in with anyone, and it's been almost half a day since she's been gone."

Silk slammed her hands on the table. "She left because of you boneheads."

I would not deny it, and neither did Hail, who stood at the other end of the room, glaring daggers at me. At this point, I didn't care one bit this man hated my guts, blaming me for taking the woman he loved.

"As much as I hate to admit it, I think Rome is right. She's been gone too long."

At least Hail wasn't as stupid as I thought.

Thunder agreed. Snow and Guy were still on the fence. Rock spoke up, "I think a woman needs her space if she's angry. If my Bee ever felt like taking time out to gather her thoughts over stinging me, well, I'd take the time any day."

As unwarranted as the information was, the man had a point.

Silk shook her head. The curls bounced from side to side. "We need to leave her alone."

I turned to look at Rayne's friend, who sat quietly in the room's corner. "What about you, Gavin?"

Gavin looked up with a shocked expression. "I..." He looked over at the black widow.

Gavin had it bad for the black widow, everyone could see it, but I didn't think he even knew if it was his own feelings or those she projected. Silk had powers she kept hidden from Unit 13. Messing with the men around her might be one of them.

"I think Silk is right; a woman needs her space sometimes." Everyone talked at once. "But..." The room stopped talking again. "Rayne isn't a normal girl, and these aren't normal circumstances."

Bravo, Gavin.

Hail jumped forward. "There you have it. I will go off to look for Rayne and bring her back."

The hell he would. I laughed, the sound more sinister than I meant it to be. "You couldn't even find her for the last five years."

The man stiffened. All this fighting needed to stop. Rayne and Hail were over the moment someone took her to the Baxters, and Hail went on his merry old way. The man needed to get over it already. My mind switched gears. I snapped my head up. The thought had never occurred to me until now.

I looked up at Hail, "You've been searching for Rayne all this time, but from the knowledge I picked up, the Baxters were affiliated with someone on the inside."

Hail narrowed his eyes at me. "What are you trying to say?"

I looked at Hail and then at the leader of the group to gauge his reaction. To anyone else, Thunder gave off nothing, but to the trained eye, I could see the tension in his shoulders and the slight aversion to direct eye contact. Thunder knew more than he was letting on, and to get it out in the open was to bluff my way.

"Ah, I see now."

Thunder placed both hands on the table. "Don't make assumptions, Roman Braggart."

Yup, the big ol' man definitely knows something.

I waved him off, looking back at Hail. "Nope, I have consistently been pretty good at gathering Intel and reading body language." I turned to look at Thunder. "I'm not far off the mark that you, my friend, knew exactly where Rayne was hidden."

The entire room erupted into a cacophony of voices—each one trying to outdo the other. Instead of hearing Thunder's loud boom, silencing the room as he usually did, I turned to see Hail scream out, "You're a damn liar."

I was confident someone here knew her whereabouts and why not the man who watched over the rest and took care in keeping them safe. Before I could shake him off, Hail had me against the wall of the Planning Room.

"I have spent five years looking for her. If anyone here knew her whereabouts, I would've known by now." The tension in the room was thick with the weight of his words.

I tried to pull his hand away, but at the moment, I was tired of fighting the man who felt strongly about the same woman I did. If I ever lost Rayne to Hail, I wouldn't ever worry about the strength of his affections. Hail's eyes glistened with unshed tears, and I knew fighting him would prove fruitless.

"Hail, let him down. He is not at fault here."

Hail didn't let me go but turned to face the leader of the group. "I won't let this man lie about things he doesn't know."

Thunder shook his head, taking a deep breath and finally planting himself in one of the rickety chairs.

The room was deathly quiet now. 1 could feel Hail's fingers tighten around my windpipe. Thunder ran a hand through his long hair, pulling the strands behind his shoulders.

Tears watered my eyes as 1 tried to control my breathing. 1 could feel the lack of oxygen reaching my brain.

"Rome is correct. 1 knew of Rayne's whereabouts and said nothing to anyone."

Hail had let go of me, dropping me on the floor in a haphazard pile.

"1 know this because 1 was the one that left her on their doorstep."

Ah, shit.

CHAPTER TWENTY-TWO

I TRIED TO adjust my clothes as I watched Hail jump over the large, splintered table with murderous intent. Thunder didn't even try to stop him. Hail tackled the leader down to the ground, hitting him in the face. The large man didn't avoid the wailing, as he took every punch, every cuss, and every beating with open arms. Hail swung with a right hook. Blood splattered out one side of Thunder's mouth. He moved in for a left, and blood rushed out from the other side.

In the chaos, I saw Gavin running after Silk, who seemed dejected and betrayed. She slunk away. There was one look directed toward me I couldn't quite place, and I could usually read it all well enough. Rock watched from his spot at the table. He didn't make a move to stop them and probably felt as if Thunder deserved the pummeling he received. He shoved a thumb into his mouth, biting his nails and spitting out the clippings.

Snow was already at the mess of bodies, helping Guy peel Hail off Thunder. The entire spectacle lasted for about ten minutes before I could no longer take the distraction and cleared my throat. "Hey, let's not forget the real reason we gathered today."

Someone pushed Guy back into the table. Snow got shoved to the far side of the room where he re-arranged the chairs he had toppled over. Rock continued to bite his nails. Thunder was bloody, but no less winded than when this all began. Hail had turned to the side and dropped to the floor, sprawled and breathing heavy. None of them said anything to one another. I wasn't sure what would happen after this, but I hoped I could get them back on track before Rayne got caught or suffered somewhere out there alone.

When the minutes ticked by, the guys all got back to their spots around the room. I expected deep hatred and animosity between Hail and Thunder, but what I saw instead made me believe real family wasn't about the bloodline one carried. I was sure it was about the people we kept around us. Thunder squeezed Hail's shoulder, and Hail responded by covering Thunder's hand with his own. There was one nod. This brief nod buried the pain and helped them move forward.

I had seen nothing like it. I didn't grow up with a caring mother and father. My mother left us years before it could bother me, and my father was a cold-hearted, egotistical tyrant who sought perfection in everything. For years, I tried making my father proud. I was in the military and highly decorated and ended up transferring over to my father's division when they presented this project to me. Not once was my father proud of who I was—nor did I have much left in me to care.

The guys were up as if nothing had happened.

Thunder used a small piece of cloth to wipe the blood from his face. A few seconds later, I heard Dr. Ferdinand rush into the room with his medical kit in hand. Either the old man listened to the ruckus, or Silk had told him. No matter, Dr. Ferdinand tended to Thunder's wounds as the big man looked around the room.

"I apologize for keeping this secret. I had promised Pops to protect her, and I thought that was what I was doing."

The guys nodded. If they thought about it, Rayne was better off never knowing about this life. If it weren't for our fateful meeting on that cold, snowy night, I wouldn't have known she existed.

"Thunder, let me go track her down," I told the Thor look-a-like.

Sighing, Thunder pointed to Snow. "Go with him."

Snow agreed and gave me a brief nod to follow him out. I didn't argue or say anything. Even though I wanted to go out on my own to track down Zane, what I saw between these men, prevented me from going behind their backs.

At least, for now.

WE WALKED THROUGH the woods, trying to catch whatever brief scent we could from Rayne. I inhaled the environment around me, hoping she had brushed against the brush. We both broke out of the tree line and walked toward one another.

Snow shook his head, "Not enough to go on. You?"

"Nothing much."

Snow walked toward an alley. He stopped and lifted his face into the air then turned to get my attention, but I was there before the man even finished. I caught the same faint scent Snow did. We both followed it. I hoped Rayne was safe and sound and hiding out somewhere. The night had disappeared, but the sun hid behind a set of clouds. The sun always hid behind a set of shadows. We walked for a while, passing people coming back and forth. Snow and I kept our heads down, trying to move as two inconspicuous townies like the others.

The trail led us to a building and nowhere else. Snow looked around. I couldn't believe she would up and disappear into thin air. Other scents were present, but none of them felt familiar to me. I spotted a ladder against the building and thought instead of staying on the ground; she might have gotten it into her head to remain above the trouble. With a burst of hope inside of me, I jumped up and grabbed the metal rung.

Her flavor assaulted me.

Without uttering a word to Snow, I made my way up the ladder onto the fire escapes connected to the building.

I ran up. Snow called out to me, but I ignored it, afraid I'd lose Rayne's scent. Once at the top, smells I didn't quite care for—and two I did—hit me like a ton of bricks. Bile rose in my throat. I ran a hand through my hair, looking around for evidence of a struggle. I found spots of blood. The smells attacked me in every direction I turned. There were so many people here on this building it couldn't have been a coincidence.

Rayne had been caught by Project Hercules. She had to have been—and by the man I trusted and called a friend—Zee.

Snow appeared behind me. "Oh, shit. Rayne was here."

I didn't want to lie to these people, but I knew that by voicing my thoughts, I'd be admitting my best friend captured Rayne. Snow dropped to the ground by the drops of blood.

"These are Rayne's."

I threw my hands up, pulling back the skin of my head and hair, squeezing in frustration. "Mother—" I screamed before saying anything further.

Snow put his hand on my shoulder as Thunder did with Hail. "Dude, it's not enough to have killed her. She's still alive. I know it."

Being captured by Braggart was no reason to rejoice. I'd worked under the man for years and had been on the receiving end of most of his punishments. Sometimes, it was better to be dead. I fisted my hand, aching to punch anything. If Rayne was in Braggart's hands, we needed to get her out of there, but I wasn't sure how. Getting out the first time was a miracle concocted by a kooky, old doctor who loved them enough to take his own life for theirs.

Rushing into and back out of the facility now would not work. Whoever took part in such a rescue would be shot down before he even knew it came. General Braggart had security measures on top of security measures. The place was harder to penetrate than chromium.

"Snow, we need to get back to the others. I have a horrible feeling about this."

Snow agreed. "Yeah, it looks like your ex-partner was at it again. Let's hope she escaped capture."

I shook my head. "No, I fear it may have been much worse than that. She eluded *this* man once and wouldn't a second time."

The white-haired man stopped walking. "What do you mean?"

Stuffing my hands inside of the loose jeans, I looked

up into the sky to feel a few drops of rain fall on my face. "I fear my friend Zane captured her." I looked back down to see Snow didn't follow. "Zane is one of the best operatives in the facility. He's better than I am. She escaped him once. He wouldn't have allowed a second time around."

"Would he kill her?"

I shook my head. Not because I was sure Zane wouldn't have killed her, because if he had orders to do so, he would, with no questions asked. The General wanted Rayne back alive—he wouldn't kill her. I didn't question the order before, but now it weighed heavy on my heart and mind. There was a reason Rayne was the only one adopted and a reason Braggart wanted her, out of all of them, back alive. If any of the others died during capture, he would chalk it up to casualties of war or collateral damage.

Braggart didn't have a trace of a heart left.

"I'm sure he didn't kill her, but because he may have gotten orders not to. We need to get back to Safe Haven."

Snow tried to catch on. "Wait, shouldn't we check the camp?"

I headed down the emergency staircase when I yelled back, "Trust me, the camp was already broken down and moved to another part of town."

Rayne was in danger.

I felt it deep in my bones and in the ache of my heart.

EVERY PART OF my body screamed out in agony. I couldn't ease the pain they subjected me to—the suffering so unbearable I had hoped to die more than once. With hands chained above my head, I was sure my left shoulder was dislocated from its socket. Metal cuffs bound my ankles. There was no way to break through the bonds. The area where they kept me had been made to break the person held captive.

I tried to swallow but couldn't get past the dry lump in my throat. Tears rushed down my battered cheeks in a never-ending flow. I dared look up at the men standing in front of me, taunting me. There was no pain left in my left arm, but my right burned with the strain of my weight. I had been chained here for a few hours now, already afraid this was where I my life would end. Trevor had zapped me over and over again with a military-grade Vuwand. The electric shocks to my body made my muscles spasm, and each time they did, I would feel the pain thrum in my whole body.

It was hard to breathe. The sound of dripping water echoed around the room. Trevor approached me once more. I flinched. My muscles sizzled again. A whimper rended the air with its melancholy sound. I didn't want to cry in front of these demons, but I couldn't handle it anymore. There wasn't a shred of hope left inside of me.

"Y'all ready now to answer some questions?"

Sniffling with trembling lips, all I could do was watch the General and his lackey perform unnatural act after unnatural act. The horror grew. The ripples of agony slammed into me like crashing waves on the shore, pointing me toward Death. My nerve-endings having gone through more trouble than physically possible.

My ears rang, but I could make out the General sending Trevor away. The cowboy pulled his hat down and bid me goodbye. His last words a testament to what I was about to experience.

"We're finally alone now, my little Rayne."

Acrid bile rose in my throat. He approached me, and I tried to move back, but my bindings kept me immobile. General Braggart looked at me as if studying a fascinating new creature. The sensation of his eyes on me equated to thousands of creepers crawling over my skin.

He walked around me. His steps were calculative and slow. I could feel his eyes burning a hole in every pore of my body. "Do you know how long I've wanted to see you like this?"

Why me?

My memories in this place were never pleasant

when it involved the General. He gave me the creeps, but now the sensation became exceedingly intense. I felt my body shake again, and a howl escaped my lips. The torture had done its job. I would break down and give the General what he wanted, or I would pass out before I could.

With my mind awhirl, I saw Braggart out of the corner of my eye. He grinned, exposing the gap in his teeth. "You have no idea how this excites me, Rayne. Punishments must be dealt with correctly to ensure compliance."

He had placed one finger on the exposed skin on my collarbone to push back a lock of hair, and I could no longer hold back the urge to vomit. I wretched on the ground in front of him. The ache in my body too much to bear. I gasped for air, pleading for Death to hurry.

Death *came* for me.

Death arrived in the form of an average man who wielded more power than the devil himself.

"You bitch," he swore as the back of his hand ripped the last remaining strength from my body. "You will learn who I am, Rayne. Whether you like it or not."

There was nothing else left for me as day became night, and my body gave up.

WHEN I MANAGED to keep my eyes open after several unsuccessful attempts, I was in a room different than the last. My body screamed with every move I made. A broken mind was a terrible thing to bear. The floor I lay on was cold. I made it toward a bench by a viewing window in the cell on my hands and knees. My muscles quivered under duress. I had pain everywhere. I couldn't pinpoint where it originated. Dragging myself from the floor to the bench took everything I had. My arms shook as I tried to pull my body onto the seat.

My line of sight shifted. I looked out the glass to see Seaa was now in front of me in a cell of her own. The sound of high-pitched rings swarmed my mind. My ears couldn't process audio. I leaned back against the wall. Short bursts of breath were the only sign my body gave that the movement had winded me. I tapped on my ear, hoping to get it to stop ringing. The room swayed. My chest vibrated with unshed tears. Looking back out the window, I saw Seaa trying to grab my attention.

I couldn't understand what Seaa said, but I could see my sister banging on her glass. Her mouth moved, but I couldn't read what she was talking about. Seaa looked to the side and then back at me with wide eyes. My stomach swirled. The sensation brought on nausea. Trevor Dallas walked into my line of sight. His hat fit so low over his brow I could roughly see his hungry eyes. I'd memorized those eyes. Every time he struck me, his eyes conveyed their enjoyment. Seaa yelled at

Trevor. I tried to understand what was going on.

I saw Trevor open the cell door and drag Seaa out into the hallway.

There was not one sound I could hear, except for the ringing in my ears, but I could imagine how loud she screamed. He threw Seaa to the floor after dragging her by her hair. Trevor beat her. He half kneeled above her. His fists pummeled my sister. I screamed my throat raw, but he merely grinned back at me. He yanked Seaa around on the polished white tiles. The smell of death grew around me. The thick air made it harder for me to swallow.

I yelled loudly while I dragged my body to the glass. I banged my fists on the hard surface, but it refused to shatter. Seaa didn't cry. She rarely opened her mouth to scream. If I had half the strength Seaa did, I wouldn't be in this situation. Violet eyes met my hazel ones, and I could see all Seaa wanted to convey in one look. Seaa told me to be strong and not give up. She demanded I not give in to their wicked schemes.

But I wasn't Seaa.

I screamed louder. Trevor got off the floor, wiping the blood off his hands with a handkerchief. Three other female operatives finished what Trevor didn't. I watched in horror as each woman took turns on my sister. My tears fell. My heart broke a little more after every hit. I could take being the punching bag, but I couldn't bear seeing the punching bag be Seaa. Trevor must have felt brave because he opened the door to my cell. I pounced, forgetting for one second I was in a lot of pain.

But my body remembered and dropped to the floor at Trevor's feet.

I could hear a little more clearly, but not enough I could understand everything Trevor told me. My body screamed louder than I ever could. I tried to breathe through the hurt. Trevor grabbed me from the back of my head, interweaving his fingers in my hair for control. He moved my head to face the travesty in front of me. Seaa's blood was a stark contrast to the white floor.

"Talk...she'll...pain..."

I could only pick up bits and pieces, but from the look on his face, I knew Trevor wanted me to talk in exchange for my sister's safety. I looked back at Seaa and knew she would be disappointed in the answer. But I couldn't continue seeing the pain they inflicted on her. Before I could answer, Trevor yelled and slammed my face into the glass. Blood sprayed the glass. My mind whirled. Thoughts faded from one thing into another.

"You...see..." he yelled.

I tried to understand, but everything was jumbled together. The only thing I could think of was the physical suffering our bodies endured. I was forced to look at Trevor and then back at the scene in front of me. I tried nodding, agreeing to anything he wanted for this all to end. Trevor laughed. He got what he wanted.

I screamed out, "I'll tell you anything. Please, leave her alone."

My arms grabbed Trevor's clothes, pleading for him to listen. His smile said he would. He patted me on the head. My brain tried to process the situation, but my nerve endings wailed. Trevor motioned for the females to stop. They got off Seaa as if choreographed. Someone threw her back into her cell. I saw my sister move a bit, but it was enough to feel relief.

Everything slowly faded.

The darkness consumed me.

I knew of the madness in this place.

The mad world I lived in.

My thoughts disappeared, and I blacked out again.

CHAPTER TWENTY-THREE

HANDS WERE ON me again. I struggled to move but couldn't get them off me. My eyes shot open. I saw a man with hungry eyes and a cowboy hat over his brow. The screams of fear interlaced with pain and defeat spun around in the air around me—suffocating, choking. He wouldn't let go. My body was still in so much pain. Each part was ready to go back into shock. I couldn't afford to be unconscious again. I blinked it away, and in the process found out it wasn't Trevor standing in front of me, but Zane.

He reassured me with his eyes.

I will not hurt you.

I wanted to believe. I tried to think that I wouldn't get hurt again, but all I knew was that this world was cruel, and I'd die never changing a thing. There was no way I could beat Trevor, let alone General Braggart. I wasn't strong enough. Tears fell from my eyes, clouding my vision. Zane pulled me up from the floor, where I had once again found my body. He dropped me on the cot. His actions confused me. To another, they would think he was forceful, but his movements made it, so I didn't feel pain.

He placed his hands on my throat. I instinctively grabbed his wrists with both my hands. Zane leaned down to my ear—the one not exposed to the camera surveying the room. "Pretend I'm hurting you."

What?

I didn't understand what was going on, but when he pushed against my throat, I assisted by sliding up toward the wall. He briefly winked. I held on tightly to his hands as he lifted me from the cot to the far wall, away from the camera view. Knowing he wasn't there to hurt me, I relaxed.

"We have little time," he whispered.

I nodded.

He looked toward the door. "They'll be here soon. Don't tell them anything, Rayne. Don't give up the others. Don't let them know about Rome." He sighed, shaking his head. "I can get Seaa out of here by faking her death, but I can't save you, Rayne."

Tears fell from my eyes, knowing I would endure this hell over and over again for God knows how long. But I didn't care. I would do anything for my family. The family I had left. At the risk of dying in this place, I would take Zane's deal. I nodded once more.

"Save her. Promise me she'll get out of here."

He nodded, his eyes averting to the side. I saw his ears move, and then he slapped me. When I looked up again, two operatives came in and grabbed either side of him. General Braggart stood behind them.

"Let me go," Zane yelled at the operatives.

General Braggart walked in and assessed the situation. "Operative Mueller, what are you doing in here?"

Zane turned to face the General with a different expression than he had shown me. "The bitch needs to pay, General." He turned the disgust on me. "Their kind killed my friend. They need to pay!"

The General nodded as if he understood the entire situation.

How could he show such a lack of remorse at the idea his son could be dead?

"Mr. Mueller, Rayne is under my authority, and I allow no one into her confinement unless authorized by me. Such a mistake, dear boy, especially after just barely leaving your last punishment."

Zane tried to pull free from the two operatives holding on to him as if coming at me with revenge. I played my part by sliding away from him, closer toward the wall.

"You can't deny me this, General." He looked up at Braggart. "Give me anything, please."

The General nodded to the operatives to remove him from the room. I watched as he fought their hold but made no dangerous moves to be unhanded until he reached the front of Seaa's door. He growled and rose from their clutches like a beast. The two operatives flew from his side. The General called in for support. I watched as he tore through Seaa's door and strangled her. My heart pounded again. I held my breath, hoping he was creating a show as he had with me.

Seaa grabbed on to his wrists. I tried to slide out the door, but Braggart held me back. I had no strength in me to hurt the man, and he knew it. So, I cried out for Seaa, pleading for them to stop. The other agents ran into the room to stop him, but it must have been too late. Seaa didn't move. She lay crumpled on the floor of her cell. I cried louder. The operatives slammed Zane against the wall as he bared his fangs. Trevor came around the corner. He looked at the mess and shot Zane with a weapon, concluding he was the threat. I watched Zane drop to the floor in a crumpled mess of limbs.

Braggart's lieutenant ran into my cell to discuss matters with the General. He took one look at me and had the soldier lift me from the floor and drop me onto the cot. Braggart walked with the man and closed the door behind them. I screamed and cried as I got off the bed and slammed my hands against the glass. I yelled profanities. I struck my fists against the glass again. If Zane would get himself killed for what he did for us, then I would play along as much as I could.

If I had one person to ally myself to in this place, I would take it.

I prayed this worked and prayed Zane wouldn't meet great judgment because of it.

Sector Bravo
Safe Haven Headquarters
Roman Braggart
ID: MIL 116.002

THE METAL FRAME groaned under my weight. The mattress squeaked as I moved from side to side, trying to find a comfortable spot. Unfortunately, I had trouble feeling any comfort right now. It wasn't about the room. I could lie on a bed of sharp nails and be alright as long as Rayne was in the vicinity. Frustrated I couldn't head back into the base and remove her from danger, I turned again, eventually giving up to stare at the ceiling above me. Zane had something to do with it, and I wasn't sure what would pull my friend off the private sector and place him in genetic retrieval.

Before I could think more of it, I heard loud voices outside the door which then disappeared down the hall. Giving up sleep, I threw the cover off me. I grabbed a pair of pants I had hanging over a chair and put them on. Before I could get the belt latched up, I had the door open and walked down the hall toward the sound of people. I ran a hand through my hair, pulling it away from my eyes. Turning the corner, I ran right into a woman I didn't recognize, with short red hair. The stranger slammed into my bare chest. I grabbed her by the shoulder and helped peel her off me.

"You good?"

She blinked several times, trying to form coherent words when Beatrice came up behind her. "Suzanne, sorry for being late. Please, let me take you to get cleaned up."

She had grime and blood all over her and some slight scrapes on her arms. I looked up at Beatrice. "Who's she?"

Beatrice looked down at Suzanne and then back at me.

Instead, Suzanne answered for herself. "My name is Suzanne. I'm a friend of Cameron's."

Cameron.

"Cameron as in Cam, the Chameleon?"

Beatrice nodded, pointing to the noise with her chin. "I have to take Suzanne to get cleaned up, so make your way to the common area."

I was about to leave when I noticed something other than how she looked right now was off with Suzanne. Not placing any further thought on it, I walked toward the loud voices. The open area was full of all the residents of Safe Haven. Silk sat against the wall with arms folded in front of her. I couldn't tell anything from her face. I never could when it involved the black widow. She was angry or straight-faced. The only time the woman showed tenderness was when it involved Rayne from what I could tell.

Thunder turned around as I approached the group. "What's going on?" I asked.

Everyone else turned to face me. Cam saw what everyone looked at, and when our eyes met, he pulled out a weapon and placed it on my forehead with the speed of one of my own batch. One side of my mouth lifted as I stared Cam down. This incident wasn't the first time I'd had a gun placed to my face, and it wouldn't be the last.

There was a lot I wanted.

For the first time, I wanted more than the orders they made me obey in the military. I wouldn't go down as smooth as Cam thought I would. To make it much clearer to the man holding the weapon, I swerved to one side. Then I dipped underneath Cam's arms and made it behind him with my blade at Cam's throat before the man could move away.

Cam may have been the foremost authority for camouflage and disappearing acts, but that was where his abilities ended. Cameron had the same enhanced skills the other members of the first batch had, but his abilities diminished as his camouflage usage increased. I was a lot stronger right now and a heck of a lot faster. Judging by the tension in his body, Cam knew it too.

"How the hell did you find this place?"

I dropped my hunter's knife. This simple piece of defense had been constructed with a metal that could cut through anything. All my weapons were custom to assist in genetic retrieval. "I was brought in."

Cameron looked at the rest of the group, who didn't argue with me.

"You guys let this asshole in here?"

Thunder spoke first. "A lot has happened since you left, Cam."

I stepped farther away from Cameron and crossed my arms, as Thunder explained.

"Rome is allied with Rayne, who has returned to us in recent weeks. But she has gone missing, and we are trying to determine how to go about finding her."

The newcomer turned to Thunder. "You let this bastard into our stronghold? Hold up. Did you say Rayne has been found?" Cam sought everyone's expressions before he said, "I thought she was lost to us during the escape. Wait, you lost her again?"

Guy cut in. "Not cool, Cam."

Cam shrugged as if to say he didn't quite give a damn about hurting feelings and turned to me again. "So, you are here with Rayne? And you were also the one hunting us down."

Finding it the perfect time to open his mouth once more, Guy grinned as he replied with, "Rome's in love with Rayne."

That brought out another guttural growl from Hail.

I had stayed away from Hail since Rayne's disappearance. Neither one of us liked the fact we were each other's competition.

"Hold on a second." Cam put a finger up to emphasize his words. "You betrayed the military and your father because you fell in love with Hail's girl?"

Cam thought it funny, but I didn't think the situation was at all humorous. The room got louder as each person spoke over the other to add fuel to the fire.

"That is enough," Thunder called out.

The group got silent. I had seen obedience in the military, but this type of compliance was brought on by trust and respect versus fear and intimidation.

"Cam, what have you found out?"

Cameron immediately flew into detail about the information the woman Suzanne had gotten for him about Unit 13's headquarters. The woman who had bumped into me earlier was blind. She couldn't see, but she compensated by having "eyes" all over the districts. Her people would contact her with out-of-character situations, and she would relate them to her paying customers. The bunker had a particular unit frequenting once a month for dead body procurement. The retrieval had continually been on the same day and at the same time. However, they noticed the truck leave the second facility this time and head toward the bunker out of ordinary route schedules.

More in-depth knowledge came back with word it was for a fish-like human female, and the entire group in front of me worked themselves into an uproar. To even hear Seaa may be dead caused the group to divide their options of getting her body from a dead body transport.

We had built the facility in Alpha as a second home to Project Hercules scientists and some of the armed forces. The difference this facility had from the one housing super soldiers was that it held the equipment necessary to break down a genetics body. That place was likewise the spot where Braggart liked to have his autopsies conducted. Each genetically enhanced human signed on to have their bodies opened to help the scientists figure out what was first to stop working in different death scenarios.

If they wanted to provide Seaa with a proper funeral, then we needed to work together and get her before she entered those ominous double doors leading into the high-tech facility in Alpha. Once inside, there was no way of getting her out unless you worked there. The facility wasn't like the one housing my former soldiers and friends. That one contained things that could only bring you nightmares. I shivered thinking about it. Hearing the group throw out one idea after another, I joined the fray and voiced my thoughts.

"Listen up."

The group turned to look at me. The majority told me to shove off, that this "had nothing to do with me," but if they planned to rescue Seaa's body from the second facility, it did.

"I'm not anyone's fan here. I know that. Personally, I could give two shits about any one of you." I punctuated by looking at each one in the eye. "Nonetheless, I will do anything for Rayne."

Hail scowled at me. "Oh, please, don't go out of your way."

"I had a few minutes to spare," I threw back.

"You self-righteous son of a..."

Snow jumped in between me and Hail, holding back his brother from taking a swing at me. Not knowing whether Rayne was in danger made me reckless. I wasn't careful about what I said or what I did. The tension was boiling over within me. This situation had done more to me than I wanted to admit.

I sighed, running another hand through my hair. "The facility DBT takes the bodies to a place built to hold unnatural things inside you guys can't even imagine. If you want to get her body, it has to be as the DBT is en route."

Thunder placed a hand on Hail's chest. Hail relaxed, and I was once again intrigued to observed the respect and comfort they get from their eldest brother and leader.

"Rome, can you recommend the safest spot for an ambush?"

I put a hand to my chin and looked up. I thought of the usual route the transport took for body disposals and got an idea. "Sector Alpha holds the second facility, but Alpha is government district and surrounded by Ground Force and military officers."

"We know that genius," Hail interrupted.

I grinned. "But I bet you didn't know someone built secret tunnels right before you get to Alpha. If you travel past Ashur where the Southern Camp was once located, you will find an independent cluster of buildings in The Waste that have housed the general populace of squatters. General Braggart thought the tunnels from below those buildings to Alpha could safely transport Unit 13 incapacitated captures or..." I left the rest to their imagination.

"Why would he transport to Alpha's second facility versus taking them to Foxtrot where the Bunkers and first facility are?"

I shook my head. "He wouldn't take captures to Foxtrot without implanting them first in Alpha."

"Implant?" They all questioned at once.

I put my hands up, a sign I meant no harm. I walked to the center of the group toward Hail. Hail's body hardened about ready to pummel me when Thunder cleared his throat. The man in front of me visibly relaxed. The rest of the group hovered around us, waiting to see what I would do. Gesturing for his arm, Hail looked at me quizzically once and then at Thunder. Witnessing the go-ahead from his brother, Hail dropped his wrist on my extended hand. I lifted Hail's arm over his head, exposing the underside of his armpit to the rest of the group when I pulled back the sleeve of his loose sweater.

Under the arm, embedded in the skin right before the axilla, were three gray lines about half an inch long each. General Braggart's scientists created a neurotoxin, assuring compliance when subjected to the brachial artery, which connected to the rest of the arteries in the blood system. Placing it in the underarm forced anyone captured or being transported to do precisely as they're told. Each shot held a person submissive for about twenty-four hours. If Hail received three, it meant he was a lot more trouble for the team after I had dropped him off for prison transport.

"Each of these bands sends neurotransmitters through the bloodstream, which control mobility until you arrive at Foxtrot and are tortured for answers or brainwashed."

Hail dropped his arm, pulling away from me. "Why not keep these bad boys in or knock us out?"

"First, they don't last long. Also, think about it. Would you honestly risk not taking all measures possible to submit a genetic human?"

No one answered me, but they knew I was right. Braggart didn't take chances, especially unnecessary ones. "If Seaa is dead, it's because torturous methods didn't work, and brainwashing failed on her. I've fought Seaa; she is incredibly tough—both mentally and physically. The brainwashing methods may not have worked on her."

"You saying I'm incompetent and capable of being brainwashed?" Hail asked.

Everyone in the room, besides Cam, probably thought the same thing. Hail got brainwashed, but not for the reasons he may believe. "Hail, you were already mentally susceptible to brainwashing." I looked at Silk, who was still listening against the wall. "Silk mentioned you didn't lose hope Rayne was alive. Being in such a frantic search for her all these years weakened your mind."

Hail didn't respond. He resembled a dog with his tail between his legs because Rayne's disappearance drove his alteration, and her return brought him back out.

"Look, if you want to ambush the truck, I recommend you do it right before the buildings where the tunnels are held. The soldiers will immediately retreat to the buildings housing the tunnels to take refuge. You will expect less backlash from them if they feel they have a safety net nearby."

Thunder nodded and looked at the rest of the group. He called out his plan, and no one complained about what their orders were. The room cleared when Thunder turned to Silk and then to me. "Both of you, here."

I walked over to Thunder, but Silk didn't look at all pleased.

"Silk, I need you to return Gavin to his home and stay there to watch over him in the meantime."

"Absolutely not."

Thunder ran a hand down his face. "Just do as I ask."

Silk balled her hands into fists at her sides. "I'm not staying in his home. I will watch from afar."

Thunder didn't argue but took a moment to turn and face me. "Please assist them. You don't have to stay long and can meet up with the rest in the desert after you drop them off. With everything going on, I don't need another person going missing."

"Aw, you care."

One eyebrow came up to hide behind the man's long blond hair. "Don't push it, Roman."

I grinned as the big man walked away and left me alone with the black widow. I turned to talk to her, but she was already giving me the cold shoulder and making her way down the hall toward her room. Gavin wasn't present at today's little pow-wow, so I made a pit stop in my room to grab some gear and a shirt and walked to the boy's room to give him a heads-up my original plan had changed.

THESE TWO GENETIC super-beings drove me bat-shit

crazy. If they weren't throwing insults at one another, they were about ready to rip each other's throats out with their bare hands. I already wasn't super thrilled to be walking in the dark with two people who could rip me in half faster than I could scream. The beautiful Silk walked ahead of me in a pair of tight, black leggings and a similarly colored tunic with white lines coming down the sides. Her hair was left out and wild as it usually was inside the compound. She climbed over another boulder, ignoring the fact I hadn't been built for this kind of extreme hiking.

Rome was a little bit more courteous with my lack of coordination and leg power. He climbed the same boulder she had and reached down to help pull me up. We were near Trēbeta after traversing the maze of underground tunnels connecting Sector Bravo with Sector Charlie—an exhausting forty-minute walk. In one way, my blood burned knowing Silk would be nearby to watch over me; in another, I shuddered, closing my eyes, afraid I'd get eaten alive by the black widow they so lovingly named. I got the heebie-jeebies, muttering an incomprehensible sound from my mouth. The thought scared the bejeezus out of me.

We turned down what we thought would have been an abandoned alley, only to find six Ground Force officers decked out in their law enforcement regalia surrounded us. Rome immediately pulled his arm back and ushered me to stand behind him. I didn't argue. I may be wicked smart on a computer, but I was nowhere near capable of fighting a Ground Force patrol-man. I saw Silk stiffen a few feet away from Rome. She gave off an incredible amount of fierce, wild energy that made the air around us harder to breathe in.

"Sweetheart, you got this?"

Silk turned around and practically cut Rome into tiny pieces—starting with his manhood—with her eyes. I heard Rome laugh, getting the reaction he wanted. Silk didn't even respond. She took two steps toward the nearest officers.

"I told you, fellas, these three were trouble. Surrender your identification and any weapons you may be carrying."

The black widow smirked. Rome took two steps back, and I had no choice but make them too. Before I could look back around Rome's massive body, Silk was already on the move. Her speed got her close to the nearest two and had their heads knocking together like two clackers on Newton's Cradle. I flinched when I heard the awful sound of bone cracking. The patrolman passed out on the floor. The other three approached with their Vuwands lit up at maximum voltage. Silk ran to the next man and threw him against a wall. She flipped over the other one with complete ease and spun him back to fall on top of the last one.

The one who hit the wall got up, and before he could take one step forward, she was already hooking him on a protruding iron rod. The man dangled from the metal. He couldn't move from the spot no matter how much he squirmed. When the other two got up, Silk had two discarded Vuwands in her hands and lit them up at her sides. The two remaining men took several steps back into a corner. She extended her arms and lit up the guards. I took a large swallow to clear the lump in my throat.

She scared and intrigued me all at the same time.

The deadly woman broke the wands in half. She dropped them on the ground and turned to face us. "Call me sweetheart one more time, and you'll meet a fate worse than them."

In one minute, she was across the alley and the next, right in front of Rome's face. I gave the guy cred-it. The man didn't even flinch.

"Clear?"

"Crystal," Rome replied.

She moved. Rome looked back at me and smiled as if we shared our own personal joke. I sure as heck wouldn't try to get on Silk's bad side, so the joke was on Rome if he thought I would be any help to him. We walked a little bit more, coming up to the street my building was on. I looked down the quiet road. At this time of night, most residents were nestled in bed. I noticed my building had doubled its front guards.

I wonder.

I knew Rome would stay back and watch from afar until Silk took me back inside to make sure the coast was clear. However, I knew security was tight in my building, and the only women who came through, looked like hookers. I stared at Silk. She looked like a death goddess ready to cause mayhem.

So, I cleared my throat. "Uh, I think you'll need a disguise, Silk."

She narrowed her eyes at me but said nothing.

"Um, the guard is used to seeing me walk inside with flamboyant female companions, and right now, you look about ready to murder someone, and with all those guards..."

Rome coughed to hide his laugh.

"Female companions, huh?"

I could feel the blush reach my cheeks and spread out throughout my entire face. I felt the need to assure her I didn't have sex with them. I invited them over to appease my father or make others believe I was a man of interest. But there was no point in saying any of that to her. Silk wouldn't care and could very well not give a damn. Instead, I looked at the cloud-covered sky.

"Maybe we should get you a disguise somewhere."

"No need," she replied.

Both Rome and I stared curiously. Silk closed her eyes and stood there. Not long after, her hair turned a bright shade of gold. Her spiral tresses straightened. Her shirt manipulated as well and became a pastel purple, with frills on both shoulders. The leggings she wore turned into purple fishnet stockings with attached shorts covering everything else. Both of us dropped our jaws. Like a white-banded crab spider, Silk changed the coloring and style of her clothes and features.

"Holy shit, Silk. It wasn't in the reports you could do this."

Silk turned to look at Rome. Her eyes were once dark with the sexiest beauty mark by her right eye, but now her eyes were green, and the beauty mark disappeared. She still looked like her pure form, except for the subtle here and there differences.

"There is a lot about me you don't know."

"I like you better the other way," I muttered without thinking.

When the group greeted me with silence, and I received a playful shove from Rome's elbow, is when I realized I had uttered the words out loud. Silk didn't respond. Clearing my throat and pulling my foot out my mouth, I patted Rome on the arm and walked away. I felt Silk walk behind me. She had made it to my side, and the moment she did, I took advantage of the situation and grabbed her silky hand in mine. She grimaced and went to pull it away. Her eyes told me I had seconds before she'd break my fingers off.

"For the guards," I whispered.

She didn't pull away again and stared straight ahead. I realized two things at once. One: I held the black widow's hand and would still live one more day, and two: I was most definitely, one hundred percent, captivated by this woman.

CHAPTER TWENTY-FOUR

Sector Foxtrot
Project Hercules Prison
General Brockton Braggart

I WATCHED FROM a spot at the end of the room as two of my assistants strapped my Rayne on a medical gurney inside of the experimentation wing. We were damn close to getting Rayne to cooperate, but since my soldier got ballsy and killed off our best tool, I would now move forward with brainwashing her. After screwing up Hail's dosage, Dr. Plumboy assured me there would be no problems this time around.

The young woman had incredible abilities. Rayne could melt down her particles. It excited the scientists to see what would make her tick, which was the reason I allowed my soldiers to break her down so badly. But I was more interested in getting my little

Rayne back where she belonged. I'd have a physically perfect experiment with superb abilities.

Once strapped into the cot, the two assistants moved away and allowed Dr. Plumboy to approach his new guinea pig. I rarely sat in for these experiments, but I wanted to make sure none of these idiots would alter her perfection. Plumboy took her readings and checked the wounds on her body. Most had already healed, and none were severe enough to cause extensive physical damage.

I made sure of it.

"Would you like the normal output, General Braggart?"

"Yes, I think we broke her enough."

With Seaa, regular was not enough to alter her mind. She was too strong-willed to become submissive. Hail wasn't so hard to place under our control, but it was easy enough for him to break from it. Seaa was another matter altogether. Rayne saw her sister beaten to death—literally. My Rayne additionally received her rounds of torture. If I weren't so peeved with operative Mueller, I would've thanked him for assisting in her mental breakdown. Zane received considerable punishment for his actions and an additional thirty days in solitary confinement. I hated disobedience. Couldn't tolerate insubordination. But Mueller was one of my best, and with Roman gone, I needed someone to take his place.

A trickle of excitement coursed through the veins

in my body. Rayne lay on the gurney, unaware of how she would wake up and who she would end up adoring. For years, my obsession over her never yielded or diminished. She was more beautiful to me than any of those other creatures created in our lab. She belonged to me.

Dr. Plumboy sent an electrical shock to Rayne's temples. Her entire body liquefied into a puddled mess on the bed. The action didn't last long. Her whole body ran back together like magnetized water. Each drop found its way around the sheets—not one bit absorbed into the cloth. Rayne's body and clothing came right back together as if nothing had ever happened. Like her genetic accomplice Hail, their bodies transmuted into abilities unlike my second batch of testers.

Dr. Richard Plumboy fiddled with his instruments—a trivial matter I was not interested in. All I wanted to see were the results. I watched with amusement as Dr. Plumboy injected Rayne with the mutated genome that would increase the power of her mysterious ability and heighten most of her senses. Rayne would become a dedicated soldier once more, and I'd have her by my side for as long as humanly possible. My scientist worked, and I watched in pure bliss. In a few more hours, Rayne would be at my beck and call.

THERE WAS A lot of noise going on around me that caused my ears to ring. Behind my eyelids, I could tell the light in the room shone above me. I tried to move my arms, but something pinned them down at my sides. My eyes shot open, and I blinked against their sensitivity to the light. After adjusting, I noticed the bands around my wrists and pulled again.

Why can't I remember my name?

A bright flash lit up the room, and I squeezed my eyes shut. After a second, images and words filtered through my mind like snapshots to the past.

My name.

My purpose.

My mission.

Everything came back to me all at once. I was a soldier fighting for Project Hercules.

But If I am a soldier, then why am I tied down to this bed?

"I see you are finally awake."

I turned my face to the side to watch General Brockton Braggart slowly approach my bed. My mind flashed with several images of the General giving empowering speeches, his courageous efforts, and the allegiance he'd earned from his soldiers. For some odd reason, my memories lacked life, but they were still my memories—a deep ache built in my chest. I must've done awfully to earn the look of caution on his face and banded wrists and ankles.

"General Braggart..."

Uttering his name brought shivers down my spine.

Is the fear of repercussion for my actions, whatever they were, making me feel this way?

I pulled on the bands again, trying to remember what I had done wrong.

"Do you recall the reasons for you being here, Rayne?"

I tried to remember the reason. All I could come up with were images of General Braggart and his purpose. Our purpose. The world was in jeopardy, and the small sectors we had left were the only things we needed to protect. The soldiers were necessary to protect the citizens from foreign warfare and rogue soldiers—rogue genetic soldiers. My mission was to eliminate the threat of genetic soldiers from Batch 001 of Unit 13 betraying Project Hercules and all it stood for.

My eyelids fluttered, so I looked back at the General. He stood with two other soldiers behind him. I could sense they weren't as strong as me. These soldiers weren't operatives like I was, but they carried weapons that could subdue me at a moment's notice.

"Did I betray you, General?"

His mouth rose on one side, hiding behind his thick, curled mustache. "You have. However, you can make amends, Rayne. Do you think you can make me proud again?"

During our training, we were taught the human brain process has two mindsets—fixed and growth. The fixed portion of my brain is made to hold the strands of my intelligence, creativity, and personality. This part of my mind remains static at all times with intermediate changes and only succeeds as confirmation of my intuitive perceptions. This static mindset tells me that to be successful, I must not fail. This part of my mind processed the information General Braggart asked of me. I didn't want to abandon him again. To seek favor, I needed to succeed in my missions.

Yet, the other part of the brain, the one harboring the growth mindset, said I wasn't a failure because I didn't succeed. That portion of my mind told me I was intelligent, and I could bounce from my past failures—whatever they were—toward success. The growth portion also said to me there was something a lot more wrong here than I thought. That part of my mind expressed something more profound troubled me. Something so intense I needed to dig straight toward the beginning point of this deficiency and strive above it.

What is bothering me so much?

I shook away my thoughts, feeling the weight of my heart crush my chest the moment I replied with: "Yes, General. I will not fail again. I promise to do as you say."

And I wouldn't fail.

They removed the bands from my wrists and ankles. There was a chaotic blur in my head, but I would look past it and do what I needed to do to win. I could feel the General's eyes on my back as they escorted me from the room with bright white walls and spotless floors. There was a tight feeling of emptiness in my chest, but I ignored it in favor of showing my creator I was not capable of failing him again.

Machinery filled up every space against the walls, while the counters held different medicinal formulas in a variety of bright colors. A shudder raced through me that said I didn't want to find myself back in this room.

I studied the interior of the facility, feeling a wave of nostalgia and longing for someone, but I couldn't recall who. There was a room dedicated to working out and another farther down tested operatives on treadmills. The scientists and soldiers who walked around the pristine hallways all pressed themselves against the walls as we moved past. Everyone avoided eye contact with General Braggart and looked at me with awe and disgust. I couldn't understand what I had done that would make them so upset.

"General," I began.

Braggart turned around to face me. The rest of the entourage stopped walking to surround the mighty general. I noted how the other guards had placed their hands on their weapons and how the operatives roaming the hall stopped in their spots to watch. Many in this facility very much favored the General, and their actions told me I had not earned enough of their trust.

"Rayne, do you wish to talk to me?"

I felt pressure behind my eyes. My insides felt strained. "Have I done something so terrible others are displeased with?"

Brockton Braggart took a step closer to me. I didn't have to look around me to hear how many of them had pulled their weapons out and aimed them at my head.

"You did terrible things, Rayne. You must do all you can to earn our trust once more." He placed one hand on my shoulder and squeezed.

The simple touch made my entire body pulse and virtually reel back in disgust. A well-trained soldier gave nothing away. I stayed put as his hand lingered a little longer. Braggart's other hand rested on my other arm. If it were anyone else, I would've broken their wrist off. For now, I feigned how I felt and listened to the General speak.

He dropped one hand to his side and used the other to twirl his mustache. "I don't give many second chances, soldier. Do not disappoint me again."

I nodded and watched as he walked down the hall. So, I followed like a good soldier and obeyed like a well-trained dog. Whatever the General wanted, I would provide him. My concerns no longer mattered.

The mission was to make General Brockton Braggart proud of me. The rest of the people in the interior continued on their way, and the mollified guards moved their hands from their weapons. I sensed I didn't belong to this group but knew I needed to make things right again no matter what it took from me to do so.

A few hours later, I was being circled by a hungry man with dark green hair and scuffed cowboy boots. I remembered from the files stored in my brain he was an operative like me. Operative Trevor Dallas walked around me as if measuring up his prey. I could feel the goosebumps litter my flesh with their tiny sensors alerting me of his every move and penetrating gaze. Something about his existence disturbed me, but he was my partner. Still, he was ready to tear me into bits should I fail in subduing him first.

Operative Dallas sprang forward with hands extended in front of him. Everything around me slowed down. I could see a panoramic view of my surroundings and the open spots in his posture allowing me to get in a good hit and jump back out unscathed. I relished the opportunity and jumped in. The movement quickened once more. I ducked under his right arm and slid around by dragging my left leg. It ended with an uppercut to the ribcage. Trevor hunched over. A large breath of air rushed from his mouth.

I had already moved away. So, I watched as he gathered himself and straightened to his full six-foot-three-inches. The crowd gathering around us cheered, but I ignored them. If I looked away for one moment, he would have me on the ground—battered and beaten to a bloody pulp. Trevor ran his hand through his green, tea-colored hair, which made the receding parts stand out more. He grimaced and drew his brows inward. Snuffing his nose with his thumb, operative Dallas moved closer. I stepped back but slipped and lost my balance. He took the opportunity to swing once. I didn't have enough time to block it. His hard fist made contact with my cheek, and everything exploded. The stars we were unable to see came to visit our headquarters. Electrified, I felt the pain shoot down my entire body—the stars disappearing one by one.

I felt like a failure for letting him put a hand on me. From his sour expression, General Braggart was not impressed operative Dallas could put a hand on me. The look of disappointment made me sick to my stomach. The pain forgotten, I made a promise to myself not to allow room for weaknesses. Trevor Dallas smiled from ear to ear. The man rubbed me the wrong way, and I couldn't understand why. Operative Dallas was my partner, and according to my memories, he had been for a long time. Although bothered, I ignored my wayward thoughts and focused on the fight before me.

The skin on my cheek swelled and tightened as I moved away from another incoming swing—more cheers from the crowd. Trevor's movements were quick, but I noticed he was reckless with his hits, preferring brute force over tactical shots. My mind filtered out everything else but him. My eyes shot to every surface of his body, seeking the weak points. I noticed he had moved closer as I studied his body. He made a swing for me again, but I walked away. This time I curled my fingers and thrust my palm into his nose. I blocked his other arm from swinging around and shoved my erect fingers into the clavicle below his neck. When he twisted his body in pain, I dropped to the ground and punched him in the kidneys.

And damn, it felt good.

Operative Trevor Dallas was now on the floor curled up in a ball, trying to control the pain in his body and his breathing. General Braggart smiled. Deep inside, I felt sick to my stomach. Although, something about how pleased it made him had me wanting to do it again. I was his soldier and creation. Sauntering over to Trevor, I reached down and lifted him off the floor in one strong pull. He looked at me askew but saw the General watched us both. Trevor dusted off his pants and walked away.

I watched him go, thinking of what he had hidden behind his eyes.

Before long, another operative, this one female, walked into the circle to spar with me. I turned around to bend at the waist in front of the woman then got into my fighting stance. The woman came in low and fast. I blocked and weaved my body around to avoid getting hit. The female operative swung toward my face. My hand shifted up to stop it. Instead, I received the female's fist into my palm. I enclosed the operative's fist with my own and twisted it at the wrist. The woman screamed when her wrist snapped. I looked at my hand, wondering how I caused so much damage to another operative built like me.

The doctor saw nothing wrong with the way my abilities ran rampant. I couldn't agree with him. Operatives should be able to take hits from one another. For me to break the woman's wrist so quickly meant I had more strength than some of the rest.

What am I? Am I an abomination or... something else?

However, thoughts of the room with its unbending scientists and extravagant equipment filled me with dread.

The woman got off the polished floor, ignoring the way her hand hung listlessly from the joint. I glanced at General Braggart, who called for me to finish the woman quickly. His intense stare and drawn brows told me to handle it. So, I did. I rushed forward. The female dropped to swing her leg around. I fell to the floor. My breath rushed out in one blow. The operative came over me, but I dodged her left blow by manipulating the waves in my body and turning into liquid. The woman struck the ground where I once lay and hollered. I had already gotten off the ground and materialized. All thoughts in my mind disappeared. I leaned down to grab the woman by the collar. Swinging the woman over my body, I watched as the momentum shot the operative toward the crowd.

She landed in the cheering crowd, causing some of them to grunt from the forced weight. The floor was cold. The air was brisk. I felt no warmth coming from the other soldiers. I felt no satisfaction in my win. And I couldn't ignore the way my body quivered in objection as the only heat I felt came from the General's glassy eyes. I didn't want to look at him.

Unexplainable energy came from his direction. I stalked over to the woman. The others around me moved away. There wasn't any mercy in my eyes or a fault in my step as I stalked closer. There was nothing but darkness enveloping every part within me. Feeling as if this woman deserved no less, I grabbed her from the floor and lifted her off the ground. The woman fought to remove my tight grip from her neck as her legs swung around in midair.

My insides ran around rampant. I couldn't linger on one emotion long enough before I felt a different way. Deep inside it felt wrong, but that uneasiness would change to assertiveness. A well-trained soldier does not allow room for weakness. I knew better than to let anyone try to make me feel inferior because I was a product trained to fight and win.

All of those rogue feelings disappeared as my body raged stronger than before. Then something inside me snapped.

The key to pleasure comes from their pain.

I squeezed tighter—distantly watching as the woman turned different shades of red, purple, and blue. Deep inside, I had an overwhelming desire to end the woman's life. My primary goal was to please my creator.

General Braggart yelled out to me, "Finish her!"

I would not end up in that medical wing again or disappoint my General. The woman gasped for air. The other agents ran forward to tackle me down. My grip on the woman didn't budge. Bodies rushed me from different directions but couldn't do a damn thing to push me. Hordes of people hovered over us. Some chanted in excitement. Others sang in fear. I ignored it all.

The female received no kindness from me. There was no room in Unit Thirteen for weaklings.

I would not disappoint Braggart.

The woman's body drooped, so I dropped her on the ground. Operatives and guards rushed to move the others out of the way. The General stood at the head of the group, pleased I followed instructions. I could not feel any pride at the moment or gather any kind of remorse.

There was nothing but numbness.

I watched as if from a distance the scene in front of me. Doctors jumped into the fray. They hovered around the woman, performing acts to revive her. Through the chaos in front of me, I heard my creator's voice call out for me.

Like a well-oiled machine, I walked over to him. I allowed him to pet me on the head. "Good job, my little pet."

Trevor Dallas ran past a few people and toward our group. "She killed her?"

I wanted to respond, but he didn't direct the question at me. General Braggart laughed with a hand to his stomach. I made him proud of my progress.

"Of course, she did. I told her to do so, and she complied perfectly."

There was caution when Trevor looked at me again. He held me at arm's length. The man didn't trust me but still didn't distrust me. I wasn't here to make friends or to please anyone else but my General. I saw Trevor bend down to whisper in the General's ear. I could easily reach my hearing to listen to what he had to say but would not do so unless General Braggart ordered me to.

Dr. Plumboy came into our little circle from around two guards. "The program was a success I take it." He turned to face me. "How do you feel, my dear?"

I turned to face the doctor. "I feel nothing."

The doctor grinned, and the General laughed again.

"She works perfectly," the doctor stated.

General Braggart grinned widely. "Of course, she does. Rayne's my daughter, after all."

CHAPTER TWENTY-FIVE

The Waste
Somewhere near Sector Alpha
Roman Braggart
ID: MIL 116.002

SNOW FELL ON top of us like a layer of clean kindness from the heavens. The ground beneath us shifted with our weight as the four of us knelt side by side in the desolate space before us. Menacing grey clouds didn't compare to the soothing, brilliant white flakes flittering toward the ground. The building 1 pointed out to the group loomed over us in a crumbling, tainted mess. Throughout the years, residents had graffitied the cement structure with traitorous verbiage and uncivilized drawings. The road had already washed away, but the tread marks of the caravan holding the DBT permanently engraved the stone and dirt like fossils found in untouched places.

The military refused to use hovercrafts for dead body transports. By using road terrain vehicles, Braggart felt assured his carriers couldn't get stolen. Although resilient and fast, hovercrafts got hacked. Braggart kept a few all-terrain vehicles in his arsenal because of it.

From a distance, I could hear the roaring engine approaching our location. I made a signal with my hands to notify the others in the group—Snow, Guy Gust, and Rock—the vehicle we were waiting for rapidly approached. I hoped everything went off without a hitch.

With Rock's ability to blend in so perfectly next to the enormous dust-covered boulders in the vast, expansive desert, we watched as he crossed over to the rock and knelt behind it. The plan wasn't a simple one, but it was the best we could come up in such a short amount of time. I not only heard the vehicle approach, but I could see it coming over the horizon. Guy Gust got up and ran away from the group as we had planned. He would conjure up all of the sand and create a whiteout effect to limit the visibility of the guards and operatives traveling in the vehicle. It left Snow and me together.

The sand lifted around us in a cloud of orange and reddish-brown bits. Snow and I lifted bandanas over our mouth and nose. With goggles protecting our eyes from the hazardous sand, we waited until Rock did the next step. The vehicle slowed down but drove through the sandstorm mixed with snow. I could feel the earth underneath us rumble as it approached. When it was close enough, I waited to hear the familiar sound of crushing metal. The noise assaulted our ears. Both of us ran toward the vehicle. Rock lifted the front of the truck. I maneuvered to the passenger door and punched the man trying to run out of the four-by-four. Snow ran to the back of the DBT and broke open the doors.

I watched as Snow kneed one man in the face and went to grab a large bag with his hands. A blunt object hit me from behind. My entire body lit up, and I writhed in pain. The sand and rocks abraded my exposed flesh, but the precipitation relieved it. I rolled over long enough to see Rock drop the front of the transport and gather the operative who had assaulted me within his arms. Rock squeezed him long enough to cause the man to shudder and drop to the floor, unconscious. The big man came around to lift me from the ground, for which I was grateful, although I felt somewhat emasculated. Rock turned us toward the chaos. With Guy's sandstorm still holding up, it was hard to see anything unless it was within close range.

When my body slammed into the vehicle, Rock growled, "Get up, you damn pansy," and bounded off to help Snow.

I tried to shake off the volts running through my body.

Did Rock call me a pansy? If I could move my body right now, I'd show the man what this pansy could do.

Until then, I waited for the tremors to stop before I could help the rest of the group. The sound of footsteps crunched on the surface of the desert floor. The steps moved farther and farther away. Able to gather stability in my legs, I turned toward the front of the vehicle to see through a brief clearing some soldiers and an operative had run toward a deconstructed building with a body bag in tow.

I turned in time to see Snow and Rock writhing on the floor as I had moments ago.

Now, who's the pansy?

Guy stopped the storm and blocked the men from entering the building. When I reached them, Guy was in hand-to-hand combat with the operative, while the rest of the soldiers dragged a body bag through a narrow opening on the side of a crumbling wall.

I ran toward the guards, leaving Guy to handle the operative on his own. My mission wasn't to protect the guys, but to get Seaa back to the compound. The soldiers were out of sight until I turned another corner and spotted them down the peeling hall hinting of urine and sweat. I needed to get to them before they made it underground. Once inside the old subway tunnels, we wouldn't get a better chance at grabbing her body. Shots rang in the interior. The men were desperate. I grabbed a piece of fallen concrete and threw it at the soldier carrying Seaa's body. Like bowling pins, I saw them topple over one another in their haste.

More shots fired. The bullet penetrated my flesh but didn't go far before it dropped to the floor. The soldiers noticed I wasn't a regular human, switching to their custom weapons. I wouldn't allow them to get a good hit this time. I avoided one round and approached them right before they cocked their new guns. Each soldier took turns trying to subdue me, but my intensity made it difficult for them to get very far. Two got knocked against the brick, and another was kicked away from me. Two soldiers ran down the hall with Seaa's body long forgotten in their haste to escape. Two more lay on the ground unconscious, so I stalked the one I had kicked. The man crab-walked away from me. I grabbed his weapon and aimed it at the backs of the two running off. With one shot, I brought both down at once.

One man fell over face first, and the other bounced off the wall and landed right-side-up on the ground. I couldn't afford them going back to my father and telling him I lived. I preferred anonymity. The one in front of me covered his face, pleading with me not to kill him. They more than likely didn't give Seaa or any of the other genetics from the first batch any kind of courtesy. I was about to take the shot when Snow and Rock came around the corner to stop me.

"Bring him in alive, Rome."

The man's eyes before me grew larger. He recognized my name, and if he went free, everyone else would know I was alive. "I'm not risking this piece of shit escaping and giving me up."

The man in question crawled farther away from us. He stopped and carefully looked over to see what obstruction was behind him. I saw the moment relinquishment crossed the soldier's face as he laid eyes on Rock. There was nowhere for him to go.

"The kid will not escape. We have what we came for and now have someone to bring in where Thunder can do what he sees fit."

Unappeased, I replied, "Fine. Whatever." I dropped the gun and lifted the body bag over my shoulder.

I walked away from the others and toward the exit. With all of the soldiers defeated, Snow started a fire and lit up a stick of dynamite. The building crumbled on one side. Smoke billowed above the mess in massive plumes of dark gray. I had ripped off my goggles with one hand and threw them on the ground as I ran back to our hidden ride. The last time I saw Seaa, Rayne had taken her away from the alley just like this. Funny how things came back around as they did. Her body hung limply over my shoulder and against my back. For the first time, I felt sorry for the poor woman who barely weighed a thing. I didn't know what torture she had undergone, but I could sure as hell guess it wasn't pleasant.

Sector Bravo
Safe Haven Headquarters

THE COMPOUND WAS a lot more hush than usual. The mood solemn. Not a word said to one another. I walked cautiously down the halls. The general gloom felt ten times thicker than it had before. Once inside the mess hall to grab some food, I spotted Beatrice sitting alone by a roaring fire. She dipped her spoon in and out of some gruel, barely paying mind to her meal. She said nothing, staring at the wall in front of her. I grabbed a piece of bread from the center of one table and walked over to her.

"You alright?"

The woman jumped. She stared at me with her one visible eye. The color on the patch she wore had faded. "You startled me," she replied.

I took a bite of the bread. No matter how hungry I was, the food sat heavy in my stomach. The mood in this place did not help me with my appetite. When I got back to the compound, I had taken Seaa's body into Dr. Ferdinand's clinic. The old man was buried under a pile of books belonging to Sebastian Lester. Dr. Lester had handed them over to Guy during the escape so long ago. I took a shower and had heard nothing else about it.

"I didn't mean to scare you. You okay?"

She turned to look at the fire as if seeing all of her problems crackle in flames. "Rock has been locked up in our room since y'all got back. All of us loved Seaa. She went off on her own, but we expected her to come back to us alive."

I nodded. The big guy was going through something and needed time to process. I could understand the feeling. "Did Dr. Ferdinand say anything about what killed Seaa?"

She shook her head. "I was going to eat and then go over there, but I guess I may have zoned out for a bit."

I got up from the table, leaving the rest of the bread uneaten. I extended my hand to her when I came around the table. Beatrice looked at it. "Want to go talk to Dr. Ferdinand?" I asked.

Beatrice wiped both of her hands on her clothes. She placed one in mine and got up from her seat. "Yeah, let's go. Maybe getting some answers for Rock would help him handle things better."

For the first time, I could sense how much the woman cared about the rock-like man. We walked in amicable silence through the stone interior until we reached the doctor's room. I heard the man shout from inside. Both Beatrice and I stared at one another, but I was the first to run inside. Dr. Ferdinand slammed into my chest. Beatrice squeaked as she bounced off my back. I steadied the doctor and looked over to the steel table where Seaa's body lay.

Seaa sat up with the sheet draped over her waist and down the sides of the table. She gasped for air. The doctor had gone as pale as a ghost. Beatrice screamed. All I could process at the moment was that Seaa was sitting up choking. I ran over to the woman whose blood-shot eyes were about to burst from her face. I didn't know what to do, so I lifted her from the table and ran toward the room we used to clean off our bodies. Once there, I dropped Seaa inside of the hydro chamber and closed the glass door. I pressed buttons in my panic. I didn't know what the heck I should do, but anything right now was better than nothing.

The chamber sprayed water.

I heard Beatrice gasp once more from behind me. But I couldn't turn around to face her. Seaa greedily sucked in the water. The scales all over her skin illuminated. It was the first time I ever noticed how beautiful the colors were on each scale gently covering parts of her body. When I turned around this time, Beatrice cried, and Dr. Ferdinand had finally gotten himself together long enough to grab a contraption for Seaa. The man approached the buttons of the hydro chamber and punched in a few digits as the rest of the group gathered at the doorway.

Their facial features were a mix between glee and shock. I couldn't relate to how they felt, but I could guess. The others came to understand the chaos going on in the room. Seaa had lived. She hadn't died in the facility.

How in the world did she make it out of there?

I took a couple of steps back when Dr. Ferdinand rushed ahead of me. The door shot open. Dr. Ferdinand knelt and attached an apparatus to the back of Seaa's neck, locking the ends around it. The technology was a silver, metal choker with glittering jewel-like lights.

She gasped—her face shooting up to the ceiling. Slowly, Seaa breathed in and out like a normal human being.

"Oh, thank goodness it works," Dr. Ferdinand exhaled.

The group cheered and pushed past me as they reached the woman. Beatrice threw a sheet over Seaa's exposed body. Knowing I was in the way, I moved to walk out of the room to leave them to rejoice on their own. The last thing I wanted to do was intrude on their moment. I was about to reach the door to the other room, when a raspy voice called out to me.

"He did this for you."

I turned around.

Hands came from every direction to help Seaa off the wet floor. Her once pale and flaking scales now seemed refreshed. They glimmered and shone as they reflected the lights of the interior. She didn't look like the fish woman I once had orders to apprehend. Seaa walked like a Roman goddess in front of me in the long white sheet hugging the curves of her body like a flowing gown. The parts exposing scales looked like adornments belonging to the make-shift dress. Her violet eyes shone brightly with tears.

"At first, 1 was surprised to see you. But you saved my life."

1 shook my head. "1 didn't do anything."

The people in the room parted to the side like the biblical Red Sea.

1 waved and walked out the door. Seaa must have moved quickly toward me because she held on to my hand, forcing me to stop.

"Please, explain what's going on."

1 pleaded with Thunder. He read the look in my eyes and came around to wrap his arm around the petite woman. 1 watched the large man envelope Seaa within his arms. She shook and cried. She cried hard and loud as if suppressing it inside for so long.

1 felt partly responsible.

To my credit, 1 thought what 1 had done was the right thing at first. 1 didn't realize all of the lies they fed me would come to light. Or that I'd fall for a woman 1 should've captured and come to depend on the kindness of those 1 had once sworn to apprehend. There were so many issues plaguing us. The problems continued to stack on top of one another—toppling over precariously.

Snow came around the corner and placed an arm around my shoulders. 1 glared at him, trying to muster up an excellent annoyed look, but failing.

Snow laughed. "Dude, Seaa is alive. You saved her life."

I had done nothing worth praising, so I shoved Snow's arm off me. The man whistled and laughed. I was about to turn the corner to get to my room; Thunder called for me. Seaa walked behind them in scrubs. Thunder said nothing else but beckoned me to follow into the Planning Room. I sighed. All I wanted to do was go to my room and think of a way to get Rayne back from my father. The rest of the group followed one another. I ran a hand through my hair. I didn't want to go in there. The one thing scaring me the most about walking into that room was hearing the worst news about my woman.

If Rayne...

I stopped thinking about the worst thoughts and squared my shoulders. When I walked into the room, everyone was already knee-deep in the discussion. So, I stood to the side of the group, leaning against the wall.

"I need everyone to stop talking and listen. We will first find out what we can from Seaa, and I will then relay what I learned from the captive," Thunder called out.

Seaa placed her clasped hands on the crippling conference room table. "As you already know, I was captured by Trevor Dallas and taken to Foxtrot."

The room remained silent, waiting for her to continue.

"I endured all types of torture in that facility. Hail..." She looked at the man in question. "I'm glad you are alive, Brother."

Hail nodded. A smile played about on his lips.

"They used him to break me. The torture they dealt us wasn't pleasant. When I heard Hail had been broken and brainwashed by Dr. Plumboy, I feared for everyone's safety here." She cleared her throat. "I was glad to learn brainwashing us only altered our emotions and thoughts. Kind of like starting with a clean slate."

Thunder moved about the room and took a seat opposite her.

Seaa continued. By this time, she had every single person's undivided attention. "Being there took all the strength I could muster to keep my wits about me. Still, I don't think I could have lasted much longer if your friend hadn't come to save me."

The news made heads pop up, and I noticed Seaa faced me. "I don't know why you switched sides, and I don't care. If my family thinks you can be trusted, then I will trust you too. Rayne, however..."

I pushed away from the wall at the mention of her name. There was no way to know what the future held for me or for that matter, all of us at this moment. Grief was a permanent tattoo on our skin. Rayne was the only balm I ever wanted. She was the only reason I fought.

"You love her, don't you?"

Hail did not bother to look back at me. Instead, he faced the ground as if giving me this moment. I was thankful. "I do," I replied in a deep, wavering voice. I cleared it.

Seaa nodded as if those two words answered all of her questions. "She cares for you too. I do not know how deep the scale of her affection, but I know she faced both General Braggart and operative Dallas, especially when she accused them of murdering you."

"As you can see, I'm alive."

The woman nodded and gently touched the collar at her neck. "She was quite forceful and believable. Did she know you weren't dead?"

I stretched my back muscles. "Yes, she knew I was alive. They left me for dead."

"I can see why she preferred if they thought you were. She was protecting you."

The room stayed quiet, absorbing every piece of information they could from Seaa. She got up from her seat and placed both hands on the table. "Operative Mueller thought you were dead. They sent him to capture Rayne. He did so thinking one of us had killed you."

At the news, I could feel the forgotten bread harden in the pits of my stomach. Zee still had my back. The small bit of news made me feel a tad bit better. I didn't like that Rayne was a captive at Foxtrot. Nonetheless, the knowledge my best friend did it because he sought revenge eased my tumultuous emotions.

As insane as it all sounded, in the world we lived in, having at least one person we could count on meant more than our weight in gold.

"Is Rayne alive?" I voiced out loud the question I knew all of us thought.

Seaa had tears in her violet eyes. For a moment, my heart dived, resting again behind my chest. I knew from her reaction it would not be good. Everyone in the room thought the same thing I was just now. The news wasn't welcome.

"Operative Mueller saved my life to save Rayne's."

I didn't understand.

She continued. "For Rayne to stop suffering, he feigned killing me to remove me from the equation."

My fingers clenched into a fist. "What the hell does that mean?" I yelled.

Seaa threw her purple and turquoise waves over her shoulder and fingered the strands in a nervous gesture. "Braggart and Dallas used torturing me in front of Rayne to break her. However, it's not all they did. Rayne had been tortured by them and made to watch as they did it to me. She broke."

I felt my entire world crash.

CHAPTER TWENTY-SIX

Three days later.
Safe Haven Headquarters
Seaa – ID: PH049.001

I LEANED DOWN to face the mirror once more. The doctor created a new contraption to help me with my breathing from the plans in Pops' notebooks. The stylish, metal choker had little lights like jewels layered on the surface from right to left. I didn't have to wear the bulky box anymore. The device recirculated water and moisture to keep me hydrated.

I stared at my reflection once more in the mirror. After a few days, my hair had regained its shine, and my scales regained their luster. Thinking of the place gave me the creeps. Staring once more at my vibrant lavender and turquoise scales, I could see areas already growing back.

Being able to see myself like this shocked me. I

didn't think I'd ever leave the facility, and if I did—it would be in a body bag. A half-laugh, half-cry startled me. I left the place *in* a body bag. If it weren't for my archenemy, I'd still *be* in the body bag. Roman Braggart was another topic entirely. After our meeting in the Planning Room, I discovered how he had betrayed his camp to join my family's cause instead, and it merely started because of his intense infatuation with my little sister, Rayne.

Rayne.

I blamed myself for bringing Rayne's life into this fight. If I hadn't made it so painfully obvious it troubled me meeting at Traces, she wouldn't have come out to find me. Rome was right. I brought an innocent into this crazed situation and caused the rippling domino effect since then. The team said nothing to me because the novelty of having me back within their fold was still so fresh and new. Once the novelty died down, I'd get blamed for causing so much trouble.

A photograph of my siblings and me lay on a small table near the dresser. I studied their faces and realized how much I had missed in the few weeks since my capture. My hauntingly beautiful sister Silk attempted a mission of her own and wouldn't be back for a while. Many things had happened. Not only did Rome join our fight, but the son of a wealthy Project Hercules investor. Having Cameron and his friend Suzanne back also meant a lot to me. There was so much I had missed.

Luckily, I was still alive to gain those lost bits back. A lot of Braggart's prisoners might not be so lucky.

The sound of someone wrapping their knuckles on the large, metal door caught my attention. I shuffled toward the connecting door to open it. My toes peeked out from beneath balloon pants, and the sleeves of my shirt got caught on the dresser's corner. Although the contraption Pops had made me was gone, I still looked like a fish out of water, belonging in a large tank with a sign over it that said *Freaks for 5¢*. Opening the door, I came face to chest with Hail.

"How are you, Slug?" Hail teased as one side of his mouth lifted into a lopsided grin.

He had called me "Slug" since we were little, and I was the last around the track for training.

I smiled back at him. "I'm better in the water than I am on land." Which wasn't so far from the truth. I possessed exceptional abilities when in contact with water—speed, strength, and the ability to manipulate running water. Unlike my sister Rayne, whose entire body dematerialized into a liquid, I could only ask water for its help in battle.

Hail looked inside my room from over my head and shoved his hands inside his worn jeans' pockets. I could always read Hail's body language. Growing up, I worshipped this man from the dark. He was the only man in my life I knew better than he knew himself. Without a word, I grabbed him by his forearm and dragged him into the room. Our rooms were side by side—separated by a door. We spent many nights chatting away about lost loves and revenge. He had repeatedly walked in without knocking and plopped down on the edge of the bed to talk or bother me—whichever he saw fit. With him knocking on the door now, it meant he was not himself, and I was sure this had to do with the love of his life either loving another man or being held captive at Braggart's facility in Foxtrot.

They would sooner kill me than they would Rayne. General Braggart had invariably had this unhealthy obsession with the poor girl. She was tortured and beaten to the breaking point, but I was certain Braggart knew how much she could take or how much he'd give. If they could manipulate and brainwash Hail, it was more than likely Rayne could be as well. There were so many things I wanted to tell him. Before sitting down to talk, I wrapped my arms around his firm waist, relieved to feel his strong arms come around my shoulders.

"I am so glad you are alive, Hail."

I felt him kiss the top of my hair, grateful I had showered a few hours earlier.

"I, too, am glad you're safe and home."

I playfully slapped him on the arm. "You're the one rarely here. Every time you got a new lead on Rayne, you'd ghost from here before any of us had the chance to stop you."

"Funny how it works. It turns out, Rayne found me."

It just so happens Rayne found me as well. A thought occurred to me. An idea so brilliant and daring, and entirely unlike me; I couldn't voice it out loud for fear they'd lock me in my room.

For years we had spent it unseen, keeping ourselves reclusive from the rest of what had been left of the world, hiding the military's dirty little genetic engineering secret. Instead of us waiting for soldiers to knock down our doors, the experiments needed to band together and go full-frontal attack. As capable as Braggart's soldiers and operatives were, I was sure my team was better. The second batch of testers didn't have the same abnormalities the first batch did. My group had abilities he could not concoct for himself. Plus, he didn't have Pops' notebooks.

However much he may control through genetic altering, the effects are temporary or amended, I remembered as I stared at the man I secretly loved. *We can bring Rayne back from the breaking point.*

"Hail, Cameron is back, but have we heard from Blister?"

Hail shook his head. "No one knows where he is at, but with Cam here, I'm sure his friend Suzanne can locate him. Why?"

"I have an idea."

I observed Hail as he shuffled to my bed as he usually did when we did our chats. His beautifully sculpted body seemed wary and worn—a warrior battered and beaten. I would do anything to make things better for him.

"We should bring the fight to them this time."

Hail's features hadn't changed. He gave no evidence he had processed my words. I continued, "It's time we start our own project. General Braggart started Project Hercules. We will punish him and free ourselves from his mind games, Hail. We will free Rayne from him."

I could see a small glimmer of hope from within his deep, indigo eyes. "Braggart needs to be hit where it hurts the most."

Hail shifted on the bed as if the conversation became too uncomfortable for him to bear. "And where would that be, Seaa? The man has no soul or moral compass." He pointed to the door as he said, "He had his son killed off, although the bastard still lives."

"We haven't hit his pockets."

My sweet man shook his head. He seemed confused, asking, "His where?"

I walked barefoot to the dresser and grabbed a few notes from the cold surface and dropped the bills in Hail's open palm. "His pockets, Hail. His sponsors. His investors. The consumer."

Hail's blue eyes shot to my lavender ones. "How do you propose we do that again? By bringing the fight to him?"

"Yes, Hail. We have the means now. With Foxhand's help, we can gather all the commercial channels open to Braggart and shut them down—one by one."

The idea was crazy as it was brilliant. For years we had spent it in hiding as if we were the guilty party. Feeling the excitement rip through me, 1 couldn't contain it anymore and ran out of my bedroom door. Hail called out to me, but if 1 stopped to hear him out, I'd lose the courage to move forward with the plan.

Three hours later. On the third day back from the dead. 1 stood in the Planning Room with the rest of Batch 001 as we concluded the first stage of plans to destroy Brockton Braggart and bring back Rayne.

Thunder placed his large hand on top of the table as he looked at all of his family. "The Rayne Project begins."

No one in the group smiled or cheered. There was no celebration. By starting The Rayne Project, everyone in the room understood it was no longer about the small battles against Braggart, but to commence a full-on war against him, his operatives, and the military. There would be a lot of suffering, and God willing, we would be spared gruesome deaths. 1 knew 1 had caused irreparable damage the moment 1 walked off from Traces, so 1 offered my plan to Thunder. All of my life, 1 lived in a metaphorical bubble. It was about time the bubble popped.

My eldest brother stared into the eyes of every single one of us as if willing us to see all of his hope, pain, and regrets for this mission. "This chapter in our lives isn't done yet."

And with that, he released us all from the room

and on to the next phase. I needed to find Foxhand and the black widow. Without them, this next mission would not pass the first phase. Roman Braggart leaned against the wall. He waited for me. I would have never thought of partnering up with a man who would have killed me if not for my sister's interference.

But here we were.

Both fighting on the same side.

In a war neither one had a chance in hell of winning.

The Rayne Project.

Acknowledgments

I have first to give thanks to my readers. If I didn't have them, then I'd be nowhere right now. There are so many things I want to say to them that it's hard to formulate into coherent words. Instead, I've decided to open up a member's only lounge of a sort on my webpage for my subscribers. As time moves forward, I will make freebies and contests available to them. But, you'd have to sign up first at www.lynalopez.com.

The next group I have to share the spotlight with is my family. My parents have supported me all my life. I remember writing awful little stories and printing them on some colored paper and then stapling it all together like a book. Oh, yes. I was that little girl. My parents never complained or cringed. They took that miserable excuse of a story and read it with smiles on their lips. That was then, and this is now. Luckily, I've been blessed with my support team as I grew up. My husband is so great at lifting me when I give in to anxiety attacks. He pushes me to finish, even when there is no finish line in sight. My kids are also so impressive. My younger ones can't read the books I write—yet, they encourage me to keep writing them. My teenage daughter is such a sucker for romance that she delves into anything I finish with gusto—like her momma.

Lastly, I have to give a massive shout-out to my team. Websterland Books, MK Editing, and CReya-Tive. Websterland Books gave me the outlet to put The Rayne Project out there for the world to see. Martha, my editor at MK Editing, is fantastic. She didn't go in there and chop up my book. She went in with eyes wide open and helped me see how we could make the story flow better. And, to Andrea, wickedly sensational book cover extraordinaire. She took an idea and created something fantastic. She helped me breathe when I thought I'd choke.

A huge thank you goes out to my online family and friends. Their support is immense, and it lightens me each time I feel I'm heading into dark spaces. My beta-readers along the way, thank you. I'm so grateful for each and every single one of you.

Thank you, everyone. Thank you. I hope The Rayne Project pulled you in as it has me for so many years.

Silk cant stand men. She can barely tolerate being around people in general except for those she cares about, and even then that's pushing it. But, now she's stuck guarding Gavin Foxhand. When matters take a turn for the worse, will Silk be able to push away her prejudice to protect and fight for those she loves?

With the appearance of a newly altered Rayne, will Batch 001 be able to complete their final mission, beat Braggart, and save their friends?

Find out in **Project Hercules's** second installment...

THE BLACK WIDOW
CHAPTER PREVIEW

CHAPTER ONE

Sector Charlie
Edge of Academic District in Trébeta

Sector Charlie
Edge of Academic District in Trébeta

THE STARS HAD always been my favorite part of the evening.

The bothersome night sky had made it its mission to hide the stars away behind thick, cumbersome clouds. No matter how far the eye could see, no stars were visible on this night—nor any night I could remember. Gavin's voice reached my sensitive hearing as I sat perched on the windowsill in the far corner of his vibrantly colored living room. There were drapes in a variety of colors and patterns from the windows to the couch cushions. Large ceramic tiles in a pale gold covered his floor from the foyer to the back of the expansive apartment. A long sitting bar with hovering stools separated his fully equipped kitchen from the living area.

Gavin had spent each night in the kitchen, creating one deliciously-aromatic meal after another to entice me enough to eat something. Each time, 1 refused. Eating a meal with him meant we were on friendlier terms—the action seemed too personal. Other than a few pieces of fruit here and there, 1 hadn't sat down to a meal in a few days. There was no use in giving the guy any false illusions. He pushed his glasses back up his nose for the sixth time since taking his father's phone call. Gavin and his father had a love-hate relationship where they both felt strong enough to get on each other's nerves.

Their bickering reminded me of my family.

Feeling somewhat depressed 1 could not find a single star in the sky, 1 removed my legs from underneath me to stretch them out. Trēbeta's lights shone from below. 1 could make out the university grounds a few blocks from Gavin's apartment. From this height, the people walking below seemed like tiny ants 1 could squash with my feet. The apartment was on the highest floor of the building, but it wasn't too difficult for me to identify the color of their outfits or hue of their skin.

Looking away from the people below, 1 played with the silver band on my wrist. Underneath the band was a thinner bracelet 1 kept as a reminder of Pops. The lightweight plastic could've been ripped off ages ago, but the weight of it kept me centered and stable. Its weight reminded me someone had loved me once, and no matter what abilities 1 possessed, his love for me had been true. The identification printed on it read, *Silk – PH062.001*. It wasn't a time in my life 1 should cherish, but the crazy spider woman inside of me couldn't part with it.

Gavin's voice filtered in from his bedroom. I'd stayed in his house for far too long. Three days was my limit. During my time here, 1 followed Gavin to his university or shops—preferring to stay out of sight. Gavin had this idea my being here would get us chatting—make us friends, but he was wrong. There was nothing 1 needed to say to him. His father was a significant contributor to my messed-up life. After finding out back in Safe Haven that Foxhand was a wealthy patron who regularly funded government projects, I'd made it a personal mission to keep the guy at a distance.

Every man 1 came across was interested in me, and Gavin was no exception. It's a curse. Any male near me fell for my black widow charm. Some women relished in that kind of power. But not me. All men made me sick—both mentally and physically. The sole one 1 tolerated was Thunder, but since finding out he had lied about Rayne's whereabouts for years, my trust in him has wavered.

For years, 1 felt guilty I'd caused Rayne's death. For years, 1 blamed myself for not being strong enough during the Foxtrot escape. For years, 1 watched my brother Hail mourn for Rayne, unable to let go—rushing off any chance he could to find her in the hopes she wasn't dead.

My lost, little Rayne.

Although not entirely religious or spiritual, I closed my eyes and prayed Rayne was alright. I couldn't bear to lose another sister because I already had so little to my name. Putting on a brave face was harder every single time something awful happened.

Gavin threw the phone across the bedroom. I opened my senses further, picking up his rash breathing and quickened steps toward the phone he had thrown. I couldn't see him, but I knew what he did and where he was at every moment.

His scent was pretty straightforward to pick up. The guy showered with rose oil that sunk into the pores of his skin and mixed with a natural old book smell he carried on him all the time. Stretching my muscles from prolonged sitting, I waited until Gavin left his room to call out that I was ready to leave his home.

Gavin Foxhand had an adorable air about him—a quality few men had. I understood why Rayne cared about him so much—not like I'd ever let him know. I'd noticed how several females unsuccessfully tried to make eye contact with the young man, but he was blissfully ignorant. Gavin either had his nose buried in a book or was absorbed in his KeViewer, which doubled as some supercomputer no one else knew about. If he took down the "fuck off" sign on his forehead, he'd see how many girls wanted to get to know him.

He'd be better off doing that than pining over me.

Not like I should talk. The same sign Gavin had on his forehead, I posted on every available surface of my body. The two of us were more alike than I wanted to admit. He came barreling around the corner. His hair flowed around his head in disarray. His glasses left behind in the bedroom. When he wore them, he was safe and adorable. But when he took off the glasses and looked at me with an air of innocence, it made him inexplicably provocative.

"Why are you leaving? Why now?" He turned to stare at the open window and the night sky I had been staring at earlier. "It's dark out there."

If Gavin needed to learn anything about me, it was that I thrived in the darkness. While the rest of the world slept, it was my time to explore. I didn't bother to reply. Gavin had not heard much come out of my mouth since being given this mission from Thunder. The last thing I told him as we made our way into his apartment building was that I was not a friend coming to stay. I advised him to think of me as a fixture. Gavin's floor bodyguards hadn't batted an eyelash when I slunk my way into the apartment in my blonde disguise and wouldn't give a damn when I left—so long as Gavin was alive and well.

I had done my job.

No one had followed him.

No one had set out to kill him.

"Damn, Silk. For three days, you've either followed me from God knows where on the outside or you've sat on the windowsill, refusing to eat or sleep." He slid his fingers once more through his dirty-blond hair while the deep air he inhaled made his sharp shoulders rise and fall. "What the hell do I have to do to be your friend?"

Gavin didn't want to be my friend.

No man wanted my friendship.

For one, I was a poisonous bitch who said or did anything I wanted without regard to someone's feelings, and two, they all asked for my friendship as a pretense to get into my pants. Nausea rose from deep within my belly as it usually did when confronted with this situation. My mind slipped into the past as Gavin ranted.

The assistant doctors and male technicians at Foxtrot had taken more than my vitals while performing their medical rounds. Their greedy hands had touched me in places they had no business touching. For so long, I thought Unit 13 had allowed it—that it was okay even though I hated every minute. Until the day Pops walked in on a lecherous male nurse, trying to place his hands into my waistband. I remembered the fury on my old man's face and learned then about molestation.

The male nurse lost the ability ever to use his hand again.

I made a promise to myself that day that no man

would ever get to touch me. For a while, I'd made things harder for Pops, who couldn't get a woman to stand to be near me long enough to perform medical tests, and because I detested all things male, Dr. Lester had had to run all the tests himself. I loved the old man very much and missed him every day since he passed. He gave his life to save us and happened to have been one of the only men in my life I didn't consider a male.

I watched Gavin inhale again as if giving up on trying to get me to say something.

"Not all men are asses, you know."

They were to me.

Men hovered around me like bees on pollinated flowers. It was a side effect of the experimentation. Because of it, I couldn't walk around like an average human female. Unless I used my cloaking ability, men and women would notice my every move, as if drawn to me like a moth to a flame. I was lucky my ability to cloak hadn't come with an expiration date because I had it on all the time. Rome was the sole person I knew who could sense me even with the use of my skill.

Although once on the same side with General Braggart, Rome's affection toward Rayne caused him to switch sides after finally seeing his father's true, deceptive nature. The guy was head over heels for our little sister and thus very much immune to my pheromones. I hated the man's guts, but he's grown on me.

Not like I'd tell him either. The man drove me batshit crazy—exactly like a new sibling would.

Gavin stomped into the kitchen. He threw open one of the four doors on the stainless steel refrigerator and perused the items inside. "I don't care what you say. If you're leaving, then you will eat something."

I felt the tiny threads of my sanity snap. One of my pet peeves was men telling me what to do. My leg muscles twitched, and my feet took me underneath the archway separating the foyer from the kitchen.

Startled, Gavin dropped the fixings of a sandwich. The blood in my veins boiled to aching degrees. "You are nothing but a plague. A disgusting, pus-filled human being I'm forced to watch because you prove to be more of a hindrance than an asset."

I watched as those sharp, blue-green eyes dimmed at the onslaught of my words, but I had no control left. "I was here to do a job, and I did it. You have no say over anything I do. Men. *All* men are the bug under my shoe, so unless you want to be my next meal, I suggest you fuck off."

Gavin's shoulders dropped, and his eyes averted contact with mine. His fingers jerked, and his chest deflated. I knew it was the wrong thing to say to him, but I couldn't bring myself to apologize. Gavin hadn't meant me any harm. I projected my feelings about disgusting, perverse men onto him. The silence in the room felt heavy. The weight of it almost crushing. Gavin shrugged those shoulders once more, depleted.

Suddenly, I didn't know if I wanted to slink away or keep my ground.

Strange, unidentified sounds approaching took the decision away from me.

Seconds into the silence, footsteps in the hallway beyond Gavin's front door reached my ears. The bodyguard posted in front of the door opened his mouth to speak, but the unexpected visitors shot both floor guards with a muffled gun. I had enough time to process; these were not welcome guests. I leaped into the kitchen. My body slammed into Gavin's. His breath shot out when we clashed and again when we landed on the other side of the kitchen floor, even though I took the brunt of the impact.

The door had exploded behind me.

Gavin's eyes shot wide open as he tried to comprehend what had happened. Debris flew throughout the once beautiful interior. Lit, splintered pieces of wood fell around us.

"Get up, Gavin."

I pulled Gavin off the floor as two men in masks came barreling through the front door with their weapons drawn.

Stuck in the small kitchen, I picked Gavin up from his pants and shirt to throw him over the bar. I didn't have time for niceties or alternative actions. Once he was over, I flew forward. A bullet whizzed to my right and another to the left. I got to the first man. Ripping the gun from his hand, I aimed it at his partner and shot. The man gasped when his partner dropped to the floor and again when I pushed him across the room. His body slammed into the wall, raining plaster all around us and through to the other side.

The Gidget dinged.

I noted three more men dressed head to toe in black gear with weapons strapped to every available pocket. They saw me at the same time I saw them. They aimed and fired as I turned to get Gavin. Bullets whizzed past me—one came dangerously close to my arm. Human weapons couldn't bring us down, but it didn't mean they hurt any less. Gavin was unconscious on the floor by the wall. I lifted him over my shoulder and ran toward the window. For days I had studied the outside of the apartment. Every brick, awning, and decorative sculpture would serve us as a means of escape.

Throwing us from the top floor, I held in my desire to scream as cuspate glass embedded into my shoulder. The sharp pain hit me like a wave. Ignoring the pain, I shot my arm out and clutched the curved window sill of a different apartment. The extra weight shifted on my shoulder, sliding down my left arm. But I held on. My right arm screamed with the strain—the blood around the glass in my shoulder trickled down my side. My fingers pressed harder into the cement as the weight pulled me toward the ground. We had at least another fifty stories down. I didn't care what anyone else thought about mutated humans. Not I nor any of my brethren could survive this kind of fall.

One stranger hung out of Gavin's window and shot a bullet my way. I pulled the arm, holding Gavin closer to myself. I could withstand the hit of a human weapon. Gavin would not.

"She's holding the boy, you idiot!" one man yelled at another.

Are they after Gavin?

"Get to the bottom."

I didn't have much time left. My hand was slipping, and the kidnappers would be here soon. I slammed my foot into the window as I hung off the window ledge above it. When I heard the glass crack, Gavin woke up and shifted in my sore arms. He shouted a few choice cuss words. My hand slipped farther.

"Gavin, shut up and stay still, or we'll both get killed."

Gavin went unnaturally still. I kicked once more. The sound of glass rang through the whipping wind of the freezing night. Blood dripped from the fingers holding us and down my arm to meet the blood from my aching shoulder. Sweat covered my forehead, causing the borrowed blonde strands to stick to my skin. Gavin whimpered.

"Hold on, Gavin."

He didn't say a word. I pulled my arm back and pushed with my forearm, letting go of Gavin as he got near the window. He dragged out a cuss word when he dropped into the open window. It was too bad I couldn't shoot webs like the comic book hero. If I could have, this would have been a hell of a lot easier.

The momentum made me lose the grip I had on the window. I couldn't get a foot on the ledge below me. I dropped. A dense, sinking feeling accosted me. My foot hit the cement shelf and sent me backward, farther away from the building.

My arms swung around to grab hold of something—anything. With nothing within reach, I knew this time I was in genuine danger. There was pressure applied to my ankle, and I slammed into the wall. A grunt escaped my lips. I looked up to see half of Gavin's body hanging out the window and both his hands on my ankle. He gritted his teeth. I saw the muscles in his arms quiver with the strain. Not willing to risk how much longer he could hold it, I bent upward at the waist and grabbed his wrists with my hands. He dropped my ankle and locked his hands around my wrists—both of us unwilling to let go of the other. He pulled up, and I assisted by using my boots on the building as leverage.

Next time, I needed to use the setules in my fingers to get us down a building because jumping out the window would not happen again. My muscles throbbed and quivered. With more than half my body through the window, Gavin released his hold on me, and I dropped on top of him.

"Let's. Not. Do that. Again," Gavin punctuated between taking gulps of air.

One of those rare smirks pulled at my lips. I pushed

myself off him, satisfied to hear a burst of air shoot from Gavin's lips.

"Which part?" I asked as I studied the dark bedroom we were in. "The part where we almost blew up, got shot at, jumped out the window to our deaths, burst through more broken glass, or when I landed on top of you?"

I no longer paid attention to Gavin as I walked towards the door, but I heard him when he said, "All of the above except for E." The sound of his footsteps told me he was following behind. "Yes, E can definitely be done again."

I stopped so abruptly that Gavin skidded to a halt right behind me. In the few minutes since our kitchen argument, I realized two things. Gavin *was* and then *wasn't* like the men out there. He perplexed the hell out of me. Not willing to comment, I took down my disguise. By manipulating the cells within my body, and thus the genes within them, my borrowed blonde hair darkened to its usual shiny, black curls. My eyes went from green to black coffee. The subtle body features also manifested on my skin, and the hot pink froufrou outfit turned back into black pants and tunic. Gavin stood there and watched. "Have I ever told you that this beauty mark" —he reached towards the tiny birthmark below my right eye— "is my favorite part about you."

Before his finger could graze my skin, my hand shot out and grabbed it. "Do not touch me," I uttered through clenched teeth.

The familiar pangs in my stomach told me his touch wasn't welcome, but a new sensation fluttered to life behind my ribcage, and I couldn't place the emotion.

A feeling similar to the one I'd felt many, many years ago.

Project Hercules Trilogy

The Rayne Project

The Black Widow

The Sera Finale

Lyna Lopez

has an obsession with reading stories that separate her from the real world, especially those geared toward strong women. After a hurricane ripped through her neighborhood, it left behind so much devastation that it got her to imagine a world in chaos, which is how The Rayne Project was born. Now, Lyna spends as much time as she can writing books that can transport her (and her) readers to whole new worlds. She lives on a mini-farm in Florida with her four crazy kids, rascal-of-a-husband, two wacky dogs, one prissy cat, and all the chickens and ducks.

Follow on Social Media

@lynalopezsauthor

&

www.lynalopez.com

www.ingramcontent.com/pod-product-compliance
Lightning Source LLC
Chambersburg PA
CBHW011507100726
47900CB00009B/2637